Chapter 1

Lucy ordered an amaretto with orange juice, nostalgic for its marzipan sweetness. Calories were irrelevant now. No need to restrict herself to the miserable vodka and soda combination that kept her slim, ready for last minute casting calls: a body on a slab at the morgue, a guest at a Regency dinner party, or maybe a belligerent employee in a corporate training video.

A tiny sip. Her mouth puckered at the sudden tartness before a honeyed warmth spread across her tongue. It was as though she was drinking the past – two-for-one Tuesdays at the Union bar, film nights in their student house, the electric charge of possibility at every rehearsal.

The pub was dense with after-work drinkers throwing their heads back to laugh at one another's jokes, shouting to be heard over the din. Stacks of empties were accumulating on the tables and the three women tending the bar moved with harried urgency, their faces flushed.

Jack arrived wearing a vintage leather trench coat, beads of drizzle weighing down his usually immaculate hair as his eyes roved over the crowd. He broke into a grin when he spotted Lucy at the table she'd just nabbed, and she experienced a warm pang of affection, swiftly followed by a constricting feeling in her ribs.

After the two of them hugged hello, Jack took a slug of Lucy's drink, then went to the bar to order her another, plus one for himself. Doubles, judging by the colour. Like her, he seemed committed to making the night feel like a beginning, rather than an end.

'Cheers.' He raised his glass and they clinked. Lucy took another sip. She couldn't help fixating on the sugar content of the orange juice, picturing flesh spilling over the top of her jeans, silvery stretch marks etched into her thighs. *Let it go,* she told herself. *Your measurements are irrelevant now. You're giving yourself that freedom.*

'You're all packed, then?' Jack shouted over the rumble of pub chatter.

Lucy nodded, trying a smile. 'Handing back the keys tomorrow lunchtime.'

He locked onto her with his hazel eyes, the irises flecked with gold. 'Are you sure about this, Luce?'

'No. But it's the right thing to do.' Lucy's last gig had been a milk advert. She'd worn a vinyl apron, adorned with cornflowers and roses, and when she'd delivered her lines, she transformed the carton in her hand into the very essence of motherly love. The producer, a woman in her mid-twenties, had nodded along enthusiastically. *Perfect characterisation. I wonder if we could try it one more time, but dialling up the smile just a little more?* Lucy's stomach had lurched as she realised how she must appear to everyone on set: a has-been, desperate for her next half-day booking. Never had she felt so foolish.

The IMPERSONATORS

Also by Angela Chadwick

XX
Ungrateful

The
IMPERSONATORS

ANGELA CHADWICK

ЯENE
GADE

RENEGADE BOOKS

First published in Great Britain in 2025 by Renegade Books

10 9 8 7 6 5 4 3 2 1

A CIP catalogue record for this book
is available from the British Library.

Hardback ISBN 978-0-349-13105-4

Typeset in Berling by M Rules
Printed and bound in Great Britain by
Clays Ltd, Elcograf S.p.A

Papers used by Renegade Books are from well-managed forests
and other responsible sources.

Renegade Books
An imprint of Dialogue
Carmelite House
50 Victoria Embankment
London EC4Y 0DZ

The authorised representative
in the EEA is
Hachette Ireland
8 Castlecourt Centre
Dublin 15, D15 XTP3, Ireland
(email: info@hbgi.ie)

www.dialoguebooks.co.uk

Dialogue, part of Little, Brown Book Group Limited,
an Hachette UK company.

For Steve

Impersonation Services Available Near You

Need someone to stand in as a partner, colleague or relative? Make the right impression by hiring a professional actor today.

All scenarios considered.
Complete discretion assured.

(Please note: we supply classically trained actors. This is not an escort service.)

A group at the bar cheered as a Bon Jovi track came on, three or so men starting singing along at the top of their voices.

Jack's eyebrows were just perceptibly drawn together. 'You could get another agent. I'd help you update your show-reel—'

'I love how you have my back, I really do. But the work isn't there any more.' Lucy couldn't afford to go on living in London, pulling pints and waitressing, sinking deeper into debt, as she clung to the belief that next week might bring the audition that would change everything.

'It's not like you're *old*.'

'I know.' But in their industry, thirty-one was considered far too late for a woman to break out and they both knew it. Lucy wasn't going to be cast as Ophelia for a run at the Globe, or as the lead in an edgy new Netflix series. She wasn't sure what it was about that milk ad, the hideous apron, that made her finally realise it, but the knowledge calcified inside her body, devastating her.

'You'll have to visit me in Portsmouth.' Lucy placed a hand on Jack's wrist. 'Come and have a day by the sea.'

Jack smiled, but his eyes looked troubled. She felt tiny bubbles of panic rising up, gathering beneath her lungs. Surely Jack knew she would pick up the phone anytime, go on supporting him as she always had? She'd never abandon him.

'When I qualify as a teacher, I might actually have money for a change,' she offered. 'I'll come up and see you as often as I can.'

Jack's lip twitched, as though he was about to once again list all the reasons why retraining as a drama teacher was such a waste of her talents. Lucy craved the hurt of it. Let him focus on her failure, if it meant he could avoid looking at his own.

The panicked call from Jack's mother, a year after their graduation, was never far from the surface of her consciousness. 'He won't get out of bed. It's like he's . . . broken. I'm frightened, Lucy.'

She'd blown her overdraft on a ticket to Hertfordshire, taken a taxi to the cottage where Jack had grown up. As she'd knelt by his single bed, careful not to recoil at the smell of his unwashed body, he'd gone on staring at the ceiling, red-rimmed eyes clouded and lifeless. Lucy hadn't been able to help feeling that her closest friend had *gone*. But where? And how would she get him back again?

In the months leading up to that moment, she'd rehearsed with him ahead of each and every audition, often for ten, twelve hours. Jack had driven himself hard, never satisfied until he'd interrogated a script from all angles, trying multiple interpretations of his character, teasing out every nuance of feeling. Lucy had told herself it was energising; he'd always strived for perfection, he flourished through effort and exertion. But later, when she was confronted by his lifeless form in his childhood bed, cold tentacles of truth had wrapped themselves around her body: his ambition was harming him.

'You just need to give it time.' Lucy had rested her hand on his pea-green duvet. 'You've got a brilliant agent. She'll find you work, I know she will.'

Jack had given no sign he'd heard or even recognised Lucy was with him. Blood whooshing in her ears, she'd tried different assurances, searching desperately for the comment, the insight, that would permeate this stupor and make her friend seem familiar again. Nothing had worked. His father had ended up packing him off to some expensive psychiatric facility where he'd stayed for almost a year.

'I've actually landed a really odd gig.' Now, Jack took a large slug of his drink and smacked his lips together. 'A friend of my dad is paying me to visit a nursing home once a week. I've got to chat to this old man with dementia and pretend he's my grandad. How mad is that?'

Lucy raised an eyebrow. 'Huh? Why?'

He cricked his neck, gave a brief roll of his shoulders. 'The family doesn't trust the staff. Reckons they neglect the residents who don't get regular visitors. They're sending me in to keep everyone on their toes.'

'The real grandson can't do it himself?'

'Lives in Dubai.'

A heavy-set man knocked into the back of Lucy's chair and she lurched forwards. 'They're actually *paying* you?'

'Hundred quid a time. Can you believe it? It's all rather fun. I mean, the poor old man doesn't know what's going on, but the carers seem nice. I was there earlier, chatting away about the weather.'

Lucy gave a thin laugh. A hundred pounds a week would have made all the difference to her, but for Jack it was pocket money to fritter away on vintage jackets and personal training sessions. She couldn't help thinking of his flat – the uniformed security guard sitting in the entrance hall, the communal garden where Jack could fall asleep in the sunshine. So very different from the cramped, mouse-infested flatshares that had marked Lucy's years in London.

'Give it a few more months, Luce.' Jack gave her a friendly pat on the arm. 'It'll only happen if you keep trying.'

She looked at him, noting the intense light in his eyes, the way he was clenching his jaw. Fear pinched at her windpipe. Jack was fragile. He needed her.

'I need to get some money together before the course starts,' she said. 'No chance of that in London.' She was being dishonest, pretending she didn't know how close Jack sometimes skirted to collapse.

'You could crash on my sofa. Instead of taking some waitressing gig, you could focus on auditions. You've worked so hard – what's it all been *for* if you give up now?' He was smiling, but his eyes were filled with a plea: *don't leave me.*

And yet: *some waitressing gig.* How casually Jack belittled the things Lucy had to do to survive. 'Can we talk about something else?' she said. 'This time tomorrow I'm going to be back living with my parents. We need to hurry up and get pissed.'

'But you know you're brilliant.'

Lucy shrugged.

Jack raised an eyebrow. 'Plenty of rich old biddies in the nursing home. You should come with me one day. Hand out flyers to the visitors. *Talented actor for hire. Don't have time to be a doting relative? Pay someone else to do it for you.*' He drained his glass, then reached over and started on the drink he'd bought for Lucy.

An unexpected sense of possibility fizzed through her veins. 'Wouldn't it be strange if there was actually a market for that kind of thing.'

Jack snorted. Several droplets of the drink he'd just commandeered landed on the table. 'I was joking.'

'But, maybe once you reach a certain age, small private gigs are all that's left. It's still *acting*, right?' Lucy realised she was flexing her ankles beneath the table. It was suddenly hard to remain still.

Jack's lips twitched with the beginnings of a mischievous grin. 'I knew you didn't really want to teach drama to a bunch of spotty teenagers.'

Her mind was racing, imagining the kinds of people who might want an actor to step into their lives. Jealous spouses testing their partner's resolve in the face of a flirtatious stranger. Single women wanting to feel safe at a boozy work function. The possibilities were endless, and London was one of the richest cities in the world. Handing out flyers would be far too crass, but a website and a few ads might just be affordable, if Jack didn't mind loaning her some money.

Lucy laid her palms down on the table. 'You've busted me. I've never been that excited about teaching. But my course doesn't start until October. We could test the idea.'

Jack stared at her. 'Grandkids for hire?'

'Impersonation services – we could be anyone people want us to be.' There was a definite click within Lucy's brain, a sense of rightness. The concept was so simple, but she'd never heard of anyone offering anything like it.

Jack narrowed his eyes. 'It wouldn't be proper acting.'

'Neither's selling milk. And come on, I bet you're perform-ing your little heart out for the staff in that care home.'

Jack sighed, but an amused sparkle filled his eyes. 'Just so I'm clear, you're *not* prepared to try and find a new agent. But you *do* want to start a business completely from scratch?'

'If your sofa's still up for grabs, I could stay in London until the course starts. We'll just see how it goes; if it's profitable, maybe I won't have to move back home after all.' If it worked, she wouldn't have to abandon Jack, she could go on taking care of him.

Jack picked up a beer mat, turned it over in his hand. 'I'll keep going to auditions, and if a part comes up—'

'If a part comes up, I'll be cheering you on, like always. Promise. But this feels like such a unique idea, don't you think? We could start our own agency.'

If Lucy managed to pull it off, Jack could be spared the humiliation of the fallow periods, the misery of unanswered calls and the creeping realisation that no one was all that interested in what he had to offer.

Jack drained Lucy's spare drink, then fished out an ice cube with his fingers, crunching it between his teeth. 'It sounds more like lying than acting.' But there was no real energy behind his words and Lucy knew she'd secured his grudging cooperation. What a gift she could offer him. A way to preserve his sense of self, keep calling himself an actor. They'd be able to go on doing the thing they loved most, holding on to the joy of performance. They wouldn't have to admit they'd failed.

Chapter 2

Lucy spent what was supposed to be her train fare back to Portsmouth on a taxi to Jack's building in the Docklands, everything she owned squeezed into two suitcases and a plastic storage crate. The flat (an investment property belonging to Jack's father) was on the fifth floor with elegant wood flooring and a balcony overlooking the communal gardens and river. Beneath them, a cluster of cherry blossom trees was in full bloom, carpeting a neat square of lawn with pink petals. In the distance, Lucy could see the glinting skyscrapers of the city, the jutting arrogance of the Shard seeming to push its way to the forefront.

As Lucy set her belongings down by the fold-out sofa in the sitting room, spring sunshine poured through the balcony door and she felt an unexpected tremor, as though she'd crossed over into a London she was never supposed to inhabit.

This was it. Seven months to see whether the agency idea could make her enough money to live on. She went to the library in Bethnal Green and borrowed a stack of books, titles like *Marketing for Dummies* and *Starting a Business*. After a decade spent watching her phone, waiting for good news, now was the moment to take control.

*

The nursing home housing Jack's fake grandfather was in a converted mansion near Hampstead Heath. The old man had a pale-blue room looking out across a striped lawn, flanked by tidy rows of daffodils. He was sitting in a tartan-upholstered armchair when Jack bounded in, delivering a peck on the cheek and a friendly rub of the shoulders. Something about this feigned intimacy made Lucy's insides twist. Performing for the care staff was one thing, but deceiving a dementia patient struck her as unnecessarily cruel. She had to remind herself that Jack's visits were intended to ensure the man's comfort and ease. The staff would be that little bit more at-tentive without really understanding why.

'Hello, Gramps. I brought a friend along with me today. This is Lucy.'

The man searched Lucy's face with watery blue eyes. He tried to mask his confusion with a weak smile, his lower lip trembling.

'Hi.' Lucy gave him a wave. Her arm felt unexpectedly stiff.

'Come in, dear.' He shifted in his seat, straightening his back, as though remembering what it was to have authority, to be a host.

Jack and Lucy sat down on the two-seater sofa opposite the man's armchair. As Jack launched into bright chatter about how the weeks of non-stop drizzle finally seemed to be over, Lucy scanned the room. There were two large watercolour paintings of sailing boats hanging on the walls; a neatly made single bed in the corner furthest from the window, with tartan pyjamas folded on the pillow. The old man nodded along as Jack described a show he and his girlfriend Emily had seen at the National Theatre, but his forehead remained furrowed and Lucy thought she saw fear in his eyes. For a second she let herself imagine what it must be like, to not recognise the people around you, to feel entirely detached. It was a visceral thrumming that subsumed her body.

A care assistant brought in tea and custard creams on a tray, and shortly after, the old man seemed to collapse into a deep sleep, his head thrown back, open mouth revealing missing molars and receded gums. Lucy felt she was violating his dignity simply by being there. He appeared so defenceless and it was chilling really, to know that she and Jack weren't who they said they were.

She took her notepad from her shoulder bag, determined to dispel her unease by focussing on her plans. Lucy had decided to spend the bulk of the three grand Jack was lending the business on digital ads; colourful banners that would pop up when people were scrolling. She was learning you could target people by age, income and education level. Even better, in most cases you only actually paid anything if people clicked your link.

She coughed gently, trying to rid herself of the tightness in her throat. 'I'm thinking we focus on forty plus. Homeowners. We only want clicks from people who can actually afford us.'

Jack gave her a non-committal nod as he sipped tea from a rose-patterned cup with a dainty handle. Perhaps, if he maintained his strict exercise regime, he'd have another ten years or so of convincingly telling himself his breakout role was just around the corner. But he'd seen the end up close and Lucy knew it frightened him. He'd told her he only felt fully alive when he was performing. If the agency worked, he'd have the opportunity to go on doing so for years to come. He might even learn to relish a new identity as a business owner.

'I still need to nail the copy,' Lucy said. 'It's got to be short. So far I've got: *Impersonation services available near you. Need someone to stand in as a colleague, family member or partner? Hire a professional actor today.*' She was secretly impressed with her own precision.

Jack wrinkled his nose. '*Partner* makes us sound like an escort agency.'

'We need it in there, though. There'll be people looking for plus ones to take along to parties and stuff. That's probably our biggest market. I was thinking we could advertise on dating sites.'

Jack shook his head. 'You're gonna be asked to give extras.'

Lucy laughed, even though Jack hadn't appeared to be joking. She was aware of a shadowy presence circling just beneath the surface of her optimism. How humiliating it had been, to accept her decade of striving, of dreaming, hadn't got her anywhere.

'I'll screen out the creeps,' she said. 'Make it clear we're trained actors. We'll create some terms and conditions.'

Jack grinned. 'No penises will be sucked as part of this assignment.'

Lucy play slapped him on the thigh, but felt her eyes stinging. Jack had never known the life of overdue rent payments, or had his card declined at the supermarket. He couldn't comprehend how radically different her decade of 'trying to make it' had been from his.

The grandfather was still sleeping, achingly vulnerable to the strangers in his room. Lucy felt a prickling beneath her skin. Was Jack experiencing it too? He was sitting back in his chair, legs splayed, no signs of discomfort on his face.

'We might have to get physical here and there, for authenticity,' Lucy whispered. 'I guess it comes down to whether it's a valid part of the performance. Just like any other acting job.'

Jack leaned forward to pick up a biscuit, wolfing it down with a single bite.

'I mean, if I need to, I might snog a client in front of their friends,' Lucy continued, trying to keep her gaze averted from the old man. 'But I'd insist on being in a public place the whole time.'

Jack threw his head back and laughed. '*Snog?* You'll do a roaring trade in fourteen-year-old boys.'

Laying her notepad down on the coffee table, Lucy turned to look him in the eye. 'Look, I'm trying, okay? This isn't how I imagined my acting career would go.'

She had his full attention now and his eyes softened. 'I know, Luce.'

'I'm being pragmatic, trying to build something.' She nearly added *for you as well as me*, but thought better of it. Over the years she'd learned to disguise every act of care, to hide her watchfulness.

He sighed, wincing slightly. 'I just don't want anyone treating you like a hooker, that's all.'

Lucy patted his knee. 'I wouldn't let them. We might actually have fun. Meeting new people, going to different places.'

Jack curled his lip and Lucy braced herself for a fresh objection. 'We should get an office. In Soho maybe,' he said.

This was the first positive sign of interest. Lucy felt a warmth in her chest, even as she recognised the impracticality of his suggestion. It was one of the things she loved most about Jack, this ability to conjure alternate futures in vivid detail, to expand on every aspiration, bringing colour and noise.

'Maybe, one day. If everything goes well.'

Jack smiled, his eyes darting to and fro. He was picturing it. With an inner lurch, Lucy thought of the anti-depressants and mood-stabilisers piled up in his kitchen cupboard, next to the teabags. He'd told her he didn't need them any more, that they dulled his creativity. Most of the time she opted to believe him, but there were moments, like now, when she could look at Jack and feel his inner ache with her own body. Thank goodness she hadn't got that train back to Portsmouth.

Chapter 3

The night of the agency's first gig, Jack appeared in the bathroom doorway as Lucy was applying her favourite red lipstick. She was listening to 'I've Got a Feeling' and he screwed up his nose in distaste, reaching for her phone to turn it off right in the middle of George's guitar slide. Jack preferred listening to obscure, unsigned bands, even though she suspected he took little enjoyment from it.

'I'm not sure about this, Luce,' he said.

She blotted her lips on a sheet of toilet roll, making a perfect crimson imprint. 'Stop worrying. I've emailed the client our Ts and Cs. He's just some lonely old soul who doesn't like going to parties on his own.'

Lucy didn't tell Jack she'd already rejected three clients who were trying to procure sex. *I'll be your audience of one,* a man had written, *and I expect you to work hard at convincing me.*

Tonight's gig looked promising, though. A plus one at a wedding reception with a man who'd seemed very polite on email. Lucy was going to be 'Eloise', a nice Home Counties girl with a bland HR job. A dreamer, who loved shopping, who believed in romance and fantasised about the perfect wedding. As she conjured these details, 'Eloise' began to instil herself, straightening Lucy's spine, relaxing the muscles of her face. It never ceased to delight her, this stepping through a membrane into a new consciousness, someone else's emotions quickening her blood.

'Text me regular updates,' Jack told her. 'I need to know you haven't been abducted.'

'I will.' Lucy checked under her arms for deodorant stains. She was wearing her special occasion dress, a backless purple number that hopefully looked more expensive than it was. With some reluctance, she'd done her roots that afternoon. She'd been planning to revert to the mud-brown of her childhood, but remembered a tutor telling her: *blondes get more work.*

Jack was still watching her, arms stiffly by his sides. 'If he tries anything—'

'We'll be in public the whole time.' This wasn't a moment for doubts. The client had already transferred over the money, hadn't even tried to haggle when Lucy set a bold rate of a hundred pounds an hour. Perhaps – for once – her optimism wasn't unwarranted. Maybe she really would find a way to make a living from acting.

The meeting point was a pub ten minutes away from the wedding venue. It was unexpectedly empty for a Saturday, and Lucy spotted her client sitting at the bar, jiggling one knee up and down as he watched the door. He was wearing a charcoal suit with a patterned shirt, flashes of purple and gold looking strangely at odds with his neatly trimmed grey hair.

'Philip?' She extended her hand.

He looked Lucy up and down and settled into a more

relaxed posture. 'You must be Eloise. Can I get you a drink while we, uh ...'

Lucy sat down on the bar stool next to him, folding her hands in her lap rather than resting an arm on the bar's sticky surface. 'I'm fine, thanks. Is there anything you want to run through, before we head to the venue?'

'Oh ... I hadn't ... should we—'

'We could go over our cover story, one last time?'

'Yes. Let's do that.'

The two of them recapped the cursory tale they'd put together through a couple of email exchanges. Eloise was the niece of a family friend and they'd met at a Christmas party. Their relationship was still in its early stages, so if Eloise didn't know every detail of Philip's life, no one would be suspicious.

Philip seemed a little naive, believing his friends would be unperturbed by him arriving with a much younger woman, when they'd likely barrage him with questions. Would he blame her, if people saw through the ruse? For the night to be a success, he'd need to become a kind of actor too and Lucy wasn't sure he had it in him.

As they headed out of the pub, the evening was entering its golden hour, the light imbuing even Philip's pallid skin with a healthy glow. A flock of sparrows were noisily taking up their positions in a narrow strip of garden alongside the river. Lucy clasped Philip's arm, fully in role as his younger, somewhat materialistic girlfriend. This was so very different from the auditions she'd attended, the sets she'd worked on, but she felt the same swelling excitement. She was performing again. Putting on a show. An actor, still.

*

When they reached the hotel, a man in a scarlet jacket with brass buttons held the door open and Lucy was plunged into a world of gleaming marble. She tried not to gawk at the crystal chandeliers and oversized flower arrangements as she walked along the red carpet running through the lobby. These brushes with the London of the wealthy used to give her an adrenalin rush, a combination of indignation and awe that had her insisting: *I'll have this too, one day, I swear I will.*

The disco was underway as 'Eloise' and Philip descended into the ballroom. It was an opulent room with floor-to-ceiling windows on three sides and a spacious dancefloor, currently empty aside from a group of three children, around ten or so, giggling as they tried to replicate the moves from a Beyoncé hit. Purple lighting bathed the ornamental columns and plaster swirls surrounding each window.

Most of the couples standing around sipping drinks were a good decade or two older than Lucy; the women dripped with gold jewellery and the men had the tanned, jaunty look that comes from copious leisure time. Lucy and Philip joined the line of evening guests making its way to the bride and groom. The bride was still wearing her wedding gown, layer upon layer of white gauze embellished with pearls, and Lucy saw a flicker of affront directed at Philip for bringing along a much younger woman.

'So lovely to meet you, I've heard so much about you,' Lucy tinkled as she shook hands.

The party soon gathered momentum, and after Philip fortified himself with a couple of brandies from the free bar, they took to the dancefloor. Lucy played Eloise a little tipsy, gyrating her body to the beat, throwing her hands up in the air. People were looking, whispering to one another, no doubt struggling to imagine this seemingly carefree woman in Philip's bed.

Lucy couldn't help enjoying herself. She was being paid to dance, to simulate having a great time. Eloise *was* having a great time and her endorphins surged through Lucy's bloodstream.

Philip had taken his jacket off and was bobbing his shoulders up and down to the beat as his eyes scanned the crowd gathered by the bar. His face was flushed and he wore a triumphant smile. If he'd gone to the reception alone, he might have been pitied. But now, his friends were re-evaluating him. Lucy's business would do more than keep her solvent, she realised; it could help people reinvent themselves, imbue them with confidence.

'Phil, you dark horse. Who's this lovely lady?' A tall man wearing a sky-blue waistcoat slapped Philip on the back. He had thinning grey hair and ruddy cheeks, the collar of his shirt bore a tiny red wine stain.

A moment of pure panic seemed to pass through Philip's eyes, so Lucy gave a wide smile, presenting her hand.

'I'm Eloise,' she said, receiving a wet kiss to the back of her knuckle.

The stranger announced himself as Rod, and he was soon joined by a cluster of older couples swaying to the beat. Lucy felt the cold gaze of scrutiny running over every contour of her body, but Eloise was flattered by the attention. Shoulders back, she pronounced the music *really fun*, appearing enchanted by descriptions of the wedding ceremony.

Philip remained quiet, so Lucy squeezed his arm from time to time, inviting him into the conversation by offering up a few, *doesn't that sound wonderful* type remarks.

She knew she was convincing, performing exactly the part she'd agreed with Philip beforehand. So when he slid his hand down to her backside, Lucy bristled but stayed in role, nodding enthusiastically to a drunk woman listing the Neil Diamond tracks she was about to request from the DJ.

'You really must bring this delightful creature to Tony's sixtieth,' she heard someone say. And the part of her that was still Lucy – that distant observer – was jubilant. Another four-hundred-pound gig would perhaps lead to another. Payment for dancing and laughing at jokes, partying in the kind of venues she'd waitressed in over the years. Poor Philip would be able to maintain the pretence of having a girlfriend, and Lucy could stay in London, being there for Jack.

The conversation was still going on around them when Philip pulled Lucy towards him, planting his lips against hers and forcing his tongue into her mouth. Everyone stopped talking, but Lucy just about managed to keep her disgust hidden. Philip was trying to impress his friends, that was all. Eloise could handle her boyfriend getting a little frisky.

She giggled as Philip pulled away, fighting an urge to wipe her mouth and putting a twinkle in her eye as she surveyed his face. There was something animalistic there, a wildness that frightened her. But they were still in public. Still putting on a show.

'That's left me rather thirsty,' she said with a flirtatious grin. Had Lucy seen that smile on another woman, she would have despised her, but Philip's buddies seemed awed as she slunk off to the bar.

She needed to steady her racing heart. Right now she was being paid to act, and that made her an actor. Her training had paid off. She was finding a way to continue in the profession she loved.

As she sat down at the bar and ordered a vodka and soda – just one to settle her nerves – Lucy saw Peter. She froze, watching him load empties onto a tray at the other end of the ballroom. It couldn't actually be him, she knew that. But the shock of recognition did something strange to her body, making her stiff and ungainly. Peter's slim build and dark hair. The waiter even parted it the same, off to one side, a kind of quiff at the front – Peter had always been pinching Lucy's mousse. She took a slug of her drink, feeling her eyes fill with tears. Eloise was slipping away as Lucy was *there*, back outside the university's theatre on graduation day, ten summers ago, scanning the crowd for Peter's face as a tannoy announcement told everyone to take their seats. She and Jack had kept returning to the registration desk where a middle-aged woman with a clipboard confirmed that Peter hadn't checked in or collected his gown.

He was supposed to have returned from his father's place in Hong Kong a fortnight before the ceremony. But Lucy's messages had all been met with silence. It was so unlike him.

'Are you sure he hasn't texted you?' she'd asked Jack.

He'd shaken his head.

'What if something's happened to him?' There had been a feeling in her belly, a seeping coldness.

Jack had taken her by the arm. 'Stop worrying. He'll be along soon.'

He'd been wrong. By that point, Peter had already been dead for a week and a half.

Philip was in front of her, clamping his hands around her waist. *This is my boyfriend,* Lucy reminded herself. *I'm Eloise. He's familiar, comfortable. I'm desperate for his friends to like me.*

'I'm not paying you to give me the slip,' Philip hissed.

Lucy threw her head back, as though sharing an intimate joke. 'It won't look right, if we stay glued together all night,' she whispered. 'I'm keeping the performance natural.'

Philip bent down, almost toppling her from the barstool as his soggy mouth connected with her neck. 'Why don't we see if we can get a room? These things are always tedious. We can order Champagne. Have a party of our own.'

'That's not going to happen,' Lucy said, in a firmer tone. 'You know the rules.'

Her very first gig, and it was descending into exactly the kind of sleazy encounter Jack had predicted.

Philip furrowed his brow, two angry lines appearing above his nose. Still, he had a hold of her, clinching her tightly, his sour breath against her face. 'I've paid. I've got you for the next two hours.'

'I'll keep going with the performance. But only if we stay in public.' Her face was still Eloise's face – she was wearing an untroubled smile, her eyes alive with a sense of fun. She wouldn't give Philip any reason to demand his money back, even though he was starting to frighten her.

He stepped in closer, scrabbling at Lucy's breast. With a swipe of her forearm, she parried him away. People were watching and she could feel a palpable sense of excitement, a barely disguised glee that this strange pairing was about to unravel. She'd let herself believe this could be easy. But really, it was the same old story – her waistline, her buttocks and breasts were what was really wanted. Lucy's acting skills weren't important to Philip at all.

Philip placed a hand on his hip, hatred igniting his eyes. 'Fine. I'll pay extra, if I have to.'

Somehow Lucy was up, off the stool, looping her bag over her arm. Even the barman had stopped serving to watch the exchange.

'Call me when you've sobered up,' she said in Eloise's sweet little voice. She made her way to the exit, not running, not pushing anyone aside.

Outside, Eloise melted away. Lucy folded her arms in front of her as she walked on past the nearest bus stop, heels clicking along the pavement as she took brisk, angry strides. In the distance she could see the towers of the financial district, thousands of lights making the buildings appear studded with gems. Alongside her, buses groaned past in groups of three, their belches and hisses strangely reassuring. She was never alone in the city, never far from help. The likes of Philip needn't intimidate her.

All the agency enquiries so far had been about female plus ones. Was Lucy really prepared to make a living out of two or three dates a week, trying to steel herself against the moment things turned ugly? If things didn't change, Jack would disengage with the business; he'd go on waiting for his agent to call, go on being frustrated.

As she continued down the street towards the next bus stop, swerving to avoid a cyclist who unexpectedly mounted the pavement, Lucy recalled the Peter-lookalike and the split-second belief that her friend was still alive. He'd recognise her humiliation at having Philip paw at her. But he wouldn't judge her for trying to make a living. He'd pity her, and somehow that was even worse.

Chapter 4

Every May, Lucy's drama class held a reunion. This was how they measured the success or otherwise of careers, through quick assessments of one another's weight and appearance, an annual audit of roles and near misses. Learning of someone's bit part role in a film or promising understudy gig could leave Jack listless and withdrawn for weeks. Each year Lucy suggested maybe they shouldn't go, but Jack wouldn't hear of missing it.

'Let's keep the agency to ourselves,' Lucy said as they exited Raynes Park Station. The sky was a cloudless blue, and she had to shield her phone from the glare of the sun as she pulled up directions to their classmate Sam's house.

'Worried everyone'll think you're a prozzie?' Jack grinned.

'No!' Lucy whacked him on the arm. 'I don't want anyone copying our idea, that's all.'

In the month since the Philip wedding, the agency had delivered just three more gigs, all of them requiring Lucy to play someone's girlfriend. To her relief, these newer clients hadn't expected anything beyond a peck on the cheek. But it still wasn't enough to make the business viable. She'd not been able to repay any of the money she'd borrowed from Jack, and there hadn't been any roles to occupy him. She'd tried to interest him in refining their website, but he'd preferred long mornings in bed, followed by afternoons exercising and pestering his agent. In the evenings they'd watch films together, unless Jack's girlfriend Emily was over and Lucy felt she had to sit and read outside in the communal gardens.

Jack peeled off his vintage denim jacket, stuffing it into his carrier bag of booze. 'I've got that crime drama I can talk about, that's something, I suppose.' Seven months previously he'd played a nosy neighbour, peering through a window and discovering a body. He'd actually auditioned for the lead and Lucy had rehearsed with him for hours ahead of his callback. When he was offered the minor part instead, they'd gone through the ritual of celebratory drinks, even though Lucy had seen the tears in his eyes.

Lucy's phone guided them onto a leafy street lined with detached houses carefully styled with wooden beams to create a mock-Tudor effect. They could hear children laughing in back gardens, a radio chat show floating out of an open window. Sam hadn't worked much in recent years either, so Lucy could only assume his parents had helped him and his wife buy a property in such a well-to-do area. As they turned into a cul-de-sac, barbecue smoke drifted towards them.

'Showtime,' Jack whispered.

Lucy smoothed her skirt and sucked in her stomach as they crunched along Sam's gravel drive. Sweat was gathering at her temples; already the forecasters were saying this May was likely to beat all temperature records.

'Here they are!' shouted Jasmine Wyatt, emerging from a side gate and ushering them in to Sam's back garden. A petite woman with a profusion of brown curls, Jasmine had officially given up on acting after her baby arrived three years ago. She put an arm around each of them and Lucy smelled the wine on her breath. 'Joined at the hip as always. Should I be dusting off my wedding hat?'

Lucy smiled and shook her head. ''Fraid not. I'm just crashing at Jack's for a while.'

'Of course you are,' Jasmine winked.

Across three years of uni, Jack had slept with at least half of their female classmates, including Lucy. By the end of their first term, he'd been nicknamed 'the slut'. Yet Lucy found their handful of drunken fumbles to be unfailingly disappointing. Jack always seemed to be performing for some hidden camera, flinging his body around, his mouth contorted into strange shapes. She remembered Peter walking in on them one time, his mouth dropping open at finding Lucy bent over the sofa, jeans around her ankles as she moaned half-heartedly.

The pace of their university course, along with the need to work four nights a week, had ultimately encouraged Lucy to explore the charms of hook-up apps. One-time encounters, no need for dinners or painful small talk.

'But don't you want to *be* with someone?' She remembered Peter's eyes filling with worry as Lucy prepared to go out one evening.

'I really don't.' Her relationship with the boyfriend of her school days hadn't survived the move to London, but rather than heartbreak, she'd experienced a joyous sense of freedom. 'What about you? You always struck me as the romantic type. Waiting for Mr Right to sweep you off your feet?'

Peter had laughed, but there had been something raw in his eyes. Why did men always feel it was so shameful to want more than just sex? 'One day. But not right now. I mean, the course barely leaves us with enough time to masturbate.'

Once Jack had unloaded the beers and vodka they'd brought onto a wooden picnic bench, he veered off to join the cluster of men surrounding the grill. Lucy poured a large vodka and soda into a paper cup, trying to resist the urge to follow. The previous year Jack had noticed her shadowing his conversations. *Fuck's sake, Lucy, I don't need a minder. I'm not going to fall to bits.*

She tried to formulate a friendly question about Jasmine's toddler. Her eyes stung from the smoke wafting over the patio and her stomach growled as she inhaled the aroma of cooking sausages. She was never sure who she wanted to be when she was around these old classmates. In the early years, Lucy had been one of the more successful ones. There'd been a couple of parts in Sunday night dramas. A few small, but nonetheless speaking roles in independent films. But these were followed by years of fruitless auditions supplemented by bar work and the odd small gig as 'drunk girl no. 2' or similar. Did she *mind* her peers knowing she'd given up? She had until October – less than five months away now – to decide whether or not to take up her place on the teacher training course.

'Nice place Sam's got here.' Jasmine grinned, her eyes meeting Lucy's and seeming to convey *acting couldn't have paid for this.*

Lucy scanned the garden, the long rectangle of parched lawn dotted with picnic tables, the spacious patio. 'Certainly is.'

'You had much work lately?' Jasmine asked.

The perennial question. And the thing was, everyone knew the answer before they even asked it. Keeping up with one another's careers was a petty obsession they all shared.

Lucy smiled. She could speak of the milk ad, talk of the rapport she had with the producer, hint that she was expecting further work from that quarter. Part of her longed to do so, to perform a version of herself still inhabiting her earlier dreams. But by the time next year's reunion rolled around, she wouldn't have appeared in a single thing and her classmates would titter about it. *Look at how the teacher's pet wound up! She'll be on the murder mystery circuit next year, or working for a corporate training company.*

'I've actually decided to retrain as a drama teacher.' It didn't feel like the truth, Lucy realised. She was still clinging to acting, to London and her friendship with Jack.

'That's great!' Jasmine's eyes were soft as she patted Lucy's arm. 'It's such a relief, isn't it? The moment you think, *fuck it, I've had enough.* I've never regretted it. It's so nice not worrying about my figure all the time, checking and rechecking my phone.'

'Yeah. I mean, I guess it's good to be pragmatic.'

'It *is* good,' Jasmine said. 'It's degrading how they make us live – traipsing round to auditions and half the time they don't even bother letting you know you haven't got the part. Fuck that.' She drained her plastic cup and refilled it with white wine.

'There was this one time,' Jasmine continued, 'I had to perform an orgasm for a bunch of middle-aged men. They were just sitting behind a desk and I was on this couch, moaning and arching my back. I wanted the part, so I really went for it, you know? Didn't get it, though. Maybe I wasn't loud enough for them.'

Lucy responded with a thin smile. Now she'd mentioned teacher training, she'd committed herself to performing Lucy-the-failure, making the best of a bad situation, trying to be happy for her peers when they discussed their understudying gigs, the appearances in hospital dramas, their elation at a call-back. The sad thing was, teaching had actually been her original goal; Lucy's very reason for going to university. Where she came from, becoming a drama teacher counted as making it, entering a professional class, the world of mortgages and nearly new cars. But Jack and Peter had taught her to want more – and made her feel capable of earning anything she wanted.

'Seen Gracie's new flick?' Jasmine asked.

Lucy felt a surge of warmth towards Jasmine for taking them to safer ground. Gracie Dorn was the only one of their cohort who'd enjoyed real commercial success. She'd snubbed these reunions since the beginning.

'Yeah. I thought it was . . . '

'Sappy as fuck?'

'Completely.' Lucy and Jack had been in fits of laughter on the way back from the cinema, with Jack pausing under lampposts to mimic Gracie's performance, crinkling his chin in dismay, widening his eyes in overblown surprise. Lucy had known it was spiteful to laugh along, but indulging in a bit of mockery always seemed to make Jack a little less envious, more able to cope.

'Do you ever think she'll get a role where she doesn't have to cry for at least half the film?' Jasmine asked.

Lucy gave a polite chortle. Gracie had been the weakest

student, every performance tipping into melodrama. But she'd been beautiful. Thick blond hair and large blue eyes. Legs that seemed far too long for her body. In the end, those were the things that mattered.

Another classmate, Katya Ivanoff, came over and asked Jasmine about her daughter. Out came a phone, a bright carousel of photos. After a few minutes of cooing, Lucy decided to check on Jack who'd migrated to a picnic table further down the garden.

'... so far it's just been people wanting pretend girlfriends.' Jack saw Lucy approaching and froze, lips apart.

Will Tanner and Sam Greene both welcomed Lucy with a hug, before turning back to Jack. There was a flush spreading across his neck. Will and Sam exchanged a questioning glance as the silence stretched beyond what was comfortable. Was Jack angry at her for checking on him? Or was he just feeling sheepish at having been caught blabbing?

'You had anything to eat yet, Luce?' Sam asked.

'I'll grab something in a bit – it smells amazing.'

'Jack's been telling us about your business venture.' Sam paused, taking a bite from a glistening burger. 'Very entrepreneurial. Wish I'd thought of it.'

'Well, if the bookings keep rolling in we might end up hiring—' Jack began.

Lucy shot him a warning glance and he fell silent.

'I'd be well up for a bit of extra work,' Will said. He'd been the only other state school student besides Lucy in their year group.

'Could you play a girlfriend, though?' Jack laughed. 'That's where all the demand seems to be.'

'For the right price, I can play anything,' Will said. 'Seriously though, it seems so obvious. Kind of insane no one thought to do it before now. Maybe you should take your post down, Jack, before anyone copies you.'

Lucy slid into the seat next to Jack and clamped a hand on his shoulder. 'You *posted* about the agency?'

Jack gave her a rueful smile, absently drumming his fingers against the wooden table. 'I'll take it down.'

Lucy drew in a breath. As well as compromising the discretion the agency needed, Jack had basically just handed their business idea to a network of jobbing actors. She wanted to tell him as much, but knew she needed to change the subject. 'So, have you guys seen Gracie's latest film?'

'Oh my God, the absolute state of it!' Sam took the bait and the group descended into sniping, distracting themselves from the feeling of failure that was winding its way around the sun-dappled garden.

Arriving back at the flat that evening, Lucy and Jack both slumped on the sofa. There was a low growl from a tug boat chugging its way along the river and the sitting room felt muggy, even with the balcony doors open. Lucy kicked off her shoes and closed her eyes.

'It wasn't a *bad* afternoon,' Jack offered.

'I wish you'd kept quiet about the agency,' she said. 'We can't go offering work to everyone; there's barely enough for the two of us. And as for putting it on your feed—' Lucy had abandoned social media a few years back, but Jack still tended his accounts obsessively.

'I've said I'm sorry. I just wanted to show Dad I was

being proactive. He got all snippy about money last time I visited.'

Lucy sat up straight. 'The people who hire us want complete discretion. If they do a search and find our faces associated with an impersonation business—'

Jack sighed and pulled out his phone. 'I'll delete the post right this second, okay?'

'Let's see it first.' Lucy extended her hand.

He passed her his phone, avoiding her eye. The image he'd used had been taken in a nightclub, five or so years ago, arms round one another, open-mouthed smiles as they leaped into the air. Lucy was wearing her purple special-occasion dress, Jack was in a tie-dyed T-shirt that was conspicuously too tight across the shoulders. They looked fun and attractive, but not in the least bit professional.

> Me and my genius buddy Lucy are now officially in business! Impersonators for hire! And no – we won't be rocking up to your party pretending to be Elton John or Madonna. We're talking high quality acting gigs only, people! First business of its kind.

He'd ended with a link to the website Lucy had created. At least this showed enthusiasm of a sort.

She returned the phone without saying a word.

Jack's fingers danced around his screen for a few moments. 'Looks like someone's filled out an enquiry form. What will it be this time? Be my girlfriend for a night, or someone trying to sell us a new website?'

'Maybe this time someone wants a boyfriend for the night,' Lucy said, tucking her feet beneath her. 'You know, you should really set your socials to private.'

Jack continued staring at his screen. 'It says: *I'm looking to work with a male and female actor in their early thirties for around six months. Would you be available to meet to discuss the brief?*' His eyes were suddenly serious.

'What's wrong? Sounds like a perfect gig to me.'

'Almost too perfect,' Jack glanced at her. 'Do you think one of the guys is pranking us? I can imagine Sam winding us up.'

'Only one way to find out.' Lucy pulled out her own phone and started tapping out a reply.

Chapter 5

The prospective client was a woman named Zelda, who suggested meeting in a Primrose Hill café the following Tuesday afternoon. The sky was a cloudless blue and there wasn't even a hint of a breeze to dissipate the heat as Lucy and Jack headed out of Chalk Farm Station. Lucy was regretting wearing her black trouser suit – it had seemed like a good idea back in Jack's air-conditioned flat, but now the fabric of her trousers clung to her legs, threatening to bring her out in prickly heat.

'It's going to be Will or Sam who shows up. I just know it,' Jack said. 'Too much of a coincidence getting the enquiry right after telling them about the agency. *Zelda* totally sounds like a bullshit name.'

Lucy stepped into the road to make way for a woman with a pushchair. 'Our ads are getting loads of click-throughs. There's every chance it could be genuine.'

'But why would someone need the both of us? And for six months too. It'll be some mate of Sam's telling us we need to infiltrate the dogging scene. Or I don't know, stand on street corners making passes at random people while Will secretly films the whole thing.'

Lucy laughed. 'If the money's real, I'll do it.'

The café's walls were covered with vintage film posters, its door and window frames painted a vibrant purple. Around half the tables were occupied with groups of mothers and babies, although there was a youngish-looking man in one of the corner seats, engrossed in his laptop. No lone woman. But no Sam or Will either.

Jack ordered an iced latte with whipped cream plus a slice of carrot cake, so Lucy didn't feel bad just asking for tap water. They took the drinks over to a table and waited.

As Jack sipped coffee through a straw, absorbed in his phone, Lucy pondered ideas for a new ad campaign to try and broaden the agency's client base beyond those simply wanting a date for the evening. She'd need to write new copy, select some less party-oriented imagery. At some point soon, she really ought to get back to Portsmouth and let her parents know she was considering abandoning teacher training. She'd been vague about her delayed return, mumbling something about *a few work opportunities*, and she felt an unpleasant knotting in her middle whenever she remembered her father's response. *That's brilliant. I always knew the work would pick up.*

He assumed she was doing 'proper' acting and would soon appear in an exciting new drama he could tell his customers about. Lucy felt too ashamed to tell him the 'work' now involved her going on dates with men his age.

The bell above the door jangled as a woman entered wearing a sleeveless floral dress that floated down to the floor. Her long auburn hair was tied back with a pale-green scarf and her earlobes stretched under the weight of heavy silver earrings.

The woman scanned the café once, then went to the counter and ordered a tea, which she carried over to Lucy and Jack's table.

'Are you—' She took her lower lip between her teeth.

Lucy stood up. 'It's Zelda, right? Thanks so much for meeting with us. Do have a seat.' Her voice was higher pitched than normal and she tried to steady herself with a deep breath. 'I'm Lucy and this is my associate, Jack.'

Jack gave Zelda a brief nod.

'We're looking forward to hearing all about your assignment,' Lucy said.

Zelda's eyes roved over their faces. 'Look at you both.'

Lucy smiled.

'I don't know how best to . . .' Again, Zelda bit her lower lip. Her hands were balled up into fists.

'Take your time.' Lucy spoke in a neutral tone, careful to hide her desperation. She was fighting an urge to pull out her phone, to play her showreel, reassure this woman that she and Jack could be whoever she wanted them to be.

'Okay.' Zelda laid her hands flat on the table. They were freckled with protruding veins and each of her fingers bore a chunky silver ring. Lucy noted a frog, Celtic markings, a skull and a hummingbird.

Zelda inhaled sharply, as though bracing herself for something physically unpleasant. 'About thirty years ago I was backpacking in Thailand. This was before such things were fashionable. There wasn't a McDonald's in every seaside town, no gaggles of package tourists like there is now.' She clasped her hands together and her shoulders just perceptibly eased themselves downwards.

'Anyway, I met this guy Sebastian. I thought we were kindred spirits: exploring, taking in the culture. He was my first love. For ten months there wasn't one cross word. We were so in tune.'

Lucy listened attentively. Zelda's forehead was smooth, but her pale-blue eyes were filled with a strange intensity.

Zelda twisted her frog ring as she went on. 'We decided we wanted to stay on in Thailand – it was easy to find work as English teachers back then. We pictured ourselves as nomads, working our way across the world, staying connected with our spiritual selves.'

'Sounds idyllic,' Lucy offered. She glanced at Jack. He was motionless, observing Zelda carefully.

'It was.' Zelda gazed out of the window and a shadow seemed to pass over her face. 'But then I fell pregnant.'

'Oh,' Lucy said to fill the silence that followed. Zelda was still looking out the window and Lucy couldn't quite gauge whether she expected congratulations or commiserations.

'I wasn't scared,' Zelda continued at last. 'Sebastian and I made each other feel as though we could do anything. He seemed excited when I told him, he really did. But the very next day I woke up and his side of the bed was empty. There was a pile of cash on the pillow, about ten pounds worth of Thai Baht. And a note.'

Zelda stopped playing with her ring and looked from Lucy to Jack, a bitter smile playing at her lips. 'Can you imagine what it said?'

Lucy shook her head.

'He'd written: *I'm sorry. I can't do this. We have our whole lives ahead of us. You should get an abortion.*'

'Gosh.' This seemed to Lucy like the appropriate response from the empathetic proprietor of a business. But beneath the role she was playing she registered a jolt, imagining the panic, the loneliness of that moment, the betrayal.

'Indeed.' Zelda sat back in her chair, taking a sip of tea. Her body seemed looser somehow, as though telling her story had freed something within her. 'I miscarried a week later. Probably down to the stress of it all. Ended up going home. You can't imagine how crushed I was.'

'I'm so sorry,' Lucy said.

'I've never forgotten the callousness of it,' Zelda went on. 'Sebastian and I did everything together. We could make the most boring of train journeys feel like fun. Do you know how rare that is? To find the person who can step into your daydreams and make everything bigger, more colourful?'

Again, Lucy shook her head. Jack didn't react at all. Why wasn't he trying to make this work? Hadn't he noticed the effort Lucy was putting into getting them customers?

Zelda looked down at the table. 'He just disappeared on me. Didn't even stick around to find out what I planned to do. He ruined my life.'

'It must have been such a traumatic time,' Lucy ventured.

Zelda closed her eyes for a moment. 'The man I loved turned out to be a fucking coward. I would have had the abortion, done anything he asked. I just wanted us to be together.'

Lucy waited for Zelda to say something more, but she didn't. Her eyes scanned Lucy's face, then seemed to settle on Jack. Her expression hinted at an ongoing sadness, as though the terror of that long-ago moment was something she revisited each and every day.

Lucy tapped Jack's foot with her own, hoping he'd murmur a supportive comment, but he remained stubbornly silent. Outside, a delivery driver leaned on his horn.

'How do you see us helping you?' Lucy offered.

Zelda gave a rueful smile, pale pink lipstick leaking into the creases around her mouth. 'I want to destroy him.'

Lucy heard Jack's breath catch, and this time they did look at one another. *What have you got me into?* he seemed to be transmitting with his eyes.

'Okay. What specifically . . . ' Bile was burning the back of Lucy's throat, she wasn't sure how to continue. She'd registered the horror of Zelda's predicament, the breathtaking fear and dismay she must have felt at being abandoned. The emotion was too strong. The pain too raw. Unexpectedly, Lucy wished today's client had turned out to be a middle-aged man asking her to pose as his girlfriend; the scope blessedly limited, the ramifications minimal.

'I know it's been a long time,' Zelda said. 'You probably think I should be over it. Some days I think that too. But the scars run too deep. To think that Sebastian's love for me could have been so easily undone. One hint of responsibility was all it took. I can't stand the idea of him enjoying his life without ever having to face up to what he did.'

Lucy nodded. She'd feel that way too, she supposed.

Zelda's face hardened, but her hands started to tremble and she quickly folded them in her lap. 'You'd think at some point in the last thirty years he might have wondered about me? But there's been nothing, he's never tried to get in touch.' The tremor spread from Zelda's hands to her arms and shoulders.

Jack leaned forwards, his cheeks reddening. 'What kind of acting would be involved?' he said.

'You,' Zelda nodded at him, 'could be the baby I refused to abort. All grown up and looking for your daddy. You find him. Try and build a relationship with him. And just at the point where he feels a connection, when he's starting to see himself as a father and get all glowy about it, you're going to cut him out of your life. You're going to disappear on him, just like he disappeared for me.' There was a ferocious light in Zelda's eyes that seemed completely at odds with the hippie clothing and herbal tea.

Lucy glanced around the café. The mothers seemed engrossed in their conversations. The young man was still tapping away into his computer.

'I'm not sure I—' Jack sounded agitated.

'You mentioned hiring a female actor too?' Lucy said. They needed time to think, to consider the gig from multiple angles. She had a sinking feeling they'd have to turn it down. It was asking a lot of Jack. Too much perhaps.

'Oh yes,' Zelda seemed animated. 'You could be a girl-friend or fiancée or whatever. More plausible if there's two of you. I want to do this properly.'

'I—' Jack was going to say no. Lucy could hear it in his voice, so she delivered a gentle warning kick. They shouldn't rush into a refusal. Six months of income. A hundred pounds an hour stretched out across multiple getting-to-know-you dinners and coffees. This wasn't supposed to be about Lucy, but it represented salvation for her. For the first time in her life, she might be able to support herself on the proceeds of acting alone.

'We'll have to draw up a schedule and a budget,' Lucy said. There might be something they were overlooking. A way of framing this gig that didn't feel quite so *wrong*. 'We'll need to agree how often we see Sebastian. I mean, assuming he believes us.'

Zelda waved her hand. 'I'll put five thousand down as a deposit. Schedule whatever you can. It's not as though you can put a price tag on closure. I've waited a long time for this.'

Five thousand? Lucy was careful to keep her features still, but the sum made her feel giddy.

'There's no guarantee this Sebastian will believe me,' Jack said. The hair at his temples was damp with sweat.

'We'll be convincing,' Lucy gave Zelda a reassuring smile.

'Do excuse me for a moment,' said Zelda. 'That tea's gone right through me.'

Lucy turned to Jack the moment Zelda was out of earshot.

'This isn't acting,' he hissed. 'What kind of sicko would think up a scheme like that?'

'I know. I just don't want to rush—'

'No way am I doing it.'

'But he abandoned her, Jack. He really *could* have a son out there – someone that poor woman had to raise by herself.'

Lucy's sister Mel had parented her son Charlie alone – she'd been nineteen and a promising politics student when the baby's father dumped her. He'd behaved as though Charlie's presence in the world was nothing to do with him, never changed a nappy, lied about his finances to avoid paying maintenance. Lucy remembered her visits home, her sister pacing round and round the living room to get the baby to sleep, never complaining even though her whole body drooped with exhaustion. 'I'm not going to feel sorry for myself. I have Charlie,' Mel had said time and again. But she'd had to drop out of university, abandon her dreams.

'Let's just hear Zelda out,' Lucy said. 'We'll talk everything through before we give her an answer.'

Jack pressed his lips together, a brief twitch of his eyebrows signalling irritation at how his morning had gone.

Zelda's form floated its way back to their table. 'Sebastian's picture is on his company's website. He's a banker now, if you can believe it. My free-spirited lover. I thought, as a start point, you might approach him at his office and tell him you've finally managed to wrangle his name out of me after many years of asking.'

Zelda reached down and produced a photograph from her hessian tote bag. 'You could have this with you.' She placed it down on the table. It was unmistakably her, auburn hair cascading over her shoulders, her figure slim in a turtle-print sarong. She was with a tall man, tanned with long sun-bleached hair, arms and legs dotted with mosquito bites.

'You can just play yourself,' Zelda said, facing Jack. 'No need to invent a whole other career or anything like that. I'm passionate about the arts. It would be very plausible for a son of mine to become an actor.' Her eyes were roving over Jack's face and Lucy was terrified as to what she might be reading there. If Lucy could make him perceive the worthiness of this gig, then she might just be able to wrangle a yes out of him. If that's what she wanted. She kept remembering that thunderous line: *I want to destroy him*. It made her scalp prickle.

Lucy braved another look at Jack and thought she saw the tiniest flicker of curiosity on his face. She cleared her throat and turned to Zelda. 'If you don't mind me asking – why now? You said it's been thirty years.'

Zelda cast her eyes downwards, once again twisted her frog ring. 'I recently came into some money. An inheritance, enough to make me comfortable for the rest of my life. And it hit me: I felt no joy. None at all. I don't think I'll ever be truly happy until I've made Sebastian face up to what he did.'

Lucy felt her insides squeeze with pity. There was something so tragic in the woman's demeanour, as though carrying this feeling of betrayal had distorted something fundamental, stolen some youthful essence that could never be recovered. 'We'll consider everything and get back to you in the next couple of days,' she said.

Chapter 6

'No way. I'm sorry, Luce, but no.' Jack wouldn't even look at Lucy as they walked alongside the elegant terraces of Regent's Park Road, passing an array of independent shops and cafés with brightly coloured awnings.

'But five grand—' It was an effort keeping up with him in the heeled boots she'd worn to the meeting.

Jack stopped outside a bookshop, wheeling around to face her. 'I'm an actor. Not some sort of slimy conman.'

Lucy conjured Zelda, the rings on her fingers, the scarf in her hair. The woman represented a world Lucy had lived adjacent to for so long – the world of money, of being able to indulge every whim. For such a person, revenge was a service that could be purchased like any other. But that didn't make Zelda's pain any less real.

It was approaching midday, the glare of the sun forcing Lucy to squint, but when they reached Primrose Hill they automatically started trudging up the hill to the viewpoint. The grass pollen made Lucy's nose tickle as they were over-taken by a man jogging, his bare back glistening with sweat. Ahead of them, a woman walking a golden retriever paused every four steps or so, putting a hand to her temple.

'I know it's not your dream role,' Lucy offered as the London skyline came into view. 'But it *is* acting.'

Did she believe that? *Five grand*. She'd be able to clear her overdraft, buy a train ticket to visit her parents. But above all, she wanted to picture Jack working hard at a role, too absorbed to dwell on the scarcity of auditions. Living with him again, after ten years, had been revelatory. She'd been shocked at how he managed to stretch out just a few activities. Gym sessions that went on for hours. Nights where he'd watch three films back to back. He was careful not to give Emily more than two evenings a week, lest she believe things were more serious than they were. It didn't seem healthy.

Jack looked around, scanning for empty benches. They were all occupied with groups of colleagues on their lunch-break, a passionately kissing young couple and a shirtless man swigging from a can of Strongbow. Jack angled his head, indicating the parched grass.

Lucy plonked herself down, stretching her legs in front of her, inhaling the scent of sun-warmed earth. She'd never tire of this view. The glimmer of the Shard, the knobbles of the Post Office Tower. It gave her the exact same feeling as arriving in London for university: here was possibility, pulsing with its own special energy.

'Our faces are out there, Luce,' Jack said. 'What if this Sebastian guy recognises us?'

Lucy stifled a smile as she unzipped her ankle boots. Her socks were damp with sweat so she took them off and laid them out to dry in the sun. *Not much chance of that*, she wanted to say.

'Like Zelda said, you could keep your cover story fairly close to the truth,' Lucy suggested. 'Tell this Sebastian you're an actor. That way, if he does come across any of your material, he won't be suspicious. Jack Moreton could just be your stage name. You're the only actor I know who could pull something like this off.'

Jack shot her a glance. Not quite grateful. On some level he knew she was flattering him. 'It's just so fucking mercenary, Luce. I mean, taking money to deceive someone. To hurt him. This isn't what I had in mind when I agreed to go along with your agency thing.'

Values could be brandished like pretty little baubles in Jack's world – he never had to worry about where he'd be sleeping the following month, or enact urgent repairs to a pair of shoes, hoping the sole could be held in place with superglue for the two weeks until payday. He didn't have a mountain of student debt looming over him, his father had simply paid his fees and rent upfront.

And yet, the idea of convincing someone they were a parent – before snatching the relationship away – was reprehensible, there was no getting around it. Lucy felt a tightening at her temples. *I want to destroy him*, Zelda had said. They couldn't be part of that.

'Fuck.' Lucy closed her eyes, trying to enjoy the sun against her face. The heat seared into her skin. If she lingered too long, she'd burn. Unexpectedly, she felt close to tears. People her age were starting families of their own, rising up the ranks in their careers, adding 'manager' to their job titles. Sometimes it felt to Lucy as though she and Jack were trying to cling to the remnants of their student lives, nursing the dreams of their younger selves in a way most people would find indulgent.

She remembered Jack taking her hand after Peter's death, a strange darkness in his eyes. 'You can't go home,' he'd told her. She felt the truth of the statement clamping around her, shutting out the light.

'Peter wanted so much for you, you know that, right?' Jack had continued. 'He believed in you. You have to give acting your everything. It's the only way we can honour him ...' Jack's pinkened eyes had brimmed over, fat tears soaking his long, dark lashes. 'I need you.'

In that bleak time, Jack's need had felt like Lucy's only consolation. There was something comforting in allowing herself to be shunted along a path he'd chosen for her. No more agonising, fretting over the very unlikelihood of an acting career. She'd do everything to make it work. And that's what she was still doing now.

Jack reached over and squeezed Lucy's knee. 'This Sebastian wouldn't have believed us, anyway. If someone told me I'd fathered a child, there's no way I'd take it at face value. It'd be so easy to disprove. I mean, anyone can order DNA tests off the internet.'

Lucy opened her eyes. 'He'd insist on a test. Of course he would.'

Jack shrugged.

A new perspective started to unfurl. Whether this Sebastian believed their performance or not depended on so much more than their acting. They'd provide a service and collect the money. Just like any other professionals. And they *needed* this money.

She placed her elbows on the ground behind her and leaned back. 'If we did it, this Sebastian would realise Zelda sent us. I mean, it would be obvious.'

'Probably.' From the corner of his eye, Jack was observing two women who'd laid out towels a few yards away and were now stripping down to their bikinis.

Lucy continued. 'Maybe Zelda actually *wants* to be found out. I mean, Sebastian would shit himself at first. And quite right too. He deserves that. But when he realises it's a lie he'll go ballistic at Zelda and she'll get to have it out with him.'

'Maybe.' Jack sounded bored. 'It's all a bit far-fetched.'

'How about we just go with it, then? If we think it's getting weird or going too far, we'll stop. But you're right, Sebastian will ask for a test straight away and it'll be over before it really begins.' *Five thousand pounds.* Just naming the sum inside her own head sent little jolts of electricity through her veins.

Jack shook his head. Behind them, up on the benches, someone started strumming 'Yesterday' on an acoustic guitar.

Lucy shifted onto her side. Her black trousers were soaking up the heat, she could feel sweat trickling along her legs. 'The man did put himself in a position where he might plausibly have an adult son wandering around. He treated Zelda appallingly.'

'That doesn't make it any less gross.'

'Yeah, but isn't it horrible to think he's never faced up to what he did? He just ran away, refused to take responsibility.' Was it right to push Jack in this way? Every cell of her body was alive with the want, the *need* to make a success of the agency.

They were silent for a moment. A fat pigeon landed by

Lucy's feet, hotly pursued by another. After a brief tussle and an attempted mounting, they flew away.

'At least your dad did right by your mum. I wonder how she'd have felt if he refused to acknowledge you.' Lucy felt her muscles tighten. She knew she was being manipulative. Jack was the result of his father's dalliance with a secretary, and even though he'd been privately educated and assigned a generous allowance, there was a raw edge to his family relationships, a barely concealed hurt. At their first university play Lucy had noticed Jack scanning the audience, hoping his father would show up. She'd felt almost nauseous at the presence of her own parents, worried Jack would make some comment about the cheapness of their clothes, the provincialism that wafted from them like the sickly-sweet scent of off-brand fabric conditioner. But his eyes had been soft as he shook their hands, greeting them warmly, making Lucy feel as though she was in fact the richer of the two.

Jack looked out over the view, screwing his lips together. Alluding to his paternity had been cheap and nasty – Lucy knew she'd gone too far. She tried to form a retraction in her mind – how could she do it tactfully, without alluding to his mental health?

'If it gets weird, we'll stop?' Jack said.

She looked at him for a moment, then drew him into a hug. 'We will. Oh, Jack, thank you. We'll make this work, I promise.'

Chapter 7

Jack loaned Lucy one of his grandmother's rings, a rectangular slab of sapphire flanked by two square diamonds, the weight of it on her finger anchoring her in her role as his fiancée, an amiable PR executive filled with gentle concern for her partner. To minimise the risk of slips over what might be a prolonged assignment, they opted to use their real first names.

They took the Tube to Liverpool Street, heading into the clamour of Bishopsgate with its stream of buses and cabs. It was another sweltering day, the glass and steel of the high-rises intensifying the white heat of the sun. Even in a sleeveless dress and sandals, Lucy could feel sweat gathering on her back and at her temples.

'You're going to ace this,' she said as the five-storey monolith housing Sebastian's bank came into view.

Jack made a sound like a growl. 'Fuck's sake! You've broken my concentration.' He stopped walking and was almost knocked over by a suited man who came barrelling up behind them.

They moved to the edge of the pavement, beneath a walkway connecting two buildings on either side of the road. 'I need a minute,' Jack said, closing his eyes.

'Okay, but—'

'It's so easy for you. You forget that the rest of us actually have to work at it.'

Lucy said nothing, hands clasped in front of her as Jack took several slow breaths. They were conspicuous. This wasn't a corner of the city that invited lingering, there were no shop windows to gaze at, only what seemed like miles of sterile office fronts.

'Right.' Jack cracked his knuckles. 'Let's go.'

Inside the building's vast marble atrium, a security guard directed them towards a reception desk. There was a profusion of tall houseplants – trees, really – and a seating area clustered around a small fountain. A group of suited people waited by the lifts, faces in their phones. This was a side of London completely unfamiliar to Lucy. What did these people do in their offices all day? She could mimic their gestures, but their thoughts and preoccupations remained a blank.

'We're here to see Sebastian Stott,' Jack said to the receptionist. She was young-looking, braids tied back into a ponytail, long nails carefully painted green with gold stripes.

'Of course. And you are?'

'Jack Hutchison.'

The woman frowned at her computer screen. 'I can't see you on his appointment list.'

Lucy clasped Jack's hand. 'It's actually a sensitive personal matter. Could you maybe give Mr Stott a call? Tell him it's regarding Zelda Hutchison. He'll want to see us, I'm sure.'

The receptionist's eyes widened, but she nodded and tapped some numbers into her desk phone. In a lowered voice, she attempted to describe the pair. *Jack Hutchison. A man and a woman. I don't know, about thirty? Regarding Zelda Hutchison?*

She smiled at them as she ended the call. 'He's coming down. If you'd like to wait over there,' she gestured to the leather sofas facing the water feature.

Jack and Lucy took a seat, both of them prim, knees together, watching the lifts in silence. The previous week they'd met with Zelda a second time to run through Jack's extensive list of background questions and now Jack-the-son lived and breathed. He'd grown up in Richmond, an only child. His mother – who never married – had worked flexible hours as a ceramic artist; his grandparents Dot and Hugh had visited most weekends. Theirs was a Labour-voting family. Bohemian, yet comfortable.

Jack-the-son was creative like his mother and growing up without a father hadn't dented his confidence, he'd been doted on too much for that. But becoming engaged to Lucy had triggered a sudden quest for understanding. He needed to know who his father was before he could start a family of his own.

Zelda had urged Lucy to play herself as an actor too, *us creatives move in the same circles, you can just be yourself, no need for invention*, she'd insisted. But Lucy liked the boundaries between her real self and the part she was playing to be clearly delineated, so she'd invented a demure PR executive.

Her body felt rigid with her character's nerves, but she flooded her eyes with compassion. She was deeply invested in Jack's quest, refusing to voice her fear that he'd ultimately be disappointed.

Before long a tall man, wearing a charcoal-coloured suit with a jade-green tie, stepped out from the lift and made his way towards them. Lucy recognised him from his website photo, although in person he seemed much older. His faded brown hair was now cropped short; his eyes were deeply set, bordered by grey skin, but he walked with long, vigorous strides. No one watching him would guess he'd been summoned to see a ghost.

Jack rose as he approached and Lucy stood up too, an apprehensive smile on her face.

'Mr Hutchison?' the man – Sebastian – said.

'Yes. I— Is there somewhere we can talk—' Jack was pitching this perfectly, his voice carrying just the slightest tremor of nerves, his eyes guarded, but flashes of pure longing seeming to escape against his will.

'You're friends of Zelda?' Two deep lines appeared between Sebastian's eyebrows. His eyes were green, the whites unusually bright and clear.

Jack swallowed. Put a hand in the pocket of his trousers. Took it out again. 'If there's somewhere private—'

Sebastian looked at his watch. 'I'm actually rather pushed for time. If you could just tell me what this is about.'

Jack lowered his gaze. 'I'm her son,' he whispered. He and Lucy had discussed this line, agreeing that *I'm your son* would be too intimidating, too likely to put the man on his guard.

Lucy watched Sebastian closely. There was a twitch in his jaw, a sudden realisation, followed by the hardening of doubt. 'I have a meeting to get to,' he said, turning as if to leave.

Lucy took hold of his forearm. The character she was playing was desperate for this to go well; ready to do anything to ward off the dismay of rejection. 'Please. You've no idea how long it's taken for Jack to build up the courage to come here. Five minutes. That's all we're asking.'

Sebastian looked at Jack, who almost crumpled beneath his gaze. 'No.' He shook his head. 'No. I'm not falling for this. No way.'

Lucy scrabbled around in her bag and produced Zelda's Thailand photograph. 'This is you, right?'

Sebastian stared at it for a moment, then straightened up, quickly glancing around the atrium. The receptionist had been watching them, but she took pains to appear engrossed by her computer screen.

'Five minutes.' He beckoned for them to follow, down a staircase, then along a corridor, using his lanyard to open a side room. He held the door, ushering Jack and Lucy into a white-walled space containing a dark wooden table and six chairs. There was a watercooler in one corner, some sort of projection equipment in another, but nothing designed to make the room feel welcoming or comfortable.

Sebastian gestured for them to sit, then appeared suddenly perplexed, unsure what should happen next.

'I'm not after money or anything like that,' Jack said.

Sebastian flinched. He picked at the skin around his thumb, as though determined not to make eye contact with either of them.

'I just want to get to know you. That's all.' Jack swallowed and Lucy placed a hand on his back, making herself a little tearful.

Lucy watched Sebastian's chest rise and fall with each breath. His lips were parted and his eyes strangely distant.

'Thailand ... Zelda ... it was all so long ago.' It was as though he was speaking to himself.

'You were young,' Jack offered.

Lucy squeezed Jack's hand. Her character was aching with empathy, desperate to help but unsure how.

Sebastian turned his back to them, taking a few steps towards the wall and resting a hand against the plaster. 'I didn't know. I thought ... '

A surge of adrenaline. He believed it was possible. He might have fathered a son.

'I'm happy to do a DNA test,' Jack said. This was a gamble, but he and Lucy felt they should be the ones to introduce the idea; remind Sebastian there was a very easy way to confirm or disprove what he was being told.

Sebastian wheeled around to face them, his expression stricken. 'This is nonsense. I can't believe— It's nonsense.'

Lucy tilted her head slightly, projecting pity. But really she was thinking, *why must it be nonsense?* Surely Sebastian realised unprotected sex had consequences for wealthy men, just as it did the poor ones?

'I know it's a lot to take in,' Jack said. 'Let me give you my number. I'm not after anything, I promise. It's just – all my life you've been this kind of mystery, and—' His voice cracked under the weight of stifled tears. Lucy had forgotten how good he could be, how precisely he considered each inflection, each gesture. She felt a pang at the performance being so fleeting. No audience to marvel at the solidity of his characterisation.

Sebastian screwed his eyes shut as though cleaving to his last remnants of disbelief. How little he'd known when he showered that morning that he'd have this new identity flung at him, that within the space of hours he'd be reborn as an errant father.

A coldness spread throughout Lucy's body as she perceived the anguish their performance might cause. It was clearly hurting Sebastian to review the last thirty years in light of this new knowledge.

'We should go,' Lucy whispered to Jack.

Jack nodded, producing a scrap of paper containing the number to a burner phone they'd acquired earlier in the week. He proffered it, but Sebastian merely exhaled, looking down at the carpet.

Jack glanced at Lucy, then at his supposed father, before laying the paper down on the table. He went to stand up, but hesitated. 'Don't be angry with Mum. She didn't want to give me your name, but I wouldn't let it drop. I had to know.'

Sebastian remained motionless, saying nothing. Lucy had the sense he was holding back tears, that trying to speak would dismantle the last of his defences. She steeled herself by picturing Zelda, remembering how she'd trembled as she described her abandonment. She thought of her sister, rummaging through countless charity shops trying to find a pair of school shoes that were within her budget. Men like Sebastian needed to take responsibility for their actions, be accountable.

Jack rose from his chair. 'Once all this has sunk in, give me a call. Please. I want to learn who you are, that's all.'

Jack and Lucy left Sebastian in the room, retracing their steps back down the corridor and up the stairs. The security guard told them to enjoy the rest of their day as they stepped outside, waves of heat rising from the asphalt to greet them.

It wasn't until they reached the end of the street and turned the corner that Jack looked at her. He gave a happy shriek, hugging Lucy and spinning her around, ignoring the tutting of a suited woman who had to swerve around them.

'You were brilliant,' Lucy said.

'You too! Fucking hell, Luce, that was intense.'

'But he believed you, right? He totally believed you. I could see it all over his face.'

Jack laughed, taking his sunglasses from his pocket and putting them on. 'Dirty bastard. This is what you get when you run away from a pregnant woman.'

The pair continued their journey, almost skipping along the pavement. At the edge of Lucy's consciousness was the memory of Sebastian's stricken expression, the haunted look in his eyes. She tried to push it away. He'd impregnated a young woman, then run away in the dead of night.

'Let's get pissed tonight,' she said, trying to cling to their sense of victory. Jack *deserved* this. After ten years of mostly fruitless auditions, something was going right. 'Bottle of vodka and a decent film. You can pick. Just not *Godfather II* again.'

'It's an Emily night. I promised her we'd go out. Do you think Sebastian'll get in touch soon?'

'I do,' Lucy said. 'He'll probably invite you for a drink and present you with a DNA kit. He'll want to know for definite.'

'He'll be furious at Zelda.'

'Yep. But trust me – she *wants* a big dust-up. That's the real reason she hired us, I'm sure of it.'

Chapter 8

'Hello, love.'

Lucy climbed into her father's taxi and was hit by the familiar smell of Murray mints and synthetic air freshener. He'd lost a second molar since her last visit, but still had a full head of brown hair and his tanned face seemed ruddy with health, even though Mel had told Lucy he was pre-diabetic and the doctor was urging him to lose weight.

She kissed his cheek. 'Sorry I can't stay the night.'

'Don't be silly, love. You're here now, that's the most important thing.'

Lucy's mother's birthday coincided with an agency booking – a garden party in Sussex – so she'd travelled home the day before and was planning to take the whole family out for lunch. It had been almost a month since they'd approached Sebastian at his office, but so far he hadn't called Jack's burner phone. Mostly Lucy felt relieved by this, but there were odd moments when she found herself pondering what they might have done wrong. Perhaps it would be natural for Jack's character to make a follow-up plea, take the initiative by ringing Sebastian's office and inviting him for a drink.

In the meantime, the agency had experienced a welcome

surge of bookings. Three weddings and six parties for Lucy, and Jack's very first plus one gig, accompanying a female engineer to an industry dinner. *It's working*, an inner voice whispered, but Lucy held on to her caution – ten years as a jobbing actor taught her that flurries of work could easily be followed by fallow periods.

Lucy's father drove away from the city centre towards their estate. The early summer heatwave had stretched into the end of June and he'd cranked the car's air-conditioning up high. Lucy flexed her ankles and gazed out at the high-rises, their balconies filled with drying shorts and T-shirts.

'Business been okay?' she asked.

'Bit slow now the students have finished for the summer. It'll pick up in the autumn.'

Lucy bit her lip. As far as her parents were concerned, she'd be joining this autumn influx, moving back home to complete a year of teacher training. She'd rehearsed telling them about the agency a few times, but none of the words she used sounded right. The fact that most clients were men seeking a young woman to accompany them to parties didn't help. But she knew her parents would be troubled by the deception involved, by Lucy helping people lie.

Her nine-year-old nephew Charlie came running into the hallway the moment she stepped through the door. His face had matured since her last visit, the full cheeks of his toddler years replaced by new contours that made him look unexpectedly serious. He stopped abruptly, giving his aunt a self-conscious grin.

'I've put some of my drawings on your bedroom wall,' he

said. He'd recently moved into the family home, after a rent increase forced Mel to give up her flat.

'It's your room now,' Lucy replied. 'You decorate it exactly how you want.'

Lucy's mother and Mel were on the sofa in the living room. The way they leaned against one another, Mel's bare shoulder resting against their mother's flesh, stirred something in Lucy's chest. Sometimes it was devastating to remember the ease of this living room. The family sprawled out watching a quiz show after dinner. The ritual of the Sunday morning fried breakfast, everyone still in their pyjamas. Rows of school photos looking down from the walls, faded shots of Lucy and Mel with missing milk teeth, their hair in pigtails, now joined by pictures of Charlie grinning at the camera.

'Happy birthday for tomorrow, Mum.' Lucy hugged her mother and handed her a Selfridges bag.

Her mother's lips sprang apart when she saw the branding. 'Oh, you shouldn't have ...'

Lucy smiled, fighting the certainty that her mother would be horrified if she knew about Zelda's assignment and the other pretences that had paid for these gifts.

Her mother carefully removed each item. As she unwrapped them, she avoided tearing the paper, folding it in neat squares and retaining the ribbons. There was a silk scarf, a box of macaroons and a Clarins gift set. Her breath caught as she opened that final one – so many times she'd led her daughters through Debenhams, looking longingly at the expensive cosmetic counters, furtively trying the odd tester, too intimidated by the starched women with their crimson lips and heavy eyebrows to linger for long.

'Goodness me … you've really gone to town. How can you afford all of this?' Her mother's eyes were wide, almost frightened.

'I've had a bit of work lately.'

'That's wonderful! Will we be seeing you on telly again?'

'Probably not for a while. It's international stuff, mostly,' Lucy felt an inner squeeze as she told the lie.

'You didn't need to spoil me like this,' her mother said. 'You ought to put something by for a rainy day.'

Lucy smiled. She was aware of how still her sister Mel had become, watching the exchange, as though she somehow recognised something dishonest in Lucy's behaviour.

'Honestly, Mum. It's your birthday.' Heat flared across Lucy's face. 'You deserve it.'

The seafood restaurant Lucy had booked was only a fifteen-minute walk from the house, but her father became out of breath, struggling to join the conversation as sweat slithered down the side of his face. He was wearing his white shirt, bought for a cousin's wedding some years ago, the buttons now straining around his belly. He seemed so much older than the father of Lucy's memories and she felt a sudden ache at the idea of him driving drunken students around the city in the early hours.

She remembered his swollen eyes after he'd watched her in a GCSE performance of *The Taming of The Shrew*, how he'd looked at her with a kind of wonder. 'You've got something really special there, love.' If only she'd been able to gift him a taste of real success: her name on a film poster, or at the very least, a lead role in the kind of drama his friends would watch.

Inside the restaurant, they were met by an icy blast of air-conditioning. Lucy's father let out an involuntary grunt of relief, but her mother adjusted her new silk scarf, taking in the pristine white tablecloths and crystal wine glasses with wide eyes and drawn-up shoulders. Mel was wearing her usual combats and vest ensemble, even though she must know the act of getting dressed up and going somewhere smart was a rare joy for their mother.

As the family took their seats and inspected the menu, Lucy was aware of something passing between her parents.

'It's a little pricey,' Lucy's mother whispered. 'We could go somewhere else?'

'This is my treat,' Lucy said. 'Don't worry about the price.'

Mel exhaled audibly, leaning over Charlie to point out the few menu options that might appeal to a child.

'I can't let you pay for this, love.' Lucy's father reached across the table and patted her hand.

'I want to treat you all. Make up for not being there to-morrow.' Absurd, but her eyes were stinging. Why did every attempt at being kind end with this sense she'd got everything wrong?

Her father was about to say something, but at that moment a tall, fair-haired waiter in a grey suit arrived at their table. 'Good afternoon, everyone. Could I start you off with some drinks?' he said.

There was a moment of dismayed silence. Her mother's eyes transmitted a silent plea and Lucy wondered whether the kindest thing might be to get up and apologise, lead the family to the all-you-can-eat buffet at Pizza Hut, or some-where they wouldn't look so uncomfortable. She'd do it, if that's what they wanted. Her being in Portsmouth seemed to have upset some delicate equilibrium.

'Can I have a Coke? As a treat?' Charlie said, looking at Mel.

Mel rolled her eyes. 'Fine. One Coke, one tap water, please.'

'I might have a drop of Prosecco,' Lucy's mother said brightly. It was calculated to make Lucy feel better, but only deepened her feelings of shame.

After the main courses, Lucy's father patted his belly and announced he was too stuffed for dessert.

'Charlie made a batch of brownies yesterday. Maybe we could have one of those with a cup of tea back at the house?' Lucy's mother offered with a hopeful look.

Lucy nodded and feigning a trip to the toilet, went over to the bar to take care of the bill.

Back at the house, she wandered out into the garden. The sight of the familiar flagstones, dandelions and tufts of grass poking through the cracks, had a soothing effect. Finally, she felt traces of belonging. Her parents had taken such delight in each B and C of her report card, never asking her to be more than she was. She imagined herself back in this house, sharing Mel's room, listening out for the click of the door as her father got home from his night shifts. She could do her teacher training then find work at a nearby school, pop home for breakfast every Sunday. She could picture her mother fighting to restrain a smile every time she mentioned, *our daughter the teacher.*

At uni, Peter hadn't shared Jack's scorn at Lucy's plan to become a drama teacher. She remembered coming back from a bar shift, the balls of her feet tender from hours of standing in heels, to find him alone in the living room, going over his

Stanislavski primer with an orange highlighter in his hand.
After Lucy had drained a glass of water, they'd got on to the
subject of their post-graduation lives and Peter's eyes became
soft, almost pleading. 'I hope you don't mind me saying. But
the way you talk about teaching – you make it sound like you
don't have a choice.'

Lucy had sunk into the plump velvet upholstery of the sofa,
a cast-off from some wealthy friend of Jack's family. 'I need
a reliable income. It's the only way I can justify getting into
so much debt.'

Peter shifted in his seat. 'I respect that. I do. But I can't
help feeling you don't realise how good you are.'

She'd felt the knotted muscles of her shoulders and back
smoothing out. Peter never exaggerated and while he was
always kind, he was too precise to dole out flattery.

'If you wanted to *try* making it as an actor, you could live
with me for a bit after graduation. You'd be doing me a favour,
I'd be lonely on my own.'

She'd felt a tingling against the roof of her mouth. Sharply
painful, yet pleasurable in its own strange way. Instinctively,
Lucy had known Peter wasn't proposing she pay him rent.
He'd chosen his words carefully, but they both knew he was
offering to put her up for free.

'Maybe,' she'd said, unsure whether she'd ever find it in
herself to accept such generosity. In the end, she never got
the chance to find out.

Charlie and Mel were coming out through the backdoor,
Charlie brandishing a small plate containing a generous slab
of brownie.

'Here you go, Aunty Lucy, try this.'

Lucy stared at the glossy brown square. Its outside was hardened and crisp, giving way to a gooey texture where the knife had gone through. Eight hundred calories, at least.

She smiled as she took the plate.

Charlie seemed to sense her reluctance. 'It's not one of Mum's vegan recipes. I made them with proper chocolate.'

Lucy felt her throat resist as she took a small bite, but was careful to feign relish.

'Yum,' she said. 'This is the best brownie I've ever tasted.'

Charlie's shoulders twitched with pride as he went back inside. Lucy would never get used to the almost violent surges of love this boy inspired in her. Sometimes all it took was a gesture, the particular set of his mouth as he pondered something, or the tiny murmurs of appreciation when he enjoyed a meal. If the agency was successful, perhaps she could do something for him, offer him the things middle class children got to enjoy. Swimming classes. Tennis coaching. Piano lessons.

Lucy put her plate down on the kitchen windowsill. Her father would eat the rest.

Mel stared at the remaining brownie for a moment, then looked at her sister. 'You've got to stop bothering with this calorie counting bollocks. Have you had your BMI checked lately?'

Lucy shrugged. If Mel only knew how many times casting directors deemed her 'too stocky', or suggested she needed to 'lengthen out'.

'Being underweight can have all kinds of health implications. Loss of bone density, fertility issues . . .'

Lucy glanced at Mel, not recognising the expression on her sister's face as she reached out and grasped her by the arm.

'Are you okay, Luce?'

''Course I am.'

'I wonder whether it's lonely sometimes, being away from your family.' The way Mel was looking at her, the blend of pity and concern, made Lucy feel unexpectedly close to tears. She had the unwelcome sense that Mel never really believed in London Lucy, in Lucy the actor. It made Lucy feel like a girl again. Middling, but content in a way that now seemed almost bovine. When she thought of who she was before Jack and Peter she always imagined a cow, placidly chewing grass in a muddy field.

'I'm never alone. Right now I'm living with Jack, for God's sake.'

'I know. But he dates people, right?'

'So what?'

Mel squeezed her hand. 'And you don't.'

'Aren't you supposed to be a feminist? I'm not *lonely* just because I don't have a boyfriend.'

'I'm not saying that. It's just, I remember what it was like after Peter—'

'Don't.' Lucy turned away from her sister. She wouldn't go back there.

'You know it's never too late to get counselling.'

'Please don't.'

Mel sighed and pulled her sister into a hug. 'It's not your job to look after Jack, you know that, right?'

'Of course.' Lucy felt her eyes stinging. She was exhausted. She had a pile of admin to do and wanted to go over the backstory for the garden party gig one last time. Her client had given her eight pages of notes to memorise.

'Make sure you visit us again soon,' Mel said. 'And don't leave it so long next time.'

Lucy nodded and took out her phone. She had a message from Jack.

> Guess who just had a text from Sebastian?! Wants to meet me for a drink!

A smile played at her lips. They'd convinced him after all, done their jobs well. Spending the day with her sister and Charlie only highlighted for Lucy how reprehensibly Sebastian had behaved by abandoning Zelda. He'd lived for thirty years without any kind of consequence, and now Lucy and Jack were about to make him pay.

Chapter 9

Sebastian didn't discuss DNA testing at his first drink with Jack. In fact, their first proper meeting went so well that they planned to meet for Sunday lunch in July. *Bring Lucy, I'd love to get to know her too*, Sebastian had told Jack.

'It was so fucking weird,' Jack said, coming into his bedroom with a towel round his waist. 'I mean, at times it felt like a quick-fire quiz. Sharing our favourite meals, favourite films. He didn't ask about Zelda, though. Reckon that says a lot.'

Lucy was tonging her hair, filling the room with a burning smell. Although she was pleased to be earning out Zelda's deposit payment, she couldn't remember the last time she'd had a lie-in, indulging in the pleasure of a Sunday morning reading in bed. She'd treated herself to the latest Elizabeth Strout weeks ago, but hadn't yet cracked the spine. Her most recent ad campaign had led to a surge of website traffic and managing the agency inbox was becoming a full-time job as the enquiries became more frequent and more elaborate. Just the other day, in among the usual attempts to procure sex, there had been a message from a woman seeking a fake doctor to soothe her hypochondriac mother. An author had emailed, wanting to hire an excitable superfan to gatecrash a meeting with his editor and underscore how beloved he was by his readers.

Jack stepped into his boxers. 'I might have actually found us an office.'

'Isn't it a little early for that?' Lucy unplugged the tongs and misted hairspray over her newly created waves.

'This friend of my dad, he's got redevelopment plans for a couple of buildings and doesn't want them sitting empty while he's clearing the red tape. He'll give us a bargain price. We'd actually be doing him a favour.' Jack flashed her a winsome smile. He'd clearly become attached to the idea of them having an office. She wondered what he'd been telling his father about the business, how much he'd exaggerated.

Careful not to let the scepticism show on her face, Lucy re-trieved her character's sapphire ring from her knicker drawer and slid it on. 'Yeah, but there'll be rates, utilities. It'll be more hassle than it's worth. All we really need right now is a laptop and phone.'

'It's in Soho.' There was something resolute in Jack's ex-pression. He was probably imagining himself hanging around the theatres, inviting young actors to 'stop by my office'. Picturing a suited version of himself, sitting in a leather desk chair, taking detailed notes as he interviewed a client about a role.

Lucy ought to be pleased. Jack was slowly weaving the business into his sense of self, which is exactly what she'd hoped for. But if he really wanted to help, he was welcome to wade through the completed client engagement forms that had started coming in faster than Lucy could process them.

'Let's at least go and look at the place.' Jack pulled on a

lilac polo shirt with a designer insignia. 'It's time to start scaling up.'

Lucy took her silver sandals from the wardrobe. She was wearing a primrose-coloured sundress that she still felt a little guilty about charging to the business. There were more pressing concerns than an office. Lucy was currently trying to manage two date clashes and would have to turn down business if she didn't quickly draft in new actors.

'I'm not sure I can handle the extra admin an office would bring,' she said, carefully.

Jack sighed, flicking through his wardrobe to find a pair of shorts. 'You're doing what you always do.'

She looked up. His mouth was pressed into a thin line. 'What's that?' she asked.

'Shilly-shallying. Chickening out the moment something starts getting big.'

'That's not fair—'

'I thought you were committed. I mean, I've been putting you up rent free so we can get this thing off the ground.'

Something inside Lucy shrank at this reminder of her poverty. The response was innate, hardwired since childhood. But just as quickly, the instinct to cower was replaced by a fierce pride. Her parents were good people. Lucy worked hard, she always had. How dare Jack belittle her?

She stood up and faced him square on. 'That's not ... you practically begged me to stay in London.'

'Whatever.' He shrugged and disappeared off into the bathroom.

Lucy sat down on the edge of his bed, catching her breath. For a brief moment she'd been on the cusp of shouting in his face. Telling him he could shove his sofa bed up his arse. Thank goodness she hadn't gone that far.

She returned to the wardrobe, searching for the small, impractical shoulder bag she used for fancier outings. It had fallen into Jack's section, where the whole bottom third was taken up by shoe boxes stacked four high. There was an array of designer trainers, some of them she'd never even seen him wear, plus boots and vintage brogues. As Lucy retrieved her bag, she noticed the corner of a photograph wedged between two of the boxes. She pulled it out and was confronted by Peter's face. He was in stage make-up, eyes ringed with kohl, a pensive expression on his face that just tipped into bitterness. This was his Iago, Lucy's favourite of all his performances. She remained very still, her insides wracked by an implosion of feeling. Loss, but paired with something happier. Love was too simple a word, it was a vivid joy at having known him, at having been his friend.

Jack never spoke of Peter. *Why upset ourselves?* he'd say, any time Lucy alluded to their shared past. But he had this picture, had gone to the trouble of printing it on photographic paper. She carefully slid it back into its concealed position, feeling a renewed tenderness for Jack, regretting snapping at him.

When they arrived at the Bloomsbury pub, Sebastian was already seated in the dining room with its large windows looking out over Russell Square. Every other table was taken with couples and small groups of thirtysomethings, looking stylish even in shorts and loose sundresses. The pub seemed to be trying hard to create a bohemian ambience, with reproductions of famous impressionist paintings placed haphazardly over the wood-panelled walls. None of the tables and chairs matched.

Sebastian stood up to greet them, shaking Jack's hand and giving him a light slap on the back. He was wearing a pristine white T-shirt and knee-length shorts and his hair was tousled with wax, making him seem younger than he'd appeared at the bank. He turned to Lucy, and after the briefest of pauses, went in for an air-kiss. 'I'm so glad to meet you properly. Jack's told me so much about you.'

She gave a demure smile, acknowledging with her eyes just how difficult this must be for him. 'You too. I'm so pleased we're having this lunch.'

Sebastian winced as he eased himself back into his chair. 'Did a six-hour run yesterday. Everything hurts.'

'Jack runs too,' Lucy offered.

'I did the marathon last year.' Jack's mouth twitched with satisfaction. Will from university had also run the race, but Jack got the faster time.

'Well done you,' Sebastian said. 'I do love the London Marathon. One of my favourites.'

'You've done it, then?' Jack asked.

'A few times, yeah. At the moment I'm more into ultra-marathoning. Want to do the Marathon des Sables before I get to fifty-five.'

'What's that?' Lucy asked.

'A two-hundred-and-fifty-kilometre race across desert.'

'Sounds horrific.' Lucy glanced at Jack. He'd picked up a menu, deciding his character wasn't going to be too impressed by his new-found father's athleticism.

Each of them gazed at the food options printed on recycled card. Jack and Sebastian ordered the roast pork belly, along with pints of craft beer that arrived in old-fashioned tankards. Lucy opted for a salad and fizzy water.

The conversation as they waited for their food was surprisingly easy. Since Jack had decided to play Zelda's son as an aspiring actor, he was able to chat about a recent-ish understudying gig at the Globe. How he'd come so close to playing Hamlet one evening, getting into costume, only to be ejected from make-up because the real star arrived eight minutes before curtain-up.

Lucy found herself watching Sebastian. His eyes seemed to be constantly working, searching for traces of himself in this stranger. Would his subconscious trick him into finding them? For a second, Lucy imagined what it might be like for Sebastian, a feeling of richness entering his life, a new layer to his identity. She registered it as a pleasure, permeating so deep that it skirted close to pain.

'It sounds a lot of fun. But is it not a little precarious? As a profession, I mean.' Sebastian spoke slowly, the corners of his mouth lifted in a smile, as though he was being careful not to appear critical.

Jack looked confused and Lucy felt a bitter laugh silently rise through her chest. Jack didn't understand the concept of *precarious*, he'd never faced not having anywhere to live or the need to make a tenner somehow cover eight days of meals.

'Well, Mum's always been really supportive.' There was just the tiniest hint of defiance in Jack's eyes.

Sebastian rested his elbows on the table. 'It sounds like a brutal industry.'

'It is,' Jack said. 'But so is everything worthwhile, right? It's not all about the money – every role is an opportunity to hone your craft, to learn something new and make the audience *feel* something.'

'It's uncanny, how much you sound like Zelda.' Sebastian raised an eyebrow.

Jack's lips twitched, taking it as a compliment. His character was devoted to the mother who'd single-handedly raised him.

'What about you, Lucy?' Sebastian turned to her. 'I don't think Jack's told me what you do?'

'I'm an account manager for a PR firm. You're in banking, right?'

Sebastian nodded. 'Afraid so. Never had a vocation as such, and after Thailand I just kind of ended up on a graduate training scheme. Totally boring, isn't it? Wish I had a better story to tell.'

There was a brief lull in the conversation and they all seemed relieved when a purple-haired waitress approached with their plates. Sebastian thanked her warmly, meeting her eye as he did so. From all her years working in the service industries, Lucy knew how rare the gesture was, how most people wanted you to be invisible.

In between mouthfuls of pork, Jack returned to the topic of acting, as he so often did, telling Sebastian about an audition for a Netflix thriller, making it sound as though it was something coming up, even though it had actually taken place a couple of years ago and he hadn't got the part. He'd stopped returning Lucy's calls for a week or so after receiving the news. In the end, she'd taken the bus to his flat, flinging open the windows and binning the half-eaten takeaway meals congealing in their foil containers.

'The scene they sent me is really well written,' Jack continued. 'I have to blackmail someone, but the dialogue is subtle. It's all very friendly on the surface, but there's this undercurrent of menace.'

Was it hurting him to recall it? Lucy wondered. Her stomach twisted as a new idea insinuated itself: she should have steered him away from playing himself as an actor. It was so obvious to her now. It could do no good, conjuring up the longing, forcing Jack to dwell inside it in the name of performance.

Sebastian gave Jack a gentle smile that seemed to convey a peculiar blend of emotion. There was definitely pride there, but Lucy also had the sense that Sebastian was troubled. Was he worried about his purported son's lifestyle? As an outsider it must be impossible not to feel exasperation when presented with endless accounts of near misses. It must be very clear to someone like Sebastian that Jack couldn't be earning enough to cover his own living costs.

'It must be hard, pinning your hopes on these kinds of ad hoc opportunities,' Sebastian said. 'Do you work part-time between acting jobs?'

Lucy saw a flicker of offence pass through Jack's eyes. It was the first crack in his characterisation.

'I can't bring myself to do work I don't care about,' Jack said. 'Maybe it's the way Mum raised me, but I'm a great believer in following your passions. Living with integrity.'

Sebastian said nothing, but his smile faltered.

'I made this pact with my drama school friends – whatever

roles we did or didn't get, our lives would always have meaning if we kept performing, kept improving.' Jack popped a
roast potato in his mouth.

'Sounds intense.' Sebastian tilted his head to one side, a
light frown settling onto his forehead.

Jack nodded. 'It's the only way to live. I couldn't be one of
those people who pours all my energy into something mun-
dane, just because it feels safe.'

Sebastian glanced at Lucy. It was a questioning look, as
though he was trying to read whether she, with her nice little
PR job, might feel wounded by what Jack had said. She kept
her expression serene.

For a moment, Sebastian hesitated, then he laid his knife
and fork down on the table and turned to Jack. The creases
between his eyebrows deepened. 'Do you not worry, though,
that there might come a point where the money runs out? I
don't mean to overstep. It's just, I've never met anyone who's
tried to make a living from the arts.'

As she witnessed the exchange, Lucy was aware of a secret
pleasure, a shaft of sunlight warming her bones. She was still
a little sore from the argument they'd had that morning; from
the reminder of how Jack regarded Lucy's financial struggles
as a kind of weakness, as though her need to pay her rent was
symptomatic of a lack of resolve.

'Thinking about acting in financial terms is guaranteed to
kill creativity,' Jack said. 'I deliver emotion. My performance
gives each and every member of the audience their own
unique reaction. It's not something you can measure with
money.'

There followed a silence that Lucy-the-fiancée perceived

to be pained. She found herself thinking of Peter, wanting to hold the photograph in her hands again, to look upon his Iago. That light in his eyes – he had such an instinct for the inner lives of his characters – intuiting the feelings they were hiding even from themselves.

She wracked her brain for suitable conversation topics, was about to utter a line about the extraordinarily hot summer they were having, when Sebastian turned to her.

'Is your food okay? You've hardly touched it.' His eyes were strangely intense and for a second Lucy had the uncanny sense he could see inside her, past the role she was playing to the shrunken remnants of her real self.

'It's lovely,' she said. 'It's just this heat, it saps my appetite.'

Sebastian continued looking at her. 'We can send it back if it's not quite perfect.'

'This is what she does,' Jack said. 'Orders something tiny and then just looks at it.'

The words were spoken without malice, but still Lucy was stung. Jack was as devoted to his physique as she was, but seemed to be able to eat whatever he liked.

At last Sebastian looked away, circling his hand around his pint glass. His knuckles were lightly dusted with hair, the nails neatly clipped.

'Personally, I don't have any truck with counting calories or any of that nonsense,' Jack said. 'If you're hungry, eat.'

Until today he'd shown no sign of noticing the careful attention Lucy paid to her calorie intake. He perhaps just assumed dieting was part of a women's lot and Lucy must be fine with it. She felt the blood rising in her face.

When Jack disappeared off to the toilet a few moments

later, Sebastian turned to Lucy. 'I'm so sorry about that,' he said. 'I can be such an oaf sometimes. It wasn't my place to say anything.'

She lowered her gaze, tried a smile, even though her face was burning with shame. How ridiculous to break character for the sake of avoiding a few hundred calories. 'It was nothing. Don't worry.'

Sebastian leaned forwards slightly, observing her closely. 'I know it's hard. What with the media photoshopping images and—' Whatever little speech he had in mind he abandoned it, suddenly self-conscious.

Lucy's eyes were starting to sting. She needed to get a handle on her performance. Calm, composed fiancée. Support to her vulnerable and somewhat flighty boyfriend. Fantasies of the perfect dress. Nice office job. Pencil skirt and heels. Cocktails with colleagues. She hardened herself from the inside out and was able to once again meet Sebastian's eye and smile. 'You know, it's so wonderful getting to know you. You have no idea how much it means to Jack, having you in his life.'

Sebastian held her gaze, his lips gently parted, his brow just slightly furrowed, as though he was deep in thought. It looked as though he was searching for something and again Lucy had that terrible feeling of exposure, as though on some primal level Sebastian could sense she wasn't who she said she was.

Once they'd parted from Sebastian and were walking back to the Tube, Jack started: 'Money, money, money! Honestly, Luce, do you think he has any idea what he sounds like?'

Lucy gave a brief laugh. She'd actually found Sebastian

rather pleasant, not at all what she'd been expecting from a banker. Even when he'd pressed Jack about his lifestyle, his face had been open, free from any trace of accusation. It seemed to Lucy as though Sebastian was trying – really trying – to forge a relationship with his supposed son.

'I think he really believes you're his child,' she said.

They walked along Montague Place, alongside the pale exterior of the British Museum. The trees lining the street provided little respite from the heat and they walked more slowly than usual. Lucy's sandals were beginning to chafe her heels.

'I know, right?' Jack just perceptibly puffed out his chest. 'Still no mention of a DNA test.'

'It's kind of a lot, isn't it?' Lucy said, as they neared the electric bike and scooter stand at the end of the road.

Jack stopped walking. 'What do you mean?'

'I guess I was so caught up in everything Zelda went through – it didn't occur to me that Sebastian might be different now. I mean, he seems to genuinely want to get to know you.' He seemed to want to get to know Lucy too, a fact that alternately thrilled and terrified her.

A group of three Dutch tourists approached, asking for directions to the museum's entrance. As she watched Jack gesticulate, pointing out the route, Lucy noticed how stiffly he was standing. He was annoyed with her and she understood why: she'd pressed him to take this gig. One of the coaches parked at the side of the road started up, its engine rattling as it emitted a fug of diesel fumes.

'We're doing exactly what we agreed,' Jack said, once the tourists moved on.

'I know. I guess I just—'

'We can't pull out, if that's what you're thinking. Sebastian would have questions and they'd lead him straight to Zelda. We had her photo with us.' Jack resumed walking, taking long strides.

'Yeah, but that wouldn't be such a terrible thing.' Lucy rushed to keep up with him, trying to ignore the relentless scraping of her sandal straps. 'If you ask me, a confrontation is just what Zelda needs. If she believed Sebastian was truly sorry . . .'

Jack watched for a gap in the traffic, waiting for a Deliveroo bicycle courier to pass, then hurried over into Bedford Square. The shrubs in the central garden looked uncharacteristically sickly, leaves yellow and wilting in the heat.

'I'm actually meeting Zelda for coffee tomorrow,' Jack said as they walked alongside the Georgian terraces with their wrought iron railings. 'I can double check she definitely wants us to carry on. I'm sure she will.'

'I didn't see an email about a meeting.'

Jack glanced back at her. It was a fleeting moment, but Lucy detected a certain haughtiness to his expression. He really did see himself as an architect of the business, an equal partner. It was exactly what Lucy had wanted, but still it shocked her.

'Zelda texted me,' Jack said. 'I guess she knows I'll be seeing Sebastian more frequently than you. She wants regular debriefs. Says we can bill her for them.'

Lucy registered unease at Zelda excluding her by going directly to Jack. It only lasted a second and was followed by a far more compelling idea. If Jack really did believe he'd built the business, was there any reason for Lucy to go on taking sole responsibility? One of their former classmates would grasp at the chance to take over the female plus one gigs. Lucy pictured herself returning to her parents' pebbledash home, lugging her plastic crate through the peeling front door. She could spend her weekends reading in bed, listen to the Beatles with her father, become a fun auntie who joined Charlie in his games. She wouldn't have to concern herself with the intricacies of others' deceit. Wouldn't have to watch her weight and keep bleaching her hair. She could be happy, or at the very least content.

Chapter 10

At the start of the new week she was woken by a phone call. She never switched her phone off, not since Peter's death. If anyone needed to talk to her in the night, she'd be there.

It was her sister, Mel, struggling to breathe. 'Dad's had a heart attack.'

'Oh my God, is he . . .' Lucy couldn't bring herself to finish the sentence.

'We had to call an ambulance. He's on his way to hospital.'

'Is he going to be all right?'

'How can I know that?'

'I . . .' Lucy's body felt cold, yet somehow light and formless. Her phone almost slipped from her hand as she clambered out of bed.

'I'm heading to the hospital now. You're going to come too, right?' There was an edge to Mel's voice, a resentment that even her tears couldn't conceal.

'I'll get the train. I'll be there as soon as I can.'

After hanging up, Lucy knocked on Jack's bedroom door. Emily had stayed over the previous evening, but Lucy needed her clothes from Jack's wardrobe.

When she heard Jack's grunt of acknowledgement, Lucy

entered the room, turning on the light and grabbing her rucksack.

'My dad's had a heart attack.' Lucy's voice splintered. 'I need to go to Portsmouth. He's in hospital.'

'Fuck.' Jack sat up, rubbing at his eyes.

Emily rolled on to her side, saying nothing.

'There are gigs – we'll have to sort cover, somehow,' Lucy's voice broke.

'Of course.' Jack lay back down. 'Just text me if you need me to do anything.'

She stuffed a few pairs of knickers into her bag, along with a couple of T-shirts and her denim shorts. When she left the flat, she realised what she really wanted was for Jack to have got out of bed and folded her in his arms. She needed him to tell her everything was going to be all right.

Once she'd boarded the train at Waterloo, Mel messaged to say their father had been pronounced 'stable'. Lucy tried to feel soothed by the word. If the doctors thought there was a real risk of him dying they would have said 'critical' or 'deteriorating', surely?

There was a ninety-minute train journey to get through. Lucy tried to think of something, anything, she could do to help. It seemed so obscene that no action of hers, no amount of longing, could affect the outcome for her father – how was that right?

She opened up the agency inbox, needing a distraction, anything to make the time go faster. Eleven new enquiries had come in since she last checked. *Eleven*. Something caught in her throat at the sight of them, at the money they represented. Eight were from men explaining they needed an attractive female companion to attend some function or other. There was a request to sabotage the sales presentation of a business rival; a message from a consultant who wanted to talk about a project with a developer, and a female who wanted a man to make a scene at her office, begging and pleading for her to take him back. Jack would relish that one.

Lucy tried to feel a kind of pride at what she'd built, but all she could see was her father's face. The still-thick hair trimmed once a month by Lucy's mother in the kitchen, his ruddy cheeks and the deep crow's feet that always made him look so genial. He'd be so disappointed in Lucy if he were to see those emails and discover what his daughter was doing for a living.

She fired off a message to Jack, asking him to meet with the consultant, who'd sounded impatient, then closed her laptop. Everything else could wait a few hours.

She recalled afternoons watching *The Beatles Anthology*, which her father had taped to VHS when Lucy was little. The two of them revisited it most years, parking themselves on the sofa under a blanket when Lucy stayed for Christmas.

'There's something about Paul's voice,' her father had said. 'It gets you in the chest.' She'd noticed his eyes were damp and had understood the emotion there. 'Not that I'm knocking John,' he added. 'I do like John's voice too.'

Lucy's favourite Beatle had always been George, although she and her father agreed on how good-natured Ringo seemed, how much of a laugh. They sent each other links to clips of his interviews here and there, quoting their favourite bits.

Jack had subscriptions to all the streaming platforms and

Lucy had been watching the newest Beatles documentary in snatched moments when she was drinking her coffee or getting ready to go out. She felt a sudden guilt at having hoarded the experience rather than sharing it. There was nothing she wanted more than to sit in the house she'd grown up in and watch all eight hours of it with her father at her side.

Lucy found her mother and Mel in the waiting area of the hospital's cardiac unit, slumped together, their faces streaked with tears. It was a white-walled space, the vinyl floor reflecting the glare from the harsh strip lights above. Rows of blue plastic chairs were bolted to the ground with ashen-faced relatives forced to sit looking out over a busy corridor where trollies clattered along. Lucy rushed over, feeling the shudder of her sister's back as she held her.

'They've fitted a stent,' her mother said, clasping Lucy's hand. 'They haven't let us see him yet. Said there might be a bit of a wait. But they told us it went well.'

Lucy looked around the room, trying to feel relief. There were posters on the wall for bereavement counselling, diagrams explaining the different food groups. She was clenching every muscle in her body, trying to stave off the threat of shaking. *Went well*, she insisted to herself. But in her stomach lay the knowledge of exactly what death felt like – the devastation at everything left unsaid, the jolt on waking each morning and having to confront the loss all over again. Mel had never experienced such a thing – couldn't possibly imagine the desolation that awaited her.

'It went well. That's good.' Lucy's voice had a strangled quality.

Her mother and sister nodded. Mel did so almost violently, but Lucy's mother's eyes were sad, as though life had taught her never to trust assurances, never to believe in hope.

Finally, they were allowed to see him. His bed was in an alcove, a semi-private space with machines monitoring his pulse and blood pressure. He had a cannula in his hand and was attached to an IV drip. When he saw the three of them he attempted a smile but his eyes were clouded with worry. Lucy felt as though she'd been violently shunted, the air pushed from her lungs.

'I'm so sorry about this,' her father said.

Lucy's mother rushed to him, dropping into the chair next to the bed and squeezing his arm. 'Don't be daft.'

'Have you let the firm know?' He was technically self-employed, but in reality was reliant on a single booking company for his passengers.

'You mustn't worry about that,' Mel said, crouching down next to her mother. 'We'll sort it.'

The nurse who'd led them there made it plain that her father was only supposed to have two visitors at a time, so Lucy hung back, drinking in the sight of her father, watching the rise and fall of his chest. This was life. One breath after another. Holding on.

He kept looking at Lucy's mother. 'The car payments . . .'

'We'll take care of everything,' Mel said. 'All you have to do is concentrate on getting better.'

He winced. The effort of talking, of thinking, seemed to exhaust him. It was inevitable he'd appear groggy, but Lucy had the sudden realisation that it was too soon to celebrate.

He hadn't been fixed, he just hadn't died. Her father, who never harmed anyone, who lived each day with a gentle kindness. Why hadn't Lucy savoured him more? Shown him what he meant to her?

The family passed the time in a state of quiet togetherness. From time to time, Lucy's father would voice a worry. He had a regular customer on Thursdays that would need to be contacted. He was down to do an airport run at the weekend. 'We'll take care of it,' Mel kept saying. 'Honestly – don't even think about these things.'

When Mel needed to leave to collect Charlie from school, Lucy took her place, squatting down next to the bed. Her father had drifted off into a light sleep. It frightened Lucy, how her parents had aged. She hadn't noticed it happening, but while her father's flesh had proliferated, her mother's had diminished. She looked frail, as though a fall would be enough to snap her bones. She gave Lucy a sad smile, tears in her eyes. 'I'm so glad you're here.'

Lucy observed her father; her eyes were drawn to the back of his hand where a purple bruise surrounded the cannula. Every once in a while his limbs would jerk, as though he was inside a terrible dream. 'What was he saying about car payments?' she whispered.

Her mother's head drooped as she looked down at the bedsheets. 'He got the Hyundai on a lease. He's tied in for two years – but surely they won't hold him to it. Not after this.'

Lucy took in the paleness of her father's face, his laboured breathing. He'd survive: she'd cling to that belief with all her strength. But returning to work any time soon was out of the question. That was assuming they'd even let him drive a taxi again.

There was Lucy's share of Zelda's deposit, the money she'd netted from her plus one gigs. She could help. 'I'll give you some money.'

Her mother's eyes widened. 'No, love, it won't come to that.'

'We can't have Dad being anxious about work. Trying to go back before he's ready. I know what he's like.'

Her mother's eyes were welling up, but she shook her head. 'We'll manage. It'll be okay, I promise.'

Lucy thought of the agency inbox, the new enquiries stacked up in bold type. She wouldn't mind going on endless dates, pretending to be enraptured by middle-aged men, if she knew it was helping her family.

'How much does the car cost him?' Lucy asked.

'Five hundred a month, I think, but you mustn't . . . '

'I want to help. I can't promise I'll be able to cover it every month, but I'll try.'

'You know your father won't take your money.'

'He doesn't have to know it's coming from me,' Lucy whispered.

'Lucy—'

'It's the least I can do. I'm not here like Mel is, I can't help around the house. Please, let me do this. I need to do something.'

'Just having you visit will mean the world to him. And you'll be home soon. He'll love having you back.'

Lucy massaged her temples, trying to dispel a persistent ache. Her teacher training course was due to start in three months. She allowed herself the indulgence of imagining it. Shedding every vestige of London Lucy and being with people who loved her. Watching her father sleep made her remember the girl she'd been before university; she'd inhabited the *now* of her life back then, relishing each day as it unfolded, the simple pleasures of a walk to school with one of the lads on their street, or a morning in bed with *Jane Eyre* or *I Capture the Castle*.

Recalling the gleeful way her father would shout out the answers whenever he watched a television quiz show, how the tears had run down his face the first time he held his nephew, Lucy felt ashamed. What goodness had London Lucy ever brought into the world? She'd been so fixated on the kind of success that was only ever granted to a few, neglecting the things that really mattered.

She had, however, come up with a way of making money. That's what her family needed right now. That's how Lucy could serve the people she loved. One day she'd come back, be with them. But for now she'd make the most of what she'd built and send her mother as much money as she could. She hoped it would be enough.

Chapter 11

Lucy had climbed the steps of the neo-Gothic building housing her university's drama department countless times. This was a place that made her schoolfriends' voices catch when they learned she'd got in. An institution that promised to bind Lucy with generations of talented British actors.

She was back in London after a week in Portsmouth. Her father had been sent home, taking the stairs up to bed slowly, clutching the banister and pausing every third step. His chin had trembled as Mel coaxed him towards his bedroom, speaking brightly of the plant-based meals she'd cook to aid his recovery. Seeing him like that gave Lucy a cold feeling, starting in her chest but trickling through her whole body. He was unhappy; humiliated, even, yet trying so hard to conceal these feelings.

Lucy had sent her mother everything in her bank account and filled her diary with gigs. Her job – the mission she'd set herself – was to strip away her parents' financial worries. The car firm hadn't released her father from his contract, so she'd assume responsibility for the payments and try to send her mother a bit extra on top of that to help with bills.

As she headed inside the university building, Lucy felt

a tensing in her core, as though her body was recalling the violent nausea of her last visit, a decade ago.

'We're concerned about Peter.' Lucy had stepped inside their tutor Claudia Gleeson's room back then, Jack at her side. 'He didn't turn up for graduation and his phone is going straight to voicemail. We were wondering if you had contact details for his family?' They'd known Peter's circumstances were complicated – his mother had died when he was five and he'd been raised by grandparents.

As soon as she'd seen Claudia's watery eyes, Lucy had a foreboding of the truth. Peter wouldn't have ignored her messages, wouldn't have missed graduation unless something terrible had happened.

'Have a seat.' Claudia had spoken in a hoarse whisper.

Jack had obeyed, but Lucy remained standing. 'Tell us.' Darkness had gathered at the edges of her vision. She knew, just *knew* what she was about to be told. She felt Jack's hand, his fingers icy as they entwined with her own.

'I'm afraid I have some terrible news,' Claudia had said. 'We've only just found out. There was a car accident. Peter ... he passed away. I'm so sorry, I know how close you all were.'

Lucy hated that term, *passed away*. As though it could mask the brutality of death, implying peace, fluffy clouds, floating. Peter would have hated it too.

'When? Why didn't anybody tell us?' Lucy had been indignant, but when she turned to look at Jack the feeling dissolved into irrelevance. Peter – dead? His keen blue eyes, the thoughtful pauses before he spoke, the way he danced with abandon, free from any trace of self-consciousness. Gone?

Later that afternoon Lucy had returned to Jack's flat – he'd just moved into the Docklands place and everything was new and pristine. Together, eyes stinging, they'd read the *Surrey Advertiser's* online account of the crash. Peter had been alone in the car. He'd collided with a tree just after midnight on a Tuesday in June. 70 MPH CRASH TRAGEDY, the headline read. The story was accompanied by an image of a mangled Golf GTI at the side of a narrow country lane and Lucy couldn't help imagining Peter's slender frame, similarly mangled. She'd retched, her stomach heaving violently. But she couldn't stop her brain forging a stream of images – Peter's hair matted with blood, his legs sticking out at strange angles.

Jack had sunk to the floor. The sound he made hadn't been human, it was more of a howl, Lucy would never forget it. She'd held him tight, the two of them rocking, clinging to one another.

A police statement claimed Peter's blood alcohol levels had been twice the legal limit. In a quote, Peter's grandfather described him as a 'fine young man with a bright future ahead of him'. It was such an inadequate summary, didn't come close to conjuring the playfulness, the intense love Peter showed his friends.

He'd been careful, so precise in everything he did; Lucy simply couldn't imagine him drink driving. 'There must be some mistake,' she'd whispered at last.

Jack had pulled away from her, eyes filled with horror. 'He . . . it says he crashed his car.'

'It doesn't make sense,' Lucy's voice was high-pitched, almost a wail. 'He wouldn't do that. He wouldn't drink and drive.'

Jack's face had become ashen and his lower lip trembled.

With a sudden ferocity, Lucy had once again folded him into her arms. They only had each other now.

Today, the university was eerily quiet as Lucy made her way along the gleaming wooden floor, heading towards Claudia's office. The dark-green walls bore headshots of famous alumni. She spotted Gracie Dorn halfway along, serene smile, hair cascading over one shoulder. The smell was just as she remembered it, the chemical sweetness of polish, undercut by something stale and musty.

She found Claudia's office and knocked on the open door. Her former teacher was still extremely thin, wearing a jade-green sheath dress and pristine white trainers. Her hair was pulled back into a chignon and her face was dominated by round-lensed glasses.

'Lucy! How wonderful to see you.' Claudia stood up from her desk, beckoning Lucy into the room and ushering her towards the sofa.

When they were seated, Claudia's gaze roved over Lucy's face. 'I still remember your Maggie Pollitt,' she sighed. 'If there was any justice ... Anyway, you're an agent now?'

'Kind of,' Lucy said. 'But it's a bit unusual. Probably not something to brag about in the alumni newsletter.'

Claudia raised her eyebrows.

'We offer impersonation services. Actors stepping into the lives of normal people.'

'I'm not sure I follow.' Claudia removed her glasses and rubbed the lenses against the fabric of her dress.

'We do a roaring trade in being people's fake plus one at weddings and parties. That kind of thing.'

'Escorting?' Claudia replaced her glasses.

'Helping people make an impression. Acting to support the little pretences our clients want to create. Like, this morning I had an email asking whether someone can sit in on a salesman's presentation and be ultra enthusiastic. Create a bit of atmosphere by nodding along and asking questions.'

Claudia sat back into the sofa, giving Lucy a sly smile. 'How intriguing. Sounds like you've become quite the entrepreneur.'

Lucy felt an unexpected glow at the word *entrepreneur*. She was surprised by just how right it felt. In a few short months, she'd created a business with just an idea and a three-grand loan from Jack. There were no guarantees it would last, but she'd given Jack a new focus and had positioned herself to help her family.

'It's all happened rather quickly,' Lucy laughed. 'I had no idea how many people would be willing to pay to deceive their friends and colleagues.'

'Oh, I can more than believe it. Nowadays anything can be bought and sold. You're hoping to sign up more actors?'

'We need to build a roster of freelancers. Most demand is for women around thirty, but we're starting to get the odd request for a forty- or fiftysomething.'

Claudia nodded, looking thoughtful. 'I could put you in touch with some people, if you're offering decent rates.'

'We pay a hundred pounds an hour. Besides the actual performance, we bill clients for prep time, normally an hour for memorising a backstory, but sometimes more.' Lucy had decided that on top of this the agency would apply a booking fee of twenty per cent to each client's bill.

Claudia swallowed. 'Goodness. With those rates you can jolly well sign me up. I've been looking for a side-hustle ever since my divorce.'

'If you're serious, I can definitely offer work.' Lucy scanned her former tutor's face.

'Could I specialise in playing cougars?'

Lucy blinked.

'That was a joke, darling. For a hundred quid an hour, I'm happy to be someone's granny if need be.'

Once she'd said her goodbyes to Claudia, Lucy headed back out into the humid afternoon for her next appointment. Zelda was already leaning against one of the pillars by the entrance, wearing a straw sunhat with a flowing turquoise skirt and white blouse.

'Thank you so much for meeting me at such short notice.' She flashed Lucy a grateful smile.

'It's lovely to see you.' Lucy realised her shoulders were drawn up, so she consciously loosened them. *I want to chat with you on your own. No Jack*, Zelda's message had said.

Jack had met with Zelda alone at least twice for debriefs. 'She's super interested,' he'd said, after the first meeting. 'She wanted to hear my take on things. Made me go over everything I talked about with Sebastian.' Was it possible that Jack had said something flippant, something that left Zelda uneasy?

'Rather than giving our money to some ghastly coffee chain, I wonder whether we might find somewhere to sit down in there?' Zelda nodded towards the university building.

Lucy wasn't sure whether non-students were supposed to be wandering around the campus, but there was no security

on the door and she'd made her way to Claudia's office without anyone asking who she was. She led Zelda inside, showing
her up to the canteen and out onto the terrace overlooking
the river. It was exactly how Lucy remembered it, the pleasure boats leaving from Festival Pier; the sun glinting against
the iconic glass frontage of Charing Cross Station; and in the
distance the Gothic spires of the Houses of Parliament. There
was a strange hush up here; the usual roar of London traffic
receding to a dull murmur. The only other people outside was
a small cluster of acting students poring over a script, their
temples damp with sweat.

Zelda sat down on one of the chrome chairs with a happy
sigh, placing her hessian bag at her feet. 'What a gorgeous
space. This is where the magic happened, I suppose? You and
Jack, making art together?'

Nodding, Lucy wondered what Jack had told Zelda about
their friendship. He always omitted Peter when he reminisced
about university. Lucy had believed him ruthless, purging
the narrative of his own life of anything painful, anything
less than perfect. But since finding the photograph in the
wardrobe, Lucy had felt strangely reassured. He *felt* the loss,
just as she did. It made her feel less alone.

With her legs stretched out in front of her, taking in the
view with a serene smile, Zelda looked completely relaxed,
as though Lucy was one of her closest friends. 'I wanted to
talk to you woman to woman. I know what Sebastian's like,
you see. He's probably already decided he doesn't like Jack.'

The comment struck Lucy as misguided and maybe even
a little presumptuous given that Zelda hadn't seen Sebastian
for thirty years. 'What makes you say that?' she asked.

'Doesn't have an artistic bone in his body, bless him. I did try and develop his sensibilities, but I don't think I succeeded.'

Lucy felt a flicker of unease she couldn't quite explain to herself. 'We could have given Jack a different backstory, if we'd known.'

'Perhaps.' Zelda shrugged. 'What's important is that we win Sebastian over to Jack's cause. That's your role in all this.'

'I'm not sure I—'

Zelda shifted in her seat, turning her body to face Lucy. Her pale-blue eyes were filled with a strange light; as though she was frightened but determined not to show it. 'If Sebastian could only understand the passion that drives Jack. The artistry. The commitment. We have to make him love Jack. We have to make him see the inherent value someone like Jack brings to the world.'

'I can steer conversations along those lines, I suppose,' Lucy said.

Zelda reached out and clasped her wrist. 'You must.'

Lucy looked down at Zelda's freckled hand. She could feel each of the silver rings pressing against her flesh.

'Sorry.' Zelda released her grip. 'I'm just very passionate about this. We need Sebastian to perceive Jack's wonderful qualities. To understand that he's so much more than his little boasts – he's a complicated human being.'

'I hope you don't mind me asking,' Lucy said, 'but are you sure you want this?'

'Absolutely. We need Sebastian to *adore* Jack.' Zelda's forehead remained smooth, but a series of lines erupted on either side of her nose.

Lucy weighed her words carefully. 'I was thinking more

generally. Having the two of them build a relationship only for Jack to disappear?'

The lines around Zelda's nose disappeared as abruptly as they emerged. A muscle in her jaw twitched as she sat back in her chair. 'That's the assignment we all agreed to.'

Lucy was shocked to see Zelda's eyes filling with tears. Had she pushed her too far? She needed the money from this gig. Needed to believe it was good for Jack.

'Here, before I forget.' Zelda reached into her bag and laid a fat white envelope down on the table in front of them. 'Another five thousand. I expect I've pretty much burned through my deposit. I want you to go to town on the charm offensive, no matter what it costs. For Jack's sake.'

Lucy stared at the money. Her share of it could buy a couple of worry-free months for her family. She imagined her mother's relief at knowing the car payments were covered, pictured her father's brow relaxing for the first time in years. But – Sebastian. He'd appeared interested as Jack had blathered on about auditions. The man was trying to connect. He seemed so set on doing the responsible thing and nurturing this new and unexpected relationship. He didn't deserve what Zelda had in mind for him. No one did.

'If you had doubts, we could maybe change course,' Lucy said quietly.

Zelda reached out and rested her fingers on the envelope of cash. There was a sense of strain about her face. Again, her jaw twitched, as though she was clenching her teeth.

'If you were to contact Sebastian, you might find he's sorry for what he did. I'm sure he regrets the way he behaved,' Lucy continued, batting away a wasp.

Zelda shook her head. She wouldn't look at Lucy, but she didn't actively dismiss the suggestion. Her fingers remained on the money envelope, every muscle in her body seemed to have become rigid.

'People change,' Lucy went on. 'They grow up. Sebastian did a hideous, cowardly thing. But doesn't he deserve the chance to make it up to you?'

Slowly, Zelda turned and met Lucy's eye. She folded her hands in her lap. Her eyelashes were damp and her mascara had smudged. She was wavering.

'You seem like a very sweet girl,' Zelda said at last. 'But it is what it is.'

Zelda's doubts were so palpable. She couldn't want this, Lucy was sure of it.

'I can't imagine what it must have been like for you, being left alone in a strange country by the man you loved,' Lucy said. 'You deserve an apology and the thing is, I'm sure he'll give you one.'

The metal legs of Zelda's chair scraped across the floor as she stood up with sudden violence, keeping her gaze just above Lucy's face. 'Arrange as many get-togethers as you can. We need Sebastian to love and respect Jack. *That's* your brief.'

Chapter 12

Jack was late for the next pub lunch with Sebastian. He'd been up in Manchester visiting a schoolfriend and was supposed to be getting an early train back, but as she was patting on her under-eye concealer, Lucy's phone vibrated with a text.

Overslept and missed my train. Going to be late x

She stared at the message. She was just about managing to squeeze her visits to Portsmouth around the agency schedule, making three-hour round trips to spend sometimes as little as a single hour with her father. He was still passing his days propped up in bed, and even though he never complained, defeat weighed down his features.

She called Jack. 'I can't believe—'

'I know. I'm a disorganised shit. Permission to scold me granted.'

'Are you going to call Sebastian and reschedule? Say you've got a bug or something.'

'No need, I'll just join you at the pub as soon as my train gets in.'

'I'm not sure . . . '

'It'll be fine. Order for me and I'll be with you before the food's on the table. Promise.'

They'd arranged to meet at a pub along the Thames Path, near Spitalfields Market. It was already crowded by the time Lucy arrived, so she was grateful to see Sebastian had secured one of the outside picnic tables. It was hot and humid; the blue skies that had continued almost unbroken since the start of summer were now swollen with grey cloud. There was a stink emanating from the river, an ever-present tang of sewage that overpowered the smells from the pub kitchen.

Sebastian wore a short-sleeved linen shirt, the top two buttons undone to reveal a thin gold chain and a smattering of dark chest hair, damp with sweat. He stood up when he saw Lucy approaching, giving her a warm smile. The character she was playing would dole out hugs with ease, so Lucy took the initiative, catching the scent of a woody aftershave as she grazed his cheek with her own.

'Jack's joining us in a bit. He met up with friends last night and is having train trouble on the way home.'

'That's the good old British rail network for you.' Sebastian returned to his seat, resting his forearms on the table, fingers laced together. Behind him, a shaft of sunlight found a space between the clouds, glinting off the steel towers of the city.

'I'll order for Jack,' Lucy said. 'He's very predictable. Always has a steak or a roast, even in this heat. He's such a carnivore.'

'Sounds like me.'

Everything about Sebastian, from the way he held his body, to the openness of his smile, seemed calculated to put Lucy at ease. She allowed herself a silent cackle: him, a banker, trying to impress a nobody from Portsmouth!

Make Sebastian love Jack, that had been Zelda's instruction. Now wasn't the moment to consider its strangeness. Lucy had scooped up Zelda's cash-stuffed envelope and put it in her bag. How could she not? It represented so much more than car payments, such a sum could insulate her family from the next crisis, whatever it may be. Lucy remembered the washing machine packing up when she was about ten or so. They'd been on a credit blacklist at the time, so it had taken three years of handwashing school uniforms and work shirts in the sink before they'd scrimped enough for a replacement. With a deep breath, she re-established Lucy-the-fiancée. Every muscle, every tendon softened as her chest swelled with her character's optimism, her love for Jack.

'I'm so glad Jack was able to track you down,' Lucy said.

Sebastian smiled as he filled her glass with red. She inhaled its sharp, fruity aroma and found herself staring at his slender fingers with their clean, trimmed nails.

'He's always been close to Zelda, but it's like you're filling this gap he didn't even know existed.' Lucy's mouth twitched. Her character had a secret pride in her own perceptiveness.

Sebastian set the wine bottle down on the table and glanced at her, suddenly serious. 'It's been nice for me too. With my ex-wife, we actually ended up doing seven rounds of IVF. Pure torture by the end of it. I'd given up all hope of ever becoming a father.'

Lucy took a sip of the wine, trying to disguise how unsettled she felt. Instead of the acidity she'd been bracing against, her tongue encountered vanilla and currants. Sebastian had longed to become a parent. She felt a sharp pang in her chest and took a longer drink, making appreciative noises to try and disguise an assault of feeling. She and Jack were giving Sebastian exactly what he wanted. But none of it was real.

'Your wife – is she . . . '

Sebastian dropped his gaze, looking down at the table. 'At your age, I'm not sure you can imagine what it's like, pinning your happiness on something that might not ever happen. It changed us. When she told me it was over, it was kind of a relief.'

Lucy pressed her lips together in sympathy. She realised she was fiddling with Jack's grandmother's ring, unused to its weight on her finger, and carefully folded her hands in her lap. 'I'm sorry.'

'You must have a very low opinion of me.' Sebastian looked up, meeting her gaze.

'Not at all. It's not for me—'

'I would have been involved in Jack's life. If I'd known. I was so young, but I wasn't a bad person.'

Lucy nodded, careful not to let her confusion show. Was this how he justified his actions? If he'd known Zelda intended to keep the baby, he wouldn't have run away?

'I'm not some sort of – I don't just think it should be down to the mother—'

Lucy raised an eyebrow.

'Every kid needs two parents. At least.' Sebastian's nostrils flared.

'I agree.' She permitted a flintiness in her character's tone. Sebastian still wasn't taking responsibility, was refusing to recognise the cowardice of his actions.

His posture softened. 'How about you? Your father still around?'

Lucy nodded. There was a tightness at her jaw, an unbidden stream of images spooling through her mind. Her father's tired face looking up from the hospital pillow. That slow shuffle up the stairs, the slightest wince at Mel's over-bright voice. Lucy standing at his bedside, desperate to help but unable to think of anything useful beyond smoothing and resmoothing his blankets.

'What does he do?'

'He's a taxi driver.'

Lucy hadn't forgotten her fake persona, she was supposed to say orthodontist, she knew that. She'd rewritten herself as a nice middle-class girl from a leafy part of Hampshire. Yet she felt in the grip of a strange new superstition: to lie about her father was to dishonour him, to weaken him in some imperceptible way.

Sebastian didn't show surprise at this hint of a working-class background. Lucy hadn't been expecting a wrinkled nose exactly, Sebastian was too well mannered for that. But his absence of snobbery was a refreshing surprise.

'And your mum?'

'A care assistant.' Lucy said it defiantly. She was hastily recalibrating her backstory, bringing it closer to the truth. Hardworking parents who encouraged their daughters to go to university. The nice PR job hadn't been gifted to Lucy-the-fiancée, she'd had to work for it.

She remembered Craig Williams coming up to her in the school corridor, shirt untucked, smelling of pencil shavings and armpit. 'Your mum wipes my granddad's arse. And she washes him. She has to touch his dick.'

Lucy's friends had formed a defensive huddle around her, expecting mortification, tears even. But after the briefest inner cringe, Lucy had felt able to shrug. 'Someone's got to do it. Better than making him wear a nappy.'

She realised Sebastian was smiling at her, and this pulled her from the memory, shaken at how distracted she'd allow herself to become.

'You and your parents are close?' Sebastian asked.

A sudden prickling behind her eyes. Lucy could feel herself slipping out of role. The late nights, the agency schedule, weren't giving her enough time to reinforce the membrane dividing her characters from her real self. She didn't want to bore Jack with the endless admin, but she was hurt at how little he'd offered to help. He'd even refused to meet with Claudia, saying *you're so much better at explaining everything, Luce.*

Lucy had to make a split decision: Sebastian had seen her emotion, she could quickly restrain it, or she could explain.

'My father actually had a heart attack a month ago, so I'm a bit ...' This was the first time she'd cried. She held her breath, trying to stifle the tears.

'Goodness ... I—' Sebastian laid his hand on her arm. His palm felt hot against her skin.

'How is he doing?' Sebastian asked.

Lucy swallowed. 'They fitted a stent. He's been out of hospital for over a month now. Has to take a whole bunch of medication. Get lots of rest.'

Sebastian swallowed. 'It's a very established area of medicine. People go on to live healthy lives for decades afterwards.'

As she nodded, Lucy felt a wave of gratitude. It was as

though he'd known exactly what she needed to hear. Yet the truth couldn't quite soothe her, her body didn't accept it, her muscles remained tight.

'I know,' she said. 'I keep trying to focus on the positives. But I guess you never really know how long you've got with people.'

Sebastian nodded and she saw, with some surprise, that his eyes were welling up. She ought to be strategising, focusing on Zelda's commission. But Sebastian's response brushed against something raw.

'I thought there'd be plenty of time to make him proud—' Lucy stopped herself. What was she *doing*? The man in front of her was a target. She was being paid a hundred pounds an hour to cement a bond with a fictional version of Jack. A fictional version of *herself*.

A waiter approached their table, looking suddenly confused by the three plates he was carrying.

'You can put the steak here,' Lucy called out, pointing to an empty spot on the table. 'Thank you. My partner will be along in a bit.'

They were silent as the waiter laid their plates on the table. Sebastian had gone for roast beef, Lucy had opted for *penne al tonno*. How had she let the conversation get so out of control? A few minutes more and she'd have been bawling.

As the waiter moved away, Sebastian gave Lucy a searching glance. 'Putting on a brave face is overrated,' he said. 'A heart attack – any kind of news like that – is bound to shake you up.'

The pasta was steaming hot, the aromas of tuna and garlic formed a pungent cloud right in front of her face. She swallowed the saliva pooling in her mouth, repulsed at the prospect of eating. The wine, too, had been a mistake, her thoughts were becoming slow and languid. It was time for a subject change.

'I'm not used to drinking in the day,' she said.

'Me neither.' Sebastian picked up his knife and fork, hungrily carving a mouthful of meat.

'I hope you don't mind me asking, but where did you end up going, once you left Zelda?'

A flicker of alarm passed through Sebastian's eyes. Perhaps Lucy had overstepped in her haste to change the subject.

'Nowhere in particular,' he said. 'Everything kind of lost its romance. I ended up coming home earlier than planned.'

'Do you regret it?'

Sebastian chewed slowly; his eyes roved around the beer garden taking in the tubs of wilting geraniums, the opportunistic crows preparing to swipe unattended chips. He sighed. 'I don't regret leaving, no. But I could have gone about it better.'

There was something so preposterous in this. Lucy felt unable to offer a platitude in response, couldn't even bring herself to give a murmur of understanding.

Sebastian took a mouthful of Yorkshire pudding, then laid his fork down on the table. 'Relationships feel more intense than they really are when you're travelling. Everything is strange and unfamiliar – it can make the person you're with feel like home.'

'But—' Lucy was straining to hold herself in character. A pile of cash on a pillow. How was he not writhing with shame?

'If I'd known she was pregnant things would have been very different.' Sebastian picked up his fork and resumed eating.

Lucy stared at him. How easily he was forking up roast potatoes, chewing with palpable relish. He appeared serene, languid even.

He *had* known Zelda was pregnant. He'd even gone so far as writing her a note telling her to get an abortion. Did he believe Lucy ignorant of that? Perhaps he'd expected Zelda to have kept the humiliating specifics of her abandonment to herself.

'You broke up before you even knew about the baby?' Lucy was careful not to sound interrogative. She was a polite girl, throwing out a simple statement, checking she understood correctly.

Sebastian nodded, picking up another Yorkshire pudding with his fingers and taking a hearty bite.

Lucy recalled an article she'd read about the fallibility of memory. A psychologist had explained how people tended to shape their experiences into stories, making sense of what happened with narratives that differed wildly from the established facts. Was that what was going on here? The treachery of leaving a pregnant woman was too hard to face, so instead Sebastian told himself a story of a failing relationship, framing his departure as inevitable? It was too much of a stretch to believe that the details Zelda described – the money on the pillow, the recommendation to get an abortion – had been embellishments invented by her in the intervening years. They were too distinct.

Lucy needed to bring matters to a head, before the deception became even more tangled and painful. If Sebastian wasn't going to make the leap and ask for a DNA test, there must be other, simpler, ways to force a reckoning. 'I think it would mean a lot to Zelda if she were to hear from you,' she said.

Sebastian raised an eyebrow. 'I very much doubt that.'

'If you were to explain what was going through your head,' Lucy began. 'Maybe ask her how she interpreted things at the time—'

'Hello, hello!' Jack bounded up to their table, pecking Lucy on the cheek as he slung his overnight bag to the floor. He wore denim cut-offs and a T-shirt emblazoned with some band Lucy had never heard of. 'Sorry, I'm late. Ooh, lovely, is this for me?' He sat down in front of the steak and chips. 'Bloody trains. What a nightmare!'

Sebastian said something about being glad Jack was here now. But Lucy could only manage a brief smile of greeting. Convincing Sebastian he had a son, letting him feel he was building a relationship was despicable. There must be a different way to help Zelda reach the closure she needed. Lucy couldn't go on taking the money, not if the goal was to make Sebastian suffer.

Chapter 13

'Okay, so now the client has put his hand on your butt,' said Lucy.

They were in the upstairs function room of a Soho pub, the tables and chairs pushed up against the wall, exposing bald patches of carpet. The windows were all flung open, the smell of cooking fat wafting in.

The actor, her name was Abigail, gave a charming giggle, angling her head as she executed a graceful sidestep. 'Easy, tiger. You'll get us thrown out if you're not careful.' Her voice was silky, but there was an undertone of assertiveness, a warning perceptible to the client alone. She'd do well. She had long blond hair too – clients specified 'blond' as often as they stipulated 'slim', a fact that revolted Lucy. If anyone became too prescriptive about dimensions, she tended to add an extra hour of prep time to their bill, but it wasn't quite enough to satisfy her unease.

'Very good,' said Jack. 'Now. Final scene. I'm a little old lady with dementia who keeps ringing 999 about my imaginary ailments. You've been hired by my daughter to impersonate a doctor. The goal is to convince me I'm healthy and put my mind at rest.'

Abigail widened her eyes for a second, then proffered her hand. 'Good afternoon, madam, I'm Doctor Smith – our practice manager asked me to pop along and take a look at you. You're having some trouble with your digestion, I hear?'

'Ooh, yes, doctor. I've been getting terrible gas,' Jack said in an exaggerated old-lady voice.

Abigail exuded brisk competence as she mimed listening to Jack's stomach, asking follow-up questions about the specific sensations and the woman's diet. As she listened to each of Jack's responses, she wore a thoughtful frown, sometimes nodding along, exhibiting a gentle patience. She concluded with a flourish, 'prescribing' indigestion tablets with the satisfaction of someone who'd just worked out the answer to a perplexing riddle.

Jack gave her a round of applause, his eyes glowing. This was the most engaged he'd been in the business – he was instantly smitten by good acting, always curious about how others would approach a role.

'Do people really ask you to be pretend doctors?' Abigail had a clipped Southern accent that suggested private school, the posture of someone who'd attended ballet classes since they were very little.

Lucy crossed her legs, trying to suppress a smile. Everyone they'd auditioned had been on the posh side, yet they were coming to *her* for work. Her father would have been tickled if he'd seen the succession of actors flashing their warmest smiles at Lucy, complimenting her on her entrepreneurialism.

'We've just got the one doctor gig,' Lucy said. 'It's well-intentioned. A weekly visit seems to settle the old lady.

We've probably saved the emergency services thousands of pounds.'

'I'm excited at the prospect of working with you both. Thank you so much for seeing me.' Abigail smiled, but Lucy recognised the hunger on her face, the desperation to go on calling herself an actor even though her showreel suggested the auditions had been few and far between.

Jack showed Abigail out. She was the seventh late-twenties female they'd seen that day, and she'd be the fourth they added to the agency roster.

'This has been rather a hoot,' Jack said as he wandered back into the middle of the room, raising up his arms to stretch his back. 'I can't believe we'll get to make money while other people do the work.'

'We're more than earning our booking fee,' Lucy said. 'Our ads are what generates the enquiries in the first place. Then there's all the pre-screening, the invoicing.' Time-consuming work that Jack showed little interest in.

'I've been in touch with my dad's friend to set up an office viewing,' he said. 'There's this place above a cake shop in Soho. Used to be a graphic design studio.'

'I'm not sure—'

'Nine hundred a month for Central London – he's giving us an insanely good deal. Come on, Luce. Next time we run an audition, we can do it in our very own premises.' He stood behind her, massaging her shoulders.

Lucy picked at the skin around the nail of her thumb. If she wanted to continue sending money home, then the agency needed to expand, and quickly – already several dates in December were double or even triple booked with Christmas parties. She turned to look at Jack. His face seemed almost radiant with excitement as he fantasised about having an office of their own. If she denied him this, would she be killing his enthusiasm?

Two nights previously, Jack's mother had called Lucy. 'Does he seem depressed to you? He was too quiet when he last visited. I've just got this feeling – are you still keeping an eye on him?'

As Jack's mother had gabbled, her voice shrill with anxiety, Lucy had tried to steady her breathing and *think*. Nothing stood out. There hadn't been any auditions to overexcite or disappoint him. He was still going to the gym, always seemed pleased when they had the opportunity to watch a film together. But then, Lucy was never entirely sure what she was looking for. The first breakdown had a swooping quality to it, a sudden, disorientating rush that had left her questioning everything.

Now, Jack was still waiting for her response. Was the expectancy in his eyes too loaded, too intense?

'All right,' she said. 'No harm in looking.'

Before they headed back to the Docklands, Jack insisted they take a detour to his favourite vintage clothing shop. The place had an overwhelming smell, a mustiness that jarred with the carefully organised rails and beautiful displays adorned with fairy lights.

'I'm meeting up with Zelda again tomorrow,' Jack said, rifling through the men's section.

'Bit over the top, isn't it? You must be seeing more of her than Sebastian.' Lucy hadn't told Jack about her own meeting with Zelda, the strange *make him love Jack* instruction. Was it remiss of her? He would be either unsettled or bemused, and Lucy wasn't sure how either emotion would help.

Jack removed a damson-coloured smoking jacket from its hanger and wandered over to a mirror to try it on. 'She likes hearing all the details.'

'Like some sort of voyeur?'

Jack laughed, rolling up the sleeves of the jacket and assessing the effect in the mirror. 'No. She's not getting off on it or anything weird. She just wants to know it's going well.'

'You're keeping a log of the time you spend with her, right? I should make sure everything's added to her account.' Lucy knew she was being a coward, defaulting to business talk. Perhaps playing a son was too much for Jack, given his distant relationship with his own father. Maybe it was unsettling him.

Jack placed a hand on his hip, still looking in the mirror. 'Do you not like Zelda?'

The question took Lucy by surprise. She felt tremendous compassion for their client. True, that wasn't the same as liking someone, but Lucy had always been polite and professional in their dealings. 'I don't know her,' she said.

Jack returned the jacket to the rail and resumed browsing. 'But you do like Sebastian?'

Lucy nodded. She hadn't expected to find a banker in the least bit likeable. But Sebastian had treated her with kindness. 'He said something strange at lunch the other week. Made out he never knew Zelda was pregnant.'

Jack looked up. 'Trying to paint himself as an innocent victim, is he?'

'It wasn't like that. He was matter-of-fact about it when he told me, as though it really was the truth.'

'Zelda wouldn't have made something like that up.' There was a firmness to Jack's tone that Lucy hadn't been expecting.

'I know. I think Zelda genuinely believes Sebastian did a runner,' Lucy said.

'Because he did.' Jack's eyes flashed a warning.

'But it might not have been as straightforward as that, is what I'm saying. They've both had thirty years to brood on what happened.'

Jack picked up a second jacket for a closer look before replacing it with a frown. Lucy found herself tensing up as he stepped towards her, but he wrapped his arm around her shoulder. 'Look – Sebastian must have known Zelda was pregnant when he abandoned her. If not, he would have asked for a paternity test by now, no question.'

Lucy swallowed but said nothing.

Jack continued: 'You saw how he reacted when we turned up at his work. He was ashamed – the past had caught up with him.'

Was it possible Lucy's judgement had been clouded by how kind Sebastian had been? A few sympathetic words about her father, and she was suddenly questioning everything? 'There is that, I suppose,' she said.

Jack tightened his hug. 'I think someone has a little crush on Sebastian.'

'Fuck off.' Her face became hot. She had to look away. Perhaps she had weakened a little at the lunch, risked the assignment by showing Sebastian glimpses of the real Lucy.

'Come on, let's find you something pretty. I'm sick of the sight of that trouser suit.'

Lucy bristled. 'You'll have to tolerate it a little longer. I'm sending any spare money to help my parents.'

Jack looked away, placing a hand against his stomach, and Lucy instantly regretted her tone.

She watched him as he moved over to the hat section, picking up and inspecting a peaked cap like Lucy's grandad used to wear.

'You are enjoying the agency, right?' She moistened her lips with her tongue.

'Yeah.' Jack was still examining the hat, running his fingers along the inner lining. 'Something to do between auditions.'

She felt a strain in her chest. Jack's agent hadn't set any-thing up for him since the previous October. 'If it gets too much ... ' Lucy's heart began to race.

With a jerk of his neck, Jack looked up. First his eyes wid-ened, almost in fear, but then they narrowed. He knew this was an allusion to his breakdown.

'I'm not some swooning heroine out of one of your Victorian novels,' he said coldly.

'I know, I just ... '

'We were having a nice day. The auditions were fun. Why do this?'

She knew there was no answer that would satisfy him, so Lucy remained silent. If only Peter was here to help her. He'd always known exactly what to say whenever Jack brooded on a negative workshop comment. *What if you were to add a little more emotion to this line here?* Peter would offer. Or: *when they said* overacted, *maybe you were just giving them too much. What if the character were to try mask his feelings?*

Would Lucy ever stop missing him? She adored Jack, he'd filled her with fire, made her twenties feel alive with possibility. But at times – like now – she knew it was Peter she really needed.

Chapter 14

In mid-September Jack travelled up to Hertfordshire for a garden party at his father's house. Lucy was trying out her new hire, Abigail, sending her to a wedding reception instead of going along herself. She planned to take the train to Portsmouth, join her father on the short walks that were an integral part of his rehabilitation programme. But when they spoke on the phone, Lucy's mother asked if Lucy could invite Mel to London instead.

'It's all getting a bit much. Mel's been giving Dad a hard time about his diet – she found out he asked Charlie to pick him up a sausage roll from Greggs. I know she means well, but they could do with a break from one another.'

'Will you manage, looking after Charlie and Dad by yourself?'

'Of course. It's not like they're any trouble. Honestly, the most helpful thing you could do right now is encourage Mel to let her hair down for a bit.'

Lucy agreed. She'd not had a night out with Mel since before Charlie's arrival, when her sister had still been a teenager. Perhaps it would do them both good.

*

Following an afternoon at the National Portrait Gallery, Lucy led Mel to a well-reviewed vegan restaurant off Sloane Square. The weather was just beginning to turn with sudden gusts rustling through the London plane trees, shaking yellowing leaves to the ground. Inside, the restaurant had wooden floors and comfortable-looking chairs upholstered in pale-green imitation leather. There was an upstairs, away from the clamour of the kitchen, where the tables were spaced just far enough apart for conversations to feel private.

'Your teaching course must be starting really soon,' Mel said, taking her seat. She was dressed in combats from the army surplus store, paired with a sleeveless top that revealed her unshaven armpits. Her olive skin looked flawless even without make-up.

Lucy adjusted the strap of her dress. 'I might not take up my place.' She still hadn't formally withdrawn from the course and over the last week the university had been chasing her up about enrolment. What was she waiting for, exactly? She was making money, helping her family while practising the craft she loved. It should be an easy decision. Yet she retained a vision of herself carrying her things through the front door of the family home, blowing up the airbed, sitting with her nephew each morning as he ate his toast and jam. It would mean abandoning Jack. But staying in London felt like a kind of abandonment too, as though she was casting some important part of herself aside.

Mel scratched at the back of her neck. 'Have you talked to Mum and Dad about this? They're looking forward to having you home. It's all they go on about.'

Lucy pictured their smiles. Imagined herself chastising

her father as he tried to help with her suitcases. She saw the softness of her mother's eyes as she asked, *what did you learn on your course today, Lucy?*

'The thing is, work has started picking up in London, so . . .'

Mel's eyes were trained on Lucy's face. 'But are you sure about binning off the course? I don't know anything about acting, but weren't you looking for something more reliable?'

'I was, but . . .'

'You want to stay in London.' Mel made it sound like an accusation.

Lucy picked at a chipped section of nail varnish on her middle finger. 'For now, yeah.' Her stomach lurched as she realised just how untrue this was. She *needed* to stay in London, she could help everyone so much better when she was here.

'With Jack. Living the student life.' Mel snatched up the menu and held it in front of her face.

'That's not . . . this isn't a lifestyle choice, Mel. I'm trying to be rational. It's not like retraining will solve everything.'

Her sister said nothing, so Lucy picked up her own menu and stared at the options. She was relieved when the waiter came along. As expected, Mel went for the cheapest option – a falafel salad – so Lucy bulked out their order with flatbreads and dips, roasted vegetables and fried sweet potato. Her sister never ate out back home, cooking nutritious meals from scratch, buying up the yellow-stickered fruit and veg at the supermarket. Tonight's meal ought to feel like a treat.

Once the waiter left them, Mel laid her forearms down on the table, leaning forwards. 'Dad was so excited about you coming home. Having you involved in his rehab would help him stick at it.'

'I visit as often as I can,' Lucy said.

Mel shifted in her seat. 'It's not the same.'

'I do my best. I'm always going up and down on that bloody train.'

Mel said nothing, gazing at her sister with her bright hazel eyes.

Lucy returned her stare. 'Spit it out.'

'What?'

'You're giving me that look. Go on, let me have it.'

Mel sighed. 'I just can't help thinking it's a little indulgent. Hanging on, taking whatever bit parts you can. I mean, I can understand in your twenties ...'

'*Bit parts.* That's fair, I suppose.' Lucy gave a bitter laugh. Why did they always end up sniping? There was no one Lucy respected as much as her sister.

Mel raised her eyebrows. There was no trace of spite on her face, she looked insufferably earnest. 'I didn't mean to sound harsh. It's just, retraining as a teacher would let you shape something; you'd be helping young people. Making a difference. Don't you want that for yourself?'

The waiter returned with Lucy's vodka and soda, plus a tap water for Mel. His smile was pained, as though he recognised he'd walked into the middle of a disagreement.

If only Mel knew about the four grand Lucy had already sent home; about the expansion plans she'd put in place for the agency. Her parents deserved to be free from worry. Lucy was going to make that possible.

*

After their meal, Lucy led them to a cocktail place on the King's Road. Jack had taken her there a year ago when it first opened – he collected write-ups of the newest places, always had a list of restaurants and bars he was desperate to try out. The bar looked almost industrial with an array of stainless-steel gadgets and expensive spirits lined up in immaculate rows.

Mel put her hands in the pocket of her combats and turned to her sister. 'It looks kind of pricey. We could just get a bottle of wine and go back to yours?'

Lucy placed a hand on the small of her sister's back. 'This is your night off. We have to make the most of it.'

None of the booths were free, so they perched on the chrome-and-leather stools at the bar. Lucy nodded her head to the club track blasting from the speakers, realising she was completely out of conversation. They'd already covered her nephew and talked about Mel's part-time job with an environmental charity. They'd discussed every aspect of their father's rehabilitation programme. She felt a sudden terror at the idea of Mel becoming more like an acquaintance than a sister.

Lucy sipped her Negroni and tried not to wince at the bitter, almost medicinal taste. It had cost her nearly twenty pounds and she'd insisted Mel have one too. 'Yum. That's delicious.'

Mel smiled, but it didn't reach her eyes. Lucy couldn't shake the feeling that her sister wished she'd stayed in Portsmouth, tucking Charlie into bed and curling up on the sofa with their parents.

'Holly?'

A man stepped between Lucy and her sister.

'Holly? It is you, isn't it?' A deep voice, plummy accent.

Mel angled her head, frowning at Lucy. 'I think he's talking to you?'

Lucy looked up at the man, sandy-haired in a white linen shirt, sunglasses dangling from his top pocket. There was something familiar about him.

'George!' Thank goodness the memory arrived in time. She'd met him at a garden party in the summer, when she'd been posing as the girlfriend of a barrister. Lucy looked around for George's wife – what was her name? – but he appeared to be alone.

The man smiled, but his forehead was creased as he looked over at Mel, taking in the combat trousers and make-up-free face. Definitely not the kind of person well-to-do Holly would hang out with.

'This is my good friend Melanie,' Lucy said. Holly had been an only child, she remembered. 'We're having a girls' night tonight.' She'd need to text her client. Adam. Adam Smythe, that was him.

'I do love a ladies' night. Let me get you some more drinks.' George looked around for an empty barstool, as though he might be about to drag one over and join them.

'Actually,' Lucy placed a hand on his arm, 'you mustn't be cross with me, but we're strictly girls only tonight, I'm afraid. Mel is having a spot of man trouble. We need to talk about how ghastly you all are.'

Again, George frowned. For a second Lucy thought he was going to disregard her comments and sit with them anyway, but at last he raised his hands in a gesture of surrender. 'Fair enough. I know when I'm not welcome. Lovely to see you, anyway. Do give Adam my best.' He walked away, rejoining a group of laughing men in a booth deeper inside the building.

Lucy exhaled and turned back to her sister.

Mel drew herself up tall. 'Spot of man trouble? Are you for real?'

'God, I'm sorry. I just needed to get rid of him.'

'Who's Holly? Why did you talk posh all of a sudden? Are you embarrassed of me?'

'I can explain, I just need to—' Lucy pulled out her phone to fire off a quick message to Adam. She was down to attend a christening with him in a couple of weeks.

Just seen your brother at a bar in Chelsea. I was with my sister, but said she was a female friend. Supposed to be on a girls' night out.

Lucy had taken far too long to respond to her fake name. It looked suspicious; at the christening she'd have to joke about how bad she was at remembering faces.

Mel drained her glass. 'Let's call it a night.' Her eyes were glistening.

'What? No! He's gone. Let me get you another drink. It's still early.'

Mel shook her head, hopping down from her bar stool and heading towards the door.

Looping her bag over her shoulder, Lucy hurried after her, hoping George wasn't observing. Her sister walked briskly, weaving through the crowd of smokers, heading for the Tube station, even though she surely wouldn't be able to navigate her way back to Jack's alone.

It was dark, but the narrow pavements were alive with young women in dresses and heels, men in their best going-out shirts, their evenings just beginning. A steady stream of black cabs and buses were stop-starting along the road, brakes hissing every few metres.

'Mel, please.'

Her sister wheeled around. 'He called you Holly. What's going on?'

Lucy swallowed, steering her sister to the side of the pavement. She felt a few drops of rain land on her bare arms. 'I've been doing a bit of acting work here and there for private clients.'

Her sister's eyes widened. 'Escorting?'

Lucy felt the heat rising to her face. 'No. I'm an actor.'

Mel took Lucy's hand and clasped it within her own. 'I'm not judging.'

'It's not *just* going on dates. I've been a fake businesswoman a few times. A mourner at a funeral. Even a doctor.'

'I don't understand.' With her free hand, Mel took hold of the neckline of her vest, pulling it away from her skin as though she was struggling to breathe.

'Me and Jack have started our own business.' Lucy motioned for her sister to keep walking. 'We've evolved our acting ambitions into something more practical. And actually, it's great. We're making money. *That's* why I have to stay in London.'

On the journey back to Jack's flat, Lucy told Mel about the ads she'd placed. How she'd forensically analysed click-through rates, tweaking the copy, making her campaigns more effective. How a trickle of requests for plus ones had morphed into regular enquiries spanning a wider range of roles, making it necessary to hire other actors.

As they reached Jack's front door, Mel's forehead remained crinkled. 'I still don't get why it's this big secret. I mean, we were talking about work at dinner and you . . . '

Lucy stepped inside, kicking off her shoes and flopping down on the sofa. 'I wanted to see if I could make a success of it before I went round telling people.'

'But I'm your sister.'

Lucy swallowed. Why *had* she hidden the truth from her sister? New bookings still gave her flashes of excitement and satisfaction. She experienced a unique relief whenever Jack became absorbed in preparation, building a character from a myriad of small details. Yet the thought of trying to explain the agency to her family triggered an inner recoiling.

'Everything has been happening so fast,' Lucy said. 'I didn't set out with a grand vision or anything. I just gave something a try and it happened to work. It still shocks me. I'm not used to things working.'

'But you lied.'

'These past few months might have been a fluke. The bookings could dry up at any time.' Lucy felt a stab of panic as she imagined checking and rechecking the agency inbox, a day without a new enquiry soon stretching into weeks.

Mel tucked her legs up beneath her. 'So – you didn't keep it to yourself because you felt guilty?'

'Why would I feel guilty?'

Mel took her plait in her hand, twisted the end around her finger. 'You're deceiving people for money.'

Lucy felt a tingling in her chest. *Deceiving people for money* made her sound like a confidence trickster, as if her sister thought she was going round selling dodgy investments, parting pensioners from their savings. It wasn't like that. Why then, did Lucy feel this niggling shame?

'There's nothing malicious in it. We're just helping people create an impression,' she said.

Mel looked over at the balcony doors. 'You must have to take what your clients say at face value?'

Lucy stood up. She almost – almost – told her sister that their father's car payments depended on these pretences of hers. But she caught the impulse just in time. She'd given Mel a lot to take in. Of course there'd be questions. It wasn't Mel's fault that Lucy hadn't quite squared the answers with her own conscience. She went around the room drawing the blinds. Made a show of stretching out her neck and shoulders. When she turned back around to answer her sister, she had full command of her tone. 'I guess that's the case with any business. I mean, the supermarket cashier who sells five bottles of gin can only ever smile and nod when the person buying them insists they're for a party, right?'

'Yeah, but, selling deception . . . '

'You make it sound so sinister. But honestly, at least eighty per cent of our work is going along to parties with some lonely soul. Trying to convince their friends they're loveable. We help people.'

Mel was still frowning. 'But . . . real, live people. To pretend to their faces.'

'I tried, Mel. I gave *proper* acting more than ten years of my life and it got me nowhere. I'm good at what I do, I really am. Why shouldn't I get to make a living from it?'

The fervour in Mel's eyes retreated, leaving her expression oddly blank as she stood up from the sofa. 'You're right. I'm sorry. I should get ready for bed. London exhausts me.'

Lucy dug her nails into her palm as she watched her sister head into the bathroom. Throughout the conversation she'd felt as though she was being pushed towards a painful realisation, that she might come to understand something important. Part of her *wanted* Mel to carry on giving her a hard time.

She closed her eyes and saw Sebastian's face. The gentle concern written on his brow as he tried to console her about her father. Her work had the potential to hurt people. It wasn't a fact she could argue away.

Chapter 15

In October the agency's monthly turnover hit five figures for the first time and Lucy agreed to the deal Jack negotiated with his father's friend. Their new office was in a three-storey brick building, in an alley off Soho's Berwick Street. The ground floor was home to a cake shop, its glass frontage displaying elaborate muffins and cakes, fondant icing in every colour.

A side door with peeling blue paint opened on a steep, narrow staircase that creaked with every step. On the second floor, they reached a small landing, barely wide enough for two people to stand side-by-side and an inner door which opened on a room stinking violently of stale cigarette smoke. The floorboards were exposed and Blu Tack stains pockmarked the once-white walls. There was a kitchenette comprising a sink and a shelf, plus a tiny bathroom with a cracked basin and pull-chain toilet. Jack enthused about the large windows and skylight that flooded the space with light. *It'll be perfect for shooting audition tapes*, he'd said. Even with the windows closed, they could hear musical shouts from the market: *lovely sweet kaki, two for a pound!* When they were opened, aromas would drift in: sizzling kebab meat and unfamiliar combinations of spices.

Jack seemed to relish furnishing the agency's new home, sourcing two desks and a velvety red armchair from charity shops. He decorated the walls with black-and-white prints of London landmarks and found a potted fern for Lucy's desk. He even gave the kitchenette a cursory clean, equipping it with a kettle and an eclectic mix of charity shop mugs.

Zelda was the first client to visit, wearing a pale-yellow linen dress with a chunky blue cardigan. Crescent moon earrings grazed the top of her shoulders. 'What a wonderful space. Right slap bang in the middle of everything. And the light—'

She air-kissed them both. Lucy caught the smell of a fruit shampoo.

'Let me give you the tour,' Jack said, linking arms. Zelda seemed to lean into him as he pointed out the furniture he'd selected. Observing the way they were with each other made Lucy feel vaguely uncomfortable, as though she was intruding on something intimate.

'What a glorious assortment. You must have spent hours rummaging around.' Zelda's eyes sparkled, her cheeks had become flushed.

'It's one of my favourite things to do. I just need to find the right curtains now. Blinds would be too clinical, I think.'

'And you need ceramics. One or two pieces. An elegant fruit bowl perhaps, and a nicer vessel for that fern. Maybe I'll make you a little something. A moving-in gift.'

Jack beamed. 'That would be wonderful. We really should have one of our next meetings at your studio. I'd love to see your work.'

Zelda returned his smile, sinking down into the armchair

and running a fingertip along the fabric of its arm. Lucy dragged her desk chair over. What *was* going on between Jack and Zelda? There was certainly something between them. Not sexual tension, exactly. It was more a mutual desire to impress, a shared excitability that didn't feel quite authentic.

'Are you happy with how everything is progressing?' Lucy asked Zelda, while Jack pulled up his own chair. Jack was seeing Sebastian around once a fortnight. They'd gone to the gym a few times and had the odd after-work drink without Lucy.

'Oh yes. You're doing a marvellous job, both of you. I'm just wondering whether now is the moment to turn up the dial.'

'Tell me more.' Jack sat himself down, placing an ankle on top of his thigh. He was wearing a pinstripe suit (another treasured charity shop find) with red Converse trainers and had given himself a severe side parting. Tell *me* more, he'd said. Lucy's stomach was sending out warning signals, plumes of acid that made her sit up straight, watching and interrogating every gesture.

Zelda observed Jack for a moment. The intensity of her gaze deepened Lucy's unease. This woman would be touching her friend if Lucy wasn't there, she was certain of it. There was a hunger in her eyes, as though Jack was a ripe peach she wanted to sink her teeth into.

'The more I think about it, spending time with the two of you must feel like a wonderful treat,' Zelda said at last. 'And Sebastian doesn't deserve that, not at all. It's time to make him suffer.'

Lucy was aware of the shouts from the market, the slow drip, drip of their leaky tap. She saw Jack plant both feet on the ground. The word *suffer* had alarmed him, just as it had alarmed her. *Good.*

'Are you're sure that's what you want?' Lucy said.

Zelda fixed Lucy with a cold stare. Her mouth twitched and she gave a high-pitched chuckle. 'We're going to have so much fun. Don't you worry. Remember, this is a man who wanted me to go and get an abortion in some grubby backstreet clinic. Scurrying off in the dead of night like a cockroach.'

No one spoke. Lucy met Jack's eye for a second. She could tell he was deep in thought, most likely trying to reconcile that word, *suffer,* with the chivalrous way he'd framed the assignment to himself.

'His behaviour was disgusting.' Jack leaned forward as he spoke. 'And he still has that entitled arrogance, it's been there, every time we've hung out. But how far do you want us to go?'

Lucy stiffened. Sebastian hadn't appeared entitled to her, not at all. 'We could bring the two of you together, so you can have everything out with him,' she offered.

Zelda twisted her hands in her lap, angling her body slightly, as though making it clear she was addressing Jack alone. 'I wonder whether you could maybe tap him up for an allowance. He can certainly afford it, and really it's the least he could do. You could pitch it as him supporting you. Helping you build your acting career.'

Jack appeared to consider this. In his worldview, money gravitating towards talent was part of the natural order. Accepting financial support incurred no shame.

'Wouldn't that be fraud, though?' Lucy was careful not to reveal how alarmed she was.

Zelda slowly turned her head to look at Lucy. 'You agreed to help me. You can't pull back now.'

'No one's talking about pulling back,' Jack said.

Zelda folded her arms. 'But you're finding reasons not to do what I want.'

'We're not prepared to break the law,' Lucy said.

For a moment, Zelda chewed on her bottom lip, saying nothing. Then: 'Your whole business is built on fraud, really, when you think about it.'

The burning in Lucy's stomach intensified. This spiteful version of Zelda was so different from the grief-stricken woman who'd briefed them. 'That's not ... we help people. But we have to draw the line, we're not going to ask for money.'

'I'm not after Sebastian's money.' Zelda pressed her lips together, forming a pout.

'We know you're not.' Jack reached forward to pat Zelda on her arm.

Zelda gave Lucy a brief smile. 'Future customers wouldn't want to work with an agency that only did half a job. You'll be dependent on reviews, I'm guessing, if you plan to grow.'

Was that a threat? Lucy took a deep breath, straightened her spine. She needed to regain control. *Calm businesswoman. Unflustered by difficult clients, used to navigating unreasonable demands.*

They *had* agreed to hurt Sebastian. It was hard for Lucy to remember exactly how she'd justified it to herself, how completely she'd believed Zelda. Every story had more than one side. Everyone's memory was fallible.

'What if Lucy were to seduce Sebastian?' Jack said.

Both women turned to look at him. His eyes shone with satisfaction as he steepled his fingers beneath his chin.

'Me seducing him would be a punishment?' Lucy said. 'Thanks a lot.'

'If we do it right, it could be brilliant.' Jack grinned.

Zelda frowned. 'I'm not sure . . .'

Jack stood up. 'Lucy-the-demure-fiancée starts showing signs she's interested. A lingering glance here. A blush there. All very English rose. Full-scale adoration every time Sebastian opens his mouth. He's arrogant enough not to question it.'

'Jack, come on.' Lucy was aware of the heavy thud of her heartbeat, a roaring in her ears. Hadn't Zelda just threatened to try and trash their business? Was her best friend really OK with this?

Jack raised a hand to silence her. 'By chance, they're left alone for a while. They're a little tipsy.' He paced around the office, starting to mime the scenario. 'Little Lucy hangs on every word he says.' He performed a brief parody of an adoring woman, angling his head, flashing a coquettish glance. 'Sebastian can't help feeling that if he were to lean in and kiss her, she'd cream her knickers right there and then.'

Lucy winced.

'And then?' Zelda raised a carefully pencilled eyebrow.

Jack stood up tall, puffing out his chest. 'Once Lucy has steered Sebastian into an indiscretion, she comes to me with a tearful confession. I go ballistic at my reprobate father. Never speak to him again. He has to live knowing he fucked up the chance to have a relationship with his son.'

For a moment, no one spoke. Lucy tried to believe that

one day this ugly predicament would be nothing more than an amusing anecdote in an otherwise inspiring story about how they came to build their business. She drew in another deep breath, folding her hands in her lap, trying not to let her agitation show.

Zelda stood up and placed her palms against Jack's cheeks. 'This is precisely the kind of creativity I hoped for when I hired you.' She turned to look at Lucy, all traces of pique gone.

'I'm not going to sleep with Sebastian for *work*,' Lucy said. She knew she was supposed to be amused, a *good sport*, but rage drove its heat into every part of her body. She was holding her mouth in an unnatural position, the lips peeled back, and quickly had to right herself, restoring a neutral expression.

'A snog will suffice,' replied Jack, cheerfully.

Lucy needed time to think. Even if she were to go along with Jack's proposal, could it give Zelda the closure she needed? The assignment seemed to have descended into petty games.

'You're such a pretty thing,' Zelda looked Lucy up and down. 'Sebastian wouldn't be able to help himself.'

'You could totally pull it off, Luce,' Jack added. 'If you start playing yourself as attracted to him, you'll draw him in. The motivation for a falling-out will be really clear. It's the perfect way to end things.'

'But—' Sebastian had clearly intimated to Lucy that he hadn't known Zelda was pregnant. What if he was telling the truth? Zelda could be misremembering. She might even be lying.

'Right,' Zelda said. 'We appear to have a plan. Keep me

informed. If it doesn't appear to be working, we'll move forward with asking for an allowance.'

'It'll take time,' Lucy said. 'If we rush things Sebastian will be suspicious.' She needed to *think*. There must be a way of reconciling Zelda with Sebastian and putting an end to this assignment. The two of them were adults now, surely it couldn't be that difficult.

For the first time, Lucy let herself imagine what Sebastian's face might look like, when he learned Jack wasn't his son. He'd wanted children enough to endure seven IVF attempts. *Pure torture*, those were the words he used, and Lucy remembered how his green eyes had suddenly turned inwards, as though the sorrow was pulling him back to a place of utter desolation.

Zelda was nodding. At least she wasn't setting a deadline for the seduction, insisting on speed. Time, that's what Lucy needed. Time to understand what was really happening. She couldn't add to Sebastian's injuries, couldn't be part of making his grief cut deeper.

Zelda gave a contented sigh. 'I hope you don't mind me asking, but are the two of you a couple?'

Small talk? Was Zelda really planning to chat, feign friendliness as though they hadn't just been discussing how best to ruin a man's life?

Jack threw his head back and laughed. 'Me and Luce? Lord, no. Lucy doesn't do relationships, she only has *encounters*.'

It was absurd but Lucy could feel herself reddening. She didn't care what others thought. Hook-ups had a cleanness to them, an efficiency she found liberating. But having Jack and Zelda laugh in unison, at her expense, felt like a betrayal.

'Sorry if I've embarrassed you. It's just, you seem so close.' Zelda leaned back in the armchair, crossing her ankles. 'You must have known one another a long time?'

Jack gave a brief account of how they'd met at university. He was animated, smiling, back to being friends again. Lucy returned her chair to her desk, feigned work at her laptop as Jack told Zelda of the shared house in Elephant and Castle, how they'd rehearsed together at all hours. Zelda seemed spellbound, asking questions about their performances, as though she'd be happy to go on chatting all afternoon.

Peter had lived in their student house too, and it unsettled Lucy, hearing a potted account of their student days from which he'd been edited out. It was as though they'd always enjoyed an intense friendship of two, when really there had been three.

Chapter 16

Lucy's mother handed her the letter from the care home. *We'd like to invite you to a meeting to discuss concerns about recent absence levels.*

'I gave them plenty of warning every time I needed to take your father to an appointment,' her mother whispered. 'And they've docked every minute from my pay. I can't see what else there is to discuss.'

They were in the kitchen while Lucy's father rested upstairs. The green-and-white lino and imitation pine cabinets dated back to Lucy's childhood, but the scraps of paper pinned to the fridge were all new. Charlie's times table certificate, the term dates for his school, a felt-tip family portrait that didn't include Lucy.

'I'm so sorry.' Lucy placed a hand on her mother's shoulder. 'I'll keep sending money. You won't have to struggle.'

'But your course. You need every penny for yourself.'

It was the perfect opportunity to explain, to tell her mother she wasn't coming back. The teacher training programme had started a month ago and Lucy had given up her place. Her parents hadn't pressed her about her plans, but they must surely be wondering. 'It's fine. I can go on helping.'

Her mother frowned, looking uncertain. Lucy was a coward. A liar. Yet how could she add to her parents' worries? Almost everyone she'd told about the agency had conflated it with escorting. She could give it a few more weeks, make sure the new roster was working, process the pre-payments for the Christmas season. Now they had the office, the agency would surely start feeling more professional, more like a proper business.

Lucy kissed her mother on the cheek. 'It's going to be all right. Dad's getting stronger by the day. I've got to run for the train, but I've got another seven hundred I can send you.'

Lucy's mother squeezed her hand. 'I can't accept that, love. You need to leave something for yourself.'

'Really, it's fine. I'll just look in on Dad, then I better get going. I'll see you all again next week.'

She would go to Sebastian, take the first steps towards a seduction. It was the most lucrative gig on the agency's books, and Lucy needed the money. Over the coming weeks she'd work on Zelda, make her understand that hurting Sebastian wasn't the answer. But for now, she had to ensure she kept getting paid.

She remembered Jack telling her Sebastian was going to be running laps in Paddington that evening. 'He's planning to keep going from seven at night to one in the morning – can you believe it?' Jack had deepened his voice in a pompous imitation of Sebastian. *'I need to adapt my body to running at all hours of the day.'*

Jack had arranged to visit his supposed father at ten that night. Again, he parodied Sebastian's voice. *'If you're able to* bring some carb-rich foods, that would be amazing. The key to ultramarathoning is to keep the calories coming in.'

From the train, Lucy messaged Jack, proposing to go along in his place. She'd say Jack wasn't feeling well and present Sebastian with sandwiches and bottled water. Sit with him while he ate.

He'll probably be too knackered to manage a hard-on, Jack texted.

Don't be gross. All I'm aiming for tonight is a rapport, Lucy replied.

Waterloo was heaving when her train pulled in. There were the usual lines of suited men and women watching the departures boards, primed to race to their platform the very moment the number appeared onscreen. Everyone seemed a bad-tempered version of themselves, refusing to step aside for others, or to acknowledge the homeless man weaving through the crowds, asking for change.

Lucy gave away the fiver in her purse, then headed up to Pret to buy four different sandwiches and some water. She took the Bakerloo Line to Maida Vale then followed her phone directions to the recreation ground. The clocks had recently gone back, and the sky was dark as she stepped out of the station. As she walked, her breath made pockets of mist and a chill settled around her shoulders, making her wish she'd thought to bring her parka. She only had a tatty old cardigan with her, but she mustn't let Sebastian see she was cold, otherwise he'd insist she go home.

The running track was floodlit, looping around the sports pitches where a lively basketball game was in progress, the shouts of the participants carrying across the night air. Lucy found a flight of concrete steps where she could sit and observe the runners. The stone felt icy against her back, but she was careful to appear relaxed and comfortable, taking deep breaths to ensure her teeth didn't chatter.

With a sudden lurch, she realised she didn't have the fake engagement ring with her. She didn't look like Lucy-the-fiancée at all, her hair was pulled back in a lank ponytail and other than a lick of mascara, she hadn't even bothered with make-up. Sebastian wasn't her friend, this wasn't real – she was being paid to deceive him. Quickly, she untied her hair, rubbing at her scalp with her fingers to try and enliven her appearance.

There he was. Arms swinging, chest lifted as he rounded the corner. He wore a long-sleeved running top in fluorescent yellow with shorts that stopped mid-thigh, and he carried a slim backpack with a drinking tube. He didn't see Lucy the first time he passed, earbuds in. She felt momentary relief as she watched his back recede and hugged her legs, trying to warm herself. Running in the night, for six hours. What drove him to test his body in this way? Come midnight, the place would be deserted, he'd just be running lap after lap, the scenery unchanging. She couldn't imagine anything more joyless.

When Sebastian rounded the corner a second time, Lucy stood up and waved, brandishing the Pret bag.

He slowed to a walk, coming off the track towards her and removing his earbuds. He was smiling and for a second Lucy felt a surge of warmth. *None of this is real*, she reminded herself. And then – almost as a penance – she remembered the hardness in Zelda's eyes, her twisted instruction to turn up the dial. *It's time to make him suffer,* she'd said. Yet Sebastian had suffered so much already. Lucy couldn't shake the feeling that the hours of laps he was putting himself through was connected to his grief, as though his aching muscles were an elaborate distraction from everything he didn't want to feel.

She sat back down, ensuring the sleeve of her cardigan covered her left hand. Hopefully this wouldn't draw even more attention to the missing ring. If he noticed its absence, she'd have to say she was worried about being mugged, had left it at home on purpose.

'I'm glad to see you.' Sebastian dropped down onto the step next to her, opening his backpack and producing a foil blanket which he wrapped around his shoulders.

There was a film of sweat on his forehead and his chest heaved with a steady rhythm.

She handed him the Pret bag. 'I wasn't sure what you liked, so I got four different options.'

'Carbs,' Sebastian groaned, diving into the bag and ripping opening a sandwich pack without even looking at the label.

'Jack's coming down with a nasty cold, so we thought it was best if I came instead.'

Sebastian smiled as he chewed. 'That's so kind. Thank you. Mm, mustn't wolf this too quickly.' He laid the half-eaten cheese and pickle sandwich down on the step next to him. Lucy was aware of the smell of him, a distilled version of London air: car exhaust and aftershave, salt and dust.

He reached into his bag again and retrieved a strange device, almost like a miniature paint-roller. 'You'll have to excuse me,' he said, attacking his calves with the tool, wincing as he ran it up and down the muscle. He met Lucy's eye, then looked away, as if embarrassed.

Exertion had made his veins prominent and his leg hairs

were damp, pasted down flat against his skin. Lucy watched him work, tracing the corded muscle above his ankle, following its graceful curve.

Once Sebastian was done with the roller device, he emptied a sachet of powder into the water bottle, giving it a shake and taking a swig before devouring the rest of the sandwich. 'Okay. I'll be normal now.' He looked at his watch. 'I'll give this thirty minutes or so to go down, then I'll need to get moving again, before everything seizes up.'

He leaned back, placing his hands on the concrete step behind him. 'How's your father doing?'

How kind of Sebastian to have remembered, not to shy away from asking her about it.

'Improving. They've created a rehab programme for him. At the moment it's just small walks, but it's a big step forward from bed rest, I guess.'

'I'm so pleased.'

'He's starting to feel more positive. Looking forward to getting back to work.' Her voice had a strangely tight quality, as though her throat was only half open.

Sebastian smiled, reaching into the Pret bag and taking out another sandwich, this time bacon and brie. 'Is there anything I can do? I have a car. I could take you to visit, if it was helpful?'

For a second, Lucy imagined heading down the A3 with Sebastian, sitting next to him as he drove. It gave her a flicker of happiness that seemed so absurd. She wasn't worthy of this kindness. She was here to *turn up the dial.*

'He just needs time.' She didn't look at Sebastian as she said it. Ribbons of guilt twined around her innards. How could she justify this to herself? If only he'd asked for a DNA test.

Why hadn't he? He was an intelligent man, trusting them was such an illogical thing to do.

Lucy swallowed. 'Are you really going to keep going round and round that track until one in the morning?'

Sebastian nodded, letting out another groan. 'A few practice sessions in the small hours is what makes the difference.' He winced as he stretched his legs out in front of him and flexed his ankles.

'But why ultramarathoning? I mean, if you want to be fit, what's wrong with an hour in the gym a few times a week?' She tried to keep her tone light. She was Lucy-the-fiancée. She'd refuse to examine her own feelings until later, away from the intensity of Sebastian's gaze.

He observed her carefully. She saw his tongue move over his teeth, dislodging remnants of bread. 'There's something about going further, pushing harder, that makes you feel truly alive.' There was a rehearsed quality to his words; he wasn't going to reveal anything to Lucy that he hadn't trotted out a hundred times before. Why would he? She couldn't help wishing that she really knew him, that she'd never pretended to be anyone other than herself.

'Distract me,' Sebastian said. 'Tell me about you.'

'What do you want to know?'

Sebastian rolled his shoulders briefly as he chewed a mouthful of sandwich. 'How did you and Jack meet? It was at university, right?'

Lucy nodded.

'So you studied drama too?'

She was supposed to have studied English at Durham, according to the backstory she'd written out on index cards.

But she'd already messed up by telling Sebastian about her father. Wouldn't it be simpler to hew closer to the truth? She could pretend she fell into a PR career after graduation, but keep the other details of her life the same. Less chance of further mistakes that way.

'I did, yeah.' The cold had seeped into her bones, she was having to work hard at repressing a shiver.

'But you decided not to pursue acting?' He was looking at her with an intense interest; she felt exposed, unsure how to arrange her features.

'I came to realise it wasn't for everyone.' She was careful to deploy fake Lucy's sweet little voice.

'How so?'

This gentle curiosity about her life stirred something in Lucy. She ran her hands over her jeans, smoothing creases that weren't there. 'There's such an oversupply of aspiring actors. It's simple economics really.'

Sebastian's eye contact was unrelenting. 'You must have been remarkably mature, facing up to the cold, hard stats at such a young age,' he said.

A dull ache settled against her temples as Lucy recalled her devastation. The milk ad and its floral apron; the producer's overdone compliments. How it had stung, realising none of her fantasies of success were going to come to pass.

'You're giving me too much credit. I knew I needed to make money, that's about the size of it,' she said. In reality, she'd been far from mature. Ten years of constantly checking her phone. Rocking up at auditions, exhausted from the previous night's bar shift. Had she really believed it was only a matter of time before she got the right part? Looking back, it seemed so implausible. If she distanced herself enough, it was even a little funny.

Sebastian sighed. 'That's the one thing that really boils my piss about the creative sector. Only those with family money can afford to keep trying for any length of time. It's not fair.'

'I try not to be bitter about it. I mean, who's to say my performances would have set the world alight?' As she said the words, Lucy realised she believed them. It was alarming to contemplate, because in the years following graduation she'd assured herself again and again that acting was all she wanted. Maybe, as she sat there pretending to Sebastian, she was the one rewriting her memories. Right now, Lucy-the-aspiring-actor seemed less real than Lucy-the-fiancée. Perhaps she'd been a conception of Jack's, a persona they'd created together after Peter died. The ache at her temples became an insistent throb: if she followed this thought much further, she might discover something she didn't like.

'Is there part of you that regrets it, though? I mean, if you'd had a trust fund to live off, you might have been the next Gracie Dorn.'

Lucy froze, just for a second. Sebastian's gaze seemed to intensify; as though he could see past her weak characterisation and observe the real Lucy, that abject, confused creature. She exhaled slowly, giving no sign she'd been unsettled.

She laughed, just a second too late. 'I'm not sure I would have wanted any of her roles.'

Sebastian took a sip of water. 'Fair point. Are you going to have a sandwich?'

Lucy shook her head. 'They're all for you.'

He smiled, starting to repack his bag. 'In that case, I'll save these for my next break.'

'I can come back,' Lucy said. 'If there's anything else you need?'

Sebastian's lips twitched into a smile that looked more like a wince. Why had she blurted out the offer? Lucy-the-fiancée would have her own plans, a hot bath with candles and essential oils perhaps, or a takeaway, snuggled up on the sofa watching a Scandi crime drama with Jack. But there seemed something so compelling about the idea of being there when Sebastian reached his six-hour target. She couldn't fight the sense that perhaps he needed someone to be waiting, someone to recognise what he'd achieved.

'You're very sweet.' Sebastian laid a hand on her arm briefly, before he stood up. He kept his eyes carefully averted as he hoisted the pack onto his shoulders. 'I'm all set, though. You've been a wonderful help.'

'You're really carrying on for another three hours?' She wanted him to look at her again. For him to waver, change his mind and tell her he'd love her to return.

Instead he stood up tall, his eyes on the track as he bounced lightly on his heels. The shouts from the courts had gone silent. 'Endurance sports tell you a lot about yourself. Everything you need to know, in fact.' He turned and gave her a final smile before putting his earbuds back in and running off into the night.

Chapter 17

The following week Charlie was in her– she really must get used to thinking of it as *his* – bedroom, playing with a schoolfriend. Her parents were in the living room, steaming mugs of tea on the table in front of them. There wasn't going to be a better time.

Lucy sat in the corner armchair, its dodgy springs forcing her to brace her feet against the floor. 'I've been thinking about the whole teacher training thing,' she began.

Both parents looked at her. Her father seemed to have regained the light in his eyes. The pallor that Lucy had found so frightening was gone. At a glance there was nothing about him that suggested illness, no hint of the stent, the hospitalisation.

'I'd been looking forward to coming home, I really had. But work's been looking up and I think that means I should go on trying to make the best of things in London.' There. Lucy felt some of the discomfort leave her body. Her fingers unfurled, she hadn't realised she'd been making a fist.

'That's wonderful, love,' her father said. 'I did worry you were giving up on acting too soon.'

A light smattering of drizzle landed against the window.

Lucy could feel Mel's eyes on her. *Don't you dare be dishonest,* they seemed to say.

'When are we going to see you on the telly again?' her mother asked.

Lucy took a breath. The forty-two gigs in the diary for November and December should be a source of pride. Just the other day, she'd added her former classmate Will Tanner to the agency roster, giving him a winter wedding and an assortment of parties. He'd be able to afford Christmas presents for his family, because of her. She was an employer. A started-with-nothing success story.

'It's not the kind of acting that comes with bragging rights, I'm afraid.' As she inched towards the truth, Lucy watched her parents' reaction to each new piece of information.

Her mother's worry lines deepened, but Lucy's father continued to smile. 'We're proud of you regardless. Hard work is hard work – whether it's for a Hollywood film or an advert,' he said.

Prior to her agent dropping her, ads had been all that was left. Of course they'd assume she was shooting adverts.

Mel still appeared to be scrutinising Lucy's face. Was she hoping their parents would be disapproving? It was uncharitable of her to suspect it, but there was a hunger coming off her sister that Lucy found unseemly.

'It's not all ads,' Lucy said. 'But I am firmly in the boring, corporate side of the industry.' *There.* Corporate was a good word. It brought her closer to the truth, without giving cause for alarm. At least now her parents wouldn't be expecting to watch her in a new series, or to crowd around the television, waiting for a fleeting appearance in a film.

Her mother loosened her shoulders. 'You always downplay your successes, love. Making enough to live on in London is no small feat.'

Lucy studied the carpet. Once beige, it was now a patchwork of spilled drinks and felt-tip marks going back decades. Why was she holding back? *Corporate* wasn't quite enough. It wasn't *agency*, or *business*. One more line to clarify, that's all it would take, then there would no longer be anything to hide.

'I'll never forget our trips to see you.' Her father shifted on the sofa, smiling. 'That *Cat on a Hot Tin Roof* play. It frightened me, how good you were.'

Lucy swallowed. Her parents' belief in her always left her with this choked feeling, as if she was about to cry. They knew now that she wasn't returning. Knew she wasn't going to be cast in the next prestige BBC drama. That was enough for one day, surely.

Despite the rain, Mel insisted on walking Lucy to the station. It was already dark as they left their estate, turning into a long, straight road lined with Victorian terraces and parked cars. Half the streetlights weren't working, but light spilled onto the pavements from illuminated windows and the security lights that clicked on as they passed.

Mel wore a navy-blue hiking jacket with the hood pulled up; she declined to share Lucy's umbrella. 'You having your own business, is that a secret, then?'

'I thought it would be a lot to take in, that's all. Me staying in London was the important bit. They're not expecting me to move back any more.'

'So I'm supposed to lie, am I? Pretend I don't know what

these acting jobs really are?' They reached the main road, and Mel had to shout to be heard above the sound of engines and swish of tyres.

'You're making it sound seedy. It really isn't.' Lucy swerved to avoid a large puddle.

'You pretend to be people's girlfriend.'

'It's not *just* being girlfriends,' Lucy said. 'We're professionalising all the time. We have a roster of actors. Terms and conditions.'

They passed a pub, an Amy Winehouse song escaping through its open door, along with the smell of stale lager. A crowd of smokers had spilled out onto the pavement, puffing away under hoods and umbrellas.

'If it's as professional as all that, then why are you keeping it from Mum and Dad?' said Mel, weaving around a woman who was lighting a fresh cigarette from a glowing butt.

'I will tell them.' Did Lucy mean that? They'd think less of her, when they understood the *pretend girlfriend* bit. How could they not?

'You let them think you're still acting.'

'I *am* still acting.'

Mel sighed. 'You know Dad failed his treadmill test, right?'

Lucy took her sister by the arm, forced her to meet her eye. 'His what?'

Mel's bottom lip trembled, but her eyes remained hard. 'Some medical test he had to do, to get his taxi licence back. They monitored his heart while he did a brisk walk. The results weren't good enough.'

'Why didn't he say anything?' That familiar pinching of fear right at the back of Lucy's throat. She'd let herself believe

it might be gone, that things might be all right after all. She
should have known better.

'Didn't want to spoil one of precious Lucy's visits, I expect.'

Lucy felt herself bristling. Mel always gave the impression
of revelling in all the things Lucy didn't know.

They reached the wide-open expanse of Guildhall Square.
A recruitment ad for the army was playing on the giant out-
door screen, men and women in camo gear, inching their way
along the ground on their elbows.

'What does it actually mean? Is he still sick?'

Mel swung her arms as she walked, purposeful as always.
As she passed under a streetlamp, the beads of water on her
coat shimmered and glowed. 'Of course he's still sick. This
isn't the 'flu. He's not going to *shake it off*. He'll need to be
careful for the rest of his life.'

They crossed the road in front of the station, weaving their
way through the row of waiting taxis as a train rumbled over
the bridge above. Lucy's toes were cold, her socks had become
soaked.

'But – do they think he's going to have another heart
attack?' Lucy asked.

Mel sighed. 'It's always a possibility. That's why I find
it so strange that you're pouring everything into staying in
London. You could be here. We don't know how long we have
left with Dad.'

It was as though her sister had scraped her nails along Lucy's
insides. They paused at the station entrance. She knew if she
attempted to speak, she'd cry. She shook the rain from her
umbrella and collapsed it down. Was Mel right? Had Lucy
gone about helping in entirely the wrong way? With Christmas

coming up, she'd been hoping to ask her sister whether there was anything special she could get for Charlie. A bike, perhaps? Or maybe an annual pass to one of the city's trampoline parks. Her parents would adore watching him open a gift like that, seeing the excitement bloom across his cheeks. But Lucy knew these moods of Mel's. The question would have to wait.

Her sister pulled her into a hug. 'What's important to you, Lucy? I mean, if you're actually enjoying what you do, then great, I'll stop giving you a hard time.'

'I'm good at it.' As Lucy spoke, she felt a flicker of rebellion. She *was* good at it. Over the next couple of months turnover was going to be in the tens of thousands. She'd reached that point in less than a year. With no experience, no advice, she'd built a *business*.

'It's just, I can't help thinking that so much of what you do is for Jack's sake.'

Lucy looked up. Rivulets of rainwater trickled down Mel's face, but her eyes were tender.

'If Peter were ...'

'Stop it,' Lucy said.

She'd never brought Jack back to Portsmouth, but Peter had stayed for a week during the Easter holidays in their final year. Mel had only been seventeen, but Peter seemed to have noticed something special in her, listening with quiet intensity as she spoke of her plans to study PPE at Oxford and her desire to get into politics one day.

'I'm just saying. He'd want you to live your life.' Mel's voice was soft, but the words had a violent effect on Lucy.

'I *am* living my life. I'm making a success of it. Don't shit all over that.'

Mel went on holding Lucy's gaze, those eyes of hers still round and pitying. It made Lucy tremble with rage.

'It's been lovely to see you,' her sister said. 'Safe journey back.'

Lucy watched her sister pull up her hood and head back out into the rain. She didn't want to leave things like that, she inhaled, ready to call out. But what was there left to say?

Chapter 18

It was close to midnight when Lucy arrived back at the flat. The lights were on, and she felt her stomach drop at the idea of Emily being with Jack in the living room, preventing Lucy from going to bed. Now she was committed to staying in London, she needed to start checking the property listings, looking for her own place to rent.

'Lucy. You're back.' Jack sprang up to meet her. He was alone.

'Is everything all right?' Lucy asked.

He placed his hands on her shoulders and she felt a sudden lurch of dread. *He's about to tell me my father has died. He had another heart attack while I was sat on the train.*

'I've been asked to send in an audition tape for *Heart Street*. It's a recurring part starting next spring. The new pub land-lord.' There was an agitated gleam in Jack's eye that make her skin prickle.

He was watching her reaction closely, so Lucy smiled. 'That's brilliant.' If he didn't get it . . . But she couldn't contemplate that, not now.

'I mean, I know it's not exactly highbrow,' Jack said. 'But the landlord is always a central figure, so I'll get loads of screen time. It could be just what I need to catapult myself towards something bigger.'

Lucy sat down and removed her sodden trainers and socks. The skin of her feet was white and puffy. 'I guess you'd stop acting for the agency if you got the part?' He'd have to. His face would become too well-known. She felt strangely numb, as though she'd vacated her own body.

Jack sat down next to her, giving her shoulder a friendly squeeze. 'We always knew this day would come.'

Still with a sense of detachment, she tried to assess the situation. Jack leaving the agency would force an ending where Sebastian was concerned. Would Lucy have to confess to being an actor too? She pictured his face, imagining his green eyes clouded with confusion, then hardening as he realised she'd lied to him. It brought her back into her body with a savage jolt; the pain, twisting up through her middle, was so sharp she winced.

Jack took her hand. He'd tried to arrange his mouth into a sympathetic expression, but his eyes were still filled with that agitated gleam. He picked up a set of papers from the coffee table. 'They want me to film a run in with Alex the barmaid. Can you rehearse with me tomorrow?'

'Sure. I've got a bit of time in the morning.' She had two new client meetings in the afternoon, plus a backlog of invoicing and enquiry-screening, then a Christmas party assignment.

'Maybe we could do a quick read-through tonight? Spark some ideas about the treatment?'

Lucy wanted nothing more than to pull out the sofa bed and curl up in a ball. But she sensed the desperation beneath

Jack's excitement, saw how fervently he was clinging to the belief that this could be *it*.

'Okay. Just let me put some dry socks on.'

The following morning, as Lucy was tidying away her bedding, Jack set about grinding coffee.

'Quite the lark this morning.' Lucy's voice sounded hoarse as she accepted a cup, savouring the nutty aroma. She'd rehearsed with Jack for two hours the previous evening and her eyelids felt heavy.

Jack bounced on the balls of his feet. 'I told my agent I'd have the audition tape done by the end of the day. But I've been thinking about the character. I'd like to have a go at making him more magnetic, less confrontational. He's the kind of person who always gets his way, but people never understand how he manipulates them.'

'But the script . . . '

'The script is dross, Lucy. We both know it. But if I play him with more depth, they'll thank me for it.'

Lucy sipped her coffee, letting the bitterness jolt her awake. 'All right. Give me an hour to get showered and check a few agency bits, and I'll run through it with you again.'

Jack smiled, but she could see he was annoyed she'd asked for the hour. The coffee was supposed to have secured her immediate cooperation.

Countless times, they went through the scene that morning, interrogating each and every line.

'This part here, where he says, "it's my way or the highway," I was thinking he could say it with a touch of irony. It would be unsettling for Alex then – she wouldn't know whether he was being serious, or whether he was making a joke.'

They tried it that way. Lucy feeling her character's uncertainty, letting it flicker through her eyes so Jack had something to respond to.

'That works.' Jack nodded to himself. 'And then maybe he could flash her a smile. But with a hint of malice in it. And pat her on the arm. Just to confuse her even more.'

If anyone else was being considered for the role of new pub landlord, they almost certainly weren't preparing to this extent. By mid-morning, Jack's delivery of the clunky lines was exceptional. He was standing differently and somehow his very face had become that of a publican, a bruiser with hidden complexities.

'I have to go and meet a client in a bit,' Lucy said. 'Shall we record it now?'

Jack looked up. 'I might just see if my agent can put me in touch with the writers' room. I should check that my interpretation works with whatever story arcs they've got planned.'

'Honestly, Jack, you've created a perfect performance. You can talk story arcs once you've actually got the part.'

Jack exhaled, scratching his chin. 'No. I think I should try and speak to someone.'

'I'm going to be out the rest of the day. Why don't you let me film you now? It's done then.' If he wasn't careful, Jack was going to mark himself out as difficult before he'd even been hired.

Jack bit the inside of his cheek. 'I have to be sure it's right. I can see you're desperate to leave. Go if you have to.' There was a tension around his forehead, so familiar to Lucy from the months leading up to his breakdown. She hadn't known what it meant back then, but she did now.

'Jack—'

'I'm not going to cut corners. It's too important.'

Lucy knew better than to argue. Without letting him see how stung she was, she got herself ready for work and left the flat, aware of Jack pacing in his bedroom as he waited for his agent to return his call. He'd probably still be up when she returned from that evening's gig, and she'd have to somehow find the energy to run through multiple takes with him. It was his first audition in over a year: how would he handle the part going to someone else?

Throughout the day, Lucy kept checking her phone, half expecting Jack to try and schedule a panicked filming session in their office. She met with a developer who wanted a couple of actors to pose as local residents at a planning meeting. *Get a bit excited, try and whip up the others, like.* She had a video call with a female accountant who wanted a young woman to appear besotted with her at the company Christmas do.

Still nothing from Jack. Lucy sent a text:

Hope the taping went OK. You really had the scene down, they'll be lucky to have you!

For her evening assignment at Battersea Power Station, she changed into a black sheath dress and applied red lippie. She was working for a regular, Tim, whose technology firm was throwing an early Christmas party for staff and their partners. The space had been kitted out as a winter wonderland, the old dials and controls decked out in tinsel and the industrial features of the ceiling festooned with holly and mistletoe. Servers wearing Santa hats were walking around with steaming jugs of mulled wine, trailing a delicious, spicy aroma. As Lucy was introduced to Tim's bosses and subordinates, she made herself appear deep in the throes of attraction, squeezing Tim's hand, stroking his arm. Every once in a while, she'd lead him away for an ostensibly private kiss that everyone could see. Her face ached from smiling, from laughing at jokes, but all the while, Lucy's stomach was knotted with apprehension. What version of Jack was she going to find back at the flat?

She returned to Canary Wharf just after eleven, having replaced her heels with trainers on the Tube. Her tights offered little protection from the cold wind that wrapped itself around her legs and found the space between the collar of her coat and her bare neck. As she walked alongside Middle Dock, the walkway still busy with drinkers and suited types finishing work late, her phone vibrated. Abigail was home from her own Christmas party assignment. Good. Just one more check-in to go, then Lucy could relax.

Even before she stepped through the door of the flat, she could hear Al Pacino, spitting out his lines through Jack's expensive surround-sound system.

Jack wasn't alone. Zelda was there on the sofa too.

For a second Lucy simply didn't trust the evidence of her eyes. But there Zelda was, wearing a floral boiler suit, her hair tied back in a green scarf. The coffee table in front of was littered with cartons from Jack's favourite Chinese restaurant and they were three quarters of the way through a bottle of white wine.

'Lucy! Don't you look glamorous.' Zelda's bare feet were tucked up beneath her; she looked so comfortable, as though this was her flat and Lucy was an occasional guest.

Jack picked up the remote and paused the film, *Godfather Part II*, his all-time favourite. He couldn't tolerate talking over the top of it.

Lucy knew she must look ridiculous, coat still on, just standing there, but she couldn't think of a single thing to say. Why was Zelda in Jack's home, at this hour? And why was Jack refusing to meet Lucy's eye?

'Oh, gosh,' Zelda said, jumping up. 'How thoughtless of me. This is your bed, isn't it? You most likely want to turn in.'

'Don't worry, it's fine.' The words came out automatically, even though Lucy didn't mean them.

Zelda approached her, putting an arm around Lucy's waist as though they were old friends. 'I've been having the most marvellous time, making a video of young Jack here. The pure talent, Lucy! Honestly, I had no idea. He transformed himself into someone different right before my eyes.'

'You got the recording done in time, then?' Lucy directed the question at Jack. He still wasn't looking at her. The remote was in his hand; finger hovering over the play button.

'We decided to interpret *close of play* as before midnight,' Zelda said, with a chuckle. 'Got there just in time, didn't we, Jack?'

Finally, he laid the remote down on the table and looked over at Lucy, his eyes dark. 'We did. I can't tell you how much I appreciate you helping me, Zelda.'

'The pleasure was all mine. I simply adore watching true artists at work.'

Lucy was aware of a sudden rage building inside her. What possible reason did Jack have for sulking? And how had he rationalised involving Zelda – their client – in the filming?

'Right. I better go and take my make-up off,' Lucy said, heading for the bathroom.

'Before you do.' Zelda grasped her wrist. 'Jack tells me you've got a dinner with Sebastian next month. We've cooked up a plan to leave you and Sebastian alone for a bit. Give you a chance to deploy your charms.'

Lucy tried to smile as she glanced at Jack. There was something going on. A palpable undercurrent she didn't understand.

Zelda let go of Lucy's wrist with a knowing smile. 'I'll let Jack fill you in.'

'Stay and watch the rest of the film,' Jack said.

'Really I should head back,' Zelda replied. 'I didn't realise it was so late. Thank you for today, though, it's been fascinating.'

'I'll see you home.' Jack stood up. Lucy glanced at his jeans and black cashmere jumper, looking for a rumpled quality that suggested sex. On some level the absence disappointed her. If it was a simple matter of fucking, Lucy would at least understand. But she registered a strange dismay, a lurch in her belly at the idea of a secret friendship kindling itself while she was busy making a living.

Zelda was at the door, seeming to hesitate. 'No. I couldn't put you out. I'll call an Uber.'

When Lucy emerged from the bathroom, Zelda was gone and Jack was back on the sofa, watching the remainder of the film.

'Sorry, but I really need to pull the bed out and turn in,' she said. 'Too many late nights.'

Jack sighed as he switched the television off. 'Just wanted to unwind a bit. Shooting the tape took it out of me.'

'You called *Zelda?*' Lucy couldn't hold back any longer. 'What were you thinking?'

Jack raised an eyebrow, his eyes still had a darkness to them. 'She's interested in the creative process. She didn't mind at all.'

'She's our client. You can't treat her like a friend—'

'She behaves like a friend. She dropped everything to come here and help me film the scene.'

'You were ready to film it this morning.'

'I wasn't. Not at all. And I would have got everything wrong. Because I found out today that the landlord has a *dark past*, so ...'

'All you had to do was tell off a barmaid, for goodness' sake. How does your *dark past* impact on that?'

Jack stood up. 'I know you don't want me to get the part.'

There was a buzzing in Lucy's ears. She felt as though she'd been slapped. 'That's not true.' Hadn't she gone without sleep to help him rehearse? Hadn't she spent the last decade of her life, there at his elbow, ready to try and soften every disappointment, soothe every frustration?

'You've always considered soaps beneath you.' Jack started to pace, walking over to the open plan kitchen, then looping back towards the balcony doors.

Lucy laughed. It sounded coarse, bitter. 'Jack, I took anything I could. I needed the money. I've been a dead body three times. I've advertised milk.'

'I know you'd rather I gave up and settled for working with the agency.'

It was true. But not because she wanted to deny Jack fame. Lucy could picture him groaning every time he received a new script, becoming infuriated by the performances of other cast members. This soap role wasn't going to catapult him to Hollywood. It wasn't going to prevent him from feeling as though he'd failed. He'd go on being pummelled by his own unrealistic expectations. Lucy could see herself, listening, soothing, and she felt a crushing weariness, an ache that permeated the depths of her bones.

'I—' Lucy looked down, at the grease congealing on a half-finished carton of chow mein. She tried to inhale, but it was a shallow, panicked effort.

Jack wouldn't look at her, was still continuing his relentless pacing. 'I'm *never* giving up. We had dreams. We promised ourselves—'

Lucy walked over to him and placed a hand on his shoulder. 'I was just wishing that Peter was here, that's all.'

He stared at her for a second, before giving a short sigh that sounded more like a hiss. 'Don't spoil this for me, Lucy.'

'I'm not – of course I wouldn't—'

'Good night.'

Chapter 19

A fortnight later, in mid-December, Lucy and Jack were in Sebastian's flat. With its white walls and pale carpeting it put Lucy in mind of a hotel room. There seemed to be a profusion of textiles she couldn't imagine a single man buying: plump cushions, linen tablecloths and heavy velvet drapes. She imagined him handing a credit card over to an assistant with the command, *take care of the furniture for me*. It had that kind of impersonal feel to it. There were no photographs in his living room, only a large canvas of an anodyne sunset, replete with palm trees and fishing boats. Lucy had been hoping for more, she realised; for a painting, a record player, a collection of books that would reveal something new about Sebastian.

He waved towards one of his black leather sofas, indicating Lucy and Jack should sit down. There was a clean tea towel slung over his shoulder, and somehow this struck Lucy as contrived. She imagined him becoming anxious ahead of their arrival, maybe even fretting about the perception he was creating.

'Can I give you a hand with the food?' Lucy used her character's voice, full of honeyed warmth.

'No need,' Sebastian said. 'The massaman will bubble away nicely on its own. Let me get you some drinks.'

Jack was staring intently at his phone. This was by design, part of the plan he'd concocted with Zelda.

'Is everything okay?' Sebastian asked when Jack didn't respond.

'I've just . . . this director I worked with at the National has just messaged me, asking if I'm free for a quick pint. Says he's been left in the lurch and wants to have a chat about a role.' Jack's eyes widened. He'd rehearsed this expression: the surge of hope, mingled with wariness about harming his fragile new relationship with his father. He executed it perfectly.

'Goodness,' Sebastian said. 'That's brilliant news. What are you waiting for? Call him. Go and have that pint.'

'But . . . ' Jack was open-mouthed, as though overawed by the suddenness of the opportunity.

'We can have dinner another night,' Sebastian smiled. 'Go.'

Jack looked at his watch, furrowed his brow just the right amount. 'What time did you want to eat? I mean, the guy's always really slammed, he's not going to give me loads of his time. I reckon I'll be an hour at the most.'

Lucy stood up. Her character did so primly, knees together, tucking her bag under her arm.

Immediately, Jack put a hand on her shoulder. 'No – you stay where you are. We can still have a lovely meal. Honestly, I reckon it'll be super quick. I can text you when I'm on my way back. Who knows? Maybe we'll even have some good news to celebrate.'

He bounded out of the flat, leaving Lucy and Sebastian standing in the centre of his living room. Lucy looked down at the pale-grey carpet and made her cheeks flush – her character had a better sense of decorum than Jack's; she knew him leaving her here like this had been rude to both her and Sebastian.

But Sebastian gave her a kind smile, just as she'd known he would. 'I was going to open a bottle of red,' he said.

Lucy followed him into the kitchen. She could hear the curry gently bubbling, smell its rich blend of coconut, lemongrass and cinnamon. Why did Sebastian have to be so *nice*? Lucy would be brave when it really mattered, she promised herself, minimise his pain, however she could. But in the meantime, here she was, enacting Zelda's plan.

'I'm so sorry about this,' she said. 'I could just go and we can reschedule for another time?'

Sebastian was going through his wine rack, pulling out bottles and dismissing them after a quick glance at the label. 'Don't be silly. Unless you'd prefer your own company?' He looked up, eyes widening in concern.

'Not at all.' Lucy smiled.

'Good. It's rather nice getting to know you, as well as Jack.' Sebastian finally selected a Zinfandel, then took a corkscrew from a long rack of kitchen utensils. He had every imaginable thing hanging there, a pizza slice, a garlic press, multiple serving spoons and spatulas, all shiny and uniform, as though from a set. There was an apple corer, an air fryer, a coffee maker and a blender. Yet the sight of all these things filled Lucy with a strange sense of desolation, as though she'd uncovered a terrible loneliness. She wasn't quite able to explain it to herself, but was aware of a palpable ache inside her ribs.

She accepted the proffered wine glass, complimented him on the tidiness of his kitchen, on the curry's aroma. She was aware now of a heavier scent, the butter and smoke of slow-cooked meat – it made her mouth water.

Sebastian matched her bright chatter, leaning against the granite countertop as he described how he finally learned how to cook after his divorce. Told her about the flavours that had inspired him in Thailand all those years ago.

Fake Lucy was at ease. She was a master of small talk, always ready to jump in with a question and interested expression the moment conversation flagged. But beneath this Lucy felt timid. She had an hour to make Sebastian desire her. To maybe go as far as provoking an indiscretion that her character could tearfully report to Jack.

'I'll just get the rice on,' Sebastian said, opening up a cupboard and revealing multiple varieties of rice and pasta lined up in neat rows.

'Let me help.'

'Honestly, there's nothing to do. I just need to give this a rinse and pop it in the rice cooker.'

Lucy placed a hand against his stainless-steel fridge, shifting her weight to ensure she appeared relaxed as he poured the rice into a colander and blasted it under a running tap. She was aware of the minutes ticking away. She tried to inhabit her character more fully. To feel a self-conscious pang of attraction, accompanied by a fluttering sense that it might be mutual. She let the longing pour into her eyes, felt a treacherous heat between her legs. Staying in role was so much easier when she wanted to avoid her own thoughts.

Once he'd set the rice cooker, Sebastian gave the curry a

brief stir, then rested his back against the kitchen counter. 'Is it hard for you, watching Jack chase after these opportunities?'

It was as though he'd tugged at a cord running through her body. 'What? No! I'm happy for Jack. Keeping my fingers crossed for him.'

The previous day, the casting director for *Heart Street* had been in touch with Jack's agent to set up a chemistry read with other cast members in the New Year. Lucy was pleased for him, but this reminder of what her working life had been – the exhilaration of hope, the immersion of preparing for auditions – felt like pressing on a bruise. How had she rationalised giving it ten years of her life?

Sebastian laid his wine glass down on the counter. 'Of course. I didn't mean ... I just know what your thirties can be like. You have to pick a path, and that means letting go of all the other lives you might have lived. It's hard.'

Lucy sighed and took a small sip of the Zinfandel. She didn't know much about wine, but this tasted expensive with a complicated flavour that lingered in her mouth. 'You seem far too young to be giving me the wise-old-sage treatment,' she said.

Sebastian didn't smile as she expected, but looked suddenly grave. 'Maybe you're right. It's strange. Over the last few months, I've had these moments where I've caught myself trying to be "fatherly". And it seems so bloody ridiculous. I want to laugh at myself. But it's all new ground for me. I have no idea who to be.'

Lucy realised she was twisting the engagement ring on her finger and stopped herself. 'Of course – I didn't think.'

He looked at her, and she saw his face soften with the relief of a confidence shared. Perhaps they really were connecting. But as soon as Lucy registered this thought, she shoved it from her mind. Such calculation felt abhorrent. How much easier her Christmas parties had been, laughing at jokes, smiling at the right moments, making her clients appear desired, then going home and forgetting all about them.

'After the divorce, after . . . I went through a bit of a tough time. I actually started seeing a therapist.' Sebastian looked down, picking at the skin around his nail.

'That's good. Not everyone recognises when they need help.' He trusted her. In spite of everything, she felt a swelling joy that made her want to wrap her arms around her middle.

'I had this whole vision of what my life was going to be like. And when Chloe couldn't get pregnant . . . I ended up loathing my own company – the incessant thoughts. I didn't know who I was, who I wanted to be.'

'That's . . .' *Chloe.* His ex-wife was called Chloe. There were no photographs of her in the flat, but Lucy pictured a blonde. Slim, maybe ten or so years younger than Sebastian.

'I guess this is my clumsy way of saying I know what it's like. I bet back when you were at uni you had this clear vision of how your life would play out. Am I right?'

'Yeah.' Lucy remembered how it felt to believe. Part of her wanted to live inside that feeling always, to stifle her pragmatic instincts and go on inhabiting the certainty Peter had instilled in her. The right role would come. She'd have her opportunity. Give a stellar performance and start receiving the very best scripts, become sought after by directors she admired. Oh, she'd believed it!

Sebastian smiled at her. 'I don't for one moment suppose

you were alone in that. I bet your friends all felt the same way too?'

'They did.' Lucy thought of Peter, the attention he gave her every rehearsal, the tender critiques. He used to sit crossed-legged on the floor as he watched her, his every comment strengthening the belief that maybe a teaching career in Portsmouth *was* a waste. Maybe she had just as much of a right to expect and want the critical adulation her classmates were seeking.

'And now you've moved on, but you have to go on watching Jack devote himself to his dreams?' Sebastian said.

The need to defend Jack was a kind of reflex, but Lucy stopped herself, exhaling, letting the retort she'd been about to utter fall away. It *did* hurt. It shocked her how much it went on hurting, long after she'd made her peace with failure. She didn't understand why she felt this way. She loved Jack. Begrudged him nothing.

'My best friend died, straight after uni.' Lucy hadn't known she was going to say it until the words were out of her mouth. She found herself watching Sebastian, as though his reaction might contain some clue, some guidance she desperately needed.

His breath seemed to catch in his throat, but he didn't launch into awkward platitudes the way most people did.

'What was she like?' Sebastian said at last.

'He. Peter. We were housemates. He was the kindest, most generous person I've ever known.' Lucy's voice cracked.

'I'm sorry.' Sebastian's eyes were welling up, his forehead was lightly creased.

'Don't be. It feels good to talk about him. Normally people

get all weird when they realise he's dead. I only knew him for three years, and so much time has passed since then. But he's always with me. Some people shape you forever.'

Sebastian took a sip of his wine. His hand shook slightly, as though Lucy's emotion had somehow passed over into his body. 'How do you mean?'

'Whenever I'm trying to decide anything, I always ask myself, what would Peter think? He was always so careful with people's feelings. But he was direct, no bullshit. No one else has ever been able to make things so clear for me.'

'He sounds wonderful.'

'I never realised at the time how hard he must have worked at being kind.'

'With the three of you – it must have been a strange dynamic. Was there jealousy? I mean, with you and Jack . . . '

Sebastian tailed off, and for a moment Lucy stared at him, confused. Then it hit her – she had a backstory that involved her coupling up with Jack at uni. This was a performance. She was Lucy-the-fiancée.

'Not at all.' As she said it, she felt a shadow pass over her, a remembered unease. There had been the occasional moment when she'd wondered whether Peter might have feelings for Jack. In halls, the two of them had once shared a drunken kiss and Jack had laughed, announcing that Peter was helping him overcome his inhibitions. *I'll be able to play gay characters from now on*, he'd crowed. For a moment, Peter had looked stunned. But it only took a second before he was laughing too.

Sebastian's eyes were moist with sympathy. He averted his gaze, giving Lucy a careful reprieve from the conversation's intensity. She couldn't help thinking how comforting it would feel, to be held by him. She took a deep breath. This would be the moment to execute Zelda's plan, if she was going to. She could cry a little and Sebastian wouldn't be able to resist taking a step forwards, placing an arm over her shoulders. Then she'd find a way for their lips to meet.

'What an ordeal for you to face when you were so young,' Sebastian said at last.

Lucy nodded. 'He was the best of us. So talented. But he was the only one in our class not to get offers from agents in year three. I couldn't understand it. He was a phenomenal actor. I think I've got some videos somewhere ...'

She was pulling out her phone, but then she felt Sebastian's hand on her arm. 'It's okay,' he said. 'You don't have to upset yourself.'

Thank goodness he'd stopped her. This was her own phone. Her own history she was about to pillage. She was light-headed. Not herself. She hadn't eaten since breakfast, and even though she'd only had a few sips of wine it was clearly having an effect.

She bowed her head and felt a tear slide down the side of her nose. Sebastian didn't show any signs of discomfort in the face of her emotion. He hadn't removed his hand from her arm. She could feel his warmth through the sleeve of her cardigan.

'We can talk about something else if you like.' His voice was tender, filled with genuine concern.

Lucy couldn't go on pretending. She'd tell him everything, even though he'd surely hate her for it. She was here at someone else's behest, helping orchestrate a scheme with the specific aim of torturing him.

'Sebastian,' she turned to face him, 'I haven't been . . . '

He seemed to understand that she was on the cusp of something important. As he looked at her, his whole face was alive with a question. Lucy couldn't remember a time when she'd felt so much curiosity, so much interest directed her way. The intensity was painful, but mingled with an unfamiliar pleasure.

She wasn't sure who instigated the kiss. It was as though they both leaned in at the same moment, hungry for connection. His lips were warm and she could taste the woodiness of the wine. Lucy wrapped her arms around him, pulling him closer. He moaned, just slightly. It was little more than a sigh, but it stoked a wild heat in Lucy. She pressed her body closer, melting into the firmness of his chest. Her hands roved along the soft lambswool of his jumper, feeling the contours of his back, the ridge of his shoulder blade, taking in as much as she could. Once she revealed who she really was, why she was here, everything would change.

They were interrupted by the door buzzer. Sebastian pulled away from her. He appeared shocked, aghast at what had just happened.

'Don't answer it,' Lucy said. 'I need to tell you something first.'

But he was up, striding over to the intercom. 'Jack! Come on up.'

He placed the handset back on the wall, then looked over at her, running the back of his hand across his mouth.

'Sebastian, listen to me—'

'I've had too much wine.' His voice was quiet. 'That shouldn't have happened. I'm so sorry.'

'Don't be . . .'

Jack was already rapping at the door. He must have taken the stairs two at a time. And he hadn't stayed out for the whole hour. How typical of him to become impatient and cut the wait short.

Somehow Lucy got through the meal, managing a few mouthfuls of aromatic curry as Jack did most of the talking. He pretended the director had offered him an understudy gig, speaking of it in bright tones, but giving flashes of a poorly concealed disappointment. Sebastian muttered the odd word of encouragement, but fortunately Jack was so deep inside his own performance he didn't notice the constrained atmosphere.

'Did he take the bait?' Jack whispered, when Sebastian went to use the bathroom.

Lucy shook her head. Whatever had happened between herself and Sebastian was private. She wouldn't subject it to Jack and Zelda's scrutiny. If Jack got the soap part, they'd be manufacturing an end to this gig very soon anyway. She could be a coward. Send an anonymous note, perhaps. *You don't have a son. Zelda paid actors to pretend.*

'Must be losing your touch,' Jack said with a grin.

Lucy smiled in return, but still she was reliving that kiss, the way Sebastian had looked at her, that tiny moan. She'd kissed him as real-Lucy, and couldn't help wondering about what it could have meant if she hadn't embroiled them all in this terrible deception. She'd never know. Once Sebastian was aware of the truth, he'd never look at her like that again.

Chapter 20

Adam keyed in a security code and the iron gates of his family home slid open, the metal groaning on its hinges. Lucy had been here before, back in the summer when the rose garden had been in full bloom, and the terrace had teemed with retired captains of industry and their impeccably groomed wives. Even now, under a darkening sky filled with dense grey cloud, the three-storey Georgian house prompted an inner gasp of wonder.

The yew hedges flanking the drive were festooned with fairy lights, a discreet nod to Christmas. The restraint contrasted sharply with Lucy's own family home: the inflatable reindeer, designed to look as though it had got stuck coming through the living-room window, the SANTA, PLEASE STOP HERE sign on the doorstep. Her parents loved nothing more than pulling on their Christmas jumpers and decorating the plastic tree that was far too big for their living room. They'd kept every craft, every bit of tat Lucy and Mel had brought home from school; paper chains and cardboard stars with glued-on glitter. How Lucy wished she was in that living room now, wearing the polyester onesie her mother would have presented her with, rolling her eyes at the suggestion of bauble earrings but enjoying them all the same.

When she told her father she'd be working Christmas and Boxing Day – that she felt she had to, because she'd been offered double time – his eyes had welled up. 'I'm so proud of you,' he'd said, taking her hand. A tiny part of her wanted to clarify she'd be playing someone's girlfriend, staying in their family home, helping her client deceive his own parents.

Sebastian's moan, that tiniest sigh of pleasure, had been constantly in her ears over the last couple of weeks. As far as she knew, he was spending his first Christmas as a father by himself. Lucy had a devastating image of him inside his flat, perhaps telling himself that it was just another day and he didn't go in for all that commercial nonsense anyhow. There hadn't been any decorations in his flat. Maybe he'd catch up with work, grateful for the lack of interruptions. Or perhaps he'd cook an elaborate meal for one. She pictured him in his kitchen, saw the determined set of his jaw as he insisted to himself that he was having a nice time.

As soon as she'd finished her assignment at this country pile, Lucy would go and have a couple of days in Portsmouth. Clear her head. Try and alleviate some of the guilt she felt by being kind and attentive to her family. Much to Mel's displeasure, Lucy had a bike delivered for Charlie. For her father, she'd bought *The Beatles Anthology* on DVD, concerned that the old VHS might not survive another Christmas viewing. The image she had of the two of them curled up on the sofa, telly blanket over their legs as they watched archive footage of early gigs in Hamburg, would have to keep her going through this Christmas away.

*

As soon as Adam parked the BMW, the front door opened and there was his mother, a very upright woman with an immaculate helmet of white hair.

'Holly,' this woman cried, opening her arms in feigned delight as Lucy approached.

'Mrs Smythe. Thank you so much for inviting me,' Lucy said.

They air-kissed, the smell of face powder and hairspray filling Lucy's nostrils as they grazed cheeks. This was her fifth outing as 'Holly', Adam's Cheltenham-and-St-Andrew's-educated girlfriend. She had no idea why Adam felt the need to feign a relationship – he was a barrister in his mid-thirties, not bad looking, with a full head of dark hair – but Lucy had gone along with him to two weddings and a christening since the garden party in the summer.

'I don't think you've seen the house properly, let me give you a tour,' Mrs Smythe said, offering Lucy her arm and leading her inside. The drawing room was cavernous, although to Lucy's eye, revoltingly decorated. There were three mismatched sofas and four armchairs, all upholstered in patterned fabrics that clashed horribly with the Turkish carpet in the centre of the room. Every surface seemed to be filled with a clutter of vases, porcelain jugs and brass ornaments that wouldn't look out of place in the jumble sales Lucy's mother used to frequent when Lucy was a child. The dusting alone must take their cleaner hours.

Upstairs, Adam's mother showed her into a large bedroom. Her suitcase had been brought here by unseen hands and positioned next to a double bed. A set of pink towels and a bar of lavender soap had been laid out on a candlewick bedspread. 'I hope you'll be comfortable here. It's en-suite.'

'Thank you,' Lucy said in Holly's Home Counties clip. 'What a beautiful room.' The wallpaper was pink and green, a headache-inducing pattern of twining roses that also featured on the curtains. There was a large white dressing table and a substantial wardrobe with mirrored doors. She was relieved she wasn't expected to share a bed with Adam, but it tickled her too, his parents imposing separate bedrooms on their grown son.

'Holly' glided her way through that evening's cheese and wine party, wearing a long-sleeved dark-green dress Jack had found on one of his vintage shopping trips. Lucy was slowly growing Holly's wardrobe, acquiring a handful of expensive-looking dry-clean only items that made her look rather drab. She'd pinned her hair up in a conservative-looking pleat and wore a nude lipstick with just a lick of mascara. There would be no bauble earrings in this house.

With a hand on the small of her back, Adam presented her to the same menagerie of older couples she'd met back in the summer. The family had hired a girl to walk around with trays of cheese and crackers, replenishing glasses of mulled wine and Champagne while the guests pretended not to see her. Not so long ago, that could have been Lucy.

She was still reeling from a text that came from Mel while she was getting ready.

Have fun with your poshos. Mum and Dad are heart-broken you're not here, especially after the year they've had. They actually believe you're shooting an advert on Christmas Day.

What if Lucy was squandering her very last chance to spend Christmas with her father? Her core turned to ice. Surely she was being unnecessarily morbid? He hadn't yet turned sixty, after all. But that failed treadmill test – Lucy hadn't been able to stop thinking about it. If he wasn't deemed safe to drive a taxi, it meant he wasn't better.

Throughout the evening she was conscious of Adam's brother George watching her, exchanging whispered remarks with his wife Charlotte who was wearing a shapeless red velvet dress and low heels. George had been suspicious of 'Holly' ever since the summer, when he'd approached Lucy and Mel in that bar and she'd taken a few moments to remember who he was.

Yet Holly was unruffled, enjoying the circuit of compliments, revelling in her competence at small talk as she charmed family friends. Her pride at being invited to share this family holiday, at the deepening of her relationship with Adam, radiated from every cell of her body.

Lucy's real self, observing from a distance, was aware of a shiver of foreboding. The longer she needed to maintain a pretence, the greater the chance of a mistake – one tiny fracture in the performance would shatter the whole.

When the party was over, Adam's mother steered Lucy and Adam to the kitchen, where the serving girl handed them steaming mugs of cocoa to take up to their rooms. George and Charlotte had already gone up to bed, and Adam's father, a stout man with thick white hair parted to one side, had fallen asleep in his armchair.

Adam squeezed Lucy's arm as she prepared to head up

the stairs and clock off for the night. 'You're doing so well,' he whispered.

It was the first time he'd remarked on her performance and she felt unexpectedly moved. Perhaps it was the effect of tiredness, being away from home, or knowing she'd have to go on acting without a break for the next two days. She felt ragged, her nerve endings crackling with wakefulness even though she was bone tired.

When she opened the door to her room, she found George at the dressing table, rummaging in her handbag.

'Oh!' She stepped backwards, slopping cocoa over the side of her cup and scalding her hand. 'What do you think you're doing?'

George came over to relieve her of the cup, placing it down on the dresser, and rubbing at the drops of cocoa that had landed on the carpet with his slippered foot. 'Just here for a chat, that's all.'

Holly wouldn't be intimidated. She'd be affronted. Lucy closed the door and placed a hand on her hip. 'It rather looked to me as though you were rifling through my things. But go on. Let's chat.'

George sat down on the bed. 'You're not really in a relationship with my brother, are you?'

'Excuse me?' She used the voice Holly would deploy in a restaurant when presented with a dirty glass. But Lucy was wracking her brains – did this room contain any evidence as to her real identity? Her phone was with her and she'd left her wallet at home. Her stomach filled with bile. Tucked in a hidden compartment of her bag, in among her stash of tampons, was a bank card carrying her real name. Had George found it? She searched his face, looking for some clue that he might be about to brandish the name Lucy White. How would she explain it? Could she invent a plausible reason for having a friend's bank card with her? For not having a single card bearing the name Holly Campbell?

George gave her a smile that seemed to carry all the confidence of this huge estate. To Lucy it looked more like a leer and it sickened her. Did he *know*?

'Adam is – how do I put this delicately – a poof,' George said.

Lucy filled her eyes with a chilly light, still firmly in character. 'You need to leave.'

George laughed to himself as he stood up. 'Don't tell me you're part of the politically correct brigade.'

'I won't tolerate language like that. And I won't let you insult me or Adam.' Her voice was icy, with a haughty quality that felt just right for Holly. But Lucy's innards were churning. Was this going to escalate into a full-blown spat? Was she about to have a stand-up row in this house, in the middle of nowhere, late on Christmas Eve? She had no way of getting home if things went wrong.

George angled his head as he looked her up and down. 'It's just – you strike me as being rather bright. I can't imagine you being taken in by Adam. Which means you must be participating in his little pretence.'

'I have no idea what you're talking about.' Lucy was imperious, her spine erect, neck long and graceful.

George snorted. 'He got caught in the act at school. Very nearly expelled. After that, he made a show of dating a girl at university, but she ended up dumping him because he wouldn't sleep with her.'

Lucy decided to show George the full extent of her capabilities. She soaked herself in Holly – the theatre trips she and Adam had supposedly shared, the fine dining. Holly knew exactly what kind of wedding she wanted, the schools she had in mind for their future children. Lucy felt all of this, and she *was* Holly, her face collapsing with dismay at the allegations George had just made. Her knees weakened, she had to put a hand against the wall.

George crossed the room and placed a hand on her shoulder. 'Listen, I didn't mean . . . Christ, you really had no idea?'

She spun around. Now Holly was angry. Furious. Teeth clamped together as heat surged through her body.

George took a step backwards. He looked bewildered and perhaps as contrite as someone like him would ever feel. Inside, Lucy was laughing.

'I should go,' he said.

'Indeed.' She stared at him and his eyes widened before he turned and stumbled out of the room.

The moment he was gone, Lucy rushed to her handbag. Her bank card, the name Lucy White proudly emblazoned on the front, was still tucked away with her tampons. If George had seen it, he'd surely have crowed over his discovery. It would have been a trump card. Evidence he could use to humiliate his brother.

She'd have to tell Adam what had happened. It wasn't a conversation she looked forward to, not least because his bedroom was four doors down the hall, and there was something farcical at the idea of approaching on tiptoes, as though she was in fact his girlfriend sneaking into his room for an illicit fuck.

She texted him:

Need to talk. Just caught your brother going through
my bag.

A cowardly part of her hoped his phone might be off.
She didn't want to admit to having brought the bank card
with her.

While Lucy waited for a response, she checked her notifica-
tions. The agency had received four new enquiries since she'd
finished up in the office that lunchtime. People didn't even
take Christmas Eve off planning their deceptions, it seemed.
There was a text from Jack:

Watching Nomadland. We must talk about Frances
McDormand. The facial expressions! The understatement!

She'd also received a text from a number she didn't
recognise:

Hi Lucy, Sebastian Stott here (I got your number from Jack,
hope you don't mind!) Just wanted to say Merry Christmas.
And please forgive me for how I behaved at dinner. I've
been feeling wretched about it. Anyway, have a wonderful
day tomorrow. Sebastian

Lucy stared at the screen. It had been just over a fortnight
since the kiss. Did Sebastian really regret what happened? Or
was he saying what any decent person in his position would
say? Lucy bit her lip, feeling the sharp ache of a wanting she

couldn't quite define to herself. It wasn't necessarily a desire to sleep with Sebastian, although she wouldn't be averse to it. It was more the way she looked forward to talking with him, how he listened, the questions he asked her. Being with him made her feel like a truer version of herself – the only other person who'd made her feel like that had been Peter.

A gentle rapping at her door. She opened it and Adam quickly ducked inside. He looked pale, frightened even.

'I'm so sorry about this. The utter, utter bastard.' He sat down on her bed.

Lucy sat next to him. This gig suddenly seemed so puerile. She wanted to read Sebastian's message again. To be alone with the feeling it had given her.

'Tell me exactly what happened,' Adam said.

Lucy recounted every detail of George's visit. Adam winced on hearing his brother had voiced disbelief in their relationship, that he'd referenced Adam's sexuality.

An owl hooted outside. Lucy had never heard the sound in real life before and in spite of everything she felt a sudden jolt of wonder.

'This whole thing must seem farcical.' There was a softness to Adam's voice.

'It's not my place to judge,' she said. But really, it astounded her that Adam's desire to hide his sexuality was behind this lucrative gig. He'd spent thousands on creating this pretence with her.

'I know what George is like. He'll make continual digs from now on. Do you think you can handle it?' Adam asked.

Lucy smiled. 'He can give me as much of a hard time as he likes. I'll be Holly till the end. What about you, though?'

'Me?'

Lucy swallowed. 'I don't know what your relationship with your brother is like. But do you think there's any chance he might goad you into saying something?'

Adam shook his head. There was a stern light in his eyes. 'I wouldn't give him the satisfaction.'

Client relations dictated that Lucy really ought to leave it there, but she couldn't help blurting out: 'Would it not be easier for you to come out to your parents?'

Adam stood up from the bed. His upper lip twitched and he looked on the cusp of saying something ferocious, but he seemed to pull himself back just in time. 'My father threatened to disinherit me if there was any sign of *that nonsense* as he put it. He means it, too.'

'But you're successful, right? A barrister.' Lucy knew she was overstepping. But this place, the lateness of the hour, the magic of Sebastian's text, had brought a haze of unreality to the evening.

Adam once again straightened his back, a flicker of defiance in his eyes. She was here to provide a service, not to ask questions. 'Even if I was a millionaire, I wouldn't be able to tolerate this place landing in George's lap by virtue of the fact that he chooses to sleep with women.'

Lucy nodded. A treacherous part of her wanted to burst out laughing. *These landed gentry types*, she thought to herself. How wonderful having such problems as *inheritance* to worry about. But she felt instantly guilty. It must be exhausting for Adam, having to pretend all the time.

'I'm the eldest son,' Adam said, sitting back down on the bed. 'And my father doesn't want to break up the estate. He's very traditional. So while George will get a tidy cash sum, the bulk of it will go to me. Unless . . . '

He didn't need to finish.

Lucy took his arm. 'It'll be all right,' she said. 'We've both memorised the backstory. I won't let George rile me.'

'Thank you.' Adam's voice cracked.

'But . . . your real relationships . . . ' She wondered whether there might be a genuine partner, and if so, how he felt about this deception.

Adam shook his head.

'I'm sorry. That must be hard.'

Adam released his arm and stood up once again. 'It's temporary. Just while my parents are still alive. When they're gone, George will have to watch me move a man in here one day. I'll hold parties. Big, gay parties.'

'I'll keep being Holly for as long as you need,' Lucy said. Part of her wished she could afford to do so for free.

'Thank you. I appreciate it.' Adam attempted a smile, but he seemed too drained to manage it.

As she finally got into bed that night, Lucy's memory flickered back to a time when Jack had laid into Peter. The three of them had been on their backs in Hyde Park, soaking up the late-afternoon sunshine. Peter had made some comment about an ex, when Jack suddenly sat up. 'You should really give some consideration to how *out* you want to be,' he'd said.

'What are you talking about?' Peter had remained lying down, but there'd been a bitter edge to his voice that Lucy hadn't heard before.

'No one casts a gay guy as a leading man,' said Jack. 'That's the sad truth of it.'

Lucy had sat up. 'Jack you can't seriously be—'

'I'm not saying it's *right*,' Jack had said.

Lucy had listed three gay actors that instantly came to mind.

Jack had shaken his head. 'A few independent films between them. No Oscars. No Marvel franchises. You see my point?'

'You can't seriously be advocating that Peter goes *in* the closet?' Lucy had been aware of Peter next to her, keeping very still, eyes hidden behind aviator sunglasses.

Jack had given her a rueful smile. 'Hopefully things will change one day. But it has to be a serious consideration.'

Peter had remained silent, but Lucy had noticed his ribs straining against the black cotton of his T-shirt as he struggled to control his breathing. She wished she'd said something reassuring, rather than simply changing the subject by blathering on about the previous day's workshop. She could still see Peter, dark hair fanning out against the grass, just the slightest tension in his jaw. She liked to think he'd be pleased at her helping Adam.

Chapter 21

The following morning, the Smythe family gathered in the kitchen for a Christmas breakfast of smoked salmon and Bucks Fizz. Everything was laid out on a marble kitchen island surrounded by spindly legged chairs upholstered in brown leather.

'Morning, Holly,' George said. 'Did you sleep well?'

She gave a serene smile. 'Like a log. Thank you, George.'

A middle-aged woman – marked as hired help by her jeans and the way the family acted as though they couldn't see her – came in to check on the turkey roasting in the Aga and to scrub potatoes at the sink. Adam's mother and sister-in-law engaged in a half-hearted conversation about their sleep hygiene regimes. Holly had plenty to say on such topics, so Lucy joined in, extolling the virtues of switching off phones several hours before bed.

Once breakfast was dispensed with, Adam's father eased himself up from his chair with a muttered curse and led the family into the drawing room. Once again, Adam kept a hand on the small of Lucy's back, his own personal shorthand for intimacy. Now she understood why he was hiring her, Lucy resolved to give him a few pointers to try and make his performance more naturalistic.

Everyone gathered by the Christmas tree; the silver star at its tip grazed the ceiling and its pine scent filled the room. Fallen needles were scattered over the gifts beneath it, each of them wrapped in demure paper, free from gaudy patterns. Adam's father sank into his armchair with a grunt of relief. He couldn't have that many years left, Lucy thought. His fingers were swollen, his wedding band cutting deep into his flesh. She found it hard to believe that a man with those rheumy eyes, that softly wrinkled face, could be such a horrible old bigot. But now she knew the truth, there was pleasure to be had in deceiving him.

'Happy Christmas, my dear,' Adam's mother said, handing Lucy a smallish box wrapped in plain brown paper. 'Why don't you get us started?'

'Goodness, you shouldn't have,' Lucy said. She tore it open with Holly's greedy relish. Inside was a green box from a London jeweller containing a set of pearl drop earrings and a matching necklace.

She was aware of George's eyes inspecting her face. *I am Holly. A thousand pounds isn't a lot of money. I receive expensive jewellery all the time.*

She beamed, pecking the air next to Adam's mother's cheek. 'These are delightful. You have exquisite taste. Thank you.'

Thankfully, Adam had added Holly's name to each of the gifts he'd bought for his family – a bottle of port for his father, a Chanel scarf and bottle of Shalimar for his mother, and cashmere jumpers for George and his wife Charlotte.

'Holly' received several other gifts that morning, including a bottle of Champagne from George and a gold watch from Adam. She was careful not to tamper with the packaging – now she knew why Adam was hiring her, she'd encourage him to return it. The earrings, though, were going straight in her ears. *A bigot tax*, she thought. Every time she wore them, she'd remind herself just how far she'd come from the humiliation of the milk ad, and how she had the power to help others in the most bizarre and unexpected ways.

Once gift-giving had been concluded, it was time to don overcoats and make their way down a narrow country lane to the small Saxon church by the village green. A wooden gate opened up on a small graveyard filled with lichen-covered headstones in various stages of collapse. Lucy had invested in a new calf-length wool coat from Karen Millen. She'd opted for black, to ensure it could be repurposed for other assignments, and it was the most expensive item of clothing she'd ever owned, although technically it belonged to the agency. With satisfaction, she saw that Charlotte's Burberry coat was very similar in style.

How surreal it felt, stepping through the church's stone entranceway, enacting rituals that seemed to belong in an Austen or Trollope novel. She tried to imagine the face Mel would pull if she could see Lucy now. The reminder of home, of the relaxed day she was missing, tugged at something deep inside her. They'd be tucking into their Christmas breakfast, around this time. It was always a deluxe fry-up: her mother would buy Tesco Finest bacon and sausages, bread from the bakery and vegan versions of everything for Mel. There would be mince pies on the table too, even at breakfast-time, and chocolate coins. Lucy supposed they would have modified the tradition for her father's sake. He'd be so disappointed not to have his usual fried bread and eggs. Lucy tried to picture everyone crowded around the glass-topped table in the kitchen. Mel would probably have taken charge of the menu, presenting her father with oats or granola that he'd pretend to enjoy for her sake.

Inside the church, there was a distinctive Christmas scent of oranges and cloves wafting down from the altar as the organist played a carol Lucy half remembered from childhood. Wreaths of holly adorned the support pillars and twined around the frames of the stained-glass windows – it must have taken someone hours to decorate the interior so tastefully. The vicar was a white-haired woman with excellent posture who gesticulated with her arms as she delivered her sermon: *Now is the time of year when we must remember, in sending us Jesus, God was sending us himself.* She spoke of forgiveness, of unconditional love, and Lucy couldn't help glancing at Adam's father. His eyes were unfocussed and he looked thoroughly bored, shifting his back occasionally with little jerks of annoyance. All that was expected of Lucy was to keep her eyes forward, a look of mild attention on her face.

Once Adam had left her room the previous night, she'd texted Sebastian:

Happy Christmas to you too! And honestly, there's nothing to forgive.

Even though it had been late, Sebastian replied instantly:

At my age I really should have better control of myself.
You're a very special woman, Lucy. Jack is incredibly lucky
to have you.

She'd stared at the message, her body still. What did he mean
by *control*? Had he wanted to kiss her? Sebastian had always
struck her as being so fully in command of his life. His divorce
and fertility struggles had undoubtedly been painful, but Lucy
thought of him as having emerged wiser, of having that rare
quality of acceptance that made him comfortable inside his
own life. Had she disrupted that somehow? The idea intrigued
her, bringing a warmth that felt compelling and dangerous.

Everyone was standing up. Organ music reverberated
through the church and the words to 'O Come, All Ye
Faithful' spooled across a freestanding screen. Lucy joined
the singing with moderate enthusiasm, just as she imagined
Holly would.

For the rest of the service, Lucy couldn't help thinking of
Jack. During the frantic round of Christmas parties, he'd
often been in bed when she returned to the flat at night, but
she remembered seeing him in the kitchen, just back from a
run. His eyes were filled with that same agitated quality she'd
seen as they rehearsed the *Heart Street* role together.

'What if I get a cold before the chemistry read?' His voice
had been higher pitched than usual. 'I'm so close. But if I
fluff it . . .'

She'd placed a hand on his back; his hoodie felt damp with
cooling sweat.

'No.' He had wheeled around, facing her square on, nostrils
flaring.

Instinctively, she'd leaned backwards, her heart racing. 'What?'

'You're giving me your doe-eyed-concern face,' Jack had hissed.

'I—' Lucy hadn't been paying attention to her expression, but she *had* been worrying. 'It's just . . . '

Jack had shaken his head, pouring muesli into a bowl, ignoring the oats and pieces of date that landed on the countertop. 'I'm allowed to want things.'

'I know.'

With a sound like a low growl he'd taken the milk from the fridge and carried his bowl into his bedroom. If she hadn't felt so guilty about lying to him about Sebastian, Lucy might have followed.

Why had she pretended nothing happened that night? The deception left her with the strangest sensation, a kind of itching beneath the skin. She'd sullied something at the core of her friendship with Jack. *Why?* She'd been supposed to kiss Sebastian. It just wasn't supposed to mean anything to her.

Back at the house, the serving girl from the previous evening had returned to help the middle-aged woman, who shared the same wild curls and was most likely her mother. The two of them worked in silent harmony, carrying platters of vegetables into the dining room and laying them out on the long, rectangular table. Honeyed carrots, crispy parsnips and fluffy roast potatoes. The family made appreciative noises as the golden-skinned bird was brought in, accompanied by jugs of steaming gravy.

'Smells divine,' said Charlotte, taking a seat next to George.

'Certainly does,' added Holly. Lucy had ended up opposite George and could sense him leering at her.

Mr Smythe – Lucy knew she'd never be invited to address him by his first name – carved the turkey, muttering under his breath as he made a hash of it.

The Smythes were not the type to wear cheap paper crowns and there was nothing as crass as Christmas crackers at this table, only neatly folded red cloth napkins and brass candlesticks bearing tall white candles. Lucy passed her plate along and received three slabs of turkey. She'd have to eat at least half of it to avoid attracting notice. It was a lean meat, at least, and she could be sparing with the vegetables, pass over the potatoes entirely.

'What is it you do, exactly?' George asked Lucy, once the meal was underway.

'I work for a communications agency. We specialise in charity clients.'

George popped a Brussel sprout in his mouth. 'How interesting. Which one?'

'Anderson Cartwright Associates – do you know it?' Lucy had learned over the course of many assignments that it was always better to act slightly excited by someone's interest. Nothing made questions stop faster than the sense she might be about to launch into a long explanation.

George raised an eyebrow. 'I don't, no. Do you have a business card with you? A friend of mine mentioned being on the lookout for a good comms agency.'

'Not with me, I'm afraid.'

'It's Christmas Day, George. You surely don't expect her to produce a card at the dinner table,' Adam growled.

George shrugged. 'Just trying to be helpful.'

'These carrots are divine,' Lucy said to Adam's mother.

'Thank you.' She smiled, taking the compliment, as though Lucy was unaware of the women who'd done the real work.

'Are you on LinkedIn?' George said to Lucy. 'I could put the two of you in touch.'

Lucy smiled as she forced down a small mouthful of turkey. She gave a little laugh. 'You mustn't think me a dinosaur, but I tend to shy away from social media.'

'Me too,' piped up Charlotte. 'The impact on wellbeing—'

'But for a communications executive, I'd say it was pretty mandatory?' George's eyes were alive with a strange combination of malevolence and humour.

Adam was up from his chair. 'What is this?' He stared at his brother, deep lines between his eyebrows.

If George harboured any doubts that the relationship was a sham, they most likely evaporated in the face of Adam's palpable anger.

Lucy reached for Adam's hand and clasped it.

'What is *what?*' George leaned back in his chair. 'I'm making conversation with your lovely girlfriend, that's all.'

'You're interrogating her!' Adam snapped.

'Sit down, Adam,' barked Mr Smythe.

'Can the two of you lay off one another for Christmas Day at least?' added Mrs Smythe. Her brow was pinched, and as Lucy looked at the lines on her face it was as though she could see the imprint of decades of sibling spats. Had it started when Adam's sexuality was first called into question? Or did it go back further, to the day when George first learned what it was to be a younger son in such a feudal family?

Lucy squeezed Adam's hand. 'I don't mind, darling.' She turned slightly, addressing the rest of the table. 'Adam's most likely worried about me boring you all. I can go on for hours once I get started on third sector PR. I'm so passionate about it.'

Charlotte and Adam's mother both gave uneasy titters, which Lucy was grateful for. But George was openly staring. He was going to keep needling at her. She could take it, but felt certain Adam would explode. Her heart quickened as her nerves crackled in empathy with Adam's. How could he endure such constant vigilance?

She turned to Charlotte. 'I've been meaning to ask you, is that Chanel?' She gestured to the red cardigan. It could have been from Primark for all Lucy knew about clothes.

Charlotte beamed. 'It's High Street, actually. I was chilly one afternoon and picked it up at Uniqlo.'

Lucy nodded. 'I'd never have guessed.'

'Can't go wrong with cashmere,' Adam's mother said.

As the meal progressed, they covered merino wool, the best brands of ski jacket, the havoc skiing can wreak on knees, and the delights of a simple hot chocolate in an alpine cabin. Adam ate his meal in silence, and this seemed to buoy George who took great care to solicit Holly's views on everything they covered.

Do you ski, Holly?

I wish I could. But two left feet, unfortunately.

You've been to Switzerland, I assume, Holly?

Oh, I adore Switzerland. Always end up coming home half a stone heavier. The chocolate!

And so it went on.

*

Once coffees had been served and a platter of homemade mince pies placed on the table, Lucy turned to Adam and proposed a walk through the grounds.

'I'm so stuffed I'll fall asleep if I stay sitting down,' she said.

After borrowing a pair of Wellington boots from Adam's mother, she and Adam tramped through the landscaped gardens and over a style into a neighbouring patch of woodland. The daylight was rapidly fading, the mist that hung over the countryside had barely lifted all day, yet there remained something beautiful about the mossy-barked trees, embracing the sky with their bare branches. The sodden leaf litter beneath their feet gave off a comforting, earthy smell.

Lucy took in the silence. Her whole adult life had played out against the background roar of traffic, of sirens and neighbours' television sets. She closed her eyes, as though imbibing the wholesome qualities this place had to offer. What had her own family's day been like? She hadn't had a moment to call them, to ask how Charlie had reacted to his bike, or commiserate with her father on the food restrictions.

'I can't believe George, I'm so sorry.' Adam's breath formed a cloud of mist.

'Don't worry about that,' Lucy said. 'I'm going to help you. But promise me, you'll turn this place into gay Mecca when you have the opportunity.'

Adam let out a single yelp of laughter. It sounded closer to a sob.

She squeezed his arm. He let her.

'When I'm back in London, I'm going to start talking to web agencies. There must be someone I can pay to create a website for this fake PR company. I pretend I work in PR about ninety per cent of the time, so it'd be an investment.'

'You'd do that?'

'Like I said, it'll be an investment.'

Adam sighed. 'Fucking George, though. He follows me sometimes. I've been out with colleagues and spotted him watching me.'

'You must have to be very discreet?'

Adam looked down at the ground and kicked at a molehill. 'Celibate, more like. He's relentless. He knows Dad can't have that much longer.'

They took a slow walk along the footpath crossing the woods. Lucy's mind was starting to whirr. It seemed so vital that George fail. Perhaps it was down to that word he'd used: *poof*. Lucy had heard that term and much worse shouted in Peter's direction. She'd always reassured him, told him to ignore people, he was so much better than anyone who sought to mock him. It hadn't been enough. If she could go back, she'd take the perpetrators by the scruff of their necks and force them to apologise.

'I wonder,' she said at last. 'Does George always live his life in an exemplary manner?'

Adam turned to her; the fog had settled in his hair, weighing down the curls. 'What do you mean?'

'Is there anything in his life he wouldn't want your parents to know about? Gambling, maybe? Or drugs?'

'A little bit of both. But Dad would just put that down to high jinks. He can be remarkably tolerant about some things.'

'Is George faithful to Charlotte?'

Adam gave a bitter laugh. 'I doubt it. But he's never been caught. Where are you going with this?'

'I'm not sure,' Lucy said. 'But I can't stand the idea of him watching and waiting for us to slip up.'

Adam said nothing, so Lucy let the subject drop. But she knew she wasn't done with George. The next time he tried to humiliate 'Holly' or Adam, she'd be ready for him.

Chapter 22

It was the first week of January and although the temperatures barely inched above freezing, the sky was a rich blue and for a few hours each lunchtime the office was flooded with sunlight. Before Christmas Lucy had created a campaign promoting honeytraps, afraid she'd struggle to find work for her new hires once party season was over. She couldn't have been more wrong. Between Christmas and New Year the agency had been inundated with requests to test the fidelity of partners and spouses. For the first time, male actors were just as in demand as females. Lucy had needed to ask Claudia to put her in touch with yet more former students. She was even considering advertising in *The Stage*.

Her second client of the day arrived at the office wearing an expensive-looking grey suit with a pale-blue shirt, no tie. He looked to be in his fifties, although his forehead was botoxed smooth, so it was difficult to be sure.

He had three print-outs of photographs which he laid out on Lucy's desk. A red-headed woman on a sandy beach, wearing a dark-green swimming costume and beaming at the camera; the same woman cradling a baby, an adoring expression in her eyes; and finally there she was again, in a pub, the client's arm wrapped tightly around her shoulders.

'Her name's Phoebe Montrose. I need you to turn up at her house saying you're from social services,' the man said.

Lucy felt a coldness spread across her stomach. She'd assumed this man was Phoebe's husband. But this was no honeytrap. Jack was supposed to be in this meeting, too, but had cried off at the last minute to go to the gym with Emily. *You're the shit-hot businesswoman*, he'd told Lucy. And she'd accepted him leaving everything to her, like she always did.

'Wouldn't that be illegal?' she asked, careful to keep her tone neutral.

The man gave an impatient sigh. 'I'm not asking you to walk out of there with the kid or anything like that. He'll be at school anyhow. You'll just be putting the frighteners on her, that's all.'

A primal instinct was urging caution. Lucy could sense a barely concealed hostility rippling beneath the man's skin. She picked up her pen and found a fresh sheet in her notepad, as though she were seriously contemplating taking this gig on.

'What's the address?'

The man gave step-by-step instructions on how to reach the woman's Notting Hill home. 'You'll need to make up a lanyard with your photo, so it looks official,' he added. 'And wear a suit. Nothing too nice, an old, tired one. You need to look like you got ready in a hurry.'

Lucy wrote it all down, consciously holding her disgust at a distance, making sure it didn't show on her face. 'What exactly do you want the actor to say?'

The man leaned in; close enough for Lucy to smell the stale

coffee on his breath. 'Right. This is very important. You need to say the school has been in touch. The boy's showing signs of emotional abuse. You need to fire questions at her. *What forms of punishment do you use? Do you ever strike the child?* Then you need to get more personal. *Are you on any medication? Have you ever suffered from depression? Do you drink? When? How much?* You get the picture.'

'Right.' From her years of dealing with aggressive bar customers, Lucy knew that the best thing to do was feign compliance. She braved an upward glance. Didn't smile, but delivered a frank, assertive gaze. 'As I said in my email, our rates are a hundred and twenty per hour, plus expenses. We'd be looking at around four hundred pounds to include preparation time and travel.'

Perhaps the man would baulk at the price. He might shout a little – he seemed the type – but then he'd leave and this would be over. Was the kid in question his son? It was so hard to believe anyone could invent such a manipulative scheme against the mother of their child, or any woman.

The man waved his hand impatiently. 'At the end, you need to tell her she's going to be monitored. There'll be unscheduled inspections. Social services could turn up at any time.'

Lucy nodded calmly and stood up, offering the man a firm handshake. 'I'll check the agency diary and come back to you tomorrow with a suggested timeslot and invoice.'

The man's lip curled, exposing his slightly crooked teeth. 'It needs to happen as soon as possible.'

When he was gone, Lucy stood with her back against the office door, listening to the creak of each stair as he headed down, making sure she heard the outer door closing behind

him. Her armpits felt clammy with sweat and she had to
breathe deeply to fight a rising nausea. How matter-of-fact
the man had been. How cruel. No amount of money would
induce her to take this on.

She went back to her desk and phoned the police. She was
passed around – with palpable distaste at some points – but
finally was handed over to a female officer who listened as
Lucy recounted everything the client had asked her to do.
The name he'd given, Tom Smith, was likely a pseudonym,
but she had an email address, surely the police could do
something with that?

The call ended with the officer giving Lucy a half-hearted
assurance that the matter would be looked into. It didn't
dispel Lucy's unease, though. What exactly had Lucy created? She couldn't shake the idea that somehow the very
existence of the agency had given this man permission to
think up his terrible scheme. She had to correct course somehow. Take charge.

The door buzzer went. Lucy froze. She didn't have any
more meetings in the diary, wasn't expecting anyone. She had
a foreboding that the man had returned, that he'd detected
a certain reticence and was going to try and push Lucy for a
firm commitment. After a minute or so, the buzzer sounded
again. She forced herself to creep to the window and look
down. A flash of blond hair. At that moment, Emily looked
up from the street, giving Lucy a quizzical glance.

She tried to breathe into her belly, letting the tension out
with every exhalation, just like they'd taught her at university. Then she pressed the button to release the outer door
and heard Emily's footsteps on the stairs.

'What was that all about?' Emily asked, as she came inside.

'Sorry. Had a tense client meeting earlier.' Lucy's voice quivered. She found herself longing to hug this other woman, to be held by her.

Emily turned her head, looking around the office. 'Where's Jack?'

Lucy remembered what Jack had told her that morning: *Emily's giving me a hard time about the evenings I've been working, so I promised we'd go to the gym together.* But Emily was wearing a tight skirt and stiletto-heeled boots – she was carrying a small handbag, certainly no room for gym kit in there.

'I'm not sure,' Lucy said carefully. Why had Jack lied? Whatever he was doing, he must have felt Lucy would disapprove.

'Isn't he working today?' Emily stood very upright, watching Lucy carefully, as if she somehow sensed she wasn't being straight with her.

'He's probably on a job. He doesn't always update the diary, you know what he's like.' Lucy tried to smile reassuringly. She didn't want to pass judgement on how Jack treated Emily, but lying to the woman's face made Lucy's stomach quiver.

Emily exhaled sharply through the nose. She placed a hand on her hip as her eyes completed a slow circuit of the office. 'So this is where it all happens?'

'Yep.' Where *was* Jack? Lucy had a sudden feeling – a conviction – that he was with Zelda. But surely if he was meeting her for one of their overly frequent debrief meetings, he wouldn't have felt the need to lie about it?

Emily was still surveying the office, taking in the black-and-white photographs on the wall, the mismatched furniture that bore the hallmark of Jack's taste. There was a tightness to her expression, a barely concealed antipathy. 'I really had no idea helping people lie would be so lucrative.'

'Me neither.' Lucy smiled, even though she was reeling from what felt like a sharp blow. At what point did acting become *helping people lie*? She wished she could ask Peter about it. The boundaries were so indistinct, so impossible to navigate – but Peter always found surprising ways to approach moral ambiguity. It had helped her at uni, letting her see depths and hidden vulnerabilities, making her realise that no one was a straight-up baddie.

'Well, I better get back to the office. I only popped in on the off-chance,' Emily said, wheeling around and heading out through the door.

Despite Emily's clipped tone, Lucy couldn't help feeling sorry for the woman as she watched her depart. She'd pulled Jack up on his infidelities before now, only to be told *Emily knows I'm not the marrying kind*. But in spite of the hauteur Emily had taken great pains to project, or perhaps because of it, Lucy couldn't quite believe that was true.

Chapter 23

There was little chance of discovering anything, Lucy knew that, but she had to *do* something. She slid her laptop into her bag and locked the office, making for Tottenham Court Road Station at a brisk pace, weaving through the clusters of tourists browsing the food stalls of the market, her chest straining in response to the unaccustomed exercise. Jack had spent the morning with Zelda, Lucy was suddenly so certain of this. She kept picturing the woman on Jack's sofa on the evening of the *Heart Street* taping. She'd looked too comfortable. Very much at home in the flat; at home with Jack. If Lucy hurried, there was the slimmest chance she might catch them together.

Of all the women Jack could fuck – why go for their client? Their much older client who'd almost made Jack shudder as she uttered those fateful words: *I want to destroy him.* Couldn't he see how dangerous, how unprofessional it was? After everything, all those years of Lucy being there to comfort Jack over every minor setback, years of shaping her own plans in relation to his, he still felt able to lie to her.

Once the Elizabeth Line deposited her at Canary Wharf, Lucy broke into a jog, her black coat flapping behind her, bag bumping against her hip. Did Jack and Zelda really think they could keep her in the dark? Did they giggle and whisper – *we mustn't tell Lucy?* Unexpectedly, she felt a wave of compassion for Emily. Lucy had seen the tiny flicker of alarm that passed through her eyes, had noticed the effort she was putting in to appearing unruffled. If Jack intended to treat their relationship as an open one, then Emily had a right to know. It wasn't fair to let her dream of bearing Jack's children, of moving into a house with a garden, when none of these things were going to happen.

Lucy gave a friendly nod to the security guard as she opened the glass doors of Jack's building with her electric key fob.

'Afternoon, miss.' He leaped up from his stool and pressed the button to summon the lift.

Lucy thanked him. It was a struggle to hold her body still as she waited. If Zelda was there, in the flat just like Lucy suspected, Lucy was going to terminate the Sebastian deception. Put an end to the whole sordid mess of it. And if she wasn't? Maybe there would be signs – an auburn hair on Jack's pillow, something Lucy could brandish.

As she imagined herself pulling apart Jack's bedding, Lucy laughed, a bitter cackle emerging from the depths of her belly. She was being ridiculous. The security guard froze – he'd been halfway back to his stool. 'Ma'am?'

'Sorry. It's nothing.' Lucy stifled her giggles, trying to muster a reassuring smile as the lift arrived and she stepped inside.

The first thing she noticed when the doors slid open on the fifth floor, was that Jack's door, at the very end of the corridor, was open. But it wasn't Zelda standing there, it was a slender man, hair bleached almost white and styled into a stiff peak. He and Jack were laughing, standing close enough to feel the other's breath against their cheeks.

When Jack noticed Lucy, he froze. His companion seemed to sense something was up, looking over his shoulder, taking Lucy in with a curious glance. He must only have been in his early twenties; his skin had a scrubbed, pink quality to it and his cheeks and lips were plump with youth. He looked back at Jack. 'I'll be seeing you, then.'

The man smiled at Lucy as he passed her in a cloud of aftershave, a sweet smell, redolent of the cheap body sprays Lucy and her friends used to mist themselves with after PE at school. His bomber jacket looked far too thin for a cold January afternoon and his trainers were starting to come unglued at the toes.

Jack's hands were in the pockets of his jeans, his back slightly stooped, but his eyes burned as he watched Lucy approach.

'Who was that?' she asked.

'No one. Just a friend. Why are you here?'

Lucy stepped inside, clicking the door shut behind her. Her body registered a knowing. It came as a sudden weightless-ness, a stream of memories, somehow retaining their clarity as they spooled outwards. The slut moniker he'd been assigned at uni. The interest he'd taken in the apps Lucy installed. That afternoon in Hyde Park, telling Peter that some things needed to be hidden.

Her heart settled into a calmer rhythm. 'Jack—' She gently clasped his wrist.

He stepped backwards. 'Are you checking up on me?'

She felt nothing but compassion. 'Look. It's okay.'

Jack shook himself free of her. 'It's not what you think.'

'Who you sleep with is your . . .'

'I'm not gay.' He faced her square on, lips peeled back. But his eyes betrayed a primal terror, and when she saw it she felt a twist of anguish on his behalf.

Lucy swallowed, heading into the living room. 'Emily turned up at the office expecting you to be there. I said you must be out on a job.'

Without saying a word, without looking at Lucy, Jack sat down on the sofa.

Lucy took the seat next to him, letting her head sink back into the plump cushions, feeling the heat of his arm against her own. Before her eyes was the picture of Peter as Iago, hidden away in the wardrobe. How blind she'd been.

She tried to laugh. 'I thought I was going to catch you banging Zelda.'

'You know I'm not . . . I've never pretended to be a saint.'

Lucy put a hand on his knee. 'You should have told me. I could have helped.'

Jack sighed. 'I don't need to tell anyone anything.'

'Fair enough.' But Lucy had been his best friend – or at least she'd thought she was – why had he felt the need to conceal his true self from her?

He adjusted his position, head high, spine unnaturally taut. 'Everyone's falling over themselves to show how liberal they are. Times are supposed to have changed, blah blah blah. But name one bisexual male who's landed a decent part. Name one.'

'Jack—'

'See. You can't. Men who sleep with men get low-budget indie trash. That's the truth of it.'

'You and Peter—'

It was as if she'd struck him. She felt him shudder.

'You didn't have to sneak around.' She'd lived in the shared house with them for two years and noticed nothing. How careful they'd been.

'Yes, I did!' Jack was up, off the sofa, flecks of white gathering in the corner of his mouth. With a gentle sadness Lucy noted the use of *I*. There was no we. Peter hadn't been given a say. Secrecy had been foisted upon him.

She almost left it there. But she remembered Peter's turquoise eyes, heard his sonorous voice telling her: *I don't think you realise how good you are.* With a crushing shame, she recalled her own drunken fumbles with Jack – he'd let Lucy believe they were engaging in harmless fun, when actually he'd been making her complicit in hurting Peter.

'It wasn't just about you, though. Peter was happy with who he was. How did *he* feel about keeping everything a secret?'

For a second Jack stood there, glaring at Lucy, his eyes conveying a violent dislike. But then his legs seemed to buckle. With a pained growl he was on the floor, cradling his knees.

Lucy rushed to him. She remembered the sound Jack had made in Claudia's office, the howl of anguish that hadn't seemed human.

'It was more than just sex?' She rubbed his back.

Jack nodded, without looking at her.

'You *loved* him?'

A soft groan.

'Oh, Jack.'

'You can't tell Emily,' he managed to say, through his tears.

Lucy felt a coldness spread across her scalp. *That's* what he was concerned about?

'You can't tell anyone. *Heart Street* mustn't find out.'

She kissed the top of his head. 'It's fine, Jack. I won't tell a soul, I promise.'

As Lucy went on soothing him, her mind filled with questions. When had it started? How had Peter responded to the secrecy? He must have been so hurt every time Jack brought one of their classmates home. She imagined Jack rationalising it, telling Peter, *no one can suspect, we have to think of our careers.*

Lucy's eyes filled with tears as she perceived the loneliness Jack had imposed on Peter. As she stroked Jack's back, assured him again and again that she wouldn't tell anyone what she'd managed to piece together, her anger started to solidify.

Chapter 24

While waiting to hear the verdict on a second in-person *Heart Street* audition, Jack arranged for himself and Lucy to spend a Saturday looking at wedding venues with Sebastian. Lucy hadn't had a chance to get back to Portsmouth for over a fortnight and it irked her that Jack hadn't thought to check with her first.

'How did this venue-hunting thing come about?' She'd just returned from the office and was preparing a salad in the kitchen. Three weeks had passed since she'd confronted him about lying to Emily. She still had so many questions, but every time she attempted to talk about Peter, Jack's expression would become like a slammed door. *I don't like talking about it, I'm not going to let it define me,* was all he'd say.

Jack leaned over and pinched a slice of cucumber from the chopping board. 'He was asking about the wedding plans and started getting all *Sebastian* about it. You know, quizzing me on what format we had in mind, asking whether I'd taken you along to any wedding fairs.'

'Sounds like normal fatherly interest to me.'

Jack frowned. 'He couldn't help making it about money, grilling me on our budget. It ended up with him doing that thing he does with his mouth, looking all disappointed at my lack of organisation.'

'Couldn't you have just kept things vague?' Lucy hadn't seen Sebastian since the kiss, nearly two months ago now. He'd likely be embarrassed, awkward with her. Would Jack notice? She'd denied getting anywhere with Sebastian and couldn't backtrack now, even if she wanted to.

'I did. He ended up offering to drive us round a handful of stately-home-type places. What's the problem? You can bill Zelda for the time. I thought you'd be pleased,' Jack said.

Lucy swallowed. 'You're right. It does make sense. I just want this job to be over and off our books, that's all.'

She pictured herself in a car, looking at the back of Sebastian's neck as he drove. How was it possible to both ache for something and dread it at the very same time?

On a cold bright Saturday, Lucy and Jack met Sebastian at his building on Grosvenor Road in Pimlico. He led them down to the underground car park, automatic lights snapping on to illuminate a smattering of BMWs, a low-slung Porsche, and Sebastian's black Tesla, parked next to a concrete support pillar. Lucy wore the serene smile of her fiancée character as Sebastian held open the door to the backseat. He was wearing a Patagonia hiking jacket, a padded affair in electric blue. There was a solemnity in the set of his jaw, something very deliberate in the way he held his gaze just to the side of Lucy's face.

'Thanks so much for arranging this.' Her voice was pitch perfect as she clambered in, no trace of the anticipation or strain she was feeling. How close she'd come to telling

Sebastian everything on the night of the curry. If Jack had been just a few minutes longer, she'd have done it. What would have happened, then? She wanted to believe Sebastian would have kissed her again, his hands in her hair, repeating that gentle moan.

'I thought it'd be nice,' Sebastian said, starting the engine. 'Give you some ideas.'

'Where to first, then?' Jack asked from the passenger seat. He was the consummate actor, his voice conveying the perfect blend of excitement and affection.

Sebastian drove up the exit ramp and pulled out onto the main road, behind a white Transit van. 'Eltham Palace. I've been to a couple of corporate functions there. It's stunning.' Was he having to consciously manage his tone, to conceal his unease? Lucy shouldn't assume what had happened between them mattered so much. There was every chance he'd moved on, viewing the moment as nothing more than a blip.

As they drove through Peckham, Jack chattered on about the latest cinema releases, then listed and ranked his all-time favourite horror performances. It was customary for his character to dominate the conversation, so Lucy didn't have to expend energy masking her discomfort. The ease with which Jack lied, to Sebastian, to Emily, to her, was starting to repulse Lucy – she'd given him so much of her life, but all along he'd been curating what she saw. It bothered her that her own deceit – the concealment of a single too-short kiss – made her feel like such a despicable liar.

From the backseat she could smell the woody notes of Sebastian's aftershave. She became preoccupied with his hands on the steering wheel, the sturdiness of his forearms.

Many times, Lucy had closed her eyes and placed herself back in his kitchen with its gleaming utensil rack and granite worktops. In these daydreams she was a drama teacher arriving home after a gruelling day, taking the glass of wine Sebastian proffered without even thinking about the calories. Her hair was returned to its natural hazelnut brown, her wardrobe was filled with comfortable shirts and trousers. Sebastian made her feel like the carefully bleached hair, the narrow waist, were the least important aspects of who she was. After a decade of craving the unattainable heights of critical acclaim, she wondered whether all she really wanted was the comfort of a shared meal, recommending books to one another and discussing what they'd read. Yet it was the one thing she'd gone and made it impossible to have.

Eltham Palace was surrounded by imposing trees and sweeping lawns that looked down over the steel towers of the city. From this distance, the urban mass beneath her seemed strangely intangible, as though the skyscrapers, the spires of the churches and criss-crossing roads belonged inside a myth Lucy could choose to believe in, or choose to reject.

The manor house itself made Lucy wish she knew more about architecture. An array of different shapes – triangular peaks, elegant semicircles – seemed to have collided, then found an unexpectedly harmonious co-existence. She was aware of an absence of odours, a freshness to the air that made her inhale deeply.

A woman called Yvonne, about fifty or so with yellow hair piled up into an elaborate bun, showed them around, her kitten heels clicking along the parquet flooring. She recounted the building's history with enthusiasm, taking specific care to address Lucy, *our lovely bride*, as she pointed out the intricate oak roofing of the great hall.

'A good proportion of our brides have the ceremony in this room, creating an aisle just along here ...'

Lucy gave the appreciative gasps that were expected of her, gazing at the majestic stone arches and wrought iron lamps in turn. She was aware of Sebastian behind them, studying the wooden panels, keeping a deferential distance.

Once they'd concluded the tour, Jack announced he was hungry and the three of them made their way to the venue's café for an early lunch. It was located inside a giant greenhouse with a brick floor and a profusion of potted plants. Winter sunlight flooded in through the glass panes, gleaming off their stainless-steel table.

Lucy ordered a coffee and a salad. Sebastian and Jack both went for bacon rolls, enticed by the scent of hot grease coming from the kitchen.

'So, what do you think, Lucy?' Sebastian asked, once they'd put their orders in.

'I love it,' Jack said. 'Just imagine how wonderful the photos would be.'

Sebastian shot him a glance.

'If it wasn't ruinously expensive, I'd say we could stop looking right now,' Jack continued. 'But we'd need one of the larger rooms and our budget wouldn't stretch to that.'

'Do you have a date in mind?' Sebastian asked.

He'd directed the question at Lucy, but once again Jack jumped in. 'We're thinking of a Saturday next June. We've got the guest list down to a hundred for the ceremony with another fifty for the reception.' On he went, recounting fictitious details, trying to assure his supposed father that he was an adult, paying attention and taking responsibility.

Jack's performances were far better when he had a script to work from, Lucy realised. The expectation that people would like him always ended up breaking through whenever he improvised.

She smiled to try and conceal stirrings of panic as their food arrived. What would she do when Jack needed the toilet? Or wandered off to fiddle with his phone? There would inevitably come a point in the day when Lucy and Sebastian would be alone. Would he speak of the kiss? She dreaded it, yet at the same time was aware of a strange fear – what if he *didn't*? She moved her salad around her plate, managing only a few mouthfuls. If she pushed it any further she'd end up retching.

On and on Jack went, speaking of the university friends they'd invite, appearing torn over who should be relegated to evening-only status. Ordinarily, Lucy would have been impressed by how thorough he was, but today it felt a little sinister. Performance and reality had become too blurred. Perhaps where Jack was concerned they always had been.

'Lucy mentioned a close friend of yours died just before graduation,' Sebastian said. His eyes were soft with compassion.

Lucy froze. She'd just been about to take a sip of coffee and her cup remained pressed against her mouth. From the corner of her eye, Lucy could see the colour drain from Jack's face. There was a faint scuffing sound, as he rearranged his feet beneath the table. He was livid with her, she could tell.

'That must have been so hard,' Sebastian added. He was observing Jack's face closely. He couldn't have failed to notice the emotion there, the loathing he was silently directing towards Lucy.

Without looking at her, Jack shrugged his shoulders. 'It was a long time ago.'

Lucy could feel Sebastian's gaze shift, coming to land on her own face. She felt hot and knew her skin must be reddening. She was aware now, of the pain concealed beneath Jack's dismissive tone. But it still wasn't right to treat Peter like an unfortunate fact, some inconvenient detail that made Jack's life less perfect than it might otherwise have been. Lucy carefully placed her cup back down on its saucer. She wasn't sure what she might do if she were to break free of her restraint. Part of her wanted to take hold of Sebastian and kiss him until her lips bled.

When a server arrived to clear away their plates, Sebastian excused himself to use the loo.

'You told him about *Peter*? What the hell's wrong with you?' Jack hissed, once they were alone.

'I can't keep doing this. It's fucked up.' She spat her words, using a tone she'd never used before.

'Oh, please, no, Luce. Don't go over this old ground again. We weighed everything up at the beginning and decided to help Zelda. We're committed.'

'I'm starting to think Zelda's unhinged—'

'That's not true. You just don't like her.'

'Think about what she's asking us to do. I mean – being someone's *son* – how did we ever square that with our consciences?'

Jack gave a bitter laugh. 'This is about justice – that's what you told me. I didn't even want to take it on in the first place. You were the one to insist.'

He was right. That's what hurt the most: Lucy had been the architect, contorting her mind, convincing herself that it was fine to accept Zelda's money. She sighed. 'Can we agree that today is the last time we see Sebastian? We'll tell Zelda we've reached a natural end point. Sebastian adores you. He'll be devastated when you stop returning his calls. Job done. We walk away.'

'He still thinks I'm a waste of space. You see the way he looks at me. I need another month or so to really get under his skin.'

So that was the real reason. Sebastian's moments of disapproval had injured Jack's pride.

Lucy changed tack. 'You'll most likely have *Heart Street* to focus on soon. You need to wrap this gig up before you're on screen three times a week.'

'What's got into you?' Jack sat back in his chair, eyes roving her face with new curiosity.

There was a roaring in Lucy's ears. 'I'm just still playing catch-up with the ethics of it all.'

He rolled his eyes. 'Is this about Zelda? You're being weird because we get on so well.'

'Oh, please.'

'I am allowed other friends, you know.'

'Get over yourself. I just want to sort this *mess*.'

'It's not a mess. It's a sustained piece of improvisation. It's actually been good for me, stretching my range. You know how much I hated improv at uni.'

Lucy sighed. Tears of exasperation were prickling the backs of her eyes. She and Jack were supposed to have shared the business. It was meant to insulate him from the cruelty of the acting profession, give him a new focus. It had failed. The agency only ever had the potential to be a diversion for Jack. And it had made a liar out of Lucy.

They sat in silence for a few minutes. Jack spotted Sebastian returning and gripped Lucy by the hand. 'Just imagine it, though, Luce. Our guests could have Pimm's on the lawn while we're having photos taken.'

Sebastian sat back down at the table. He was holding a bundle of literature. A brochure with a bride in a close-fitting dress, open-mouthed smile showcasing perfect teeth.

'I've been thinking about how I can help,' Sebastian said. 'I'd really like to do something nice for you both.'

Lucy felt a shadow pass over her. Sebastian was smiling, but his body language was all wrong, his movements seemed jerky, as though he was thrumming with nervous energy.

'That's really kind.' Jack gave a supplicating smile.

'Well. I can see you've fallen in love with this place. So I've put the deposit down. Secured you the last Saturday in June of next year.'

Lucy's mouth became unbearably dry. 'We can't let you do that. It's too much.'

'Think of it as an early wedding present.' Sebastian didn't look at her, he kept his eyes on Jack.

'Thank you!' Jack raised his arms in delight, his mouth falling open.

'No,' Lucy said. 'Honestly. We can't – you don't have to . . .' She was aware of Jack reaching for her hand and gripping it tightly. She was sabotaging his performance, ruining everything they'd worked for.

Had Sebastian done this out of guilt? Lucy couldn't shake the idea that this expensive down payment was his way of atoning for the kiss. Yes, he could probably afford it. Twenty grand was a small sum in his world. But things had gone too far.

Sebastian finally met her eye. 'Why ever not? Think of all the birthdays and Christmases I missed.'

Lucy tried to swallow. If she admitted everything now, her friendship with Jack would never recover. But how could they go on with this?

'We're really grateful,' Jack said.

She was aware of Sebastian handing the paperwork to Jack, pointing out the receipt tucked inside the brochure. And for the first time in her career Lucy was capable of precisely nothing. She'd never dried up before now. Never experienced stage fright. But this is what it must feel like. She felt powerless, unable to say a word.

Chapter 25

On Monday, as sleet fell across the city, they took the Overground to Hackney Wick to meet Zelda at her studio. It was inside a repurposed warehouse next to a canal lined with brightly coloured houseboats. A vinyl sign next to the door declared the space to be a 'talent incubator'. As Zelda led them down a narrow corridor with small studios on either side, Lucy glimpsed an array of half-finished canvases, an assault of colour. One room contained what Lucy thought must be a loom, another a silk screen printing press.

Zelda was wearing dungarees with an old black shirt, the sleeves rolled up to her elbows. Her hair was plaited into two loose braids, but her eyebrows were carefully pencilled in and she'd swept blusher along the apples of her cheeks. She ushered them into a light-filled room with an exposed concrete floor and high ceiling, filled with pine shelving units bearing an array of dishes, vases and pots, some of them glazed, others unfinished. A window dominated one wall, overlooking a roundabout and graffiti-covered warehouse.

The centre of the room was home to a work table, covered in paint-streaked sheets of newspaper and next to that was a potter's wheel. The damp, earthy smell of clay reminded Lucy of her secondary school art room.

'Let's sit at the table,' Zelda said, dragging over a stool.

Lucy was aware of Jack drifting towards the shelves to inspect the ceramic items lined up in neat rows. She found herself observing him, trying to detect any signs of familiarity, any indication that he'd been here before. His curiosity suggested this was a first visit, but Lucy no longer trusted what she saw – he'd been lying about Peter for over a decade and it left her with the dislocating sense that she didn't know who he was at all.

Lucy sat down on a plastic chair. She needed to get ahead of any digressions; it looked very much as though Jack was going to start asking about the ceramics.

'Thanks so much for seeing us,' Lucy began. 'At the weekend Sebastian caught us off-guard by putting down a deposit on a wedding venue.'

Zelda's lips sprang apart and a flush spread across her nose and neck. 'I ... goodness ... that's very generous of him.'

'It's left us in a bit of a difficult position, so we wanted to talk next steps.'

'How much are we talking about?' Zelda seemed startled, her eyes wide as she took deep, open-mouthed breaths.

'Twenty grand.' Lucy felt an inner tremor. She'd been bracing herself for a battle, imagining their client would insist they keep the money, perhaps even ask for more. But Sebastian's generosity appeared to have left Zelda stunned.

Jack turned away from the shelves, placing a hand on Zelda's shoulder. 'We're still a hundred per cent committed to our work,' he said. 'Lucy's just worried about the money element. Says we need to find a way to give it back.'

'It could be interpreted as fraud,' Lucy said. 'We've accepted financial support under false pretences.' She and Jack had argued on their return from Eltham Palace; he'd refused to see the danger they were in, insisting it couldn't possibly be fraud when Sebastian had made the payment of his own volition.

'Goodness,' Zelda said. 'I wasn't expecting him to do a thing like that.'

'It would help enormously if we understood how you see the assignment ending,' Lucy added. 'Then we can figure out how best to return the money.'

Zelda looked down at her ankles. Her face was now blanched of colour, all traces of the confident client who wielded envelopes of cash seemed to be gone. On coming here, Lucy had rehearsed the arguments in her mind: *I know we made a commitment to you, but unfortunately that commitment doesn't extend to engaging in illegal activity.* She didn't know quite how to meet Zelda's quietly shocked reaction, but it gave her a flicker of hope. Perhaps the woman was having second thoughts.

'I need to think,' Zelda said at last.

Jack turned back to a row of unglazed vases. 'These are exquisite. The curvature on the stem – it feels so unexpected, yet so perfect.'

Zelda smiled at him. 'They're inspired by Peruvian folk art. A new passion of mine.'

'What specifically *do* you want us to do next?' Lucy asked Zelda. 'You alluded to making Sebastian suffer. We'll get there by giving the money back, then ghosting him. He won't understand what's happened.' Lucy felt bereft as she imagined Sebastian's perplexity, the gut-piercing blow of rejection.

Zelda inhaled, lifting her chin so that she was looking Lucy in the eye. She was about to say something, her lips forming a new shape. But then she appeared to quickly abandon the thought. 'I don't think we're ready to wrap things up yet,' she said.

'It could work perfectly.' Lucy kept her voice gentle. 'Us rejecting him right now, when he's been so kind, would really hurt.'

She couldn't go on being answerable to Zelda, couldn't risk being charged with fraud. But was Lucy really ready to disappear on Sebastian without a word?

'No.' Zelda's nostrils flared, but her eyes seemed to turn inwards.

'In that case, when?' Lucy was having to breathe deeply to manage her exasperation, to stay in her role as business owner. *I am proprietor of a successful agency. I can handle any uncomfortable situation.* 'I'm unclear on what prolonging things will achieve.'

Zelda bit her lower lip and turned to stare out of the window. She said nothing.

Jack had picked up one of the jugs and was turning it over in his hands. Any moment now, he'd ask Zelda a question about her creative process and Lucy wouldn't be able to stand it.

Suddenly, Zelda placed a hand on Lucy's wrist. 'You've become fond of Sebastian, haven't you?'

'What makes you say that?' Lucy's cheeks felt bathed in heat.

'He's a charmer. I can perfectly understand it.' Zelda didn't look angry. Her eyes were unfocussed and a sad smile played at the corners of her mouth.

Lucy looked at Zelda, filling her eyes with an urgent appeal. 'We really do need to get that deposit back to Sebastian somehow. If we knew exactly what you want, we can work out the best way of handling things. Maybe you'd like to confront him, explain what the abandonment felt like?'

Zelda swallowed. 'Just give me a couple more days. I'll mull it over.'

'We do have to give the money back, though – you understand that, right? We can't leave it too long. If anything were to . . . we all could end up in trouble with the police.'

Zelda drew herself up. 'Are you threatening me?'

'Of course not,' Lucy said. She glanced at Jack. He was still holding the jug, eyes down as though he was inspecting it.

'There's nothing to prove my involvement in any of this.' Zelda sounded close to tears.

A shiver of apprehension darted along Lucy's spine. It was true. Zelda had hired them in the very early days, before Lucy had started drawing up formal agreements for each client. She'd even paid in cash, so there were no bank records to prove the relationship.

'What's that supposed to mean?' Lucy was careful not to raise her voice.

'All this talk of fraud,' Zelda said. 'I don't like it. It feels as if you're trying to pin something on me.'

'Not at all.' Lucy searched Zelda's face, trying to read where she was going with this. There seemed to be a tightness to her expression, as if she was expending enormous effort

just to remain still. Her pale eyes were once again turned inwards, either in reflection, or because she wanted to conceal
what she felt.

'We're on your side,' Jack added.

Zelda placed her knuckles to her eyes for a moment. 'Then
you need to go on doing as I say. I'll figure out what to do
next. Work out how to bring everything to a close. As long
as you stick to the plan, we'll keep the police out of this and
there'll be no more talk of fraud.'

'Sounds good,' said Jack, finally returning the vase to its
shelf. 'I'm sorry things got so tense for a minute there. But
you see how worried Lucy is.'

Lucy was about to respond. To calmy lay out the facts,
stressing the need to act quickly. The venue likely had
policies and time limits regarding refunds. But a feeling of
futility weighed down her muscles. She was alone in this.
Jack was wilfully choosing not to see the danger they were in,
and Zelda was wildly unpredictable. Reasonable arguments
weren't going to get through to either of them.

Zelda's face broke into an overly sweet smile. She reached
across to ruffle Lucy's hair. 'Dearest Lucy. Such a worrywart.'

Lucy forced herself to smile in return. She'd have to come
up with a plan of her own.

Chapter 26

Later that week, Lucy arranged a morning of rental viewings. She'd been bold, opting to see self-contained bedsits rather than flat-shares, and as she took the train to Greenwich a familiar voice rose up inside her. Could she really justify shelling out an astronomical sum each month? Thousands of pounds gone from her bank account, enriching some buy-to-let landlord who probably drove a Jag and sent his kids to private school. Lucy's father still wasn't back at work; his doctor had insisted he wait a few months before taking another treadmill test and reapplying for his taxi licence. Although they'd never ask for help, Lucy's family still needed the money she sent them.

Throughout her twenties, she'd become used to moving every six months. Invariably, Lucy would reach the end of a contract and her rent would be hiked for no tangible reason. She'd made small talk with a constant succession of strangers, hearing their arguments and excretions, loathing them when they didn't empty the bins or clean their dishes. The idea of her own front door had always been a fantasy, representing the very pinnacle of success. Surely this was the time? Even after sending money to her mother,

Lucy's bank account continued to grow at an astonishing rate. In December – not a typical month, true – the hourly billings just for her own assignments had totted up to fifteen grand. It was a figure that made her knees weak. There had been entire years where she'd barely scraped together that much.

It was one of those grey, late-winter days that left Lucy feeling starved of light and warmth. She had a thick woollen scarf around her neck, and a cable-knit jumper under her parka. But still she shivered as she walked to her first viewing in Corvette Square in Greenwich. The route took her along a quiet road with tall brick houses on one side and a high wall enclosing parkland on the other. It was almost unnerving how little traffic there was. It didn't feel like London at all.

Her phone vibrated with a call from Adam. The night before she'd texted him, asking whether he'd mind discussing a legal situation with her. Navigating the hushed streets now, she told him about the Zelda gig and the wedding deposit. She felt her face burning at just how naive she'd been.

'Goodness. This is a complicated situation,' Adam said at last. 'Allowing him to pay the venue deposit does constitute fraud. The fact that you're answering a client brief wouldn't stand up as a defence, I'm afraid.'

'What are my options?' Lucy turned into a narrow side-street lined with spiked iron railings. 'I mean, if you've got time. You should probably bill me for this.'

Adam laughed, a little nervously. 'I don't mind at all. And actually it's pretty simple – I'm afraid there's no such thing as undoing a crime, you could still be charged even if you give the money back.'

Lucy gasped.

'Returning the money *might* lessen your chances of being prosecuted. But it all comes down to this Sebastian and whether he has an appetite to press charges. I'm sorry, I know that's probably not what you wanted to hear.'

Lucy's legs felt heavy as she processed this. If Sebastian found out he was being lied to, he could report them to the police and have them charged for accepting the venue deposit. Why hadn't she been more assertive on the day? She should have marched him back over to Yvonne's office and insisted he cancel the order.

She thanked Adam, doing her best to sound composed and professional. Somehow she managed to speak about a rabbit shoot she was due to attend as Holly. It would involve another overnight stay in Sussex.

'Has George given you any more trouble?' she asked.

'The two of us don't really speak outside of family events.'

'I'll try and hang out with Charlotte. See if I can learn anything that might rein George in a bit.'

'I can't say I'm hopeful,' Adam said. 'But I love the website you commissioned. Holly even has her own email address now, I see. It was really good of you to be so thorough.'

Lucy managed to smile as she hung up. When she worked with Adam, she felt she knew exactly what she was doing and why. It couldn't be further from the mess with Zelda and Sebastian.

Lucy's heart leaped when she arrived at the first address. It overlooked a small park filled with mature trees. She'd be met with greenery each morning, her own little patch of nature.

Inside however, the entranceway smelled of wee and the flat itself had a pervasive damp odour. It looked as though it had been recently painted, but already patches of mould were blooming around the windows.

No one turned up to let her into the second flat and the estate agent didn't answer her calls. As she waited by the communal entrance, Lucy texted Sebastian asking to meet later that week. She wouldn't give herself the luxury of hesitation. Return the money or confess – those were her options, and a meeting would impose a deadline.

With a sudden burst of inspiration she called the wedding venue.

'My partner's father put a deposit down for our wedding at the weekend. Unfortunately, the ceremony won't now be going ahead. Is there any way you could refund the money? He paid by card.'

A pause. 'I'm very sorry to hear that,' came the sing-song voice of Yvonne who'd showed them around.

'He went to so much trouble on our behalf. It really would mean the world if he could be refunded with the minimum of fuss. I was hoping it was something we could take care of over the phone.'

'You're officially releasing the date?'

A surge of hope. 'We are, yes.'

'Well. A refund might be possible. But we'd need the card holder's authorisation.'

'The wedding is most definitely off. Can't we just arrange for the money to be put back on the card?'

'I'm afraid I do need to speak to Mr Stott. Just ask him to give me a quick call and we can take it from there.'

Lucy sighed. She imagined confessing to Sebastian, pictured his eyes filling with tears. Perhaps he'd slump forward for a moment, but then the anger would come. She imagined him trembling with rage, directed not just at Jack and Zelda, but at Lucy too. Why wouldn't he report them? If someone had deceived Lucy for months on end, she certainly wouldn't hesitate to press charges.

Yvonne hesitated, then: 'I really am sorry to hear about the wedding. You seemed like such a lovely couple.'

By the time Lucy reached her third viewing, at a high-rise in Dowell Street, she was bored of flat-hunting and it made her feel strangely reckless. The walls were a horrible pink, and the window looked directly into the block of flats opposite. But Lucy would mostly use the place to sleep, and even though the block was situated in a sea of tall buildings, the area did seem clean and well-maintained. The rent was double what she had paid each month for her previous flatshare, but in a fit of bravado she agreed to go back to the estate agents' office and sign the contract then and there. She could move in next month. She wouldn't have to rely on Jack any more, which was probably just as well.

After leaving Zelda's studio the previous week, Lucy had fought with Jack on the train platform.

'She was threatening us,' she'd said of Zelda. 'Things are getting dangerous. We need an exit strategy.'

Jack had rolled his eyes. 'She wasn't *threatening* us. She just wanted time to think. It's not unreasonable.'

'That thing she said about us not being able to prove we're working with her. It sounded like a threat to me.'

'She was just panicking because you were getting all heavy. Honestly, Luce, if you're serious about continuing the agency, you need to be a bit nicer to people.'

Lucy had felt her anger rising. 'This whole situation is *heavy*, Jack. Being done for a twenty-grand fraud is pretty bloody *heavy*.'

'There's no need to be melodramatic.' Jack had sighed and pulled out his phone.

'Why are you so loyal to her? You're so ready to believe her, and you don't know her, not really.'

'I'm allowed other friends, Lucy.'

'Fuck off.' Lucy had said it louder than intended and sensed the couple nearest them on the platform looking up.

'You turn against anyone I get along with,' Jack had said.

Lucy felt as though she'd been slapped. This characterisation of herself as the possessive best friend, always lesser, always dependent somehow – Jack probably believed it to be true, even though he'd never attended an audition without devouring hours of her time, making her critique every line and gesture. She'd worked so hard to build him up after his breakdown, enthusing at every opportunity, reinforcing his sense that every disappointment was an injustice. When had he ever shown her such consideration? Whenever Lucy spoke of her father, Jack would simply nod and go quiet. He never asked how the recovery was going or if there was anything he could do to help.

'Get over yourself,' Lucy had said. 'I turned against Zelda because she's involved us in fraud.'

'It can't be fraud because we didn't ask Sebastian for anything. If you'd actually managed to seduce him, we wouldn't
have reached this point.'

The train had roared in and they'd stepped on board, sitting opposite one another in sulky silence.

Chapter 27

Sebastian responded to Lucy's text with the suggestion of a lunchtime walk the following Friday. She found it impossible to sleep on the Thursday night, the springs of the sofa bed mattress dug into her back as her mind circled and probed the deceit. She rehearsed the words of a direct confession, admitting she and Jack were actors hired by Zelda. She pictured the dismay blanching Sebastian's face, the slow dawn of understanding, followed by disgust. There had to be a better way of doing things, a way Lucy could spare Sebastian at least some of the pain. Listening to Jack's soft snores emanating from his bedroom, she alighted on a plan.

The sky was a slate grey as she waited for Sebastian outside the cladded cube housing his bank. She was wearing the black coat she'd bought for her Holly assignments and had a red pashmina around her neck, but her legs had only thin tights to protect them from the bitter wind gusting between the skyscrapers. She was still in character as Lucy-the-fiancée, sapphire ring on her finger, although her grasp on the role had become shaky. She'd mined her own experiences too deeply and the shift from one person to another no longer felt complete. She was having to act mechanically, thinking about each expression and consciously planting it on her face.

'Hello, you,' said Sebastian, emerging from the building. 'I thought we might walk towards St Paul's. Take a stroll round Festival Gardens if you don't mind the cold. Always nice to get some fresh air at lunch.'

'Sounds good.'

She observed him from the corner of her eye as they walked. He was wearing a well-brushed black overcoat over a navy-blue suit. His shoes were shiny and stiff-looking, making a distinct click every time the heel hit the ground. With his lean physique and full head of hair, Sebastian could pass for a fortysomething as he took long, vigorous strides along Queen Victoria Street. This part of London with its wide roads and elegant high-rises usually stirred something in Lucy; making her feel connected to history, significant in some intangible way. But this afternoon her stomach was too knotted for such things.

'So,' Sebastian said as they reached Cannon Street, 'as lovely as it is to see you, I'm assuming you wanted to talk to me about something?'

Lucy swallowed. Time to enact her plan. It would alienate her even further from Jack, but it was the right thing to do.

'It's Jack's mother.' Lucy had to shout to be heard over the roar of traffic. It didn't quite set the confiding tone she hoped for.

'What about her?'

Lucy could see St Paul's now, its pale grey stone rising up to meet the swelling clouds. She would be strong, see this through. 'There's no easy way ... Zelda's said a few things lately that kind of suggested you might not be Jack's father. I thought you had a right to know.'

Sebastian said nothing, ploughing on towards the park.

Lucy continued: 'I'm so sorry, really I am. But the way Zelda's started talking about Thailand ... she made it clear there were other men, other possible fathers.' She'd done it, uttered the words that could destroy the new identity Sebastian had constructed for himself. She was barely acting as she spoke the lines she'd concocted the previous evening, aware of the thudding of her heart as she waited for a reaction.

'You should ask for a paternity test. You have the right to be sure.' She needed Sebastian to look at her, for him to see in her eyes just how much she ached on his behalf.

He stared straight ahead, crossing the road with brisk efficiency, as though the two of them were colleagues, hurrying along to a meeting.

'In the meantime, I was thinking you should call Eltham Palace and get your deposit refunded,' Lucy said. 'I'll square everything with Jack. It's just – I can't bear the thought of you being so generous when there's an element of doubt.'

Please, she was thinking. *Please, hear what I'm saying and do the sensible thing.*

Finally, they reached the gardens. Even in February, the lawn was vibrant green, offering an oasis of colour amid the concrete and stone. Despite the freezing wind, all the benches were taken with office workers in their smart coats, forking salads from plastic boxes or staring at their phones. Sebastian paused by the fountain, scanning the space, his arms rigid at his sides.

'It must have been very difficult for you to work up the

courage to approach me,' he said finally, still refusing to look at her.

Lucy gazed at the fountain, watching water spurt from the mouths of intricately carved lions. 'I can't stand the idea of thinking you have a son, when ...' Lucy felt the searing disappointment of the unsuccessful IVF rounds with her own body. Cycles of hope followed by tense waiting and then crushing misery. Sebastian had wanted so badly to believe he was a father; he'd pushed all scepticism to the side. How despicable it had been to *use* that.

Sebastian sighed. A woman vacated the bench nearest them and he moved towards it, sinking down, his face drained of colour. The need to touch him was overwhelming.

'Have you spoken to Jack about this?' Sebastian asked. 'Does he share these doubts?'

Lucy sat down next to him, drawing her coat tightly around her. 'No. He doesn't know I'm here.'

'Everything is ...' Sebastian faltered. 'Jack and I are still very early days.'

'I know,' Lucy said. 'That's why getting a test now would feel so natural. I mean, Jack kind of expected you to ask for proof. He's not going to mind, I promise you.'

Sebastian looked down as his feet. For a moment the two of them were quiet. Lucy looked up at the cathedral, taking in its colonnaded dome, the ring of windows and tall cross that pierced the clouds. *I'll be better,* she vowed to herself. *I won't allow myself to become a vehicle for pain, not ever.*

Lucy shifted her gaze to the man sitting on the low stone wall opposite them, throwing crumbs from his sandwich to the pigeons gathered at his feet. An ambulance went by, sirens blaring. Had she done enough? The organic discovery of a 'mistake', an error on Zelda's part, would hurt Sebastian the least. He didn't need to know he'd been actively deceived, that Lucy and Jack had lied to his face countless times.

She heard Sebastian sigh. 'Jack is so ... I've tried to feel a connection, I really have. But we're so different. At times I find him infuriating. Isn't that an awful thing to admit?'

'Not at all,' Lucy said. 'Jack can be *very* infuriating.' Perhaps some tiny part of Sebastian would be relieved to know there was no biological connection. He wouldn't have to persist with a relationship that at times must have felt frustrating and unnatural.

Sebastian turned to her. The wind had stung his cheeks pink. 'But you love him. You must see things that I ... '

Instinctively, Lucy reached for Sebastian's hand. It felt unexpectedly hot. She squeezed it briefly, then forced herself to let go. She couldn't let her own feelings come into this, couldn't distract herself from what she needed to do.

'Tell me what Jack was like at university,' Sebastian said.

Lucy wasn't sure how this linked to the question of paternity, but in that moment she would give Sebastian anything he wanted.

'Me, Peter and Jack lived together. We shared the same mindset. Driving ourselves really hard to try and be the best. Everyone else in the class thought they were pretty great already, only bothering with the course because they saw it as a tried and tested way of getting an agent.' This was Lucy's origin story, the foundation on which her ten years of trying to make it in London had rested. But the words were poison in her mouth. It was all lies. She couldn't fight the feeling that she hadn't just lost Jack – his deceit had contaminated her memories, taken Peter from her.

'But what was it that made you actually *like* Jack? Or was it all purely transactional: you push me and I'll push you?'

Lucy drew her hands up inside the sleeves of her coat, trying to warm them. 'Mutual encouragement is a pretty decent basis for a friendship. Or any relationship, really.'

Sebastian said nothing.

'It was exhilarating,' Lucy insisted. 'Before uni I'd never met anyone with Jack's drive. It inspired me. Gave me permission to think more boldly about what I wanted and who I might become.' It *had* been true. Lucy needed to hold on to that.

'But . . . ' Sebastian's eyes were starting to water. He pressed his lips together, then tried again: 'Was it not damaging? Encouragement is all well and good. But when people push their friends into going after something unachievable – there's a kind of cruelty in that.'

Lucy looked down at the chewing gum spatters and cigarette butts decorating the path. A single snowflake drifted down and melted by her foot. Then another. She felt as though Sebastian had shaken something loose inside her. Some long-hidden kernel of knowledge was now exposed; all she had to do was look at it and she'd understand the truth about herself. But no. She would not tolerate this. Her friendships, her shared ambitions were the scaffolding on which she'd built her whole life. She would not let her sense of self unravel in the face of Jack's lies.

'You weren't there,' she said. 'I was the first person in my family to go to uni. All I really hoped for was a job that let me earn more than my father gets driving his taxi. Peter and Jack *made* me.'

Sebastian shook his head. Lucy was dimly aware that she'd fractured her performance even further, but it was vital that Sebastian understand she was no victim, she'd willingly embraced everything Jack and Peter had offered her.

'I was a nobody.' It came out sharper than Lucy intended. 'With Jack and Peter I created scenes that were transcendent. They encouraged me to believe in my talent. Gave me drive. They made me want more for myself. And you know what? I had a *right* to want such things.'

Sebastian gave her a brief sideways glance. She searched his face, looking for signs of softening, anything to indicate he'd heard her and recognised the validity of what she had to say. His features seemed oddly rigid, as though his mouth had filled with an unpleasant taste and he was trying to conceal his disgust.

'You use the word "drive" a lot, whenever you talk about Jack. Does he still drive you hard, even now?'

Lucy inhaled. Her skin prickled with sudden dread. What was Sebastian really asking? Did he somehow *know*? She wasn't sure where the suspicion came from, but it seized her by the throat. It was completely irrational.

She braved a glance at his face. He looked so broken, his eyes were filled with a strange new despair. He must be starting to doubt the paternity. Lucy had done the job she'd set out to do. She'd push the refund one more time, then perhaps she'd never see him again.

'I think you should seriously consider the test,' Lucy said. 'In the meantime, get the wedding deposit back. I'll tell Jack

I had second thoughts about the venue. He doesn't need to know we've talked about this.'

Sebastian said nothing. He looked at her for a moment, his eyes soft, lashes damp with quiet tears. It was as though they'd both silently spoken a want they knew could never be fulfilled. Lucy's chest burned, but she wouldn't let herself interrogate the feeling, it would hurt too much.

'I'd better get back.' Sebastian rose, putting his hands in his pockets.

After they said their goodbyes, Lucy walked back to Soho, flakes of snow landing in her hair, dotting the black wool of her coat. Her boots were no protection against the chill of the pavement and her toes soon became numb. With every step, she vowed to herself: never again. It might mean giving up the agency, letting go of everything she'd created. But sitting in that small park with Sebastian had made her realise: she would rather be poor, let go of acting entirely, than go on being a liar.

Chapter 28

After a week went by without Zelda issuing any instructions regarding the wedding deposit, Lucy sent a message to chase her:

> Sorry to be persistent, but we do need to return the venue money to Sebastian asap.

Zelda remained infuriatingly non-committal (*I told you, I'll think of something*), but did agree to meet, setting a date in early March.

Lucy spent that morning moving her things from Jack's place to the Greenwich bedsit, unboxing her books and setting them into place in her very own bookshelf. She reached the office twenty minutes before the meeting was due to start, but Zelda was already sitting in their red armchair, wearing a knitted green dress with riding boots, blow-dried hair cascading over her shoulders. She was drinking from one of the crystal tumblers Jack had recently found, a bottle of Moët at her feet.

'I got it, Luce.' Jack rushed at her, lifting her up and whirling her around. 'I'm officially a cast member of *Heart Street*. Start filming my first scenes in May.'

'That's amazing!' Lucy was perhaps the single person who knew that for Jack, a soap role represented failure. For a second, they looked at one another and Lucy felt certain he was searching her face, looking for traces of this knowledge, or maybe even expecting to see disapproval. She showed him only joy.

'I'm so excited,' Zelda said. 'To think, I was the one who recorded Jack's audition. What a privilege.'

Lucy glanced at Zelda. Her cheeks were rosy and her eyes seemed to sparkle when she looked at Jack.

'Get yourself a glass, Lucy.' Zelda picked up the Champagne bottle.

All the other tumblers were sitting unwashed in the sink, so Lucy rinsed one under the tap and forced herself to smile as Zelda filled it to the brim.

'Cheers,' Lucy said, clinking glasses. She felt muddle-headed as she stood in the centre of the room taking the tiniest of sips, the bubbles tingling against her tongue. It was as though she was staring at the answer to a problem she couldn't quite recall asking herself.

If Zelda hadn't been there, surely Lucy wouldn't feel so constrained. She wouldn't be fighting this sense of bereavement that made her want to hug her knees to her chest. Jack was to become a soap actor, and Lucy was going to be left to navigate the agency alone. She tried to summon Peter's presence, to cling to his image so she didn't feel quite so lonely. But her mind wasn't able to form him. It was as though the cord connecting her with the past had frayed and come apart.

'Sorry to spoil the atmosphere with talk of business,' Zelda said. 'But I've been thinking about the Sebastian sitch and I've decided what I need you to do.'

Jack perched himself on the edge of Lucy's desk while Lucy remained standing, holding her tumbler. The Champagne's acidic aroma filled her nostrils; it was disturbingly close to the smell of vomit.

'Jack getting this glorious news about *Heart Street* rather settles matters,' Zelda said.

Lucy felt a spasm run through her stomach. Her secret hope that Sebastian would ask for a DNA test and discover the truth about Jack's paternity was something she cradled deep within herself.

'What are you thinking?' Jack asked Zelda.

'Let's tell Sebastian you have an opportunity with a soap,' Zelda said. 'You just need a little money to get you started. Cover your rent while you do a few final auditions, that type of thing. I'm sure you'll think of something convincing—'

'I'm not sure . . .' Lucy was aghast.

'Lucy, Lucy.' Zelda was smiling as she shook her head. 'This is the perfect way to end things. Jack disappears from Sebastian's life, then suddenly pops up on his television screen. It's as though all along, Jack knew Sebastian was good for one thing and one thing only – a bit of cash to help him get his career off the ground.'

Jack was nodding along. 'I'm guessing he'll try and contact me? He won't necessarily accept being ghosted.'

'We'll send him a snarky little message. *I've realised we have nothing in common and I don't see you as someone I can have a relationship with.* That type of thing. He deserves something brutal. The man ran away from a pregnancy, left me to face everything alone.'

'But it's another layer of fraud!' Lucy said.

Zelda raised a hand. 'If you'll let me finish. We'll give it a month or so, have Jack appear on screen, watch the reviewers fawn on him as he becomes the success he was born to be. Then, I'll contact Sebastian myself and return the money. Tell him Jack asked me to give it back because he wants nothing more to do with him. The father he's been wanting to meet his whole life turned out to be a massive disappointment.'

'That's perfect,' Jack said. He was looking at Zelda with wide eyes, as though awed. Lucy was aware of a tightness in her forehead. For years she believed she was the best friend Jack had – the only person besides his mother who was constantly looking out for him. Now she barely recognised him.

'I'll even throw in the wedding money,' Zelda said. 'Give everything back to him in a lump sum. A giant "fuck you".'

'He'll go on thinking Jack is his son?' Lucy asked.

Zelda's expression betrayed nothing as she turned to look at Lucy. 'Of course. A son that despises him.'

Lucy feigned a sip of Champagne, forcing herself to step outside her feelings and view the situation objectively. If Zelda returned Sebastian's money quickly, it would tie things up. He wouldn't be out of pocket, so would have less of an incentive to press charges. But the cruelty of the plan opened a chasm inside her. They'd made Sebastian feel as though he was needed, as though he was forging a family.

The only insulation against the pain would be for Sebastian to discover he wasn't Jack's biological father. Had Lucy sown enough doubt? She'd been constantly checking her phone since their lunchtime walk, hoping Sebastian might message her and share what he intended to do, telling herself they were allies of a sort. There'd been nothing.

'Text him,' Zelda said.

Lucy looked up, but Zelda was addressing Jack.

'Arrange a nice father–son drink somewhere. Just think – this'll be the very last time you have to see him.'

Jack grinned. 'I must say, I won't miss the supercilious bastard one bit.'

Chapter 29

Lucy went back to Portsmouth that weekend. Although the agency had five gigs across the Saturday and Sunday, Lucy wouldn't be acting in any of them. Will Tanner was attending a wedding in Essex, while Claudia would be having afternoon tea at the Ritz, posing as the mother of a young woman. The other three – two women and a man – were heading out on various honeytrap assignments. Lucy would have a valid reason to keep checking her phone, waiting for confirmation that everyone was home safe. Perhaps Sebastian might finally message her too.

Once she'd arrived at her parents' house and had dumped her bag in Mel's room, Lucy accompanied her father on one of his daily walks. He moved slowly along the promenade; beneath them the waves were a murky green, crashing into the shingle in bursts of white foam. In the distance, before the shoreline rounded a sharp corner, Lucy could see the cars of the Ferris wheel, looking like brightly coloured lozenges against a grey sky. They were walking against the wind and strands of hair broke free from Lucy's ponytail, whipping around her face. She felt as though her lungs were being purged, every breath of salty air stripping away London's black residues.

'Got another shot at the old treadmill test,' her father said. 'Hopefully they'll clear me to drive the taxi this time.'

'Fingers crossed.' Above Lucy came the screech of gulls, the sound of home.

'I can't go on taking your money, love.' Her father said it quietly.

'Huh?' Her father wasn't supposed to know about the grand or so a month she'd been sending her mother. Money they almost certainly needed, given that the lease payments were still due on the Hyundai, even though it had been sitting idly in the street for months.

'Your mother doesn't have it in her to fib,' her father said. 'As if I'd believe those tight buggers at the nursing home would pay her compassionate leave.'

Lucy let out a small laugh. But she was fighting a sense of desolation. Every time she'd seen a payment to her mother going out, she'd felt a tiny pang of relief. She was helping from afar. Part of her was still good, in spite of what she was doing to Sebastian.

'But I want to help.' Lucy was aware that her father was becoming out of breath, so she steered him towards the long stone bench of the war memorial, just as the sun found a gap in the clouds. 'Let's rest for a few minutes.'

Her father grunted with relief as he took a seat. 'You need to be building a nest egg for yourself, sweetheart. Acting work comes and goes, doesn't it? I'm so proud you're having a good run. But you earned that money. You should be the one to enjoy it.'

There had been nothing substantial for her parents to watch her in, not for years. Yet still, they'd found it within

themselves to believe Lucy was an actor. They were so determined to think well of her. She didn't deserve it, not at all.

'I failed as an actor,' she said. 'The last thing I did was that
god-awful milk advert.'

'You were great in that, love. Had me totally convinced.'

'But I'm trying to tell you – that was the very last time I
acted professionally. The work I've had on lately, it's been . . .
different.'

Her father looked at her, saying nothing as he took her
hand inside his own gloved paw. She noticed his cheek bones,
newly prominent now he'd lost weight. He looked younger,
but somehow more grave.

'Why aren't you disappointed?' Lucy said at last.

He gave her hand a squeeze. 'You've always worked so hard.
And you've been brave, going after things that your mother
and I couldn't even dream of.'

'But I failed. I spent most of the last decade pulling pints
and now—' Lucy hesitated, but only for a second. She needed
her father to see what she was. Part of her craved his disapproval, wanted to feel the pain of it twisting inside her. If she
could look in his face and see disgust, she might begin to feel
as though she was atoning.

'I run my own business selling deception,' Lucy said.
'Hiring out actors to do all kinds of nasty things.'

Her father wrinkled his forehead. 'I don't—'

She held his gaze. 'Are you a sad loser who can't get a partner? I'll find you an actor to impersonate one. Want to cause
trouble for a business rival? Send me along to a meeting and
we'll humiliate him for money.'

Her father's eyes were welling up and Lucy felt a sudden

terror. She'd gone too far. He was supposed to be avoiding stress.

'You've started a business?' His voice was filled with wonder.

Lucy exhaled. 'The irony is, I'm raking it in. After all these years, I've finally made acting pay.'

'But that's wonderful.'

Lucy listened to the sound of the waves crashing into the shingle; a sudden boom, followed by an extended rattle as the water dragged along the stones, back into the sea. What would it take to make her father understand what she really was? 'I earned it by being a liar, Dad. Creating a liars' agency. Liars for hire.'

'Isn't that what acting is, though? Pretending. Making people believe you?' her father asked with a smile.

Lucy swallowed. She'd been self-indulgent, laying her worries at her father's feet. It wasn't his responsibility to punish her, to force her to extricate herself from this mess. 'I don't think Florence Pugh offers herself out for targeted deception like I do,' she said. 'You probably wouldn't catch her playing the paramour of a dirty old man.'

Her father let go of her hand and wrapped an arm around her shoulders. The gesture was so unexpected, so comforting that Lucy could feel her eyes stinging with tears.

'Tell me this,' her father said. 'If you'd retrained as a teacher, do you think you'd be sorted for life? Able to buy a house. Support a family?'

Lucy sighed. 'Probably not.'

'And who exactly would have been up in arms about that? Do you think anyone would be outraged at how society failed you, letting you rack up debt just so you can earn enough money to get by?'

'No.'

A woman with a black Labrador walked along the memorial, glancing at the names carved into the stone. The dog paused to sniff at Lucy's legs and she reached down to stroke the top of its head.

'No one else is looking out for you, my sweet,' Lucy's father said. 'Just your family. And it's not like we're in a position to do anything for you.'

'When did you become so cynical?'

Her father tightened his grip around her shoulders. 'I'm not saying you should do what you like, to hell with other people. But the system's rigged, Lucy. You can be brilliant and still have nothing to show for it. Nothing wrong with trying to play the game on your own terms.'

Lucy swallowed the saliva pooling in her mouth. 'I'm just not sure it's right.'

'You're a smart cookie, Lucy. You've found a way to make money. I'm sure you'll be able to figure everything else out too.' He eased himself up off the bench. 'Let's go back. It's freezing.'

Later that evening, in Mel's room, Lucy told her sister about the conversation she'd had with their father. The two of them were sitting on Mel's single bed while Mel rolled a joint. It was a tidy room with apricot walls covered in plastic-framed photos of Charlie at every stage of his life: swaddled and pink, progressing to gummy smiles, then teetering around in the garden wearing a woolly hat. Next to the bed was a tiny desk with a lamp and a small pile of books. The chair had been moved onto the landing so that Lucy's airbed could fit on the floor.

Charlie was asleep in Lucy's old room, and their parents were downstairs watching a police procedural.

'I can't believe you told Dad everything. Did he think you were confessing to being a prostitute?' Mel reached over to open her bedroom window, then lit the joint and took a long drag, blowing the smoke outside.

'Surprisingly, no.' Lucy motioned for her sister to pass her the joint. 'He was actually very supportive. Unlike some.'

'I've been supportive,' Mel said.

Lucy took several long pulls on the joint, then started to giggle.

'Jesus,' Mel said. 'The absolute state of you.'

'The thing is,' Lucy said, 'some days I fucking love it – I mean, I built my own business. There's something so satisfying about taking cash from image-obsessed people.'

Mel nodded. They heard footsteps coming up the stairs towards the bathroom.

There was a light knock at the door. 'Are you girls *smoking* in there?' their mother hissed.

'No,' Mel called. She looked at Lucy who doubled over trying to keep her laughter inside.

'You better not be,' their mother hissed. 'You're supposed to be grown-ups.'

The sisters listened in silence as their mother retreated from Mel's door. They heard the clink of the bathroom light going on, then Lucy's phone buzzed. It was a text from Jack.

I'm meeting Sebastian for a drink tomorrow. How much
should I ask for? Thinking 10k

Lucy felt the skin across her forehead tightening. The light-
ness of Jack's message astounded her. She handed the joint
back to Mel and tapped out a reply.

It's fraud, Jack. You can't do it. Even if Zelda gives the
money back, you're still guilty of a crime.

How could he not see the danger he was putting himself in?
A text came straight back. Even this was different; normally they'd call and speak to one another.

I'm going to see this through. After that you can run the
agency however you like

Lucy stared at her phone. She expected to feel upset, but
instead was aware of a rising anger. There was something so
patronising, so intolerant in Jack's tone, as though she was an
annoyance, someone to be placated.

'Everything all right?' Mel stubbed the joint out against
the exterior of the house and buried the butt in the tiny bin
beneath her desk.

Maybe it was the weed, maybe it was her sense of alienation
from Jack, but Lucy found herself telling Mel the whole sordid
tale of Zelda and their deception of Sebastian. She nearly mentioned the kiss, but at the last moment she hesitated – she was
desperate to hold the memory tight, to keep it vivid and safe
inside her. It might be all she and Sebastian would ever have.

Mel managed to refrain from interrupting, but her frown deepened as Lucy recounted the wedding deposit and everything that followed. She omitted the discovery of Jack's lies, the bomb detonated inside their friendship. Jack had made her swear to keep his bisexuality secret.

'I'm going to talk to a solicitor, formally dissolve mine and Jack's business partnership,' Lucy concluded. She'd previously harboured a hope that he might remain a silent partner, that they might audition new actors together here and there. But this evening's text exchange had clarified something important for Lucy. The agency was *hers*.

Still, Mel remained silent.

Lucy couldn't help laughing. 'I suppose you think I've become a rabid capitalist?'

Mel exhaled. 'That thing with Sebastian, though ...'

'It's sickening, I know. I never should have agreed to it.'

Mel lay back, head on her pillow. 'You need to put an ethical framework over everything. Get really specific about the kind of work you will and won't take on. I mean, in future, impersonating a biological child is probably something you'll rule out, no?'

Lucy lay down next to her sister, looking up at the white artexed swirls of the ceiling, feeling Mel's plait against her cheek. She couldn't help thinking of the awful man who'd wanted her to impersonate a social worker. There would perhaps be more enquiries like that as the agency grew. Sinister requests that made her afraid. 'I know I need to tighten up. But people aren't always candid about why they're hiring us.'

Mel rolled onto her side, her eyes boring into Lucy's face.

'You're entitled to ask your clients questions. To apply any ethics test you want.'

'They aren't always going to be straight with me, though.'

Mel ran her tongue over her teeth. 'I say this with love, Luce, but it sounds to me like you're wallowing a little.'

'It's not as straightforward . . .'

'It could be. You've got every right to assure yourself you're not being drawn into anything unsavoury. I'm sure most clients won't mind answering a few questions, or even signing a formal agreement with you, for that matter. It's basic due diligence.'

'I suppose you're right.' Why did Lucy always feel so scolded when she spent time with Mel?

Her phone went. She snatched it up. Abigail confirmed her target had weakened and kissed her; she had a recording of the whole exchange, and now she was in a taxi on her way home. Lucy tapped out an acknowledgement, then opened up her text history with Sebastian. She found herself hoping there'd be a message she'd somehow missed. But there was nothing new.

Chapter 30

On the slow Sunday stopping service back to London the next day, Lucy tried to work. The honeytrap campaign was still bringing in an astonishing amount of business; most clients wanted a second actor to be in the vicinity, ready to snap pictures or video footage that could be used in divorce proceedings.

She spent the journey tackling her email backlog, pinging out texts to the actors on her roster, trying to match availability with the times targets would be heading out for after-work drinks or attending parties. There were also backstories to memorise for her own assignments, and Lucy filled out index cards with key details, preparing to drill herself before bed. Tomorrow, she and Jack were to be mourners at a funeral. *Dennis. A political historian. Occasional contributor to* The New Left Review *and* New Statesman. *Home in Islington. Passionate mentor to young intellectuals.* The following weekend she was doing another turn as Holly, accompanying Adam to the rabbit shoot while trying to gather intelligence on George, specifically any upcoming events he'd be attending without his wife.

What *was* she going to do about Sebastian? There was

no way she could let him go for that drink with Jack and be guilted into providing an allowance. But what were her options? Even as she asked herself the question, Lucy realised the answer had been with her the whole time, sitting heavily in her gut. The truth. It was time to tell Sebastian the truth.

Sebastian buzzed her into his building and was holding his front door open as she climbed the sweeping staircase. 'Lucy?'

She'd come straight from Waterloo in her jeans that were fraying at the bottom, rucksack over her shoulder. No trace of Lucy-the-fiancée. She stood before him as her real self.

'Sorry for disturbing you. Can I come in?' There was a tremulous quality to her voice; she sounded so young, even to her own ears.

Sebastian's forehead was creased. 'Of course. Is Jack not with you?'

'No.'

'I'm meeting him for a drink in an hour.'

'Yeah. I know.' Lucy brushed past him and headed into the sitting room, hesitating for a moment, then sitting down on the sofa, clasping her hands tightly in her lap. There was a ringing in her ears.

Sebastian sat down in his armchair. He was wearing jeans with a plain black jumper, navy-blue slipper boots on his feet. On the coffee table was a tray bearing a few remnants of pasta and tomato sauce that filled the room with a tang of garlic.

'Are you going to ask for a DNA test?' Lucy asked.

Sebastian bit his lower lip. 'I can't. Not yet.'

There was only one thing left to do. She felt her body tense, as though even now, she was trying to hold the words inside.

'I actually need to get going fairly soon.' Sebastian looked at his watch. 'Are you joining us?'

Lucy shook her head. 'Listen. There's something I need to tell you.'

It was as if Sebastian hadn't heard her. He hopped up to retrieve his shoes from the rack in the hallway then sat back down, trying to tug off one of his slippers, his hands suddenly clumsy. 'I don't want to be late.'

'Sebastian, I'm so sorry. I really am.'

He looked up, meeting her eye and then recoiling, as though he'd seen something that disturbed him. His mouth was open and Lucy caught the slightest tremor of his lower lip as he bent down to fuss at his shoes. He seemed to know she was about to tell him something appalling, something he wasn't ready to hear.

'I'm really sorry to be the one to tell you this. But Jack isn't your son. He's an actor. We both are. Zelda hired us to deceive you.' There. It was done.

Only the tiniest flexing of his jaw indicated Sebastian had heard. He was holding his shoe mid-air, the tendons of his hand protruding as he gripped it tightly. 'I don't understand,' he said. 'I mean – I know Jack's an actor. It's pretty much all he talks about.'

Lucy felt as though she might vomit. She tried holding the sensation at bay with deep breaths. Clarity was the only kindness she could offer. 'Jack's been performing for *you*, Sebastian. You don't have a son. Zelda miscarried, or so she said. She cooked up this whole pretence and hired me and Jack to act in it.' Even as she said the words, Lucy was conscious of trying to absolve herself, to put all the culpability on Zelda. She remembered the envelopes of cash she'd taken, the satisfying weight of them in her hand.

Sebastian stood up. Took a couple of steps towards the door, then wheeled around and paced in the other direction.

Finally, he stopped and faced her. 'You're telling me the truth?'

Lucy stood up and placed a hand on his arm, but he pulled away from her. 'I'm so sorry, Sebastian.'

'You let me believe I was a *father*? And I'm not?' He said it in a whisper, but his eyes were fixed on her and they were shouting.

'I can't tell you how sorry I am. We never should have gone along with it.' Lucy tamped down the urge to mention how broke she'd been at the time.

'So, who exactly are you, then?' Sebastian said at last. 'And why are you doing this?' His wide-eyed stare made Lucy feel monstrous.

She inhaled. Tried to steady herself. 'My name really is Lucy. A big chunk of what I've told you is true. Jack and I were friends at uni, studying acting. But we're not a couple. And I don't have a tidy little PR job. I'm a failed actor who set up an impersonation agency.' She was unbearably hot. She shrugged her arms out of her parka and threw it down on the sofa.

'You do this for a living? Deceive people for money?' Sebastian's upper lip was curling. He was disgusted.

'No! I mean, most of the time it's straightforward. A client might want a plus one to go to a party. Or, a salesperson might want an enthusiastic audience member to attend a presentation.' Lucy's voice cracked. She refused to cry. She was perhaps giving Sebastian the most devastating news of his life; she could not make this about her.

'Does Jack know you're telling me this?' Sebastian rubbed at his cheeks.

Lucy shook her head. *Jack.* How would she find the words to tell him what she'd done?

'Does Zelda?'

They were standing so close, she could hear Sebastian's breaths sliding in and out. 'No.'

'Then why are you here?' He sounded defeated.

'Zelda had a plan. They – we – have been building up to Jack rejecting you. I thought the truth would be less hurtful.' Lucy placed a hand on Sebastian's back and this time he did let her touch him. He bowed his head and was very still, as though trying his hardest not to cry.

After a moment of silence, Lucy tried to compose herself. Sebastian deserved every scrap of the truth. Nothing should be omitted or remain hidden. 'At the start, Zelda fed us this story about you knowing she was pregnant, saying you scarpered in the dead of night.'

She heard Sebastian's breath catch.

'I don't believe her. Not any more,' Lucy quickly added. What *had* happened between them? Now probably wasn't the moment to ask, but Zelda's behaviour confused her. Lucy had been certain she'd seen regret, or at least hesitation on the woman's face. Yet at other moments, her determination to hurt her former partner had appeared almost frightening in its single-mindedness.

Sebastian was shaking his head, eyes closed. More than

anything, Lucy wanted him to put his arms around her and tell her she was forgiven. But such a thing was impossible.

'You made me think it was real,' Sebastian said at last.

Lucy's eyes were stinging. 'I'm so sorry. Zelda told us you knew about the baby. She said you disappeared in the middle of the night and left her money for an abortion.'

Sebastian's eyes widened. For a moment, he was entirely still, not even breathing. 'What a thing to say. I'd never do anything like that.'

Lucy was conscious of her fingers on Sebastian's back. She'd let her hand rest there as long as possible; after this, he'd probably never let her touch him again. 'Why do you think she wants to hurt you so badly?'

He searched her face. She could smell the spiced wood of his aftershave, feel the pull of his lips. 'You must think I'm a total idiot,' he said.

'If I could go back, I'd handle things very differently.' The words tangled in Lucy's throat. Her nose was starting to run and the tears were pushing through. She'd remember this moment forever. Unveiling her real self and watching Sebastian recoil. Knowing she was sundering herself from Jack, would never be forgiven for this betrayal. How would she go on, knowing the people she cared about, the people she most wanted to help, scorned the affection that bloomed inside her?

Sebastian continued observing her closely. Lucy-the-fiancée's composure, her pretty manners, were all gone. Without them, Lucy felt painfully exposed. She drew back, finally removing her hand. Now it was done, she wanted to hide herself, retreat into her shame.

Reaching out, Sebastian grazed her cheek with the back of his knuckle. Lucy froze. He seemed to recognise how unsettled she was and a faint smile played at his mouth. Then, with a sudden motion, as if he had resolved something within himself, he leaned in and kissed her.

At first, Lucy was too stunned to react. Then she was kissing him back, her arms around his neck. His lips were soft, but he pressed against her with unexpected urgency. She could feel his teeth and beneath his aftershave she could smell his skin – a sweet, earthy scent that imprinted itself in her memory.

She fumbled at his belt buckle and in a single, swift motion he lifted her off her feet. There was that moan – just like before, soft, but urgent – it crackled through Lucy's every nerve ending. She wrapped her legs around him as he carried her through to the kitchen, setting her down on the granite countertop. It was going to happen. Lucy was about to have the thing she wanted most. She kissed him hungrily, pausing only to remove her top and throw it to the floor.

Sebastian's hands roved over her middle as he kissed her. But then he stopped, stepping back, a single finger tracing the outline of her ribs. He was looking at her body not with desire, but with what seemed like a crushing sadness.

'I can't do this,' he said, dropping his hands to his sides. 'I'm sorry.'

'You can.' She pulled him towards her, so forcefully he almost lost his balance. 'Please.'

He reached out, running his finger along the jut of her collarbone. Was he weakening? She tried to transmit with her eyes, just how much she wanted him to go on touching her. But he bent down to pick up the top she'd thrown to the floor and placed it on the counter next to her. She was being dismissed.

Lucy's face burned with humiliation as she dressed herself. Sebastian was careful not to look at her, walking over to the sink and staring into it for a few moments. She deserved this rejection, how could she have even dreamed otherwise?

He lifted his head, wheeled around to face her. 'I'm not ready to . . . Jesus, I'm supposed to be meeting Jack. I've got to go.'

'You're still going to meet him?' Lucy tried to read his face, but Sebastian's expression had become impassive.

'Are you going to have it out with him?' she asked, dread trickling down her spine.

He shook his head. 'I just . . . I'm not ready to . . . '

'Sebastian. Jack's an actor. He's going to sit there, pretending to be your son.'

Sebastian bit his lower lip. Looked down at the gleaming floor tiles. 'You coming here, everything you've told me – it's so unexpected.'

'But it's over now. You know the truth.'

He shook his head. 'I need time to think before I decide what to do. I need to find out what Zelda's up to.'

'She just wants to make you suffer. She's unhinged.'

'There must be more to it.' Sebastian placed a hand on Lucy's shoulder. 'You did a good thing, telling me. I won't forget. But please, can you keep this conversation to yourself? Just for a little while.'

Lucy stared at him. 'I don't understand.'

He attempted a laugh, but it sounded more like a defeated sigh. 'I'm not sure I do either. I'm just not ready to stop being Jack's father. I mean – fuck – I just . . . '

'You're going to let Jack go on deceiving you?'

Sebastian flexed his fingers at his sides, then balled them into fists. 'I need to let everything sink in. I'm not ready to have a big confrontation tonight.'

Coldness wound its way around Lucy's middle. 'You'll break down. You'll watch him acting for you and you won't be able to handle it.'

'I'll just have to do my best.' He turned and walked back into the sitting room to resume putting his shoes on.

Lucy followed him. 'Sebastian, he's going to ask you for money.'

He glanced up at her, then shrugged. 'Look, I know it sounds weird, but please, Lucy, let me go on pretending to be duped. Just for a little while. Just until I know what I want to do. You owe me that at least.'

There was nothing Lucy could do but nod her consent. She'd given him the truth. He had every right to do whatever he wanted with it.

Back at her flat in Greenwich, she worked into the night, keeping the sound on her phone. Any moment, she expected the call. Jack shouting down the line, telling her there'd been a scene in the pub. He'd be furious with her. Indignant that she'd betrayed him, then let him walk into a confrontation.

Over the past couple of months she'd laid trap after trap on behalf of her clients. Arranged for husbands to encounter pretty women who made them feel interesting and funny.

Now it was Lucy's dearest friend who was walking into a deception.

The night stretched on and no message came; the silence made her deeply uneasy.

Chapter 31

It was a perfect day for a funeral. Leaden sky and a fine drizzle that gusted under Lucy's umbrella and sat in little beads on the wool of her black coat. She was waiting at the entrance to the West London Crematorium, standing by the iron railings as traffic whooshed past, stirring up clouds of spray. On the other side of the road was a play park where mothers hunched beneath their hoods while toddlers in bright-coloured water-proofs played noisily, their happy screams carrying across to the cemetery.

Jack pulled up in a cab. He looked dashing in the black suit and tie he'd charged to the agency; his dark hair was ruffled, but stylishly so. He greeted Lucy with a half-hearted smile, a wan echo of what their friendship had once been. Something tightened around Lucy's heart. She'd betrayed him, made it impossible for things to be as they once were.

'How'd it go with Sebastian last night?' Lucy asked as they walked through the entrance, following the path to the crematorium. She was aware of her heart thudding, an un-comfortable squeezing in her bowels.

'Good,' Jack said. 'He shelled out the money.'

Lucy faltered, stopping in the middle of the path. Sebastian allowing the pretence to go on was odd enough. But to give Jack money? It didn't make sense.

'Are you sure?' she said.

Jack took hold of her umbrella, positioning it over them both, steering her forward with a hand on the small of her back.

'Yes, I'm sure. Fuck's sake, I'm trying to stay in role,' he hissed.

'But did he take much persuading?'

'Not really. Ten grand is nothing to someone like him.'

'But . . .'

'Let me concentrate.'

Lucy walked on in silence. It didn't feel right. True, Sebastian probably wouldn't feel the lack of ten grand the way a normal person would. But he'd known Jack was lying. How had he been able to tolerate going through the motions, acting as though he was still ignorant of the pretence? And why endure such a thing?

'*How* exactly did he give you the money? He'd need your real name for a bank transfer.'

'Lucy! Do you want me here today or not?'

'Of course, I . . .'

'Then, please, let me focus. I'm trying to feel my way into grief for Dennis.'

Lucy exhaled. Jack was right, they should be focussing on the job at hand. She tried to push Sebastian from her mind with a quick mental recap of everything she knew about their deceased client. She'd never met him, but in the emails from his hospital bed he'd been very specific about the effect he wanted at his funeral, asking to see photographs of Lucy and Jack so he could assure himself they had the 'right look'.

The hearse was already outside the crematorium and a small cluster of mourners was waiting to go in. Jack closed the umbrella and handed it back to Lucy before homing in on a bald man, about fifty or so with very upright posture. 'You must be Edward?' Jack shook the man's hand. 'I'm so sorry for your loss. Your uncle had such a profound effect on me. I don't know what I'll do ...' He broke off, appearing to struggle with his emotions. The performance was as naturalistic as ever, a small moment of artistry.

Lucy moved forward. Already tears were coursing down her face. She'd purposefully worn waterproof mascara and forgone eyeliner. 'Your uncle was such a formative influence on me. He really shaped how I see the world. I owe him so much.'

The nephew nodded, eyes darting over to Jack who'd rested his forearm against one of the tall pillars at the front of the building, as though trying and failing to compose himself.

'Thank you so much for coming along.' The nephew's voice was deep, filled with decorum, but his eyes were rapidly scanning her face in confusion.

Lucy went over to Jack, giving him a comforting hug before they stepped inside the building. Would this really be the last time? There was something so heartbreaking in impersonating best friends, replicating the ease they'd once shared. As soon as Jack realised she'd gone behind his back, he'd cast her off like a pair of scuffed shoes. Nothing she'd done had ever succeeded in making him care for her the way she'd cared for him. She'd poured all the love and affection she had for

Peter into Jack, and he'd let her, as though he recognised she needed something to fix and he could be the beneficiary.

The chapel was in a wood-panelled room with rows of highly polished pews, most of which were empty – there were only four other mourners dotted around inside. Gentle organ music emanated from speakers mounted on the ceiling. Had Peter's funeral been like this? Even after a decade, it still distressed Lucy that she hadn't been invited, hadn't known when or where it had taken place. Would it have helped her to attend a ceremony, to have cried and told his grandparents how much Peter meant to her? Their friendship was something unfinished in her life, an ache at her temples, a whispering voice. She was afraid that if she ever stopped being sad, she'd no longer be able to summon her friend's presence.

Lucy and Jack sat together, choosing a pew towards the middle. As she dabbed beneath her eyes with a tissue, she was aware of the other mourners glancing at her and Jack in turn, as if trying to place them.

She put her arm around Jack, leaned in as though she was about to whisper words of reassurance. 'Did Sebastian give you cash?'

'No,' Jack replied quietly. As irritated as he must be, Lucy knew he wouldn't lash out, he'd preserve his grief-stricken demeanour to the very end.

'*How*, then?' Lucy whispered.

'Zelda set me up an account under the name of Jack Hutchison.'

'How did she manage that?' Lucy didn't know much about banking, but she was pretty sure you couldn't set up an account under any old name.

'Drop it.' Jack's voice was a low growl.

Lucy had promised Sebastian she'd say nothing. It was the only promise she'd made him as her real self. But didn't Jack have a right to know that his cover was blown?

The organ music stopped. Everyone shuffled to their feet as the undertakers brought the coffin in. It was a heavy-looking mahogany affair, covered in floral wreaths. Poor Dennis had evidently spent a lot of money on his funeral and Lucy couldn't help feeling a profound sadness that there were so few people to absorb the carefully curated effect.

The mourners were invited to sing 'All Things Bright and Beautiful'. A white-haired lady read a Christina Rossetti poem. Then the nephew stood up to give a eulogy. Dennis had used the word 'keening' in his instructions, so as the nephew read from a crumpled sheet of paper, Lucy's sobs intensified, building to a low moan. Jack was audibly fighting for breath, pausing every now and then only to blow his nose.

Lucy was aware of the turning heads. Of the nephew faltering as he looked over at them then struggled to regain his place in his speech. *This is what Dennis wanted,* she insisted to herself as she cradled her head in her hands and brought forth more sobs, her whole body shuddering as she imagined telling Peter her friendship with Jack had died, picturing his blue eyes laden with sympathy as he listened. He'd say something wise, something comforting. *Focus on what this friendship brought to your life. You got to be a Londoner. You rehearsed for hours, honing your craft with someone who was committed to being the best. Just because it's ended doesn't make it a failure.* Lucy heard Peter's words inside her head and wept with ease.

She and Jack cried their way to the end, building to a

crescendo as a switch was pressed and a grey curtain slowly surrounded the coffin. There was to be no wake, which was fortunate as already Lucy felt weakened by the grief she'd pulled from the depths of her body.

When it was time to file outside, the other mourners approached her and Jack in pairs, eyes lit with unseemly curiosity. *Did you know Dennis well?*

She and Jack reeled off their fake histories, wiping their eyes. *I contacted him after reading his work. Such an astute political thinker – it still astounds me that he was so under-appreciated. He took it upon himself to mentor me, gave me hours of his time. Wrote the reference that got me into LSE. His work has shaped so many lives.*

The drizzle had eased off by the time they made their way back down the path. Lucy held on to Jack's arm and together they walked slowly, as though reverently contemplating Dennis and his legacy, committed to the performance until they could be certain they were out of sight.

'So this is it,' Lucy said. 'Your last impersonation.'

'Yep. I was thinking I might still use the office now and then as a rehearsal space, if you're cool with that?'

Lucy swallowed, trying to rid her mouth of a sour taste. He'd said nothing of her. Given no promises of drinks here and there or invitations for her to visit him on set.

'Maybe it's best if I buy you out of the agency,' she said. 'I could get a solicitor to draw up an agreement.' Her legs felt shaky. Was this her being spiteful? No, this was what asser-tiveness felt like. If all Jack cared about was the office, then it was only right to detach from him completely. Lucy would take sole responsibility from now on.

He shot her a surprised glance. 'We don't need to make things so formal, do we?'

Even now, to hurt Jack was to hurt herself. Lucy could feel sharp stabs of confusion in the pit of her stomach. 'You'll be so busy, with *Heart Street* and any opportunities that follow on from that.'

For a time, Jack said nothing. Amid her anxiety, Lucy felt an unfamiliar pride at the idea of the agency becoming fully her own, any suggestion of reliance on Jack gone. It wasn't wrong to insist on something for herself. She was only taking what he didn't want.

'You don't need to pay me anything,' Jack said at last. He wasn't going to argue, then. Had she expected him to plead with her? No. But she'd wanted something more, a quiver, a slight hesitation, or perhaps most of all some kind of concern around how often they'd see one another.

Lucy bit the inside of her cheek. 'It's your money. We can negotiate the final figure, but I was thinking twenty grand would be fair.' On paper, the business would probably be worth more than double that. But Lucy had put in so many more hours than Jack: hiring new actors, screening the enquiries, drafting the ad copy.

'Just give me five,' Jack said. 'We'll call it back rent for the months you spent on my sofa.'

Lucy swallowed. She caught herself scanning Jack for some sign of resistance. Or at least recognition that something profound was ending. Something that had shaped him as well as her. It didn't come.

'Deal,' she said at last.

Chapter 32

Since neither of them disputed the terms, the process of dissolving their business partnership proved straightforward. Lucy hired a solicitor to draw up an agreement, and she and Jack attended a ten-minute appointment to sign the papers. They headed to the office after, so Jack could retrieve a couple of the photographic prints he wanted to reclaim for his flat.

They walked through Chinatown as the lunchtime rush was beginning, weaving their way past tourists pausing to look at the menu boards outside restaurants, or holding their phones aloft to take in the red lanterns and the Chinese characters on the restaurant signs. The distinct smell of durian fruit lingered in the air and a busker was strumming a guitar, singing 'Wish You Were Here' by Pink Floyd.

Jack gabbled on about *Heart Street*. Although rehearsals hadn't started yet, he'd been invited on set a couple of times and was now rating his castmates, highlighting the inadequacies of their performances one actor at a time.

Lucy laughed in the right places, murmured sympathetically when it was required of her. She was performing friendship rather than really feeling it, and she wasn't even sure Jack noticed the difference.

'Has Sebastian been in touch at all?' she asked as they turned into the alley leading to their building.

'No. It's all in Zelda's hands now. She'll contact him when the time's right.' There was an impatient quality to his voice and Lucy felt a sharp pang. They'd shared more than most couples – having him yell at her would be so much easier to bear than these moments of clipped tension.

When they reached the peeling blue side door to the office, Lucy unlocked it with the heaviest of her set of keys. 'We're still friends, right?' she asked.

A pained expression settled between Jack's eyes. 'Of course. What makes you ask that?'

'You know. The solicitors. The dissolution agreement.' Lucy nearly added, *Peter, the lies*, but the previous weeks had told her this would be met with a curt 'No, Lucy' and a furrowing of Jack's brow.

She clomped up the narrow staircase, the bare floorboards creaking beneath her feet. There was no banister, and she placed a hand against the cold exterior wall for support.

'It did seem a little over the top,' Jack said.

'I just thought it was important to have clarity.'

'I wasn't going to swoop in and demand half the profits.'

'I know.' They reached the second-floor landing and Lucy opened up the office.

She put the kettle on and made them both cups of instant coffee while Jack stood on her desk to take down the framed photographs of Tower Bridge and Borough Market. The wall looked strangely uneven without them there in between the shots of the London Eye and the birds' eye view of the river.

Would he stay to drink his coffee? She'd made him one

without thinking and now the idea of him walking off without drinking it seemed devastating.

The buzzer went. Jack automatically walked over and pressed the button to release the outer door, even though Lucy wasn't expecting anyone. She heard more than one set of footsteps on the stairs. There was no rational reason for her unease, but she felt a pang of foreboding so sharp, she had to place a steadying hand against the draining board.

Two policemen stepped into the office. A middle-aged man wearing a turban and a slim youth with a constellation of acne across his cheeks.

'Good morning,' the older man said. 'I'm Sergeant Singh, and this here is PC Gayle. We're hoping to speak with a Jack Moreton.'

Jack was standing in the centre of the room, holding the two framed photographs against his chest. 'That's me.' His eyes widened. Were they here to inform him of a death?

'Super. We wanted to have a little chat with you,' Sergeant Singh said.

'What's this about?' There was a slight tremor in Jack's voice.

The sergeant glanced at Lucy with a cocked eyebrow.

'It's all right,' Jack said. 'We can talk in front of Lucy.'

The officer faced Jack square on. He wasn't smiling but he still managed to look cheerful with his glowing eyes and relaxed forehead. His radio crackled, a female voice saying something incomprehensible. 'We're investigating an allegation of fraud.'

There was a moment of silence. Lucy felt light-headed, too many thoughts rising up all at once, shouting inside her head, a cacophony of sound. Jack's skin had become dangerously pale. His eyes had a faraway look, as though the reality of what was happening hadn't fully hit him yet. This had to be about the ten-grand 'allowance'.

'Are you arresting him?' Lucy said quietly. This couldn't be happening. Jack had been idiotic, true, but he hadn't coveted the money, it had been transferred into an account he didn't even have access to.

Sergeant Singh turned to look at Lucy. She felt a tingling in her chest as she realised she might be arrested too. There was the wedding deposit – she hadn't managed to persuade Sebastian to get it refunded.

'No,' the policeman said. 'At this stage we're inviting him for a voluntary interview. A chat at the station to clear a few things up.'

'Now?' Jack said. 'Do I have to come now?'

'It doesn't necessarily have to be right now,' Sergeant Singh replied. He looked mildly irritated, as though he had in fact hoped to put his questions to Jack there and then.

'You should get a solicitor, Jack,' Lucy said. They'd both been extras in police dramas often enough to know you should only ever be interviewed with a solicitor present.

Sergeant Singh handed Jack a card. 'Call the station in the next couple of days. We can arrange a time for you to come in. And yes, you are very welcome to attend with a solicitor.'

'What is it you do here?' The younger officer's eyes were roving around the office.

'We're an actors' agency.' Lucy said it defiantly. Just let them say something about escorting, just let them try it.

The officer smirked, then he and his colleague turned and left.

Lucy and Jack remained standing exactly as they were, listening to the creaking of the stairs, hearing the muffled *whump* of the outside door closing.

'Shit!' One of the framed photographs Jack was holding slid to the floor, its glass shattering.

They didn't have a dustpan, so Lucy bent down gathering up the largest shards with her fingers and placing them in the bin. Jack remained completely still, watching her.

She placed a hand on his arm. 'It'll be okay.'

Slowly, he turned to look at her, wearing a solemn expression she'd never seen before. 'What a ridiculous thing to say.'

Her desk phone rang and Lucy answered it reflexively. 'Impersonation Services. How can I help?'

'Ah, hello. Rachel Clough here. You set a honeytrap for my husband last weekend.'

Lucy felt her cheeks become hot. Why had she answered? Jack could be arrested. Lucy, too. 'Hello, Mrs Clough. Do you mind if I—'

'I've been looking at the photographs from the weekend, and honestly that woman you sent was far too good-looking. Ashley didn't stand a chance, really. I'm not sure it was a fair test.'

'Right ... maybe we could ... '

Jack was staring at her, eyes wide, a slight wrinkling around his nose. She really should have let the call go to voicemail.

'So, we'll try again,' Mrs Clough continued. 'But this time I'd like you to use an ordinary-looking woman.'

Somehow Lucy got through the call, keeping her eyes on Jack as she confirmed a second booking, agreeing that the actor used wouldn't be too pretty or too thin. Poor Ashley wouldn't know what to make of this recent run of women snogging him in pubs. When Lucy finally hung up, she rubbed at her eyes.

Jack placed his unbroken picture down on the armchair, then walked over to the kitchenette and downed the coffee Lucy had made. 'I suppose I'd better call my father. He'll know the best person to hire.'

Lucy nodded. Her mouth had become intolerably dry, so she crossed the room and drank half her own cold coffee. She tried to give Jack a hug, searching desperately for words of reassurance, but he shook her off.

'I need to get this over with.' He stepped out onto the landing, cradling his phone in his palm.

Returning to her desk, Lucy called Adam. 'Hi. Listen, I'm so sorry to tap you up for legal advice again, but the situation with Zelda that I told you about has kind of escalated. At least, I'm pretty sure that's what's happened.'

'Go on.' There was no trace of irritation in his tone.

In a low voice, she told him about the police visit. About how Zelda had tasked Jack with asking Sebastian for money, assuring them she'd return it after a brief interlude. How Lucy had confessed everything to Sebastian, but he'd given Jack ten grand anyway. 'I don't know quite what Zelda's playing at. But I've had this feeling – sometimes the way she looks at Jack – it unsettles me.'

'So you think this Zelda might have reported Jack?' Adam asked.

Lucy glanced at the door. Still closed. No sign of Jack. 'It couldn't have been Sebastian. I mean, he knew the truth. But Zelda didn't know he knew. Fuck! I know this must sound like such a farce.' Adam was a client. He needed to trust her professionalism.

'Take a breath for a moment. If the police ask to interview you, or arrest you, then you need to hire a solicitor and have them handle everything. Don't be tempted to try and clear things up on your own.'

'Okay.'

'The most helpful thing you could do in the meantime, is write out a timeline of events for Jack's solicitor. When Zelda commissioned you, what the brief was. Sebastian knowing Jack was an actor could be crucial.'

Lucy nodded. 'Thank you. I really appreciate your advice.'

'No problem at all. You were magnificent at the weekend, by the way.'

Despite herself, she smiled at the memory. 'Holly' had worn a Barbour and hadn't flinched at the sight of bleeding rabbit carcasses being swung along by their feet. No one besides George had any suspicion that she wasn't who she said she was. She felt a stirring of pride, quickly followed by the most crushing guilt – Jack was in trouble.

'I'm briefing everyone this week. We'll be all set for Goodwood.' She hoped this panicked call hadn't given Adam cause to doubt her abilities.

'I'm still not sure it'll work.'

'We'll give it our best shot. Danielle, the actor I've lined up, is gorgeous.' She'd been the one to weaken the resolve of Mrs Clough's husband – and she'd done so in under ten minutes.

'Okay. Well, we'll finalise everything later in the week. If there are any developments with the police, then do call, any time.'

'Thanks, Adam. That's really good of you.'

After hanging up, Lucy laid her head down on her desk. She found herself recounting each and every meeting with Zelda. The malevolent glint in her eye when she spoke of *turning up the dial*. How satisfied she'd appeared, sharing a takeaway on Jack's sofa. Zelda had seemed so smitten with Jack. Nothing made sense. But if Lucy didn't get a grasp of the situation, and quickly, Jack could be in serious trouble.

Chapter 33

Lucy was about to start writing out a timeline of her Zelda meetings, when Jack came back through the office door. Now the initial shock had passed, his cheeks were flushed and his eyes were filled with a restless energy.

'How did it go?' Lucy asked.

'I had to endure a long spiel on how much of a disappointment I am. But he's putting me in contact with someone.'

Lucy pressed her lips together.

'Sebastian must have reported me,' Jack said.

Lucy straightened her spine. 'What makes you say that?'

'He's had this disapproval thing going on, right from the very start. He must have found out I was an imposter somehow and decided he wanted revenge.'

Lucy was aware of her chest tightening, a buzzing inside her ears. She stood up and walked over to Jack. For a second her hand hovered over his arm, but she couldn't bring herself to take it. 'He did know. I told him.'

Jack stared at her, aghast. 'When? Why?'

'Right before he gave you the money. I went to his place and confessed everything. I had to do something.'

'You just went and did your own thing? Without telling me?'

Lucy dropped her gaze as heat washed over her face. 'Sebastian didn't deserve what Zelda had in store for him. I couldn't be complicit. And I wasn't going to let her make a criminal out of you.'

'So Sebastian *knew*? He met up with me, knowing I was an actor? Transferred the money, even though he knew I was deceiving him?'

Lucy nodded, forcing herself to meet Jack's eye. 'But this is good. It means you didn't defraud him. Not really. Because he knew it was an act. Zelda was behind everything.'

Fury contorted Jack's features, screwing up his face until it was almost unrecognisable. 'Fucking hell, Lucy! Sebastian *must* have reported me.'

Lucy flinched. 'No. He was crushed. He was confused. He wouldn't . . . '

'Why the fuck not? I mean, it's pretty bloody perfect – he realises I've been lying, that I've got a job to do, and he lets me walk right into a trap. Jesus. I knew it was too easy. He didn't even ask me what I needed the money for. Not one single question.'

'Sebastian wouldn't do a thing like that. It's not how his mind works.' Lucy spoke more loudly than she'd intended.

Jack's mouth snapped shut. He looked at her curiously. 'What would you know about how Sebastian's mind works? How many times have you seen him behind my back?'

'He's decent,' Lucy whispered.

Jack snorted.

'He *is*.'

Jack paced around the office. 'Did something happen between you? Have you been fucking him this whole time?'

Lucy felt herself redden. 'No. And you're one to talk. Zelda looked pretty bloody comfortable in your flat.'

Jack stopped pacing and stared at her. His face became completely still. 'I'm not sleeping with Zelda. She's become a friend. A very good friend, actually.'

'She's unhinged, Jack, surely you can see that? She was the one who devised this whole twisted scheme. *She* was the one who told you to ask Sebastian for an allowance.'

Jack was shaking his head.

'Did you upset her somehow? Did you knock her back?'

'You're being ridiculous.'

'Sebastian wouldn't try and get you into trouble. It's Zelda. It has to be Zelda.' Lucy walked over to the kitchenette and rested her hands on the cool steel of the draining board.

'Is this about *Heart Street*?' Jack's voice was quiet and somehow this was worse than when he'd been shouting.

Lucy felt her spine pulling itself taut. 'What do you mean?'

'You're jealous.'

With a bitter laugh, Lucy shook her head. 'Fuck off, Jack.' She felt more deflated than angry. How little Jack knew her. How little she knew him.

He took a step towards her as she filled the kettle. 'You *are* jealous. I didn't roll over and give up like you did. And now I've got a part in one of the country's favourite shows.'

She swung around to face him. Clapped her hands sarcastically. 'Congratu-fucking-lations! Twenty-year-old you would be so proud.'

Jack drew back. For a second, he was paralysed with shock. But he quickly composed himself. 'You were jealous. So you thought you'd sabotage me.'

Lucy shook her head, flicking the kettle on. She wouldn't respond. She'd already gone too far.

Was it possible that Sebastian had snapped, and decided Jack deserved to be taught a lesson? She had to admit it was possible. It must have been galling, sitting opposite him in a pub as he made his allowance pitch, knowing all the while that he was a paid actor. Maybe Sebastian had just wanted to scare Jack. Shake him up a little.

'If this police business fucks up *Heart Street*, I'll never forgive you.' There was something theatrical in Jack's delivery, an overdone iciness.

That their friendship had come to this was unthinkable. Part of Lucy wanted to hold him tightly, rest her head against his shoulder and transport them backwards. To the place where every hurt made sense, because it was just one more milestone on an important journey. To the adrenaline rush of callbacks. Rehearsals that went on into the night. Feeling as though they set the very highest standards for one another. That it mattered, that somehow it set them apart. She'd believed they were living the lives Peter had wanted for them, that they were honouring him with every audition, every attempt to manifest the careers of their student daydreams.

Lucy could see the moisture gathering in the corners of Jack's eyes. She put a hand on his shoulder. 'We'll sort this. I'll call Sebastian, I'm sure he'll be happy to clear things up . . . '

Jack screwed his eyes tightly shut. With a sudden jolt, Lucy realised just how frightened he was. *Heart Street* was the thin border that separated him from failure.

She made them both new coffees, carrying them over to her desk and gesturing for Jack to sit opposite.

'Why don't you get in touch with your dad's solicitor contact? I'll try calling Sebastian.'

Sebastian's phone went straight to voicemail and Lucy left a message asking him to ring back. She tried Zelda's number, but heard the same electronic voice saying her call could not be taken.

Five minutes later she tried both numbers again, this time calling from the office landline. The result was the same. Jack had stepped out into the hallway to speak to his solicitor, and she could hear his incessant questioning through the closed door.

Frustrated, Lucy looked up the number of Sebastian's bank and rang the switchboard. Once an operator transferred her, she was greeted by a bright female voice. 'You're through to Lynne, Mr Stott's assistant. How can I help you?'

'I need to speak to Sebastian on an urgent personal matter. Could you tell him Lucy is calling.'

'Lucy ...' The assistant paused, expecting to be given a surname.

'Just tell him I'm calling about his son.'

There was silence at the other end of the line. Too late, Lucy realised that Sebastian probably hadn't mentioned Jack to his colleagues. 'Hello?'

'Is this ...' the assistant faltered. 'I don't know who you are. But Mr Stott's son is dead.'

Lucy's stomach heaved, she clamped a hand over her mouth as bile surged up into her throat. After a moment or two, the assistant hung up on her, but Lucy continued holding the phone to her ear, her heart hammering inside her chest.

Chapter 34

After two days of regularly trying Sebastian's and Zelda's phones and having the calls go straight to voicemail, Lucy made her way to Zelda's studio in Hackney Wick. It was a bright April day and a cold breeze coming off the canal made Lucy glad she hadn't given in to the urge to leave her parka at home. She harboured a vivid fantasy of grabbing Zelda by her hair, dashing her pots to the ground. To have arranged such an elaborate deception for Sebastian, when he was a bereaved father, was twisted beyond anything Lucy could have imagined.

Jack had stared uncomprehending when Lucy told him about the call to Sebastian's office.

'*Mr Stott's son is dead*, those were the exact words?'

Lucy had nodded. 'Why didn't he tell us about this other child?'

Jack's lips had sprung apart. He blinked several times, wiping his palms against the fabric of his jeans. 'None of this makes sense.'

Sebastian had told Lucy about the failed IVF rounds. *Pure torture*, he'd said, and Lucy had felt the warm glow of a shared confidence. The idea that there had been this greater pain, this bereavement, filled her with dismay.

'Maybe the two of them were working together.' The set of Jack's jaw seemed to convey a longing for violence.

'No ... I mean, ... ?' Lucy had faltered. Could it be possible? All those times Sebastian had appeared so interested in her, were they mere performances? The idea was so terrible, she had to shove it from her mind.

Jack's shoulders had dropped, his jaw unclenched. 'Zelda wouldn't do that to me.'

Since then, Lucy had been to Sebastian's flat a couple of times, but he hadn't answered his buzzer. He had every right to ignore her, was likely still angry. But she needed to see him. She remembered the way he'd lifted her from her feet, the sudden frenzy of desire. He'd wanted her, she was sure of it. Yet all the while he'd been nursing his grief over a dead child. Lucy ached with a need to comfort him, to hold his head to her chest, inhaling the scent of his skin.

When Lucy arrived at Zelda's warehouse, the front door was wedged open as a group of three young women unloaded planks of wood from a van.

Lucy slipped inside, walking with purpose down the corridor that led to Zelda's studio. Part of her was looking forward to Zelda's shocked reaction at her coming here. Did the woman really think Lucy would accept her not returning their calls? Jack hadn't been able to believe it at first. He'd sent Zelda a stream of increasingly desperate texts. Had called her relentlessly. But the outcome was the same: silence.

The door to Zelda's unit was closed. Lucy turned the handle. Locked. Standing on her tiptoes she peered through the glass panel and saw that the studio had been stripped bare. The shelves, the pots, the table – everything was gone. She stared into the emptiness for a few seconds, then lowered herself down onto her heels.

Zelda had made herself disappear. She'd drawn them in, persuaded them to commit fraud, and now she had evaporated. Her scheme was more calculated than Lucy had dared suspect. They had no way of proving Zelda ever existed. Why hadn't Lucy addressed that earlier on? Insisted on a written contract? All they had were a few emails from a Hotmail account; they'd even returned the Thailand photograph she'd loaned them. When Jack attended his police interview, Zelda and the assignment she'd given them would seem like a wild invention.

She rested her back against the locked door and closed her eyes. The temptation to cry was irresistible, but she fought it with everything she had. There *must* be something else she could do. What had Zelda *really* wanted? Had she planned to entrap Jack right from the beginning? If so, why? And what was Sebastian's role in all of this? Failing to mention he had a son who died; giving Jack the money, when he knew he was an imposter – none of it made sense.

Jack was meeting his solicitor later that day, so she broke the news with a text:

I'm at Zelda's studio. It's cleared out. She's gone. I'm so sorry.

'Hiya. You taking this unit?'

Lucy looked up from her phone and saw a tall man with long fair hair pulled back into a bun. He was wearing a paint-spattered shirt and jeans, with bare feet.

'What's your practice?' he asked her.

'Oh, I'm not an artist. I was just visiting – but she's gone.'

'The ceramics lady? Yeah, she moved out a couple of weeks back.'

Lucy felt a sudden prickle of hope. 'Do you happen to know where she went?'

The man shook his head. 'Said she couldn't afford a studio any more. Was going to try and fit her wheel in her kitchen.'

Lucy placed a hand against the wall to steady herself. Her mind grappled with the rising certainty that she and Jack had been targets, that Sebastian might even have been in on Zelda's scheme. To what end? She had the uncanny sense that the truth was close at hand, she just hadn't been looking in the right place.

'She was all right,' the man said, turning on his bare heel. 'Said she might come along to my private view next week.'

'Your what?'

'The opening of my exhibition. Me and two friends are putting on a group show.'

Lucy took a deep breath, trying not to reveal her desperation. 'Yeah? Is it open to everyone, or . . .'

The man gave her a broad smile. 'You should totally come along. I've got some flyers in my room.' He inclined his head and Lucy followed him to a unit three doors down. The smell of oil paint hit her as she stepped inside, making her light-headed. Abstract paintings, bold colours in surprising combinations, were propped up against every spare inch of wall.

The man picked up a leaflet from a small table by his easel and handed it to her. 'The Tyranny of Beauty,' read the heading in bold purple letters. It gave the time and date of the opening, along with the address of a pop-up gallery in Hackney. It was happening next week.

Lucy held it tightly in both hands, wrinkling the paper. This was her sole, tenuous link to Zelda.

Chapter 35

With everything that was happening, it felt ridiculous for
Lucy to be gussying herself up, squeezing herself into an
off-the-shoulder dress in pale pink, pinning her hair into an
elaborate twist, then adding a fascinator. She'd had to enlist
the help of a personal shopper to select the outfit, having no
idea what people wore to horse racing events. Jack always
used to advise her about such things, but it didn't feel right
asking him for help any more.

She and Adam travelled down to Goodwood in his BMW.
It was a bright spring day as they drove through the South
Downs National Park. The wooded hillsides were veined
white with dead ash trees reaching towards the sky; their
bleached, naked branches appearing to make a final plea for
life. They passed a pig farm, field upon field dotted with
small domed structures, where pigs rooted in the mud, or
basked in the late-spring sunshine. The car filled with a
strange odour, redolent of manure but mixed with something
almost meaty that settled inside Lucy's mouth and refused
to shift.

'You're certain George will be there?' Adam asked her.
'Imagine going to all this effort and he doesn't even show.'

Lucy smiled. 'He'll be there. Charlotte referred to it as a lads' weekend.'

Adam gave a theatrical shudder. He was wearing a well-cut navy-blue suit and aviator sunglasses. 'The man's thirty-six.'

'Indeed. There's a group of four. They have passes to one of the VIP bars.'

'How will I recognise your staff?'

'You won't. It'll look more authentic that way.'

'And you're sure the police aren't going to swoop in and arrest you, part of the way through?' Adam turned his head to give her a wry smile.

'Not amusing.'

Today was the day of Jack's police interview. He and his solicitor had an appointment at Charing Cross Police Station, something Lucy was trying to push to the side of her mind for the duration of this assignment. The interview might lead to him being arrested.

'I'm just nervous.' Adam braked as the traffic in front of them ground to a halt. Up ahead, Lucy could see a parking marshal in a fluorescent jacket directing cars into a field.

'Don't be. If it doesn't work, then we haven't really lost anything. But if it does, you'll have something on George.'

Adam flashed her a smile. 'You know, you've busted all my preconceptions about actors being airy-fairy diva types. I think you're the most pragmatic person I've ever met.'

When she stepped out of the car, she was Holly. Which meant she had to avoid looking this way and that and appear completely unawed by the spectacle of the event, the Rolexes and designer handbags, sculptural hats with plumes nearly a metre high.

Back in her twenties, she'd dreamed of attending such events, wearing such clothes. Now she was actually making money, these things left her cold. Wealth for her meant a flat she didn't have to share, the gift of being able to help her parents and buying her favourite authors' latest releases in hardback. Even if she became super rich, she'd always prefer a morning in bed with a book to this kind of thing.

Playing Holly, she had to suffocate her intrinsic distaste of horse racing, the cruelty of the whip, the braying of drunk spectators clutching their betting slips. She and Adam were supposed to be here by sheer coincidence. It was a date, a birthday treat, the kind of thing Holly would enjoy. She and Adam watched two races, cheering as the hooves thundered past even as Lucy ached with compassion for the poor animals, foaming at the mouth, their flanks heaving. Adam stood stiffly at her side, waiting, unease marked clearly on his face. The only thing that appeared to distract him were legal questions, so Lucy kept turning to him, asking about the burden of proof required for a fraud conviction.

'You're really going out of your way to help your friend,' Adam said.

'Well, I'm the one who got him into this mess.' She ensured Holly's smile remained on her face, keeping her expression light.

'Does he have your back?'

For a moment, the fake smile dropped. 'Absolutely,' she said. But it wasn't true. She wasn't sure it ever had been.

It was much later in the afternoon when Lucy's phone buzzed.

She clutched Adam's arm. 'Time to get ready.'

They made for one of the VIP bars, Lucy's spike heels sinking into the turf with every step. She was aware of the tension rippling out from Adam's body as he moved with quick, long strides.

'Relax. This is just you and your partner off to get some Champagne.'

He gave her a terse little nod.

Lucy's phone went again. This time it was Jack:

Interview went okay. I've been released under investigation. Solicitor says you telling Sebastian about the acting is a crucial detail. Also would be ideal if we could produce Zelda.

They hadn't arrested him, then. Surely that was significant. Lucy turned to Adam, about to ask what 'released under investigation' meant, how worried she ought to be. But the sight of his hunched shoulders made her hold her tongue. He was having to expend enormous effort to appear nonchalant. She couldn't break his concentration. Since learning about Peter and Jack, Lucy had become more invested than ever in freeing Adam from his brother's threats of exposure.

The bar was alive with a well-dressed crowd, everyone speaking in exclamations, honking with laughter every few minutes. Light poured in from the terrace overlooking the track and a garlicky aroma came from the kitchen.

It took Lucy a few moments to spot George in a far corner with his back to them. He'd broken off from his friends and was speaking with twenty-two-year-old Danielle who looked extraordinary in a sleeveless green dress, dark hair trailing down her back. She was just perceptibly leaning towards George and when he appeared to make a joke she threw her head back, as though he was the wittiest man she'd ever met.

Lucy steered Adam towards the bar, ensuring they were out of George's sightline.

'Seems to be going well,' she said. 'Keep your eyes on the bar, then once you've been served, get into a deep conversation with me. Don't look this way and that.'

'Yes, boss.' Adam swallowed; he was twisting the gold ring he wore on his little finger, looking as though he was waiting to be called in for a particularly gruelling job interview.

Lucy ordered them Champagne and Adam produced his card to pay. They waited, hemmed in by a crowd of braying men in tailcoats. Adam tried to enact a shouted conversation about the race they'd just seen, but clearly didn't know what he was talking about. Lucy stood with Holly's tidy posture, nodding along, doing a good job of looking enraptured. Even though she couldn't see them, her attention was trained on the corner where George and Danielle were gathered.

Her phone buzzed for the third time. 'Now,' she said.

They stood up, holding their Champagne flutes and fighting their way free from the crowd at the bar. Lucy took Adam by the hand, leading him towards the terrace, as though excited to take in the view. 'Would you just look at that scenery,' she said in Holly's voice.

She was aware of angry voices on her left, of people interrupting their conversations to see what was going on. It was the most natural thing in the world for Holly and Adam to take a look.

Will Tanner was there, wearing a three-piece suit, an expensive-looking camera around his neck.

George currently had hold of the camera strap.

'You had no business . . . delete it right now.'

'George? What's going on?' Adam did a reasonable job at sounding shocked.

Lucy raised her arms, feigning surprise. 'My goodness – Will, is that you? It's Holly. Holly Campbell. We were at St Andrews together.'

George let go of the camera strap and jabbed a finger at Will's chest. 'This prick here has just been sticking his camera in my face.'

'Holly' turned and glared at the people who'd crowded around to watch. As one, they averted their gaze, making a show of shuffling back to their drinks.

'I'm on assignment for *High Society*,' Will said, drawing himself up. 'I'm their pictures editor.'

'Oh, congratulations!' Lucy said. 'That was always your dream job.'

'I'm not going to be in any society pages,' George snapped. 'Give it here.'

Behind him, Lucy noticed Danielle retreating. Her lip gloss was smudged, her hair slightly messed. She saw Lucy observing her and winked. She was so in command of herself for a woman of twenty-two. It gave Lucy a deep sense of satisfaction to keep funnelling money her way.

'What's the problem?' Adam asked George. 'I thought you'd enjoy having your mug plastered everywhere.'

'You and your lady friend are very photogenic. Such a good-looking couple.' Will's forehead was crinkled in sincerity.

Lucy couldn't help feeling a flicker of pride at just how well he was doing.

'Lady friend? Is Charlotte here?' Lucy said, looking around.

'Just give me the camera,' George's face was a dark pink and Lucy noticed a smear of Danielle's red lip gloss just above his top lip.

She put a hand on George's shoulder. 'Let me handle this,' she said. 'Will's a dear friend of mine.' She turned to Will. 'You can see George here is rather upset. Could I trouble you to give me the memory card? Just as a special favour?'

Will appeared to vacillate. Then he sighed. 'Since it's you, Holly.'

He took a few steps backwards as he extracted a tiny piece of plastic from his camera and handed it to her. Lucy immediately passed it to Adam who placed it in the inside pocket of his jacket.

George followed the transaction, his eyes coming to rest on his brother's lapel.

Will sighed. 'I better get back to it. I've got pages to fill. I'll get you and your chap to pose for me later.'

Holly smiled as he left, then turned her attention back to George. 'There. What a ruckus! But no harm done.'

George took a step towards his brother, his eyes narrowing. 'What are you even doing here?'

With the appearance of being completely unruffled, Adam tilted his glass in Lucy's direction. 'It's Holly's birthday. I swear I told you I'd be bringing her here for a day out.'

George's eyes flickered inwards, as though searching his memories. But then his gaze seemed to harden. His jaw jutted forward, as though he was grinding his teeth. 'Give me the card.'

'Why?' A smile played at Adam's lips.

'Just give it.' George lunged at his brother's jacket, but Adam sidestepped him.

'George,' Lucy began cautiously, 'were you photographed doing something you shouldn't be?'

George froze, then glanced behind him. Danielle had disappeared.

'My goodness.' Lucy placed a hand against her own throat. 'How could you do that to Charlotte?'

'I . . .'

'What am I going to see, when I look at the photos?' Adam asked.

George balled his hands into fists. It looked as though he was holding his breath. But then his posture softened as he attempted a knowing smile. 'Look. A bit of harmless fun, that's all.'

Adam raised an eyebrow. 'Well, you're lucky Holly was here to help you out. Divorces can be very expensive.'

George stared darkly at Adam, then at Lucy. 'What is this?'

Adam patted him on the shoulder. 'You stay out of my business and I'll stay out of yours.'

Chapter 36

There was a pub diagonally opposite the pop-up gallery, a plucky hold-out against gentrification with its patterned carpet and nineties rock soundtrack. Homemade posters advertised quiz night Wednesday and a Sunday meat raffle in large type. Older men were clustered loosely at the bar, sipping from pint glasses as they pursued conversations that seemed to have been going on for decades. Lucy and Mel took a table by the window, keeping watch for Zelda's auburn hair.

'I feel sick,' Mel said. 'I'm not sure I can do this.'

'You'll be fine.' Lucy placed a hand on her sister's arm. 'Step one is just getting a photo. You can pretend to be snapping one of the paintings.'

Mel nodded, biting her lower lip. In her combats and vest, upcycled cotton shoulder bag, she could easily pass as one of the artist-types trickling through the entrance.

'After that, just do the best small talk you can,' Lucy added. 'If it was me, I'd try and catch her viewing a painting, and start with some just-look-at-the-use-of-colour-type observations.'

Mel wrinkled her forehead. 'I honestly don't know how you do this for a living.'

'You just need to be interested in her. Act enthusiastic when she says she's a ceramicist and ask for a card or a web address. Anything that anchors her to a place or a business would be a massive help. Jack's solicitor says "producing" Zelda is his best chance of not being charged.'

'No pressure, then.' Mel sipped her lager and lime.

'Even if you only get her photo and real name, it's more than we have at the moment.' Lucy eyed the gallery entrance as a cluster of art students made their way inside.

'I really appreciate you helping out this evening,' Lucy added, still gazing out of the window. 'I've been thinking a lot about the ethical side of the business. What you said about screening clients, that type of thing.'

'That's good.' For a moment, the worry lines on Mel's forehead smoothed out. The eager, interested look she gave her sister filled Lucy with hope.

Lucy steeled herself as she prepared to make her request. 'You're so much better at this stuff than I am. I've been wondering whether you might consider getting involved.'

'Fuck, no,' Mel said. 'Just the idea of trying to get Zelda's business card is making me want to puke.'

Lucy was surprised by how crushed she was. She had to concentrate hard on maintaining an unconcerned expression. 'You wouldn't have to do acting. You could be in charge of client relations. Weeding out anything dodgy.'

Mel drained her half pint. 'I couldn't be doing with living in London. Sorry, sis.'

'But you could take care of the enquiries from home, fit it around school hours. I could make you operations director, or any fancy title you like. It'd free me up to focus on the creative side – hiring actors, briefing them, that type of thing.' There was a desperate note creeping into Lucy's voice; she took a sip of her vodka and soda to try and steady herself. The drink was such a disappointment compared to the delicious smell of Mel's lager and lime. Now she had a roster of actors, was there any reason to be so severe with herself?

Mel screwed her nose up. 'Are you sure there'll still be a business after the fraud investigation?'

Lucy closed her eyes for a second. 'Thanks a lot.'

'It's a sensible question. One you should be considering yourself.'

'Sure.' Lucy glanced out the window again, at the painted white exterior of the gallery, where a small cluster of students outside stood smoking. The shop next door looked like it had been closed a long time, the windows covered up with sheets of newspaper. A van went by, overtaking a female cyclist far too closely.

'I haven't said no.'

'Maybe I've changed my mind about wanting you involved.'

Mel grinned. 'That's a shame. Because – against every better instinct – I am a *little* bit excited at the idea.'

Lucy felt a ripple pass through her – it wasn't elation, exactly, it was more a feeling of safety. Before she could reply, she caught the flash of auburn hair she'd been waiting for. Zelda was approaching the gallery wearing a pea-green trench coat. Even from this distance Lucy could see she was smiling, her gait relaxed.

'That's her.' Lucy glanced at Mel, making sure she had a good visual on Zelda.

'I guess I'm up?' Mel's eyes were wide with anxiety as she watched Zelda pass the smokers and step inside the gallery.

Lucy nodded. 'You can do this. Remember, photo first. If all else fails, we at least have evidence she's a real living breathing woman.'

Mel stood up, hesitating for the briefest moment before she marched out of the pub.

While her sister was gone, Lucy produced her laptop from her bag and tried to concentrate on the agency inbox. There were the usual attempts to procure sex that needed deleting and blocking. A stream of requests for attractive women to act as plus ones. Endless enquiries about honeytraps. She'd need to run another recruitment drive if she was to keep up. Lucy found herself totting up the likely income in her head as she fired off responses and confirmed dates. It was still astounding to her, that she'd found a way to access the wealth of the city, to take a tiny part of it for herself. She wouldn't let Zelda destroy everything she'd built.

Lucy had considered telling Jack about the exhibition, and the possibility that Zelda might be there. But he hadn't responded to her calls in the days that had passed since his police interview. She decided it was too risky – he might turn up, eyes flashing, demanding an explanation. She'd been calling Sebastian incessantly over the past week, varying the time of day, trying to catch him off guard. Sometimes it rang, but he never picked up, even when she withheld her number. He was done with her, that much was clear. But Lucy still couldn't find it in herself to believe he'd knowingly got Jack into trouble with the police.

'Here.' Mel was back, slightly out of breath as she laid a business card down in front of Lucy.

KATE DWYER CERAMICS, it read, giving a phone number, email and web address. Lucy felt a shiver as her suspicions were confirmed: there was no Zelda. Their client had been pretending all along.

'You did it!' Lucy stood up and hugged her sister.

'Made up some shit about my mother being a pottery enthusiast.' Mel sounded breathless, shuddering slightly with each exhalation. 'I got the photo too. I'll ping it over.'

'How did she seem?'

Mel shrugged. 'Relaxed, I guess. I mean, I'd never have put her down as a con woman. She was nice.'

Anger flared in Lucy – how could she be relaxed with everything she'd done? Storing the card carefully in her wallet, Lucy gathered up her laptop and phone. 'Right, time for me and *Kate* to have a little chat.'

Mel reached out, placing a hand on her sister's shoulder. 'Be careful. I'm heading back to Waterloo. But I will have a think about what we were discussing earlier. I mean, what you do for a living is wild. Someone's got to keep an eye on you.'

Lucy gave her sister another hug. 'Thank you. I can't help thinking you've just saved me from a whole lot of shit. Safe journey.'

Halfway to the gallery, Lucy realised she was marching, swinging her arms with purpose. She slowed to a deliberate saunter. *I'm here to browse. To expand my mind.* She didn't want to attract notice, for Zelda to look up and have time to retreat as she saw Lucy approach.

No one checked her invite, or marked her off a list; she was able to easily step inside and pick up a glass of white from a table near the entrance. She took in as much of the gallery as she could without making it obvious she was looking for someone. The exhibition spanned two high-ceilinged rooms, both of which were filled with people, clustering together in loose groups.

'Hey, you made it!' It was the long-haired man from the warehouse, wearing a black suit with a white shirt and no tie. As before, his feet were bare, the toenails caked with dirt. 'You want a tour of the work?' His eyes were expectant.

Lucy smiled. 'Maybe in a little while. First I'd like to catch up with Kate – the ceramics lady.'

The man nodded, making sure Lucy observed the disappointment in his eyes. 'She's over there in the second room, I think.'

Thanking him, Lucy weaved her way through the crowd. A club track thudded from a sound system. It seemed to interact with the slashes of colour on the canvases, making it feel like the room was pulsing.

She spotted Zelda in front of a large canvas filled with indistinct swooshes of purple. Her coat was now slung over one arm, revealing the floral dress she'd worn to her very first meeting with the agency. She was standing with a group of three women of a similar age, all of them wearing chunky silver jewellery with clothes that were contrived to look cheap, but most likely weren't.

Lucy approached, laying a firm hold on Zelda's shoulder. 'Kate! I was hoping to run into you here. Can I borrow you for a moment?'

Zelda turned, eyes widening as she saw Lucy. Her posture visibly stiffened and, although her lips had sprung apart, she didn't seem capable of saying a word. Lucy couldn't help feeling a jolt of satisfaction – after the helplessness of the past three weeks, she was finally back in control.

She craned her neck to address the other women. 'Please excuse us. We'll only be a few minutes.' She took Zelda by the arm and led her over to the emptiest corner of the gallery, next to a series of paintings composed of green and yellow paint daubs.

They faced one another, shoulders squared.

'I thought you liked Jack.' Lucy had to shout to be heard over the music.

Zelda blinked several times in quick succession. 'I did. I do.'

'Then why are you trying to get him in trouble with the police?'

'I'm not. I—' Zelda placed a steadying hand against the whitewashed wall.

'You talked him into committing fraud, then a few days later the police are knocking on his door. Don't tell me you had nothing to do it.'

'Oh, God.' Zelda screwed her eyes shut. 'He really went through with it.'

'Why did you betray him?' Lucy felt a fresh surge of indignation as she remembered how Jack's face had blanched at the sight of the police officers.

'Everything okay, Kate?' her companions approached, eyeing Lucy with suspicion.

'Yes. All good.' Zelda drew herself up, startled. 'You carry on, I'll catch up with you in a bit.'

She and Lucy were silent as the women moved along, congregating in front of the next painting.

'It was your own ads. The post on Jack's socials,' Zelda said. 'That's where the idea came from.'

'Idea?'

'He said he wanted to get to know you. I thought he deserved that. You have to understand – I thought it might bring him closure.'

'Who? What are you talking about?' Lucy felt a coldness trickle through her belly.

Zelda lowered herself to the ground, sitting with her back against the wall. Lucy joined her, setting her untouched glass of wine on the floor as she sat cross-legged. A drip of condensation ran down her finger.

'You went to university with Sebastian's son,' Zelda said.

Ice spread through Lucy's body, fanning out into her fingers, freezing her ribs. She couldn't breathe. 'No. That's not possible.'

'His name was Peter Hawkins.'

It was unconscionable, hearing Peter's name on this woman's lips. A violation. Lucy balled her hands into fists, digging the nails into her palms. Zelda was saying Sebastian's son was Peter? This had to be a sick joke. One more layer to her twisted deception. Lucy forced an exhalation, attempting an audit of everything she knew. Too many thoughts rushed at her at once, scouring the wet meat of her brain, roaring in her ears. Peter was raised by his mother's parents. His father worked abroad and Peter always implied that he disapproved of drama school.

But she'd spoken of Peter to Sebastian. Surely, he would have told her? It couldn't be true.

'You're lying,' Lucy said.

Zelda pressed her lips together, angling her head, as if she pitied Lucy. 'Sebastian was living in Hong Kong when Peter died, but they were close. They spoke regularly.'

Lucy swallowed. 'You're trying to tell me that Sebastian knew Jack wasn't his son? He's been pretending?'

Zelda nodded. Her eyes were welling up, the tiny red blood vessels seeming to swell and become more prominent.

'Are you Peter's mother?' Peter had told Lucy his mother died when he was very young. She'd had breast cancer.

'No,' Zelda said. 'She was a uni friend of Sebastian's. He didn't find out about the baby until after we got back from Thailand.'

Lucy remembered Sebastian's listening eyes. How he'd reminded her of Peter at times, not because of any physical resemblance, but through his kind, unobtrusive attention – the feeling that talking with him could help her resolve any problem. 'I don't believe any of this,' she said.

'Sebastian used to dip into Jack's social media here and there. He saw the post about you setting up an agency and became obsessed with the idea of getting to know the people who'd been so important to Peter.'

'All he had to do was send an email, for fuck's sake. We'd have jumped at the chance to meet with Peter's family.'

Zelda shrugged. 'I told him that. But he wouldn't be persuaded. He had his plan, and he wanted to stick to it.'

'What about you? What are you to Sebastian?' Lucy's vision darkened as it struck her that Zelda was probably his partner. All along they'd been in cahoots, letting Jack and Lucy believe they were in control. Those thick envelopes of cash must have come from Sebastian.

'We went to school together,' Zelda said. 'Lived very different lives since then, but he's my oldest, dearest friend. When he needed help, I had to be there.'

For a moment, Lucy felt a surge of relief. They weren't together. Perhaps Zelda knew nothing of the kiss, of the fever with which Sebastian had hoisted her onto the kitchen countertop.

'So, what – he got you to pose as a client? You've been deceiving us this whole time?' Lucy's voice was cold. She wouldn't have been able to control her tone, even if she'd tried.

Zelda looked down at the floor. 'Two years ago, when his marriage ended – everything seemed to catch up with him. It was terrifying.' She lowered her voice and it became difficult to hear her over the bass. 'He became so single-minded. Had to *do something* for Peter, he kept telling me.'

Lucy shook her head. 'None of this makes any sense. Why is Jack in trouble with the police? Why have you been pushing him to commit fraud? And how can it even *be* fraud if Sebastian was driving the whole thing?'

Zelda's eyes hardened. A shadow loomed over Lucy and she looked up to see the long-haired artist. 'Hey! You found your friend. Are you ready for that tour now?'

'No. Not yet.' Lucy's tone was blunt and she saw a flicker of annoyance on the man's face as he retreated.

'We've all been on Sebastian's payroll,' Zelda said at last. 'Sebastian got the idea of impersonation from Jack's post. Said he'd underwrite my studio costs, give me some money for materials, if I pretended to be your client. It gave me a chance to work on a new collection. I was desperate.'

This couldn't be right. Lucy stood up, towering over Zelda.

'You were acting? Sebastian paid you to act?'

Zelda picked up Lucy's wine glass, wincing as she eased herself up off the ground. 'Yes.'

'Why should I believe you?'

Zelda handed Lucy her drink. 'In many ways the two of us are alike. Devoted to our art but lacking the means to survive.'

Lucy stared at her, her lip curling in offence. Again, she had that rushing sensation – thoughts slamming into her brain, too fast for her to make sense of anything. Without another word, she turned and made for the exit. She couldn't recall a time when she'd been so angry. She felt Zelda take her arm and she wheeled around to face her. All around them, people paused their conversations to watch the exchange.

'I'm sorry,' Zelda whispered. 'I thought Sebastian just needed to get to know you. But he kept pushing and pushing – he's my oldest friend. He lost his son. I couldn't deny him—'

Lucy shrugged her off and kept walking. Zelda was lying. She had to be. Perhaps she'd become obsessed with Jack. Maybe she'd made a pass at him and he'd rejected her. Or maybe he'd slept with her and then backed away when Zelda thought it could become serious. The trouble with the police could be Zelda's disturbed form of revenge. All this time Lucy had been looking for a logical explanation – but Zelda was unhinged. There was no logic to be had with the likes of her.

It was still light when Lucy emerged into the street. She realised she was still holding her wine glass and hurled it into a nearby litter bin, the sound of it shattering giving her the release she needed. She cried and growled all at once, a strange animal noise that made the people walking past avert their eyes.

Chapter 37

It took Lucy more than an hour to reach Sebastian's place in Pimlico. She was light-headed and nauseous as she endured the interminable stops on the Overground from Hackney, changing to the Victoria Line at Highbury and Islington. There would be no rest until she'd looked into Sebastian's eyes and demanded the truth.

When she emerged from the Tube at Pimlico, the sky had taken on an indigo hue and the streetlamps were coming on. She strode towards Grosvenor Road, her heart thudding, sweat gathering on her back despite the coolness of the evening. When she arrived at Sebastian's Regency building, he buzzed her in straight away, as though he'd known she was coming. Zelda – Kate – must have called to warn him. He would have had an hour to compose himself, whereas Lucy was flushed, trying to manage the threat of vomit as she climbed the stairs.

Sebastian leaned against his door-frame wearing grey tracksuit bottoms and a matching hoodie. The dark circles beneath his eyes were more pronounced than usual and Lucy felt unexpectedly stirred – in spite of everything, she longed to brush her hand against his cheek.

Without speaking, she went into his sitting room and stood by the coffee table, bracing herself for the truth. Zelda had been lying. She was a former fling gone bad, who'd lied and lied, becoming obsessive about Jack as she tortured Sebastian. They were all her victims and if they pulled together they'd be able to help Jack. They could fix this.

Sebastian followed her into the room, then stood perfectly still, allowing Lucy's eyes to rove across his face. His forehead was creased and his jaw seemed slack, as though weighed by an unfamiliar fatigue. It went entirely against reason that being near him made her feel so reassured.

'Lucy ...' Something in Sebastian's tone wasn't quite right. Lucy took in the hooded eyes, the perfectly straight nose and well-defined Cupid's bow. Not a clear resemblance, but there were tiny vestiges, darts of familiarity. Why hadn't she noticed them before? She raised her hand, just grazing Sebastian's temple with a finger. Traces of Peter.

Sebastian took her hand and cradled it inside his own. He really was Peter's father. Every single interaction they'd shared had been false. Lucy had been acting for Sebastian. Sebastian had been acting for her.

'I feel sick.' She'd come so close to sleeping with him. Had wanted it, more than anything.

'I don't know what to say.' Sebastian released her hand, pressing his lips together as he searched her face. There was a desperate light in his eyes, as though he was hungry for something only she could give him.

'The supportive, interested future father-in-law thing was just pretend?' Lucy's voice sounded thin, defeated. The feelings he'd stirred in her had been grounded in lies. Once again, she'd failed to recognise a deception playing out in front of her. Was there nothing she could trust?

Sebastian gave a sad smile, a film of tears coating his eyes. 'There's a certain irony. You chiding me for deceiving you.'

Lucy sank down into his sofa. She'd let herself believe she meant something to him. Even as she'd performed, in some twisted way she'd felt herself being truthful, exposing sides of herself that usually remained hidden. Drawing close, even though it had felt dangerous.

Bile rose in her throat. This wasn't a moment to wallow. Jack needed her help. 'Why are you out to get Jack?' she asked. 'He was just doing his job. Following Zelda's instructions. Working for *you*, without even realising it.'

Sebastian sat down on the opposite sofa, massaging his temples. 'All this time, I was wondering if you knew.'

Lucy was aware of a faint hum coming from Sebastian's fridge in the kitchen. She could feel each beat of her heart, not just in her chest, but in her neck, in her ears. 'Knew what?'

'About Peter and Jack.' Sebastian's chin quivered.

She bit into her bottom lip. Had Peter told his father about his secret relationship? She couldn't know for sure.

Sebastian clasped his hands tightly together, placing them decisively in his lap. 'Peter and I were close. We spoke on the phone once a week. He used to stay with me every summer.'

Those trips to Hong Kong. Peter had been visiting Sebastian, his banker father. Her mind fizzed as she tried to process this alternate history. When Peter described his father taking him to a dumpling restaurant, he'd been speaking of Sebastian. Peter's allowance, his rent payments had all come from Sebastian.

'He's a good guy,' Lucy remembered Peter saying. 'One of those ultra-competitive types. Complete workaholic.' Sebastian hadn't come to watch any of their student performances. Hadn't seen for himself just how talented his son was. It was unfathomable. A tragic waste.

'Jack killed him.' Sebastian's voice broke as he made this bald statement.

'What?' Lucy dug her fingers into the arm of the sofa. 'That's not true. There was an accident ...' She could feel her eyes straining, as though they'd suddenly become too big for their sockets.

Sebastian sighed. His nose and cheeks reddened, as though he were about to cry. 'You didn't know.'

'I was with Jack when he found out – there was no way ...'

Sebastian wiped his eyes. 'You knew they were lovers? For two years. Jack wouldn't let Peter tell a soul, but I wondered if you suspected. Peter thought the world of you.'

Lucy swallowed. 'I didn't know back then.' *Two years?* Emerging from their own rooms each morning, so careful to ensure Lucy never saw the touch, the brushing of fingertips or lips against a shoulder that would have made her suspect.

'When he stayed in Hong Kong that final time, he'd never been so happy.' Sebastian cast his gaze downwards. 'He told me Jack was finally going to come out. They would be together. No more hiding.'

She felt a searing pain in her lungs. Lucy had sent Peter off to the airport. His face had been radiant as he told her he'd start looking for a flat on his return. She remembered being secretly relieved that Jack's father had sorted him a place, that she and Peter would flat-share without him.

Sebastian wiped his eyes with the back of his hand. 'He'd gone to Jack's the night of the accident. Was supposed to be staying with him in Hertfordshire.'

Lucy screwed her eyes tightly shut. Was she to believe that as they'd waited in their graduation gowns, Lucy fretting about not hearing from Peter, Jack had kept this final meeting to himself? It couldn't be true. She remembered asking whether he'd heard from Peter, and Jack had said no.

'They'd been drinking, Lucy.' Sebastian looked up, a darkness in his eyes as he met her gaze. 'Then Jack told Peter he wanted to end it. He must have known Peter was over the limit, but he decided he didn't want Peter staying over after all. He sent him on his way. Sent him to his death.'

There was a stiffness to Lucy's jaw. She couldn't speak. Couldn't regain control of her hands. 'Jack wouldn't . . . '

'I told Peter to pull over, but he wouldn't listen, he was too upset.'

Lucy placed a hand over her mouth. 'You spoke to him *in the car?*'

Sebastian nodded. 'He called me on speakerphone. Gave me this whole spiel about how coming out would limit Jack's career prospects. That he understood, in some way, why Jack had ended their relationship. I'd never heard such horseshit and I told Peter as much. I had no idea it was going to be our last conversation.'

Lucy doubled over, every muscle in her body tense, as though some ancient reflex was drawing her into a ball-shape. What must it be like for Sebastian, knowing he was the last person to have spoken to Peter? Knowing his son had died heartbroken. Had got into the car because of Jack. She had a sudden vision of Peter's face, stricken, tears staining his cheeks. It made everything feel so much worse.

'All those hours you spent with Jack ... you've laughed at his jokes, listened to him gabble on,' she said.

'All I wanted was one sign that he was sorry. Anything that let me believe he'd changed.' There was a flintiness to Sebastian's tone that made Lucy straighten up.

'You cooked for us. You smiled. You ... all along, you believed he killed your son?'

'It's not a matter of believing. He let Peter get drunk, then asked him to leave. Jack's responsible.'

How had Jack lived with the memory of Peter driving away, knowing what had happened next? Lucy couldn't take this. She needed to be alone. Only then would she find the strength to revisit her memories, to confront the things she might not have been able to see. She hauled herself up from the sofa, placing her hand on the arm to steady herself as her knee buckled. There was still so much to say, so much to ask, but there was also part of her that wanted to cover her ears and run.

'Lucy,' Sebastian reached for her hand.

She snatched it away and silently left the flat.

Chapter 38

The next morning, Lucy hammered on Jack's door. She'd forced herself to wait until eight, even though she hadn't been able to sleep at all. Emily answered, wearing Jack's dressing gown, her strawberry-blonde hair dishevelled. She looked Lucy up and down. Lucy was wearing yesterday's jeans and hoodie; hadn't showered or even brushed her hair.

'Wasn't expecting to see you here, not after the trouble you've made for Jack,' Emily said.

Lucy didn't have the patience for whatever sniping Emily had in mind. She slid past her, stepping into the hallway. 'Jack!'

'Hold on a minute.' Emily took Lucy's arm. 'You can't just barge in here.'

Lucy stared at Emily. She knew her eyes must be wild, because the assured set of Emily's lips suddenly collapsed. She released Lucy's arm.

Jack emerged from his bedroom in just his boxers. The corners of his eyes were crusted with sleep and it looked like he hadn't shaved for at least three days.

'I need to talk to you. In private,' Lucy said.

Jack looked at Emily and shrugged.

Emily's smile faltered for a moment, then she gave a theatrical sigh. 'Fine. I was about to get in the shower anyway.'

Without speaking, Lucy followed Jack into his bedroom, her hands clasped in front of her as she watched him pick up his jeans and an Aran jumper from the floor and pull them on. From the bathroom, she heard the whoosh of the power shower.

'You saw Peter the night he died.' She didn't phrase it as a question, but saw the sudden calculation in Jack's eyes, as though he was preparing to deny it.

She reached out, grabbing a handful of his jumper, clutching the rough wool between her fingers. Inside her mouth, her teeth itched. She slid her jaw from side to side, straining with the effort it took to control herself. 'You loaded him up with booze, broke his heart, then saw him to his car.'

'What are you talking about?' Jack looked down at her hand.

'Peter. The night he died.' Tears fractured her voice into high-pitched fragments.

Jack swallowed, making several false starts before he was able to reply. 'It wasn't . . . it was a difficult evening.'

Lucy stared at him, still clutching his jumper, not trusting herself to let go. There was something about Jack's expression, a tinge of righteousness that made her crave violence. She imagined driving her fist into his face, colliding with the hard bone of his cheek, a sound, wet steak slapping down on a countertop. Her face became hot with tears.

'It wasn't my . . .'

'Don't you dare lie to me!'

Jack's eyes widened, he inched his head backwards, away from her.

For several moments, they remained still. Lucy could feel her nails separating the fibres of his jumper as she maintained her grip, her knuckles white, tendons straining. She tried to breathe. If she let go, she would hurt him. What she felt was too large to be contained, to indistinct to name. All she could do was hold herself motionless, until its force finally began to weaken.

She let go of his jumper. 'Sebastian is Peter's father.'

Jack had been gazing out the window, his eyes glassy, but he suddenly snapped to attention. 'You can't be serious?'

'I tracked Zelda down. She's been working for Sebastian. He hired her to pretend to be a client.' Lucy wiped her face with the sleeve of her hoodie.

Jack shook his head. The colour drained from his face; his skin had a grey tinge to it. 'That can't be right.'

In spite of everything, Lucy felt a tugging through her middle. Jack *believed* in Zelda, had truly felt he was helping her achieve a kind of justice. She tried to steel herself, straightening her spine and pulling her shoulders back. 'This whole gig, the mission Zelda sent us on, has been about revenge from the start. Sebastian's revenge. Against you.'

Jack's face appeared to crumple. He folded his torso forwards, placing his hands on the tops of his thighs. 'Sebastian's been trying to get at *me*? I knew something was off with him.'

'You killed Peter.' Lucy took a step backwards. She'd tended to Jack for a decade, let herself feel responsible for him, and all the while he'd been concealing this terrible secret.

Jack's back heaved with each breath as he stared down at his sheepskin rug. 'He'd only had a couple of glasses. I thought he was fine to drive. We both did.'

There was a sudden bursting feeling in Lucy's chest. 'How have you lived with yourself?' she whispered.

Jack shook his head. His eyes were wild.

'You broke up with him the very night he crashed his car. You must have connected the two things. You must have felt responsible.'

A purple flush spread across Jack's cheeks, there was a mottling along his neck. Again, he shook his head.

'You could have been together. Made each other happy.'

He wouldn't meet her eye. 'It's not . . .'

'Where's your Marvel franchise? Your Austen hero? Your action man? You gained nothing by letting Peter go. Nothing. Do you understand that? You've lived a lie, made yourself miserable, for *nothing*.'

Jack sank down onto the bed, pressing his hands against his forehead. She'd not seen him overcome like this since the breakdown. Her body responded, pinpricks of empathy across her chest. But Peter – Lucy felt a fresh stab of anguish at him being in love and having to hide it. At how crushed he must have felt, getting into his car that final time.

'You let Peter love you when you had no intention of being with him. You used him, just like you use everyone.' Again, the rage was swelling inside her, that desire to hit him, so strong she wasn't sure she could trust herself not to act on it. She tucked her hands into her armpits, holding them there tightly.

Still, Jack remained doubled over, elbows on his knees as he cradled his head. Lucy's body was filled with a strange electric crackle, as though she'd suddenly been jolted awake. Jack's breakdown hadn't been about acting at all. It had been about Peter. He must have been tortured by guilt, perhaps terrified of exposure, and he hadn't felt able to share it with anyone.

She sat down on the bed next to him, her anger gone, her body flooded with compassion. 'Things could have been so different.'

'What's going on this time?' Emily swept into the bedroom in a grey shift dress and black tights, her hair wrapped in a towel. She saw Jack's face and hurried over to him, wrapping an arm around his shoulder. 'Jack? What is it?'

'We just need a minute,' Jack managed to say. 'Please, Emily. I'll explain later.'

Emily looked at him in disbelief for a moment before retracting her arm, snapping it down by her side. Her nose wrinkled as she turned to address Lucy. 'It isn't right, the way the two of you carry on. You take the best-buddy thing way too far.'

Lucy's eyes met Jack's. He attempted a smile, his lips heavy with sadness. It felt like a question, one she couldn't answer, not yet.

Once Emily had left the room, Jack closed the door softly, then returned to the bed.

'Please don't tell anyone about this,' Jack whispered.

That's what he was concerned about? Not his betrayal, or the lies by omission, but *exposure*? Lucy's kindly feelings evaporated as a bitter laugh rose in her throat. She shook her head in disbelief. She'd hoped his guilt would come pouring out, making it easy to forgive him. What a fool she'd been. Jack might be able to perform empathy when it was written in a script, but looking at him now she wasn't sure he understood it at all.

'Are you sorry for what happened?' Lucy's voice quivered. She needed to hear one word of tenderness. Proof that Jack hadn't been indifferent to Peter's pain.

Jack placed a hand on her knee. 'If people knew . . . it would ruin *Heart Street* for me.'

'That's your first thought?'

'I've waited a long time for this. And Peter . . . he understood.' His voice broke when he said Peter's name. At least there was that.

'I'm glad it hurts.' Lucy stood up from the bed.

Jack took hold of her wrist. 'I didn't do anything wrong. Peter was an adult. We were both thinking of our careers.'

She shook him off. He had no right to speak for Peter. No right to tell her what Peter had thought.

Jack frowned, his eyes darkening. 'Peter found you stifling, you know that, right? Friendship with you can feel like a death grip sometimes.'

Lucy held her breath until her lungs burned. Her lips twitched as she tried to form a question. Had Peter really said that? Had he used that specific word, 'stifling'? She tried once more to speak, but her throat tightened.

'Lucy.' Jack stood up and placed a hand on her shoulder. 'I'm sorry. I didn't mean it. I was just . . .'

He'd hidden the truth for all these years. He must have known how responsible she felt, after his breakdown, but he'd accepted her support and encouragement as if it was his due. She turned and started to walk away.

'Lucy, wait!' Jack took hold of her wrist. 'You tracked Zelda down? I should tell my solicitor . . . '

She shook herself free of his grip. 'Sort it out yourself.'

Chapter 39

The next day, Lucy visited the website on Zelda's – or more accurately Kate's – business card. It gave the address of her home studio in Balham. Lucy wasn't entirely sure why she felt compelled to confront the woman for a second time. She could simply text the address to Jack, let him plead with her himself, or have his solicitor reach out. She owed him nothing. The ordeal of Sebastian and Zelda could be over for Lucy now, if she chose.

Yet here she was, standing outside a terraced house with soot-blackened bricks and a front door opening directly onto the street. It had been drizzling all morning and the clouds had a solidity to them, bunching together to shut out the light. She needed answers. And she wasn't ready to face Sebastian again, not yet.

Kate winced when she saw Lucy waiting on her front step.

'Can I come in?' Lucy hated the idea that this woman could say no to her, that the truth was a gift she could withhold.

Silently, Kate stood to one side, ushering Lucy through a narrow hallway where a bicycle was resting against a wall, into the kitchen at the back of the house. The potter's wheel had been crammed in by the backdoor, next to a kitchen

table covered in newspaper and a series of small unvar-
nished pots.

'Tea?' Kate asked.

Lucy shook her head. She stood by the backdoor, looking out
over a small paved garden filled with potted plants. It was a
riot of colour, crimson roses and orange marigolds, a profusion
of tulips, their petals buckling under the weight of raindrops.

Kate shrugged. 'I'm making one for me.' She filled the
kettle and switched it on, producing a box of mint teabags
from a cupboard and placing one into a large yellow mug. The
worktop was cluttered with various jars and packets. There
was a single bowl and spoon in the sink.

'I'm not entirely sure why I'm here,' Lucy said to
Kate's back.

Kate turned, giving her a sad smile. 'You want to
understand.'

'That's probably it.'

The kettle clicked off and Kate poured water into her mug.
'I thought it would be so easy for Sebastian to let go of his
anger once he got to know Jack. It's impossible not to like
him, he's so passionate about what he does, so full of life.'

A tortoiseshell cat emerged from the clutter of cardboard
boxes crammed beneath the kitchen table. It meowed, rubbing the side of its head against Lucy's leg and she bent down
to stroke it.

'I understand why Sebastian is angry at Jack,' Lucy said.
'I am too. But if he wanted to punish him, surely there were
other ways?'

Kate rested her back against the kitchen counter, regarding
Lucy with fresh curiosity. Today, Lucy looked nothing like the

business owner she purported to be. Instead of her black trouser suit, she was wearing jeans and a waterproof jacket she'd brought from Aldi, no make-up. But Kate looked different, too, dressed in pyjama bottoms and a black vest, her hair in a topknot. The row of chunky rings across each knuckle were the only remaining trace of Zelda.

'He wanted the coroner to force Jack to take the stand at Peter's inquest. But there wasn't any appetite for that. Inquests aren't about attributing blame, they told him.'

Lucy shook her head. 'Peter wouldn't have wanted his father to go after Jack. I'm sure of that.'

'Maybe not. But Sebastian needed to *do* something. He became tortured by his own inaction, by the idea that he was standing by and letting Jack get away with everything. You should have seen him after his divorce, Lucy, something inside him seemed to break.'

Lucy rubbed at her eyes with the heels of her hands. It was so difficult to rid herself of the certainty that she'd known Sebastian. Sadness bloomed inside her abdomen at the absence of any hint or sign that she'd meant anything to him. That was why she'd really come here, she realised. She was being pathetic. Holding on to an affinity that hadn't been real.

'When you told us it was time to turn up the dial, that was Sebastian, pushing to escalate things?' Lucy asked.

Kate looked at her sharply. 'He never said anything about the police. As far as I was concerned Sebastian just wanted to explore what kind of man Jack was now. Get to know him. Then maybe confront him further down the line.'

Lucy felt the retorts rising up. Kate's capacity for self-deception was truly astounding. But Lucy restrained herself.

In spite of everything, she hadn't quite let go of Jack. He needed her help.

'If you were to explain that to the police—'

Kate sighed. 'You and I are really quite alike. Fiercely loyal to much wealthier friends. My own studio, Lucy. You can't imagine how long I've waited. The money was nothing to Sebastian, but he still only let me have it for nine months. There was no offer to extend the lease, even though I did everything he asked.'

The previous night Lucy had lain in bed going over each of her meetings with 'Zelda'. She'd viewed her as eccentric, unhinged; possessing that dreamy relationship with reality that was the preserve of the monied. What she'd really been seeing was bad acting. A crude caricature of a wealthy, vengeful woman.

Kate angled her head slightly. Pressed her lips together. 'Sebastian really was quite taken with you.'

These were the words she'd longed to hear, but Lucy couldn't trust them. Sebastian's interested gaze had been fake, so had the kind enquiries about her father, even the kiss and his tiny little moan. Believing otherwise would only make a fool of her.

'If you spoke to the police, you could end the fraud investigation hanging over Jack,' said Lucy. 'Can you imagine how relieved he'd be?'

Kate twisted one of her silver rings. 'I'd be happy to. But—' She looked down at the floor. It was linoleum, made to look like tile.

Cold air seemed to rush over the back of Lucy's neck. 'What?'

Kate drew her brows together. She was about to say something, formed a shape with her lips, but then recoiled before she'd uttered a sound.

'What is it?' Lucy's stomach tightened.

'Involving the police was just a way of putting the frighteners on Jack. Sebastian knew he wouldn't get a fraud charge to stick.'

'Right, and . . . ?' Lucy hadn't meant to sound quite so demanding. Kate was the only person who could help her make sense of things.

'He's been onto the *Heart Street* people. Told them Jack pretended to be his son for months. Made sure they knew about the police investigation. He's determined to get him booted off the show.'

'He wouldn't be able to manage a thing like that.' Lucy placed a hand against the moist plaster of Kate's kitchen wall. If *Heart Street* was taken from Jack, he'd be destroyed. She could picture his face crumpling.

'I did try,' said Kate. 'I really did. I told Sebastian Jack doesn't deserve this. He really is a fine young man, but Sebastian can be so single-minded . . . '

Maybe there was a chance the *Heart Street* executives would dismiss Sebastian's account. Perhaps they'd even embrace a colourful past, they could shape Jack's involvement in the agency into a tale of plucky pragmatism, feed it to their media contacts to build expectation around his appearance in the show. But he hadn't started filming yet. No scenes would be wasted. Jack's contract likely included a good conduct clause which would make it easy for them to fire him.

'Fuck,' Lucy said. Jack was going to be crushed.

She felt Kate's hand on her forearm. 'You know, I did always enjoy drama at school. If you ever needed me—'

Lucy stared at her, not comprehending.

'Your agency must need the occasional fifty-year-old?' Kate's eyes roved Lucy's face. 'I could really use the money.'

Lucy couldn't laugh, even if she felt light enough to see the funny side.

'Sure,' she said. 'I'll call you if anything comes up.'

Chapter 40

Sebastian seemed to understand and respect Lucy's need for silence as he drove her to the natural burial site. Small talk would have been insufferable, yet she was still too choked with emotion to speak of Peter. They came off the dual carriageway and passed through a village of new brick houses, detached but tightly packed with the tiniest strips of garden. There was a primary school and a Co-op shop, along with a pub advertising Pizza Tuesday on a chalkboard. Soon, the pavements disappeared as Sebastian joined a country lane, the verges overgrown with cow parsley and brambles. They had to overtake several cyclists, standing up from their saddles as they took on a steep hill.

Sebastian was taking her to Peter's resting place. Lucy had been strangely relieved to learn that her friend hadn't been cremated, that his grandparents had organised an eco-friendly burial. Sebastian turned off, seemingly in the middle of nowhere, parking his car on a barren patch of mud that bordered woodland. 'This way,' he said, pointing to a narrow footpath. Lucy could see a small wooden hut off to one side, it bore a green sign reading SUSTAINABLE BURIAL CENTRE in plain white letters.

'How's your father doing?' Sebastian asked.

'Improving. He's just got his taxi licence back.' Lucy's voice sounded unnaturally airy, as though she was back serving in a bar, making idle chat with a regular.

'That's wonderful.' Sebastian glanced over his shoulder, flashing her an open-mouthed smile. He really did look pleased.

Lucy said nothing. It had been a fortnight since she'd confronted Sebastian in his flat. The charges against Jack had been dropped, but *Heart Street* had nonetheless sacked him. *Suppose it's for the best. Might have made the transition to film a bit tricky*, he'd said in a text. He could have blamed Lucy – she'd been the one to talk him into working for Zelda – but he'd opted to keep things friendly. Still, Lucy didn't feel ready to start messaging again, nor was she able to meet up in a pub like they always used to, speaking of auditions, of the films they'd watched and throwing in the odd barbed comment about Gracie Dorn.

The previous fortnight had seen Lucy conjure elaborate fantasies. Sebastian holding her in his arms, recounting his happier conversations with Peter. His warmth encircling her, giving her the consolation she'd been searching for but never quite found over the past decade. Lucy would kiss away his tears, her lips salty as the two of them grieved for Peter together. Could such a thing come to pass? It was a twisted thing to crave.

'Here.' Sebastian took a few steps off the path and placed his hand against a narrow tree trunk. It had vibrant green leaves with reddish veins, its branches reaching high up above Sebastian's head. 'This is where we buried him.'

Lucy approached the tree, remembering Peter's long eye-lashes, his wavy hair. He was here. His body beneath the earth. By now, he'd be nothing like he was, only bones would remain. But she could *feel* him. She closed her eyes and it was as though he was standing next to her, his affection resonating through her body. Peter had made her feel life could be savoured, drop by delicious drop. Told her she could become whoever she wanted, nothing need constrain her. She would have lived a different life perhaps, if he hadn't died.

She was aware of Sebastian retreating, giving her space as she held Peter's presence close. *I'm sorry you loved someone who wasn't worthy,* she said with her inner voice. *I'm sorry you couldn't talk to me about it.*

Above her, the trilling of a blackbird. This whole place was teeming with life. She'd seen robins, blue tits and round black pellets that indicated a healthy deer population. Each of the trees around her represented a person who had loved and been loved, decaying in the warm embrace of the earth, providing nourishment for new life.

She stretched out her fingers, registering a vague surprise at not feeling in the least mournful. All these years it had bothered her, not knowing where Peter was buried, not being part of his funeral. The absence of any kind of ritual, any opportunity to say goodbye, left things feeling unfinished. Now, she let Peter's presence seep into her heart. Her loving friend. With her always.

Her eyes searched for Sebastian. He'd found a wooden bench a little further down the path and was waiting for her, hands on his knees.

'How are you doing?' he asked.

She could only smile. She didn't have the words.

He made no move to get up, so she sat down next to him inhaling the scent of sun-warmed wood.

'I still miss him,' Lucy said at last.

Sebastian nodded. He didn't touch her. She supposed it was respectful of him, but she couldn't help imagining the heat of his fingers against her bare knee.

'Did he ever talk about me?' Her voice cracked. *Stifling.* Jack had told her Peter found her stifling. It sounded too specific to be a lie.

Sebastian shifted on the bench, turning his torso to face her. 'He adored you. I remember how desperate he was to house share with you in your second year. He was so afraid London rents would force you to drop out.'

'I might have done,' she said. 'No one else noticed I was struggling.'

'Peter seemed so aware of how Jack took advantage. He told me how he used to wait up for you to return from your bar shift, make you run through his scenes.'

Lucy swallowed to try and combat the dry feeling in her mouth. *Had* Jack taken advantage of her? It hadn't felt that way at the time. She'd been so grateful to be included, to feel as though these wealthy new friends of hers saw something special in her.

'I've felt responsible for Jack for so many years,' she said at last. 'He had a breakdown a year after Peter . . . '

'At least he felt *something*.' Sebastian flexed his fingers, then balled his hands into fists.

'I thought he was so fragile,' Lucy continued. 'I spent more time helping him prep for auditions than I did on my own stuff. The whole point of the agency was to give Jack something to focus on. I had no idea it would grow the way it did.'

'He's manipulative.'

Was that the truth? Lucy couldn't help feeling it was more complex than that. Perceiving the damage, doing what she could to help, had made her feel as though she was earning her place at Jack's side. Maybe it was down to class. The feeling of not quite belonging, not having a lifetime of theatre trips to draw on, having to put a price tag on her time. She'd never been able to see herself as Jack's equal. And so she'd tended his wounds, made herself into the balm that soothed each tear.

'All these months ...' Sebastian unfurled a hand, raised it so it was hovering just above her knee. But then he seemed to think better of it and placed it in his own lap.

Lucy experienced a sharp pang of disappointment, right beneath her ribs.

'Why now?' she asked. 'If you'd known about Jack and Peter right from the beginning ...'

Sebastian looked at her with the frankness she remembered from the few times they'd been alone. 'I had this sudden moment of clarity as things were ending with Chloe. Peter was dead and I hadn't done a single thing to make Jack pay. I'm not sure I can describe ... I felt so dirty I wanted to tear off my own skin.'

She longed to kiss him. He would kiss her back, she knew he would. But she was aware of an echo inside her skull, a warning issued by some wiser part of herself. This would be the continuation of a pattern. One damaged man exchanged for another. Did Lucy really want Sebastian? Or was it his injuries calling out to her, offering her a purpose?

She drew herself up. What would Peter tell her in this moment? She heard his voice as clear as it had been in life. *You have to live your own life, Lucy. You cannot spend a life fitting yourself into other people's cracks.*

What did she want for herself, really? A business empire? It struck her that she'd never really asked herself the question before. It had been impossible, all the while she'd been surviving from one paycheck to the next, uncertain where she might be living in two months' time.

'I hope you feel some sort of closure,' she said. 'I hope it's been worth it.'

She saw his Adam's apple bob. A flicker of recognition in his eyes. 'Maybe it could be a new beginning for both of us?' He tried to smile, but couldn't quite manage it.

'I need a break from intense friendships, I think,' Lucy said. 'I need to take some time to figure out what I want.'

The not knowing didn't frighten her. Her sister was coming up to London that very afternoon to be inducted into her new role as operations director. She was planning to surprise her father with tickets to see Ringo Starr. She no longer had a grand plan, the beauty of a shared ambition. But there was a lot to look forward to, a lot she still needed to discover.

Chapter 41

Sam Greene offered to host the annual class reunion at his Raynes Park home for another year running. Lucy had pretty much resolved not to go, until Will Tanner told her at least three of their classmates were hoping to collar her. 'They want in on the action,' he'd said. 'Everyone I've spoken to is sick with envy about me getting paid to go to parties.'

Lucy couldn't go on avoiding Jack, she realised. They were still supposed to be friends and maybe – now she didn't feel the need to watch over him, ready to console him the moment he heard someone else's good news – she might actually enjoy the occasion.

She approached Sam's street wearing jeans and a light jacket in her favourite shade of teal. Beneath it, she wore a Beatles T-shirt; she'd laughed to herself as she picked it out, knowing it would irritate Jack.

Katya Ivanoff was standing at the end of Sam's driveway, smoking a cigarette. She quickly stubbed it out with her narrow heel. 'Lucy! How are you?'

Lucy greeted her with a hug. 'Good. You?'

'I've heard you can make me rich,' Katya grinned, ushering Lucy around to the side gate.

When she arrived in the garden Sam quickly wrapped up his conversation with Jasmine to hurry over and offer Lucy a drink. She hadn't been this popular since her second year after graduation, when she'd landed a promising role in a BBC drama.

As she caught up with her classmates and accepted invitations to have coffee, she became aware of the ripple of attention that heralded Jack's arrival. He was wearing tight-fitting jeans in slate grey with his leather jacket, flashing his white teeth as he hugged old friends and nodded along enthusiastically to their small talk.

His capacity to be dazzling – regardless of what he felt – astonished Lucy. Whenever she thought of their last exchange, the poison of his words – *friendship with you is like a death grip* – Lucy wanted to double over.

'I often think how sad it is, looking around and Peter not being here,' Sam said.

Lucy's shoulders twitched.

'Sorry. I'm never sure whether I should mention it or not.' Sam rested his hand on her arm.

'Don't be sorry. I feel it too.' Lucy tried to imagine Peter in his thirties. Would his brown hair be starting to thin? Would his habitual pensive expression have taken its toll, carving deep lines around the eyes? She experienced the familiar wave of grief, sudden and intense. It wasn't a feeling she feared any more; she felt a strange affection for the sensation, it was an old friend, part of who she was. Peter *mattered*.

'He'd be more famous than Gracie Dorn, I reckon,' Sam offered.

'I always imagined he'd go into directing,' Lucy said.

'He had a real talent for bringing out everyone's best performances.'

Sam angled his head and nodded. 'I think you're right. Anyway – here comes your . . . ' He didn't know how to complete the sentence.

Jack was approaching, his smile serene. He reached in his jacket pocket and handed Sam a silver envelope. 'Looks like I'm going to be joining you in suburbia. Here's an invite to my engagement party.'

Sam looked at Lucy, suddenly perplexed. She was just about managing to keep her expression neutral.

'He's not marrying *me*.' Lucy gave a tinkling laugh. Just like Jack, she was impersonating a relaxed person.

She felt her smile tighten as Jack gave Sam a quick overview of who Emily was. Family in Devon. Works for a PR agency. *Makes more money than me, that's for sure*, said with a knowing titter.

She felt a flicker of alarm as Sam went off to tend the barbecue.

'How've you been, Luce?' Jack's voice was tender.

'You're *marrying* Emily?' If they could train themselves to speak frankly, then perhaps there was a chance they could go on being friends. With her eyes Lucy extended an invitation for Jack to confide in her, to speak the truth.

He pretended not to see. 'Thought it was about time.' He gave her the grin he used with other people, full of happy-go-lucky charm.

'Does she *know*?' Lucy knew the question would be unwelcome, but couldn't help asking it.

Jack moistened his lips with his tongue. Shook his head.

'I've got an invitation here for you,' he said, producing another silver envelope from his jacket pocket.

Lucy took it in silence.

'I'd love you to be there,' Jack said.

She stared at him, open mouthed. 'But Jack ... you're ...'

He drew his eyebrows together. 'Don't.'

It didn't make sense. He'd been with Emily for three years, but it always seemed to Lucy as though the relationship was a kind of habit. He approached their nights together with the same sense of duty as he regarded his long runs or his weight sessions. Did Emily believe he loved her? Had Jack convinced her he wanted to spend the rest of his life with her? Had he convinced *himself*?

'But ... Peter.'

Jack raked his fingers through his hair. 'I've got a few more of these to give out. I suppose I ought to do a circuit.'

As she watched him approach the group of men around the grill, Lucy took a sip of her white wine. It was fruity, calorific and delicious. She drained her plastic cup with a satisfying slurp, aware of a great absence. That roiling vortex of worry. The churning thoughts. The feeling of responsibility. They were all gone. Jack's happiness wasn't *her* responsibility. It never had been. Her breath caught and she found herself contemplating, *what shall I do next?*

Acknowledgements

My heartfelt thanks to Steve, Lucas, Mum and Kim for being so unfailingly supportive and believing in me more than I believe in myself. I am also deeply indebted to Kalika Sands for reading my early drafts and offering her wise feedback so generously.

Thanks to my agent, Cara Lee Simpson, for her brilliant advice throughout the writing process. And special thanks to Christina Demosthenous for being everything a writer needs in an editor and much, much more. I am so proud to be published by Renegade Books, and am grateful to the whole team at Dialogue for their bold vision and outstanding author care.

Bringing a book from manuscript to what you are reading is a team effort.

Renegade Books would like to thank everyone who helped to publish *The Impersonators* in the UK.

Editorial
Christina Demosthenous
Eleanor Gaffney

Contracts
Anniina Vuori
Imogen Plouviez
Amy Patrick
Jemima Coley

Sales
Caitriona Row
Dominic Smith
Frances Doyle
Ginny Mašinović
Rachael Jones
Georgina Cutler-Ross
Bukola Ladega

Design
Meg Shepherd

Production
Narges Nojoumi

Publicity
Annabel Robinson
Sophie Goodfellow

Marketing
Mia Oakley

Operations
Kellie Barnfield
Millie Gibson
Sameera Patel
Sanjeev Braich

Finance
Andrew Smith
Ellie Barry

Audio
Ellie Wheeldon

Copy-Editor
Jon Appleton

Proofreader
Saxon Bullock